Praise for New York T

"An action-packed plo
Publishe

"Michaels's snazzy tales   d

Booklist on *Late Bloomer*

Praise for *New York Times* bestselling author Linda Lael Miller

"Pure delight from the beginning to the satisfying ending . . . Miller is
a master craftswoman at creating unusual storylines and charming
characters."
Rendezvous on *Springwater Wedding*

"A fun read, full of Ms. Miller's simmering sensuality and humor, plus
two fabulous brothers who will steal your heart."
Romantic Times on *Two Brothers*

Praise for Theresa Alan

"Alan does a masterful job . . . As the three women face the trials and
triumphs of life, they assist each other in ways that only best friends
can—through unconditional love, unrelenting humor and unwavering
support. Reminiscent of *Bridget Jones's Diary* and *Divine Secrets of
the Ya-Ya Sisterhood*, Alan's is a novel to be savored like a good
box of chocolate."
Booklist on *Who You Know*

"A gorgeous book, superbly written with compassion and caring. *Who
You Know* should absolutely be number one on everyone's list."
Rendezvous

Praise for Jane Blackwood

"If you can read the first paragraph of *The Sexiest Dead Man Alive*
and not buy this book . . . you may want to seek therapy."
Kasey Michaels

"Readers who like quality romantic comedies such as Lisa Plumley's
Perfect Together will be quick to add Blackwood's excellent mix of
humor and pathos to their list of favorites."
Booklist on *The Sexiest Dead Man Alive*

Books by Fern Michaels

About Face
Annie's Rainbow
Celebration
Charming Lily
Dear Emily
Finders Keepers
The Future Scrolls
The Guest List
Kentucky Heat
Kentucky Rich
Kentucky Sunrise
Listen to Your Heart
Plain Jane
Sara's Song
Vegas Heat
Vegas Rich
Vegas Sunrise
What You Wish For
Weekend Warriors
Whitefire
Wish List
Yesterday

Books by Theresa Alan

Who You Know
Spur of the Moment
The Girls' Global Guide to Guys

Books by Jane Blackwood

The Sexiest Dead Man Alive
A Hard Man is Good to Find

Published by Kensington Publishing Corporation

JINGLE ALL THE WAY

FERN MICHAELS
LINDA LAEL MILLER
THERESA ALAN
JANE BLACKWOOD

ZEBRA BOOKS
KENSINGTON PUBLISHING CORP.
http://www.kensingtonbooks.com

ZEBRA BOOKS are published by

Kensington Publishing Corp.
850 Third Avenue
New York, NY 10022

Copyright © 2004 by Kensington Publishing Corp.
"Santa Unwrapped" copyright © 2004 by Theresa Alan
"Maybe This Christmas" copyright © 2004 by Jane Goodger
"The 24 Days of Christmas" copyright © 2004 by Linda Lael
Miller
"A Bright Red Ribbon" copyright © 1995 by Fern Michaels

All rights reserved. No part of this book may be reproduced
in any form or by any means without the prior written con-
sent of the Publisher, excepting brief quotes used in reviews.

If you purchased this book without a cover you should be aware
that this book is stolen property. It was reported as "unsold
and destroyed" to the Publisher and neither the Author nor the
Publisher has received any payment for this "stripped book."

All Kensington titles, imprints and distributed lines are available at special quantity discounts for bulk purchases for sales
promotion, premiums, fund-raising, educational or institutional
use.

Special book excerpts or customized printings can also be
created to fit specific needs. For details, write or phone the
office of the Kensington Special Sales Manager: Kensington
Publishing Corp., 850 Third Avenue, New York, NY 10022.
Attn. Special Sales Department. Phone: 1-800-221-2647.

Zebra and the Z logo Reg. U.S. Pat. & TM Off.

First Printing: November 2004
10 9 8 7 6 5 4 3 2 1

Printed in the United States of America

CONTENTS

SANTA UNWRAPPED

Theresa Alan

CHAPTER ONE

Have you ever longed for something so much, every fiber in your being is *consumed* with desire and yearning? It's as if you've been overtaken. Your thoughts, your mind, your body—they are no longer your own. That's how I feel now. The world has stopped. I can think of nothing else. I have invoked the stars, the Heavens, God above, the powerful forces of nature and the universe, and with all my will from the marrow of my bones and the center of my heart I urge the clock at the bottom of my computer screen to speed ahead to five o'clock, but no, no. It mocks me. Every century or so, it will crawl to the next number, 3:01, which after many eternities will toss me a bone and change to 3:02. It's like a slot machine in Vegas: every now and then it will surprise me with a win, just enough to keep my hopes, my dreams, my greed, alive. Oh, how those three little digital numbers at the bottom of my screen taunt me.

I try to trick the clock into thinking I don't care what time it is. I do on-line searches for recipes as if I'm very interested in something other than my workday coming to an end at long last. But it knows the truth. It knows I'm glancing at it approximately 876,543,281 times per minute, and so the numbers get their kicks by nearly standing still. Whole mountains have been eroded by wind and water into flat prairie lands at a faster pace than my clock is moving.

It's 3:02 on Christmas Eve eve. Naturally, neither my office-mate Olivia nor I have done a shred of work today on principle. It's wrong to be asked to work on Christmas Eve eve. That's just a fact. Especially when I have a ton of last minute Christmas stuff to do, and I clearly have no time to pretend to be productive at my job.

Olivia and I are underwriters, which means we approve loans or deny loans. We make dreams come true or squash dreams into oblivion. Our lives are an endless scourge of paperwork. But not today. Today is goof-off day. Read the 'Net day. Take a two-hour lunch day. Spend endless hours gossiping day. Fret about hosting Christmas for the first time in my adult life day.

My entire family is coming to Colorado to visit me from Montreal, which is where I'm from. I'm looking forward to seeing them, and I thought I was ready for their visit. Then today I realized I completely forgot to buy stocking stuffers, and I'm feeling like I really should get one more gift for each of them, and while I'd plotted our Christmas dinner in intricate detail, it slipped my mind entirely that we'll want something to eat on Christmas morning, so I have to go grocery shopping for breakfast food.

And I'm going to have to get it all done tomorrow before they get here tomorrow night because instead of being able to shop and clean this evening, I have to go to a children's hospital and give gifts to little kids. I signed up for it a few weeks ago when I was in this deranged frame of mind where I thought that I was a good person who gave back to my community. Today I remember clearly: I am not a good person. I have no desire to go to the hospital and be nice today. What was I thinking?

The organization I signed up to do the volunteer work

with is called For the Children. They do stuff for needy children all year round. Even as I signed up to give gifts away for Christmas, I knew how insignificant this one little gesture was when all year long there are children who are sick and don't have enough food or a warm place to sleep. So the truth is, I do want to give back, I really do. Just not tonight. Tonight I want to finish getting ready for my family's visit and then be one with my couch and my TV.

There's just so much left for me to do before they get here. Right now I'm frantically searching recipe sites online, trying to plan a suitably exotic breakfast to dazzle my parents and younger sister with on Christmas morning. Meanwhile, Olivia has spent the last hour reading every on-line horoscope there is and subjecting me to the predictions for both herself—Aries—and myself—Pisces.

"Listen to what this one says here about Pisces," Olivia says. " 'Before the New Year, you will meet a love like you've never known before. It will transcend all of your expectations.' See, I knew breaking up with Sean was the right thing to do."

That's a big fat lie. Olivia had strongly urged me not to break things off with Sean. He was, after all, perfect marriage material. Sean and I were together for four years, three of which we lived together. We didn't fight. He didn't beat me. He was good with money. He was kind. And because of all those things, it had been easy to keep on dating him, even though I knew he wasn't the guy I wanted to spend my life with. We just didn't laugh enough together. There was never enough passion. Our relationship was close to being what I wanted but never quite right. I kept trying to talk myself into being happy with him, but eventually I just couldn't do it anymore. My body knew it before my mind did. It shut off from him sexually months before we technically broke up. We eventually got to a place in our relationship where he'd literally beg me for sex, and I'd be like, "We just had sex two months ago, and you want it *again?*" As if he were the one being unreasonable. I knew in some faraway place in my mind that when you get to a point in a relationship in which you can't stand having sex more than once every other month, things aren't going well, but I did my best to ignore this little tidbit of truth because it seemed easier to go on being miserable than to risk the fear of the unknown. Breaking up with Sean meant I might be alone forever or that my heart might get broken again and again or that I'd go on an endless number of awkward, horrible dates and never find true love. It seemed safer to stick with a low-grade misery I was familiar with.

Also, because we lived together, there was the added bonus of a breakup leading to an ugly snarl of fiscal entanglements. For the last several months of our relationship I just quietly moved into the guest bedroom of my two-bedroom townhome and did my best to be really mean to him, hoping he'd get fed up and break up with me. Very mature, I know. But he didn't break it off, so I had to be the villain, the heartbreaker, the reviled ender of a long-term relationship.

It took a lot of courage for me to end things with him, but I know I did the right thing because I miss the DVDs I lost in the breakup more than I miss him. I hadn't realized it, but apparently during the three years we lived together, almost every DVD I bought, I'd bought "him" as a gift, because when you live with someone, every book and DVD you buy "him" also just happens to get added to your collection. Then you break up, and suddenly property ownership becomes a very big deal. We had about a thousand conversations that went like this: "I didn't buy that for you as a gift. I'm sure of it." Then he'd say, "Yes, you did. You got it for me for Christmas." "Well, maybe you're right, but I'm sure *Being John Malkovich* wasn't a gift." "Yes, it was. You got it for me for my birthday." "Are you sure? Damn!" Etc. etc.

Even so, now that the holidays are here, I'm thinking about him a lot. I miss him. I can't deny it. Right now I'm thinking about how, even though we were only pretend happy together, maybe that's as good as I'll ever be able to get.

Olivia continues reading the Web site's predictions. "It also says that 'You should be open to the unexpected.' " She looks at me and says, " 'A transcendent love.' " She gets a spacey, wistful look in her eyes. "It's going to happen for you."

I roll my eyes. Olivia has a little trouble with a concept I like to call "reality."

"Great. I'm glad to know a love will be delivered to my door. That's fabulous. Do you think Mom and Dad will give him to me wrapped up in a bow or will Santa be bringing him by?"

"I think you need an attitude change, Aimee. Good things are going to happen to you. Christmas is a magical time."

"Like hell it is. It's a giant plot to separate people from their hard-earned cash just so we can have some lame gifts to unwrap. Magical time my ass."

The truth is that I really don't hate Christmas. I'm just a wee stressed out by getting ready for it. Even though I bought a lot of gifts on-line, I feel like I've gone back and forth from the mall to Target to the local post office every single day this month. And I've spent a lot of money I didn't really want to spend. And my fingers are permanently cramped from all the endless wrapping. But even though the holidays are a lot of work, I'm looking forward to it because I'm excited to see Mom, Dad, and my younger sister Bridgette again— I haven't seen them in months. I moved to the States eleven years ago to go to college, and then I got a job right after graduation, and somehow I never went back to Canada. I visit them when I can, but it's never often enough.

I actually get along with my family. Mostly. Although I fully anticipate that my mother will pester me about having children the whole time, and we'll have at least one fight about it, but we have this fight every time we see each other, so it's not really a problem. I'm used to it. The thing of it is, I wouldn't even mind her bugging me about it if she'd bug me in the right order. She never gives me a hard time about not being married. She never urges me to run out and snag myself a husband. But for the last few years, her urging me to get on with making grandbabies has bordered on relentless. I genuinely don't think she'd care if I had the kid out of wedlock. She's just obsessed about me getting knocked up. The thing is, Bridgette has a boyfriend, so she seems the much better candidate to harass about procreating. But because I'm the eldest, Mom has all her grandmotherly hopes set on me. She doesn't care if I get preggers from a one-night stand, immaculate conception, or a drive-by insemination. She just wants me to generate babies. Mom acts like some mythical kingdom is going to fall if I don't produce an heir to the throne IMMEDIATELY.

I turn my attention back to the Internet browser I have open. I'm just writing down all the ingredients for a spinach quiche when my cell phone rings.

"Hello?"

"Hi. I'm looking for an Aimee La . . . La . . ."

"This is Aimee Lachaussée."

"Hi. This is Vince Contreras. For the Children gave me your name and number to talk to you about tonight."

"Yes?"

"Well, I wanted to know if you were going to be getting to the hospital early so I could get you your elf costume."

"Elf costume? What are you talking about? Nobody said anything to me about an elf costume."

"Yeah. You're the elf. Me and my buddy Gerry will also be elves, and my friend Ryan will be Santa. Do you want a ride or anything? If you want, we could pick you up."

An elf costume. *Merde!* I will never forgive myself for getting myself into this. I will never be charitable or nice ever again.

"Yeah, actually a ride would be great." The children's hospital we are going to is in the suburbs, and as I am a city girl,

I have no idea how to get there. I'd printed out Mapquest directions and had armed myself with my mapbook of Colorado, but leaving the navigation up to someone else seems a much safer plan.

"What time were you thinking we should leave?" I ask.

"With traffic . . . I was thinking we should head out of Denver at five."

"Could you pick me up from my office, then?" I give him the directions and then click my phone off. I look at the clock at the bottom of my computer screen. It's still only 3:29 P.M. How is that possible? Five o'clock seems like a distant dream.

It takes a few millennia, but eventually five o'clock does roll around. I shut off my computer, bid Olivia a *Noël joyeux,* and bound down the stairs. I wait for Vince in front of my office building, and very quickly become bitterly cold. The cold isn't so bad when the sun is out, but between the sun going down and the bracing winds, it's freezing. Still, I stick it out because I'm worried I won't be able to see Vince from the foyer of the office building.

I check my watch: 5:11. He's not that late, but every minute seems like an eternity because it's so cold out. Also, I have to wish happy holidays and Merry Christmas to my coworkers who are leaving work, and I'm just not really in the mood to be cheerful and friendly right now. I'd better get in a better mood, though. Otherwise I'll be snarling at the sick children tonight, and that will do awful things to my karma.

I realize I stupidly didn't ask Vince what kind of car he was driving, so every vehicle that goes past I squint at expectantly and full of hope, only to be disappointed.

I hear a strange beeping sound, and I realize it's coming from my cell phone. It's the sound it makes when it's running out of juice and is going to shut itself off. I'm pretty hopeless about remembering to charge the thing. I just hope Vince either calls me very soon to tell me he can't make it or gets his butt over here quickly.

My nose hairs weld together from the cold. Fabulous—I have icicles in my nostrils. That's just great.

I try to rearrange my scarf babushkalike to better cover my nose, ears, and head, but then my neck is exposed, and it instantly hurts from the biting wind.

At last, a van stops in front of the building. It has the words "For the Children" emblazoned on the side. It hadn't occurred to me that For the Children would have lent out a van. A man rolls down the passenger side window.

"Are you Aimee?" he asks.

"Yep."

"Hey. I'm Gerry. I'll open the door. Hang on."

He gets out of the van and shakes my hand. He's wearing baggy green velour pants, pointy elf shoes, and a white T-shirt. He's got crewcut blond hair, rough skin, and pale blue eyes.

"Hi. It's nice to meet you. I'm Aimee."

When he opens the van door, I realize there's something weird about this van, and I'm struck by the sudden knowledge that I'm getting into a vehicle of total strangers. Maybe they painted "For the Children" on it as part of an elaborate ruse. These three guys could be serial murderers who have outfitted their van so they can trap me inside it and then gut and flay me in a particularly brutish manner. Then I see that the only real thing that's different about this truck is that it's got a fold-out ramp, and that's when I realize this van hasn't been designed to kidnap random women; it's a van for somebody who uses a wheelchair.

I get in, and there is a very attractive man sitting in the backseat. Before I tell you what happens next, I have to give you some more background on me. You need to know that I'm not normally a woman who gets crazed with lust over a good-looking guy. I've never been out just for fun, meaningless sex. It's important to me to care for somebody and for that somebody to care for me before I get physical with a guy. I tend to be practical with my choice of boyfriends. I'm not looking to reform a bad boy who treats me like crap.

Give me a sweet guy with a good job who treats me well over a jerky pretty boy any day. Because I care a lot less about dating a hunk than choosing a sweet guy, I usually go through this whole evaluation of a guy that's not based so much on initial attraction but on things like whether he's smart and has a good career and so on. Having said all that, you'll understand how surprised I am when, with one look at this guy, my body is rocked by this intense carnal craving. In just moments, the wave of desire eases, and I decide to pass off the powerful surge of emotion to the fact I haven't had sex in several months.

Then I see the wheelchair folded up against the wall beside him, and that jars me even more.

"Hi, I'm Aimee," I finally manage.

"I'm Ryan."

I wave up front at what must be Vince. "Hi. Thanks for picking me up."

"No problem. Sorry we're late."

Gerry closes the door and gets in the front seat, and Vince takes off. I smile shyly at Ryan, feeling a little awkward.

I'd put all three guys to be about my age. Vince is Hispanic and very good-looking, with dark hair, dark eyes, and a nice smile framed by two small dimples. Vince is also wearing green pants, and I think it's an interesting choice to have the guy in the wheelchair play Santa while the rest of us are the elves. I wonder how the kids will react.

Ryan has curly brown hair and friendly brown eyes. He looks like he was once a jock. He has large, muscular arms and a powerful chest. He's not wearing a winter coat, just his red Santa pants and a white T-shirt. He doesn't need a jacket because the heat is cranked up to levels you'd expect to find in the center of the sun. Within a minute or two, I'm all warmed up, and a couple minutes after that I start to sweat, so I peel my jacket, scarf, and gloves off. I catch a glimpse of myself in the rearview mirror and discover that my hairstyle can best be described by the word "disastrous." I have curly hair just like my mother and sister, but unlike the two of them who always blow-dry and straighten their hair into sleek, orderly styles, I'm far too lazy to bother with much in the way of primping, and today I regret it. The scarf has completely flattened the curls on the left side of my head while causing the curls on the right side to spring all over the place in lunatic coils. Lovely.

"So, Aimee," Vince says, "how'd you get roped into doing this? Did your office make you so it looks like your company is full of charitable, well-meaning employees?"

"No, no. I volunteered by choice. I get a little delusional every now and then and think I want to be a better human being, and then I remember being a good human being takes a lot of energy, and I'm not really up for it. But here I am. How about you guys?"

"We've been doing this every year for three years," Vince says. "It's actually really fun. Well, Gerry and I have done it for three years, and Ryan has done it for two."

"I was recovering in the hospital three years ago, so that wasn't my fault," Ryan says with a smile.

Again, I feel uncomfortable, and I absolutely hate myself for feeling this way. *So he's in a wheelchair, get over it!*

"How do you guys know each other?" I ask.

"High school. We went to high school together," Vince says. "We were all on the football team together. You like football?"

"I don't much like watching any sports," I say. "I like playing them. Volleyball, skiing, swimming, tennis, really just about anything. I was a jock in high school and college, but football has never been one of my favorites."

We talk some more, and I learn that Vince owns his own motorcycle repair shop and Gerry is in the air force. Ryan once worked as an organizational management consultant in the medical industry, but since he got out of rehab from his accident, he's been reexamining his life and trying to figure out if he wants to go back to doing that or take his career in a new direction.

The traffic is absolutely unbearable, which I don't understand. People should have taken the day off to fly home to be with their families. They should not be in our way, anyway. I feel strongly about this.

"Is there an accident? Why aren't we moving?" Ryan asks.

"I don't know. I don't see anything," Vince says.

When we finally get off the highway, we're able to go a little more quickly, but we still seem to drive and drive and drive for an eternity. I don't understand how it can take so long to get to a suburb.

"Where is this place? I feel like we could have driven to the Himalayas in the same amount of time," I say.

"Welcome to urban sprawl, Aimee," Vince says.

To kill time, Vince and Gerry tell very explicit off-color jokes. I can tell a racy joke every now and then, and I don't usually get offended easily (although if something strikes me as sexist, I can go from calm to outraged in seconds flat), but because these guys are strangers, it makes me a little uncomfortable.

At long, long last, we get to the hospital, and Vince hands me a plastic bag. "You can change inside."

Oh, goody.

Inside the women's washroom, I change into the green velour top and pants that could comfortably clothe a rhinoceros. I tuck my hair back beneath the green felt cap and add a ton of red lipstick and pink blush to affect looking merry.

I join the guys in this waiting room area just outside the children's ward. They are completely dressed in their Santa and elf attire. They are the youngest, buffest, hottest Santa and his helpers I've ever seen in my life.

"Okay, so what is it I'm supposed to do?" I ask.

"Well, here's the scoop," Vince says. "The gifts are color coded. Red is for girls and green is for boys. On the bottom of the gifts, it says what the gift is and what age group it's appropriate for."

He flips over a red box, and written faintly in pencil it says, "Age 3. Doll."

"We can't guarantee that every kid will get what he or she wants, but Santa will ask, and we'll do our best to accommodate. I was thinking we should have one elf sort of entertaining the troops while they wait and the other two elves picking out the gifts for Santa to give out. Aimee, how about you do the girls' gifts, I'll do the boys' gifts, and Gerry, you can maintain order while the kids wait their turn."

"Sounds good," I say. Gerry nods his agreement as well.

With our plan in place, a nurse ushers us into a large room where the kids are waiting for us, and the stressed-out, bummed-out feeling I've been battling all day lurches toward a full-on depression because these kids look very, very ill. Several are bald, a couple are bedridden and hooked up to machines, and all of them seem pale and weak. It is heart-wrenching and soul-diminishing at the same time.

The walls are painted in relentlessly cheerful primary colors. Kids' artwork—crayon drawings and watercolors that range from discernable images to abstract, Rorschachian shapes—is taped to nearly every available inch of wall space. There is a Christmas tree with ornaments that were obviously crafted by the kids, and the handmade decorations, with their perfect imperfections, put a smile back on my face.

It turns out my worries about how the kids would react to a Santa in a wheelchair were unfounded. They seem thrilled by him. Some of the kids don't mention the chair at all. Others ask how he got hurt or why he needs the chair. Each time he tells a new made-up story that makes the kids laugh, and then he turns the attention to them, asking what it is they want for Christmas. A boy who is also in a wheelchair seems especially excited to meet this particular Santa.

"Do you really need a wheelchair?" the boy asks.

"I really do," Ryan says.

"What happened?"

"It was when I was going down a chimney. I came down the wrong way and blammo! Wheelchair City."

The boy giggles.

"But it's not too bad being in a wheelchair," Ryan says.

"Yeah it is; you can't skateboard or anything."

"But just think. Your feet never get tired when you're going through museums or the zoo. You get special seating at the movies, and you always get a parking space."

"Parking space?"

"You'll care about it when you're older, trust me. Now, what is it you want for Christmas?"

"An X-box."

I watch Vince do some frantic searching through his bag of gifts, and then he leans in to whisper something to Ryan. Ryan nods, and Vince hands him the gift.

"Now, since you don't have your own TV to use while you're hanging out in the hospital, why don't you check this out?"

The boy unwraps the package, which turns out to be a Gameboy, a handheld computer game player.

"All right!" the boy says. "Cool. Thanks."

"No sweat. You have a Merry Christmas, okay?"

The boy hugs Ryan, and my heart melts. It's easy to see Ryan as a former football-playing hunk, but it takes a little suspension of disbelief to get my mind around the idea that this cute, brawny, young guy could bond so well with little kids. It's the stuff of made-for-TV movies, cotton candy, and greeting card sentiments—sickeningly sweet, but also irresistible.

The next kid in line is an adorable blond girl with slightly chubby cheeks and ringlets of curls springing out from her head. She looks like she's around five or six years old.

"What's your name?" Ryan asks.

"Madelyn."

"So, Madelyn, what is it you want for Christmas?"

"See her?" Madelyn says in a whisper. She points to one of the little girls who is asleep in a bed and attached to various scary, futuristic-looking machines. "Her name is Sarah. Can you bring her a new heart? She's been waiting a real long time. She's real sick."

A stricken look crosses Ryan's face, and for a moment, he's rendered speechless.

"I'll see what I can do, okay? But what about you, what would you like for Christmas?"

She shrugs. "Just the heart for Sarah's all I want."

I lean in and whisper into Ryan's ear, "Give her two stuffed animals. One for her and one for Sarah."

"Good thought," he says.

I hand him two boxes marked "Age: 4–8. Battery operated stuffed animal (cat)."

"Why don't you take this one for Sarah and this one for yourself so you can play together?"

Madelyn smiles. "Yeah. 'Kay. Thanks, Santa."

I'm impressed with how comfortable Gerry, Vince, and Ryan—three tough-guy-looking types—are with the little kids. As I watch the guys with the kids, my dark mood softens, because there is no possible way anyone can feel grumpy when little kids are scampering around, squealing and laughing with delight.

I'm not sure how long we've been at the hospital when the nurse tells the kids that Santa has to go home because it's getting close to their bedtime. I can't believe how quickly the night has gone. There are many protests—plaintive choruses of "Nooooo!" fill the room—and I understand a little of what it's like to be a beloved celebrity.

We leave the hospital still dressed in our outfits, and that's when I feel the fatigue of the long day—the long month—hitting me. As Vince pulls out of the parking lot, I say, "Weren't the kids adorable?"

"That girl with the red hair is going to be a babe when she grows up," Vince says. "She is going to be one juicy morsel."

I know technically that kids grow up and become adults with sexual feelings, but I don't want to talk or think about it, and I *really* don't want a man I barely know to talk or think about it.

"She reminds me of that girl that was after me the other night at the bar," Gerry says.

"She wasn't after you. She couldn't have been less interested in you if she tried."

Vince and Gerry start arguing loudly about whether this girl they met at a bar the other night was flirting with Vince or Gerry. They are each quite convinced that *he* is the one she had her sights on. They go on and on about what great tits she has and how great her ass is. As they go into greater and greater detail about how they'd like to sexually service her and be serviced by her, I get more and more uncomfortable. I realize that Gerry and Vince may be the kind of guys who volunteer their time to bring cheer into children's lives, but they are also sexist bastards.

From the purgatory of the backseat, Ryan and I exchange looks and half smiles, trying to pretend we can't hear the gutter talk going on in the front of the van.

"That was fun tonight, wasn't it?" I say.

"Yeah. The kids are really great."

"I was really touched by that little girl who didn't ask for anything for herself but for a new heart for a friend."

"I read this article about this charity—shoot, I can't remember what it's called. It might be the Make a Wish Foundation or another one like that. Anyway, the charity takes poor kids out shopping for Christmas, and the director of the project said the hardest thing about it was trying to get the kids to buy things for themselves. The kids always want to buy things for their family instead."

"That is so sweet."

Our conversation is cut off when we hear Gerry say, "Where the hell are we?"

I look out the window. We're in a subdivision, with cookie-cutter houses as far as the eye can see.

"What are we doing in a subdivision?" I ask.

"Shit. I'm not really sure. Mapquest told me to turn on Ida, which I did," Vince says, "but I'm not sure where I went wrong. What does Mapquest say?"

"Well, where are we now?" Gerry asks.

"We're on . . ." Vince slows the van down and squints at the street sign. "Man, could they make these signs any smaller? Streetlights, anyone? It looks like Grape Circle. Wait, how'd we get on Grape? I thought we were on Ida."

We drive around in circles for fifteen minutes, which may not sound like that long of a length of time, but in the context it's an eternity—after all, we're in a major suburb, not the Australian outback. How hard could it be to find civilization?

"We have to get back to Tower Road," Gerry says.

"Thank you, genius, I hadn't thought of that." Vince slows the van down to inspect the street sign. "Grape Drive. What's that street?" We slow down again a little ways ahead. "Grape Circle! We're back to Grape Circle!" At the next block, we slow down again. "Grape Road. Aah! We need to get to Ida to get back to Tower. Where'd Ida go? We're in an endless maze of Grapes."

"We've done a good deed tonight," I say, "and how are we rewarded? By being banished to the farthest hinterlands of subdivisioned suburbia! We'll be lost here forever! Why do they name every single street Ida and Grape? Why?"

"Because they are out to get us, obviously," Ryan says dryly, and I can't help but snicker.

"That way!" Gerry yells. "That street is Tower Road! That's the road we came in on!"

"Where?" Vince asks.

"Back there. You passed it."

Vince does an abrupt and extremely illegal U-turn and goes careening into the curb, which makes a horrible noise and gives us all a very hard jolt.

We get onto the road Gerry thought was Tower Road, only it turns out to be Smoky Mountain Road.

"Shit. I've never heard of Smoky Mountain. Is it on the map?" Vince asks.

"I'm looking," Gerry says.

"Where are we?" Ryan asks. The subdivision we were driving in is behind us, but ahead of us it looks like farm country, just endless empty fields that will no doubt one day become more subdivisions, but right now just seem like an endless expanse of wastelands.

I can't believe we were lost for fifteen minutes only to be spit out onto some unknown street in the middle of nowhere.

"I feel like we're in rural Nebraska or Kansas or something," Ryan says.

Just then the van makes a horrible sputtering noise, and Vince starts swearing up a storm. The van dies just as Vince pulls over to the side of the road.

Vince, Gerry, and I go outside to see what's going on, leaving the van door open so we can easily talk with Ryan.

"You must have knocked something off the van when you hit the curb," Gerry says.

Vince lays in the rocky, snowy terrain on the shoulder of the road so he can inspect under the wheel of the passenger side where he rammed into the curb.

"I knocked a little paint off, but that's it," he says.

"Guys?" I say. Vince stands, and his and Gerry's gazes look in the direction where I'm pointing. There is a trail of oily-looking liquid all down the street.

Vince pops open the hood of the van as Gerry loudly curses him for ramming into the curb. "This is all your fault!"

"It's transmission fluid that we leaked," Vince says. "The transmission is hosed. It had nothing to do with me crashing into the curb. It's just a beat-up old van of an underfunded charity. Get a grip."

"We need a tow truck. Who's got a cell phone?" I ask.

Gerry and Vince look at me blankly.

"Ryan, do you have a cell phone?"

"Sorry."

"Who doesn't have a cell phone in this day and age? What do you think this is, nineteen-fifty?"

"What about you? Why don't you have a cell phone?" Gerry says.

"I do have a cell phone!" I pronounce triumphantly. Then, in more humble tones, I admit, "I just forgot to charge it and it died."

"We'll just go back to one of those houses," Vince says.

"It's after eleven. You can't go knocking on somebody's house in the middle of the night; you'll get shot," I say.

"We'll just wait here. A car will come along soon," Gerry says.

"It's freezing out here," I grumble.

We stand outside for a minute, and I take a look around. "Look, there are lights coming from over there. It could be a gas station."

"I think you're right. It is a gas station," Gerry says. "Vince and I will go jog over there and call a tow truck."

"Way, way out there?" Vince whines. "It's going to take us forever to get there."

"Well, what other choice do we have?" Gerry says.

Vince shrugs. "I guess."

"Are you just going to leave Ryan and me here to freeze to death?"

Quietly, Gerry leans in and whispers, "What do you want us to do, try to get a wheelchair through fields and snow?"

I'm about to suggest that I could go with Vince or Gerry and one of them could stay with Ryan when I realize that if I'm going to be stranded with a strange man, I'd much rather be stranded with Ryan than with either of them. "Okay," I say.

"Dude," Vince calls to Ryan. "We'll be back in fifteen minutes. Twenty at the most."

I climb in the van beside Ryan and swing the door shut.

"I hope they get back as quickly as they say they will," I say. "I have guests coming tomorrow, and I'll feel like a terrible hostess if I'm in the hospital recovering from frostbite."

He smiles. "Are you French by any chance?"

"French Canadian. You can hear my accent?"

"It's very faint. I can only hear it on some words. Your English is great. Where in Canada are you from?"

"Montreal."

"I've heard that's a great city."

"It is. It's kind of like a cross between Paris and San Francisco. It's got great Parisian-style food with San Francisco-style houses and zillions of ethnic restaurants and cool shops all over the place."

"Then, I think I'd like it. I like both those cities a lot."

"You've been to Paris? I was there for a week. I fell in love with it."

"I was there for about a week, too. I traveled through Europe one summer when I was in college. I think Paris was my favorite city. The food was to die for."

"I like to cook a lot, and French food is my specialty." As I say it, I realize I'm flirting with him. The words "Would you like to come over for a home-cooked meal sometime" are on the tip of my tongue, but I chicken out of actually asking him on a date.

"Oh, a woman who can cook. You're bright, you're pretty, and you can cook. You are the perfect woman. I can't even cook toast."

While my heart is doing a happy dance (did you hear what he said? "Bright"? "Pretty"? "Perfect"?) I try to exude a calm exterior. "Toast is all you need in life; you don't need to know how to make anything else. There's cinnamon toast, French toast, melba toast . . ." I say.

"Don't forget English toast, rye toast, white toast . . ."

"You see, the variety is endless. And needing only to have

a toaster would cut down considerably on cookware expenses."

"It could put Bed, Bath, and Beyond right out of business."

"We could form a whole toast-only movement," I say.

"I seriously think I might be able to live on bread alone if it was as good as all the bread I ate in Europe. Those Europeans know how to do bread right."

"Yes, they do."

We start talking about our European adventures and food and college, and we don't stop talking until a tow truck with Vince and Gerry in the passenger seat pulls up. I don't notice them until Vince knocks on the van door, nearly scaring my elf pants right off me. I slide open the door.

"Sorry we took so long," Gerry says, getting out of the tow truck. I take a glance at my watch. It's nearly one in the morning, which means Ryan and I have been talking for an hour and a half! It seemed like just a few minutes. "We weren't sure what cross streets were closest to the van, so we figured it was easier to wait for the tow truck at the gas station."

The tow truck driver gets out of his truck and comes around to where Gerry and Vince are standing. He's shaking his head, which I'm not taking as a good sign.

"The dispatcher didn't tell me you were in a van."

"We told her we were in a van," Vince says.

"Well, she didn't tell me. I'm going to have to go back and get a flatbed truck."

"Oh, man," Vince says.

I suddenly realize that I am absolutely freezing cold. My nose and fingers feel as if they could drop off my body like an icicle breaking off from a gutter. And I'm tired. This means we won't get home until two or three in the morning. And I have so much to do tomorrow before my parents and sister get here, so I won't be able to sleep in.

"Could you please take us someplace warm while we wait?" I say.

"All four of you can't fit in the cab of my truck, unless a couple of you sit on the other's laps."

"We'll be fine right here," all three of the guys say in unison.

"You guys are such *men*. You can't sit in a guy's lap for the five minutes it'll take to get somewhere warm? Somewhere warm with beer?" I say.

The allure of beer is strong, that's obvious. I can see them all perk up a little at the prospect.

"Could you fit his wheelchair into your cab?" Vince asks.

"How about this: how about I take the three of you someplace and then come back for him and his chair."

"That is so nice of you. Thank you," I say. The guys all agree to this plan, and after closing the van door with Ryan inside, the three of us pile into the tow truck.

"Sit in my lap," Vince says.

"We'll be fine. We'll just be a little snug," I say.

"There's not going to be enough room," he insists.

And he's right. We're practically—but not technically—sitting on each other's laps We're uncomfortable as hell, but I'd rather be uncomfortable than sit in Vince's lap.

We drive down a couple streets, and within minutes we can see a strip mall ahead and the gas station where the guys called for the tow truck.

"There's a Hooters up ahead," Vince says.

"We are not stopping at a Hooters!" I say. "There's a bar. We'll go in there."

"That place looks like a dump. Come on, what's wrong with Hooters? They have good wings," Gerry says.

"Do not give me that 'they have good wings' crap. You guys can go there if you want, but I have a little something called self-respect."

"What do you have against Hooters?" Vince asks.

"Oooh, where do I begin? The logo itself is enough to make me send the place up in flames. The owl with the lascivious eyes saying it's perfectly okay to ogle women, to treat them like sex objects, it burns my butt."

Vince tells me I'm reading too much into it and I need to relax, which may be true, but the driver drops us off at the rinky-dink, no-name bar anyway.

The bar is, in fact, an absolute dive. It feels like we've somehow wandered into some small rural town instead of a bustling suburb outside of a major city. Their beer selection is feeble, and the bartender has hair that looks like it hasn't been washed in a very long time and teeth that demonstrate why dental insurance should be mandatory for all.

We each order a beer and retreat to a table. Vince and I both reach to pull away the wooden chair at the same time to clear a space for Ryan to roll up to the table.

A few minutes later, the tow truck driver pulls up again, and I slip my coat on and go to hold open the door for Ryan. I watch the tow truck driver pull out the wheelchair and basically carry Ryan out of the truck. Ryan sees me, and a look of humiliation crosses his face. I feel like my presence has made him feel ashamed when he has nothing to be ashamed of.

When he gets to the door, I smile my warmest smile. Then I realize that there is just the slightest incline from the outside to the inside, and when you're in a wheelchair, the smallest bump may as well be a mountain.

"Here, let me see if I can help," I say.

I go outside and lean on the back of his chair to get the front wheels elevated, and with only minor trouble, we get him inside.

"Good to see you, man," Vince says.

"Good to be here out of that damn cold." Ryan inspects the beer list. "Is this it? They've only got four beers and they're all crap."

"I still don't know why you wouldn't go to Hooters. They have a much better selection of beers," Vince says.

"Could we just drop the subject?" I say.

But they don't drop the subject. Instead Gerry and Vince keep talking about it, and then the subject morphs into a discussion of strippers, and I get more and more pissed off. *I will never, never volunteer again. I'll send checks off to charity, but I'll never volunteer again, so help me.*

"It was so wicked when, what was her name—" Gerry says.

"Cinnamon," Vince cackles.

"Cinnamon," Gerry laughs. "We hired this prostitute for Ryan—"

I feel abruptly nauseated. Ryan had seemed like such a nice guy, not the kind of guy who would pay for sex.

"You paid for sex?" I ask him.

"No! Don't be ridiculous! I would never do anything like that," he says.

"We tried, though. It's been three years since he's gotten any. Not a single date since the accident," Vince says.

"So you can still—" I begin to say; then I realize I can't ask a complete stranger whether he can still get it up. My face flushes with embarrassment.

"He can get it up, all right. He couldn't resist Cinnamon's charms," Gerry says, snickering like a little kid.

"She did this . . . striptease," Ryan says. "But I'm telling you, nothing more happened. It was one of the most mortifying experiences of my life."

Phew. So he's not a total scumbag.

I immediately wonder what it would be like to have sex with him. He's hot as hell, for one thing. And nice. And smart.

Mon Dieu! What am I doing thinking about having sex with him? Is it simple curiosity? Is it that I think he's a great guy and I want to be the one to usher him back to enjoying the pleasures of life? Is it just simple attraction and I'm blowing it out of proportion because I'm uncomfortable with the stupid wheelchair?

But the image of making love with him is strong. I'd probably always have to be on top, but that'd be okay—it's much easier to come that way.

Ahh! Aimee, it's wrong to think dirty thoughts about a guy who's sitting right across from you. You're as bad as Vince and Gerry.

"Is it okay if I ask you . . . I mean you don't have to tell me . . ." I begin.

"A car accident," Ryan says. "Three years ago. Vince and I were driving back from skiing in the mountains. I was in the passenger seat—"

"And I asked him to get something out of the back," Vince says. All his previous jocularity has drained from his face, and he looks serious, almost distraught. "He took off his seat belt, just for a moment—"

"And an oncoming car didn't make a tight enough turn on the mountain road."

"We ran straight into them, and Ryan went flying through the window. It was so awful. I really thought he was dead."

"I thought I was dead, too."

"I'll never forgive myself," Vince says.

"It wasn't your fault. It was the other guy's fault."

"But I was the one who asked you to get the CD case from the back."

"He really can't stop beating himself up over it. He started volunteering like crazy after the accident."

"Guilt charity, huh?" I say.

"Is there any other kind?" Vince says.

"There's also the intrinsic reward you get because it feels good to help other people," I say, and I realize that it's true. Even though giving up my night was kind of a drag, and even though seeing the sick kids was sort of depressing, bringing a little happiness to those kids felt really good. And it made me appreciate just how good I really have it, and how lucky

I am to have my health. Maybe I'm happy I volunteered after all.

"You seem like you've adjusted well to the change," I say to Ryan.

"I was bitter for a while. I think the hardest thing for me was coming to accept that I wouldn't be able to play sports anymore. That was a huge part of my life."

"You seem like you're in really good shape, though."

"I lift weights. And I have to rely on my upper body a lot more now, so that helps keep my arms and chest in shape, but my legs have really atrophied."

"So you lift weights and volunteer, is that enough to keep you busy? Do you ever get bored?" I ask.

"Sometimes. Definitely."

"Do you think you'll go back to work anytime soon?"

"Well, from the money I got from the insurance settlement, I don't really need to work again for a few years."

"I have to close up the bar," the bartender says. "You kids need to get going."

"You're not really going to throw us out into that cold, are you?" I say.

"I'm sorry. You need to get going."

The tow truck driver—this time with a flatbed truck—gets back just in time before we're sent out into the cold. The flatbed truck has an extended cab, so all four of us are able to squeeze in. The driver drops us off at my office so I can get my car. The plan is that I will then take the three guys to the For the Children office where Vince's car is.

When the tow truck driver parks behind my car and we all get out, I watch how deftly Vince and Ryan work together—Vince unfolds Ryan's chair and lifts him into it; then Ryan rolls the few feet to my car and is able to use his muscles to pull himself from the chair to the backseat. Vince folds up the chair and puts it in my trunk.

After a short drive, I pull into the For the Children parking lot and follow Vince's directions to where his car is. I pull up behind it, pop the trunk, and get out of my car to say goodbye.

Once again I watch Vince and Ryan work together like dancers with a carefully choreographed routine. Vince unfolds the chair, and because the chair is even with the car seat, Ryan is able to slide from one to the other with relative ease, using his arms to support himself like a gymnast on a pommel horse.

"You know, even though the night didn't turn out like I expected, and even though I'm going to be exhausted all day, I actually had a lot of fun tonight," I say.

"I did, too," Ryan says.

"Me, too," Vince says.

"You should come with us next time we do volunteer work," Gerry says.

"I'd like that a lot. Vince has my cell phone number, so you guys should give me a call next time you're going to do something. Well, have a Merry Christmas!"

"Merry Christmas!"

"Have fun with your family!"

As I drive off, I smile. My bad mood is completely gone, and I'm feeling surprisingly cheery.

CHAPTER TWO

I get home at four in the morning and collapse on the couch because it's the first soft surface I come to. I sleep in until almost ten, and since I have to pick my family up at the airport at four this afternoon, there's no way I'm going to make it to the mall today, so that means no more presents. I have to streamline. I go to the grocery store to buy food *and* stocking stuffers—gum, batteries, and Planter's Nuts for everyone! Then I come home and sprint through my house armed with Windex, paper towels, a duster, and a vacuum, trying to make it look as presentable as possible in a limited period of time.

Even though my day goes by in a mad rush of activity, I can't stop thinking about Ryan. I haven't had so much fun talking with a guy in years. Literally years because Sean and I never really joked around together. We never connected like Ryan and I did in just a few hours. I'm mad at myself for not having the courage to ask Ryan for his phone number last night. I'm just going to have to hope they call me to volunteer again soon.

By 2:50 I've hidden all my cleaning supplies, and I'm

tearing through the house peeling off my clothes to take a shower. And by 3:15 I'm out the door, heading for the airport.

Using our cell phones, I tell Mom how to find me outside at the passenger pickup area. When I pull up and see them all standing there, I smile broadly. I pop the trunk and get out of the car to greet them properly.

"Bonsoir, Maman," I say, hugging her. It feels so good to have her in my arms. My mother is a classic French beauty. Very thin, always immaculately dressed, with sleek black hair that's always cut in a new, trendy way. My sister Bridgette looks just like her. I didn't get their slim builds. I have a much more athletic, sporty frame. Even so, the similarities are enough that anyone can tell the three of us are related.

After a long minute, we part and I hug my father. *"Bonsoir, Papa. Noël joyeux."*

After hugging Bridgette, I help them put their bags in the trunk, and we all pile into the car.

On the drive home I tell them all about my little adventure last night. It feels so good to be speaking French again. My entire family is bilingual—at least half of Montrealers are—but when we're together we speak our native tongue, and speaking it makes me feel like I'm home. I have so little chance to talk in French in my daily life. It frequently intrudes on my dreams, which are often a mishmash of French and English, but in my day-to-day grind, I can almost forget I'm a native French speaker.

"So I didn't get home until really late and didn't quite get enough sleep last night," I say in French. "And I didn't get my townhome cleaned up quite as much as I wanted."

"Is that why you look sad, because you're tired?" my mother says.

"I'm not sad. I look sad?"

"Oui. There is a sadness in your eyes. What is it?"

I think about it for a moment.

"Well, maybe I'm a little sad about breaking up with

Sean. And I'm sad because I met this nice guy yesterday—
he was the guy who played Santa last night. And I haven't
been able to stop thinking about him all day. The thing is, I'd
really like to see him again, but I don't have his number and
I don't even know his last name."

"Can't you call the organization you volunteered for and
see if they'll give you his name and number?" Bridgette suggests.

"Oh, maybe. That's a good idea. But won't he think I'm
stalking him?"

"I think he'd be flattered."

"Maybe I will. But I've never asked a guy out before. I'll
think about it."

When we get home, I take their coats and show Mom and
Dad to the guest room (Bridgette gets to sleep on the couch).
Then I heat up some spiced cider spiked with Goldschlager,
and we sit around the kitchen table and catch up.

In the morning, I get up to make breakfast while Mom and
Bridgette take turns in the shower. When breakfast is ready,
Mom and Bridgette are still styling their hair and putting
makeup on. I keep yelling for them to hurry up or the quiche
will get cold (even though I'm keeping it warm in the oven),
but they still take forever getting ready. Why they feel the need
to get decked out as if they are going to the Academy Awards
and not opening Christmas presents at home with their family eludes me. I'd forgotten how nuts this drives me. When I
still lived at home, I'd sleep in half an hour later than the two
of them, go for a half-hour run, and still be ready for school
before Mom would be ready for work or Bridgette would be
ready for school. They are beautiful women, though; I have
to give them that.

After we finally get to eat we sit around the Christmas
tree to open gifts. I miss the Christmas tree I grew up with,
which was decorated largely with ornaments Bridgette and I
had made. Naturally, they involved lots of popsicle sticks,
pipe cleaners, and glued-on googly eyed creatures. Neither

Bridgette nor I have ever had a shred of artistic ability, and our whacky-eyed reindeer ornaments and green felt creations were pathetic excuses for decorations, but I liked them anyway. Each year we'd add new ornaments to the collection, and I liked how looking at the tree each year would bring me back to memories of Christmases past. Then one year when I was about fourteen, a pipe burst in our house, destroying most of what we had in storage, including our Christmas tree ornaments. Mom went out and bought a slew of boring bulbs and mass market decorations without heart. That's the kind of tree I have now. It's a beautiful (though fake) tree, with a white and blue theme and lots of glittery snowflakes dangling from the branches. It looks picture-perfect, the kind of thing you'd see in a department store or magazine. But I miss the popsicle sticks and misaligned eyes and strangely painted faces of the decorations of our youth.

We tear into our gifts, ribbons and paper flying. As usual, Bridgette has gotten me a bunch of funky jewelry and hip, low-maintenance clothes. She knows my taste exactly. She knows I like artistic, unusual jewelry as long as it's not big and clunky, and I like to wear fashionable outfits as long as they don't take an hour to zip up and fight my way into. And as usual, Mom and Dad have gotten me stuff for my home. Since I have never had a wedding to pile up on dishware and towels, etc., every year they get me stuff-I'd-get-at-my-wedding type gifts. When I was just out of college the gifts were super practical—a colander, a big pot, a frying pan. But as the years have progressed and my salary has increased, the gifts have gotten less practical and more fun. This year they get me a set of very simple yet elegant sterling silver serving bowls and trays. I suspect Bridgette acted as a consultant on this purchase because if my mother had been left to her own devices, she would have probably gone for something very ornate, with detailed etchings of flowers and vines engraved into the servingwear, whereas I am all about simplicity and casual elegance.

After we exchange gifts, we watch one of the DVDs Bridgette got me for Christmas. Mid-afternoon I get started on dinner. There are no traditional French-Canadian dishes on the menu today, except for dessert. My grandmother used to make this ground pork and veal pie called a tourtière for Christmas every year, and while her recipe is a delicious one, I don't eat much red meat these days, so I opt for a stuffed goose instead. For dessert, I do make the traditional Christmas dessert called *Buche de Noel,* a yule log made with genoise sponge cake and buttercream that is to die for.

We enjoy a pleasant meal and more wine than is really good for us. It's a very nice, relaxed holiday, without the usual loud racket of little cousins running around whooping it up. But in a way, I sort of miss them. Yes, little kids hog all the attention when they are around, but they are also a lot of fun.

I make a comment about how I miss our cousins, Adeline and Rochelle. "Of course, if they were here, we couldn't hear ourselves think, but they're so much fun."

"Well, you should be having your own kids soon," Mom says. "Then you'll always have kids around to have fun with."

Ugh, I can't believe I inadvertently brought the you-should-be-having-kids-soon lecture upon myself. I left myself open for attack. Now for a defensive block: "I don't even have a boyfriend. How do you expect me to have a child?"

"But you will have children someday, right?"

"Mom, please don't bug me about this."

Mercifully, she lays off. Instead the conversation turns to how Rochelle and Adeline's parents are doing. I'm glad Mom isn't giving me a hard time, but usually we have to argue about this for at least an hour or two, so the fact that she dropped the topic so easily is highly suspicious. Something is going on.

The reason we argue about me having kids is because one time I said I wasn't sure I wanted to have children. It was at a time when I was watching my officemate Olivia's marriage disintegrate, and I saw what a challenge it was for her to become a single mother.

Olivia and I have worked together for seven years and shared an office for the last five, so we've had a chance to become pretty good friends, though it's the kind of friendship that rarely extends beyond the office since she's busy being a mom. Back when she was still married, I would share tales of my dating woes, and she would tell me about the everyday stresses of being a wife and mother—things her husband did that drove her crazy, the arguments she had with her mother-in-law, that sort of thing. Even so, she always seemed pretty happy with her life. Yes, she had her struggles, but we all do. So when she broke down crying one day at the office and said she wasn't sure if she should leave her husband, I was flabbergasted. I had no idea things had gotten so bad at home for her.

Marriages are like icebergs to outsiders. No matter how close you are to your friend, you can only really know about one-tenth of what her marriage is really like. Nine-tenths of it lurks beneath the surface in the dark, deep unknown.

That was the time Olivia started becoming obsessed with horoscopes, psychics, and tarot cards. She was so confused about her life, she wanted guidance from any source she could get her hands on. Her life had gone in a direction she'd never expected. She was lost and scared, and I don't begrudge her her desire to be comforted with predictions that assure her that, in the end, everything will be all right.

As it turned out, her husband left *her*. I was there to see the entire separation and divorce. I heard her talk about how angry her children were that they had to move from their three-bedroom house with a big backyard to a two-bedroom apartment with busy streets surrounding them and no yard at all. I heard all her fears about how tight money was now that she was a single mother (the child support her ex sent was a far cry from the fiscal stability she'd had living in a two-income household), and how scared she was about the possibility she could lose her job one day because how would she support her kids then? It made me realize that while many marriages fail and you can easily go from "wife" back to "single girl," once you become a mother, you're a mother forever. Did I really have the courage to shepherd another human being through life, no matter what financial, health, or personal circumstances might be thrown my way?

Really, my mother's haranguing makes me want to go out and get my tubes tied just to spite her. My father takes a much better approach. Dad pretends to be a stereotypical French male letch, but he may well be the most hard-core women's rights activist I know. (Hence my low tolerance for all things sexist.) He's always saying that the world needs more female leaders and politicians because women aren't nearly so eager to send their sons and daughters off to get killed in war as male leaders seem to be. He appreciates the beauty of women of all shapes and sizes. He's very European that way. Europeans don't see an extra few pounds or a kink in someone's nose to be a flaw that needs to be surgically changed but as what makes people unique and therefore beautiful. And he talks at length about how amazing women's bodies are for being able to carry another life within us and then give birth to brand-new human beings. If Mom would focus more on the magic and beauty of having children and less time simply antagonizing me (which causes me to get defensive and contrary), she might have a better chance of helping me overcome my fears.

The next day, Mom and Dad go to check out Denver on their own for a few hours so Bridgette and I have a chance to catch up. In Canada, the day after Christmas is called Boxing Day. It has something to do with some saint and some legend. The story has a few different versions, but the one I grew up with was that it was the day noblemen "boxed up" gifts for their servants. (Clearly an early form of regifting.)

Bridgette and I usually go for sushi when we have time alone together since there is no way we could drag our parents to a sushi restaurant, so this is really our only chance to go.

We order far too much food, but we can't help ourselves. It's so much fun to sample all the different possibilities. When our waiter brings us our spicy miso soup to start, I study my sister across the table. It finally hits me that she has been unusually quiet since she got to Denver. She looks sad. Has she been sad this whole time and I just didn't notice because my mind was too wrapped up with thoughts of Ryan?

"Bridgette, is something wrong?"

"Yeah, as a matter of fact, I have something I need to tell you."

"Mon Dieu, you're pregnant. That's why Mom didn't give me a hard time about not having kids yet yesterday. I *knew* something was up!"

"No. I'm not pregnant. Mom will bug you about having kids, don't worry. I think she was just trying to avoid a fight on Christmas."

"Oh, well, what's up, then?"

"I broke up with Tristan."

"You're kidding! When? Why didn't you tell me? Why?"

"About a month ago. I told you just now. And as for why . . ."

"I thought you two were talking marriage."

"We were. Well, it was mostly me talking marriage. I was bored with our relationship and I wanted a change. I decided that the change should be that we should get married. And then when you finally worked up the courage to break up with Sean, I realized that getting married wasn't going to solve the problems we were having; it was going to make them a whole lot worse. So I finally broke it off."

"I'm so sorry, Bridgette."

I reach across the table and take her hands in mine.

"I know. I wasn't expecting it to be so hard."

"What problems were you having?"

"We were just bored with each other. Bored with the sex, bored with having the same conversations over and over, bored with doing the same things night after night. I know you have to work at keeping things fresh in a relationship, and I tried, I swear I tried. It wasn't like we never had fun together. Sometimes we did . . . Aimee, how do people keep their relationships interesting?"

"Phpt!" I grunt, pushing air through my bottom lip and upper teeth. "How should I know? Do I look like a happily married person to you?"

"Do you think we expect too much from relationships? Do you think we can ever get married, or will we just get bored someday?"

"I don't think it's easy to keep any relationship passionate and interesting, but I think it's possible if the relationship is strong enough to begin with. I can't speak for how things were between you and Tristan, but as for me and Sean, I don't think the foundation was ever strong enough for the two of us. I think things were really exciting in the beginning, because meeting someone attractive and new is always exciting, and because we got along, our relationship was able to coast along for a really long time after the initial excitement wore off. I just don't think we ever communicated at the level we needed to to make our relationship long-term."

"I feel so scared. I'm not really used to being alone."

"I know how you feel."

"At least you have a possibility of having someone to date. What was that Santa guy's name?"

"Ryan."

"He sounds great. You should go for him."

"I have to tell you something about him."

"D'accord."

"He's in a wheelchair."

"What do you mean? He'll never walk again?"

"Barring some scientific medical breakthrough, he'll never walk again."

As she takes in this information, her eyebrows furrow, and her lips make this odd pucker-and-twist expression.

"You don't approve?" I say.

She exhales a deep sigh. "No, it's not that, it's just . . . you're so into sports, I can't really see you with a guy who isn't also into sports."

"He used to be into sports. He was driving home from skiing in the mountains when he got into his accident."

"That's all fine, but it's not what I mean. I mean the next time you want to go skiing, you won't be able to go with *him*. Relationships are hard enough even without a major obstacle built in before you even get started."

"Look, all I know is that I had so much fun talking with him the other night, and I find him so attractive, and he's really kind and—"

"I'm not saying I don't approve. I'm just . . . concerned. What if things don't work out?"

"No relationship is guaranteed to work out."

"I know that, Aimee, but just think about how hard it was for you to break up with Sean. Can you imagine how hard it would be to break up with a guy with a disability?"

I nod. I see her point.

"But you know what," she goes on, "if you're into this guy, you should go for it. You'll never forgive yourself if you don't see if things can work out."

"You think so?"

"I do."

That afternoon, my mother takes Bridgette and me for our traditional post-Christmas spa day (although granted, it's just half a day). We get facials, manicures, pedicures, and massages. Mom says it's so we girls can bond and relax, but secretly I think she's appalled by the state of my cuticles and pores, and this is an excuse for her to get me cleaned up, even if it is just once a year. And while I may not be all that into makeup, I have absolutely nothing against being pampered, so you won't see me complaining.

All through the day, as my face is being steamed, my feet are being pumiced, my nails are being painted, and my back muscles are kneaded into a heavenly state of relaxation, my thoughts turn to Ryan.

I'm just going to call him. What's the worst that could happen? He could turn me down. I'll get over it. Eventually. I'll probably never have to see him again, so what's the big deal?

When we get home, I stare at my telephone for a long time.

I'm definitely going call him. Just not today.

CHAPTER THREE

On the last day my family is in town, we drive to the mountains for a day of snowmobiling. The snowmobile rental place outfits us in suits, boots, gloves, and helmets. The black outfits and helmets make my family members look like Evel Knievel wannabees.

We each get a snowmobile and instructions for how to use them, and then we take off through the snowy woods.

We all go rather slowly and cautiously at first. I'm the first person to increase the speed so I really feel like I'm flying, but soon the rest of my family is following suit. I'm not surprised by my dad hurtling through the woods at a pace that feels like it could break the sound barrier, but I'm impressed that my elegant mother and sister are adventurous enough to speed through the forested mountains.

Racing through the snow and trees feels exhilarating and liberating and scary, all at the same time.

Then it occurs to me that Ryan will never be able to go snowmobiling like this. I wonder if he'd ever gone before his accident. Will he ever know what it's like?

* * *

When we get home, my parents and sister lie down to take naps before we go out to dinner.

I go into my bedroom, close the door, and do some deep breathing and positive visualization exercises like I used to do before a big swim meet or a softball match. Again, I stare at the phone for several minutes before I finally pick it up and call For the Children as fast as ripping off a bandage. I tell them that I went to the Children's Hospital on Christmas Eve eve and the guy who played Santa lent me his gloves and I'd forgotten to give them back to him. (I figured that lie sounded better than saying, "I thought Santa was a babe and I want to ask him on a date.")

"So I was hoping you might be able to give me his number so I could call him. His first name is Ryan. I'm afraid I don't know what his last name is."

Fortunately for me, For the Children has very poor privacy policies for its volunteers, and the girl gives me his name and number as soon as she's able to find it. I thank her and hang up the phone, and then I pick it up again to dial Ryan. Before I can even punch a single number, my heart starts doing its impersonation of a basketball being dribbled at a furious pace. I try to take a few deep breaths to calm myself, but I'm having trouble finding air. I don't want to give myself any time to chicken out of this, so I go ahead and dial his number anyway.

"Hello?"

"Hi, may I speak to Ryan?"

"This is he."

"Hi, Ryan. This is Aimee Lachaussée, I uh . . ." I expel an embarrassingly loud gasp for air since I'm about to keel over from lack of oxygen. "We met the other night at . . ."

"Yeah, of course, I remember you. What's up?"

"Oh. Well, uh, sorry, I'm a little nervous. Uh, so, how was your Christmas?"

"Fine." He says "fine," but his voice is suspicious, like what he's really saying is, "What is it you want?" What happened to how easily we were able to talk the other night? He *does* think I'm a stalker. I knew it!

"The thing of it is, I really enjoyed talking to you the other night, and I was hoping maybe we could get together sometime and talk some more. Like maybe get some dinner or something?" Thank goodness, I've said it. The words are out. I'm able to breathe again.

"Do you mean like on a date or something?"

"Uh, yeah, that's sort of what I was thinking. I really haven't been able to stop thinking about you since I met you. And, of course, none of that guarantees that anything would work out between us, but, well, I was hoping we could see . . . if maybe things could . . . work out." Ugh, I have the aural dexterity of Daffy Duck. *Get it together, Aimee!*

"Look, Aimee, you may think I'm some sad schmuck who can't get a date and hasn't gotten laid in three years, but I don't need your charity." His voice has this hostile tone that throws me.

"I didn't call you out of feelings of charity . . . I . . ." I want to say "I'm attracted to you. I don't care about the stupid wheelchair," but I'm too nervous. Nervous about having made the call in the first place and a little freaked out about his reaction.

"Well, I'm not interested. Goodbye."

And with that, he slams down the phone. I stand there in shock, staring at the telephone as if it can tell me what the hell just happened. I really want to call him back and ask him if he's just not attracted to me, or if it's too soon after his accident for him to start dating again. Whatever it is, he didn't have to slam down the phone on me. Does he know how much courage it took to make that call in the first place? What a jerk!

I lay on my bed, stewing with anger until Bridgette comes

to tell me that Mom and Dad are ready for dinner. I take them to a family-owned Italian restaurant, and Mom and I spend the duration of the meal arguing about me having children.

At least there's something in this world that's predictable.

CHAPTER FOUR

I see my family off to the airport the next morning and get into work a little late. Only a skeletal workforce has shown up to the office since so many people have taken extended vacations to visit family.

"Good morning, Olivia," I say when I get into the office.

"Hey, Aim. How was your Christmas?"

"Good. It was good to see my family." I tell her about some of the stuff we did, and then she tells me about how Christmas for her involved much shuffling of children from one family event to another, from her ex's house back to her apartment and back again. She and her ex squabbled at length over everything under the sun. (Which she repeats to me verbatim. It isn't very interesting, but it also isn't work, so who's complaining?) He gave the kids hundreds of dollars' worth of presents while she only spent a "mere" hundred on each of them, so they now think she's selfish and he loves them more. So naturally he's the hero and she's the villain. At this she starts to tear up.

"Olivia, I know it seems hard now, but eventually the kids will grow up enough to understand that you were the parent who did the brunt of the parenting—making them eat their broccoli, brush their teeth, clean their rooms. It's not the fun part of the job, but it's one of the most important parts. Someday they'll understand that their father swooping in every now and then bearing gifts like Santa Claus is a much easier way to express love. It's much easier to sign a check than to give up your time." She nods. She knows this is true, but that doesn't make any of it easier. So I just keep talking, to keep her distracted from her dark thoughts. "Speaking of Santa, doesn't it piss you off that Santa gets all the credit for everything? You just know it's Mrs. Claus in the background getting all the gifts ready and wrapped, the holiday cards written, the food ready. And who gets the credit? A man, of course. So typical."

She smiles at this. "Speaking of men, did you meet your transcendent love?"

"No. I'm afraid not."

"Oh. Well, it said you have till the New Year. What are you doing for New Year's anyway?"

"I'm going to a party at a girlfriend's house."

She nods, and there is something about her expression that makes me realize she's got nothing to do that night.

"If you'd like to come with me, you're more than welcome to."

"Oh, no. I couldn't go out with a bunch of kids."

"Olivia, I'm only five years younger than you. Give me a break."

"I wouldn't know what to wear. And I probably couldn't get a sitter on such short notice."

"I'd help you pick out something to wear. You could come over to my place and we could get ready together. I'm sure there is some teenage kid out there somewhere who'd rather earn twenty bucks watching your kids than sit home alone on New Year's. You should really get out more. You're never going to meet anybody if you never leave your house."

"I know, but I *probably* won't meet anyone, and sitters are so expensive, and I won't get to sleep until late, so I'll be tired the next day, and . . ."

"You're right; you probably won't meet a guy, but you might. More importantly, you might just have yourself some fun. Even if you have an awful time, at least that's an experience. Sitting in front of your TV is not an experience; it's a waste of your life. Living is about having good experiences and bad ones. It's about making memories and meeting people."

She thinks about this for a moment. "Are you sure you really want me to come? You're not just inviting me because you feel sorry for some frumpy old single mother?"

"Why does everyone think I do things out of charity? You know me well enough to know I'm not really a good person. If I didn't want you to come, I wouldn't have invited you. I see you enough at work as it is."

"Well, I probably can't get a sitter. I'll see."

"You just let me know."

I'm pitifully unproductive at work. I try to get stuff done, but for every minute of work I do I spend about ten minutes daydreaming about Ryan. I think about things he said, or the way he was with the kids, or how we laughed together. And then I think of how he treated me when I called him yesterday, and the memories of that really piss me off. I want to call him and get some explanation. I really thought we connected the other night, but it's happened to me many times before that a guy I wasn't remotely attracted to thought we'd "really connected," and I had to do that awful tap dance around the truth where I try to come up with a reason not to go out with him without hurting his feelings. *I really like you . . . but the timing just isn't right.* Then, of course, the guys I *am* interested in brush me off with some lame excuse like they don't "see a future between us," which I usually interpret to mean, "your breasts aren't big enough." I just want to know if the fun I had the other night was all a figment of my imagination. Plus, I'd love to tell Ryan off for hanging up on me.

I'm still feeling resentful toward him when Olivia leaves for lunch. Before I can talk myself out of it, I close the office door and dial his number. After three rings, I get thrown into voice mail.

To leave a message or not to leave a message, that is the question.

For several seconds the only thing recording is the sound of me breathing. Then I realize it'll be much easier to tell him off to his machine than personally, so I forge ahead.

"Hi, Ryan, this is Aimee Lachaussée. I just wanted to say that I was sort of surprised and confused about your reaction yesterday. I mean, if you're not interested in me, that's fine, but I just think you could have been a little bit nicer about telling me that. It took a lot for me to work up the courage to call you. You seemed so nice the other night. And cute. And fun. But if you're not attracted to me . . . I mean, you certainly wouldn't be the first guy . . ." *Shut up, Aimee, shut up! Stop talking. Set the phone* down. *Drop your weapon!* "So, I just wanted to call you and get that off my chest. Goodbye."

I hang up the phone. My insides rumble volcanically, and for the second time in as many days I feel like I could pass out from a lack of oxygen.

CHAPTER FIVE

For the next several days, I come to the office and pretend to work while actually spending my time thinking about Ryan, and my sister and Tristan, and about Sean, and about relationships in general. Then at night I come home and think about how I should put my Christmas tree and all the Christmas decorations away. I have a fake tree, so really, I could just take the entire thing, decorations and all, down to my storage space in the basement of my townhome and leave it there, all ready for next year, but even that seems like more effort than I can summon. So instead of returning my living room to its natural state, I come home, strip off my clothes, and sit on the couch watching TV in the calming glow of the Christmas tree lights.

Even though I normally like to cook, this week I just can't face doing all the dishes that cooking creates. So one night for dinner I have M&Ms, another night it's microwave popcorn, and the next night I go crazy and order in something resembling a balanced meal: sesame chicken and fried rice. Close enough.

We have to work on New Year's Eve—we just get New

Year's Day off—and Olivia comes in that morning looking happier than usual.

I, immediately suspicious, ask, "What are you smiling about?"

"I found a baby-sitter for tonight. I can go out!"

"Awesome! That's great. You'll have a lot of fun, I promise."

"Do I need to bring anything to the party?"

"Something to drink. Wine, beer, whatever you like."

"We're going to drink? Do you know how long it's been since I've had a drink?"

What did she think we were going to do at a New Year's Eve party, play pin the tail on the donkey?

"You don't have to drink if you don't want to."

"Oh. I want to," she says, with the wide eyes and breathy voice of a woman possessed with thoughts of debauchery on a grand scale. The look of a woman who has found a baby-sitter and has been given the all-clear for a night away from the kids.

What have I gotten myself into?

"What time is the party?" she asks.

"Well, it starts at eight, so we'll want to get there at nine. Come over to my place at seven-thirty and bring a few different outfits. We'll do each other's hair and makeup, have a glass of wine, consult each other on what to wear, and then go to the party together."

"That sounds like fun. It's a plan."

I'm glad to be able to consult with Olivia on her appearance. I'm not a fashion maven or beauty consultant, but there are many days when I want to pull Olivia aside and say, "Girlfriend, what were you thinking when you got dressed this morning? How can you not see that couldn't possibly be less flattering for your figure?"

She's overweight, but that's not why she looks frumpy. I know lots of overweight women who are as stylish and good looking as any model. It's not about her weight; it's about the tragic fashion choices she makes. I couldn't tell you what cuts or fabrics or colors would look good on her, but I do know that I can look at her and know whether she looks good or not. And tonight I'll finally have my chance to let my thoughts known.

Before Olivia gets to my place, I begin the what-should-I-wear-to-the-party ritual. Because I don't get dressed up very often, I find it a particular challenge to try to figure out how to look sexy and festive while simultaneously being comfortable. I don't mean just comfortable in that I want to avoid wedging my feet into impossibly narrow shoes or comfortable that I'll be able to do fancy things like breathe. I mean I want to feel confident that I won't be offered money in exchange for sex and I'll be secure in the knowledge that my boobs won't come tumbling out for all to see in the event that I should laugh or sneeze. I'm wearing my sexy, too-tight jeans and the multicolored sequined bustier that Bridgette got me for Christmas. I put my fitted black blazer on over the bustier, but I still worry it's too sexy for me. I look good, but I fear the possible boob-pop-out factor might just be too strong. I take the blazer off and am about to free my breasts from their sequined confines when the doorbell rings. It's 7:30 on the dot. That can't possibly be Olivia, can it? I hadn't actually expected her to be on time. She's never on time for work, usually because of her kids. (I'm always late to work, too, but that's just because I don't like work.) I grab the blazer and am putting it on as I make my way to answer the front door.

"You look so, so sexy," Olivia announces.

"Yeah. I was thinking I look *too* sexy. I'm probably not going to wear this." I finish buttoning up the blazer. "What do you think?"

"You look gorgeous. Sexy but not slutty. Very hot."

Olivia enters my place, and I close the door behind her.

She is carrying a dizzying array of plastic bags—both of her arms have bags dangling all up and down them. She looks like a shabbily decorated Christmas tree.

She begins peeling off the bags, and then frees herself from her layers of outerwear and I see what I have to work with.

Not much.

"I brought most of my wardrobe and all the makeup I own," she says.

"I'll open a bottle of wine, and we'll get to work."

I pour us each a glass of wine, and I show her around my place. It's small, but nicely decorated, and Olivia makes all the appropriate cooing noises about how great the place is. I am proud of it. I redid the kitchen cabinets and the kitchen floor myself, and no wall or ceiling is the same color it had been when I bought the place. (The previous owner had apparently suffered from a very serious drug problem to come up with the combinations she did. Three words should be kept in mind if one is going to attempt sponge painting: "tasteful" and "in moderation." And the places she'd wallpapered looked like she'd taken magic-eye paintings and plastered them over pebbled, rocky terrain—it was so bumpy I wondered if she'd somehow managed to wallpaper over entire colonies of bugs that were spread out across the walls at the time the gluey paper came down.)

In my bedroom, I tell Olivia to spread out the clothes she brought. We sip our wine and inspect the selection. It's grim, that's all there is to it.

"The outfit I'm wearing now is the one I thought looked best. What do you think?"

"Well, you look good," I lie, "but having your shirt tucked in at your waist makes your figure look kind of boxy. Why don't we put you in a blazer?"

"I don't have any."

"But I do."

"But you're so skinny."

"Yes, but I'm also broad-shouldered. Just try this on. I really think it'll fit."

"What will I wear under it?"

"Let's just see if it fits first."

I let her try on my chocolate brown blazer. We have to roll the sleeves up, but otherwise it fits her surprisingly well. The color is well suited to her hair and eyes.

"See how flattering that is? It gives you a waist. You have nice curves; you need to show them off, not hide them."

I watch her watch herself in the mirror. I can see the corners of her mouth bending upward, just a little, as she tries to absorb the possibility that her curves are actually a good thing.

"What am I going to wear under it?"

"Let's figure that out after we get our hair and makeup done. Take the jacket off so it doesn't get full of makeup."

I take my bustier off and put on a tank top, and the two of us, half dressed as we are, go into the bathroom.

"Why don't you let me style your hair," I say.

"I've already done my hair."

"Let's try something a little funkier tonight."

She looks at me for a moment, considering. With the blazer victory fresh in her mind, she decides to trust me. "Okay," she says with a definitive nod.

"Why don't you get your hair wet in the tub, and I'll blow-dry it."

I help her get the water started, and she bends over the tub, leaning her head under the faucet. As she gets her hair wet, I begin putting on makeup. I only put minimal makeup on for work, but sometimes it's fun to pretend I'm a drag queen and really paint it on. I put on foundation, powder, blush, and lipstick, and then I begin the tricky process of putting my eyeshadow on. I brush a dark brown color on across the crease and the outside of my left eye, and that's when the doorbell rings.

Olivia shuts off the water and gives me a look.

"I have no idea who that could be," I say.

I walk across my townhome to my door and open it so that my body is shielded by the door and just my head is peeking out.

Ryan is sitting on the path just outside my door. A rush of emotions surge through me: excitement, nervousness, desire, and then, when I remember my partially made-up face, embarrassment.

Immediately, my hand goes to shield my one made-up eye.

"Happy New Year's," he says.

I notice that Vince and Gerry are in a dark blue van in the parking lot. They wave, and I wave back, and then immediately return my hand to covering up my one made-up eye.

"Hi, what are you doing here? How did you find my house?"

"I have caller ID, so I got your number when you called me. You're in the book, so I was able to look on-line and match your number to your house."

"Oh, so . . . why are you here?"

"I'm here to apologize. I've been thinking a lot about what you said when you called—left the message, I mean—and . . . I feel really bad about how things went between us."

It's freezing out, and the cold air has made me hyperaware of my nipples standing at attention. I feel like my nipples have taken over the entire house.

"I'm sorry, but I'm freezing. Can you—" I was going to ask him to come in, but he won't be able to make it over the cement step you have to cross to get inside with his wheelchair. "Hang on a second. Let me put a jacket on. I'll come out."

I run over to the sink, wash off the makeup from my eye, then grab my coat from the back of the kitchen chair and put it on as I go outside.

"Hey," I say.

"Hey. So, I mean, I just wanted to say that—that I'm sorry. Of course I think you're attractive. And I had a lot of fun talking to you, too. I'm just not sure I'm ready to start dating."

"Well, that's fair. I understand that."

"Okay."

"Okay."

We stare at each other for a long moment. I shift my weight from my right foot to my left, feeling confused and awkward.

"So, you're going out?" he asks.

"Yeah. My coworker, Olivia, and I are going to this party at my friend's house. How about you?"

"Gerry, Vince, and me are going to see a band downtown."

"Cool."

We stare at each other in silence for several more seconds.

"God, this is really awkward, isn't it?" he says.

"Yeah. It sort of is."

"Well, I guess I'll get going. I . . . uh, would you be interested in seeing the exhibit at the art museum with me sometime?"

"As friends, you mean?"

"To start."

"Yeah. Sure. I think I'd like that."

"Well, I have your number. I'll call you. Have fun tonight. Happy New Year."

"You, too. Happy New Year."

I wave him off, watching him for a moment before I return to the warmth of my townhome.

"Who was that?" Olivia asks.

I tell her the whole story, and she reacts as I knew she would, which is why I haven't told her before: she goes bonkers, shrieking about how he was the transcendent love my horoscope told me about.

"I don't know about love. There's definitely attraction." I tell her about his accident and how he's not ready to date. I ask her if she thinks it'll be a problem for me to date a guy who can't walk.

"You guys could have fallen in love and then he could have gotten in the accident. What would you do then, leave him?"

"No, of course not."

"Every relationship has its challenges. Real attraction, real connection—that doesn't come along very often. I think you should see where this goes."

"Well, the real obstacle is whether he actually calls. I'm not counting on it."

I blow-dry and curl her hair; then I help her with her makeup and finish doing my own. I end up wearing a fitted black sweater that is sexy without being too revealing. Olivia and I would never be mistaken for movie stars, but I think for two ordinary underwriters, we clean up pretty well.

The party is at my friend Cindy's house. Cindy and I were roommates our freshman year in college. We were, and still are, very different people, but somehow we became friends, despite getting off to a terrible start. When she learned I was French Canadian, she told me she'd taken French in high school and proceeded to ramble off some horribly mangled sentences in a pitiful attempt at French. I couldn't help myself—it was so awful—I burst out laughing. Needless to say, this didn't endear me to her.

"I'm sorry, I'm sorry, I'm sorry," I'd said. "That was very French of me. We're snobs about our language. But that was a good try, really. No, really."

We managed to become friends despite me nearly keeling over with laughter at her butchered French the first time we met.

Though she never spoke French in front of me again.

Nowadays we hardly ever see each other. I swear if e-mail hadn't been invented, most of my friendships would have disintegrated like a sandcastle in a windstorm. Much like a Christmas newsletter, once a month or so I e-mail my friends, telling them about what's going on in my life whether they care or not and doing my best to pry out a few details about their lives as well. In this way, we're able to stay in touch, even if it is a tenuous link.

As soon as I get to the party, I start scoping the scene for guys who look to be about Olivia's age and aren't wearing wedding rings. I see one who looks promising. I'm pretty sure I've met him at one of Cindy's parties before. He either goes to her church or works with her, something like that.

"What about him?" I whisper to Olivia.

"What about him?"

"For you, silly. What do you think about him for you? Come on, let's go chat him up."

"Oh, I don't—"

But before she can protest, I've got her by the arm and am essentially dragging her across the room.

"Hi," I say to the guy. "I'm Aimee. We met at one of Cindy's parties . . ."

"Her barbeque last spring."

"Oh, right, right. What was your name again?"

"Bob."

"Bob, this is my coworker, Olivia. I was just going to get a drink. Bob, do you need a refill?"

"Sure, that'd be great."

"Olivia, what's your poison?"

"Oh, I . . . I'll have whatever you're having."

"I'll be right back."

I cross the room to the kitchen, where I take as long as I possibly can to retrieve a beer out of the fridge for Bob and pour two glasses of red wine. I sneak covert glances at Bob and Olivia, and things seem to be going well. There are smiles exchanged, gazes are met, the usual flirtation regimen. Just as I'm about to stop dawdling and return, I see Bob make a hasty retreat and a look of disappointment flash across Olivia's face.

"What happened?" I ask.

"As soon as he found out I had kids he couldn't get away from me fast enough."

"Oh. I'm sorry."

She just offers a resigned shrug.

Not for the first time, it occurs to me that this whole dating thing really sucks. There is so much possibility for rejection, so many things that could go wrong. For two people to have things in common, *and* want the same things in life, *and* be attracted to each other . . . well, really, sometimes I think it's amazing that a couple ever hooks up and stays together at all.

It's hard, because I want everyone to be partnered off with someone they love and who loves them back. You see two single people and want them to hit it off and live happily ever after. You think that if you can just finagle a way to get them together, they'll be drawn to each other like cat hair to black pants—they'll become inseparable. Sometimes I have to remind myself of the lesson of Sean and me and Bridgette and Tristan: Just because somebody is in a couple does not mean he or she is happy. Sometimes it's better to be single and free than to be shackled in an unhappy relationship.

I really want Olivia to have a good time tonight—she gets so few nights out on the town—so to get her mind off Bob, I quickly gather a group of eight of us together to play Cranium. She does her best to avoid doing any singing or art or impersonations, but at last her teammates force her to do the next round, and when she's called upon to do a Copycat of Marilyn Monroe, she starts laughing and doesn't stop for the rest of the night.

When midnight approaches, Olivia whispers to me that she's worried about not having anyone to kiss when the clock strikes twelve. I tell her we'll kiss each other like the

French do—once on each cheek. That's exactly what we do. Then we hold our champagne glasses high and toast. Amid the yelling and shrieking and cheering, I have a moment where I think about the year that has gone by and the year that is to come. That's the thing about the holidays—they force you to reflect on your life whether you like it or not.

I realize this: This past year, I made some hard, but good decisions. I had some fun. I went on a trip to the Bahamas I'll never forget (a little present to myself after breaking up with Sean). I don't know what this new year will bring for sure, but I can make a guess that some of it will be good, some will be bad, most will be forgettable, but maybe, just maybe, this year has some exciting possibilities in store for me.

CHAPTER SIX

On New Year's Day, I spend the morning sleeping in and then work out to a step aerobics videotape in my living room. I'm just contemplating what I want for lunch when the phone rings.

"Aimee?"

"This is she."

"Hey. This is Ryan."

Excuse me, does anyone have a defibrillator handy, because I do believe my heart has stopped.

"Hi! I'm glad you called. How are you?"

"Good. I'm good. Are you hurting from last night?" he asks.

"Actually, I drank pretty sensibly last night. How about you?"

"Me, too."

"I guess that means we're growing up, huh?"

"I never would have thought I'd see the day. What is the world coming to?"

"It's a scary, scary day indeed when you can drink in

moderation on New Year's. Rogaine and incontinence diapers are all that much closer."

He chuckles. "Look, would you still be interested in going to the art museum with me on Saturday?"

"Absolutely."

"Would you be able to pick me up?"

"Sure."

He gives me directions to his place, and we decide I'll pick him up around one.

I spend the next two days out of my head with excitement, even though I tell myself that we're going to the museum as friends and I shouldn't expect anything.

When Saturday finally comes, I pull into his driveway a few minutes before one. He lives in a ranch-style house with a ramp fashioned from his front door to a cement path that connects with his paved driveway. I wonder if, before the accident, he lived in a two- or three-story house with lots of stairs. Or maybe he lived here all along and the only change was the addition of the ramp.

I ring the doorbell, and he's at the door in about a split second—he must have been watching for me from the window. As soon as I see him again, a charge of excitement rushes through my body.

"Hi," he says with a kind smile.

"Hi," I say. And with just those two words and a couple of smiles exchanged between us, I feel like whatever weird blip happened with us is a thing of the past and everything is okay again.

We spend a couple hours tooling around the museum. Then we walk (or roll, depending) several blocks to the 16th Street Mall, which is a pedestrian mall in the heart of downtown Denver. There, we go to a café and order lattes.

We talk a little more, and then I ask him if we can move our conversation to some place where they serve real food.

We go to the Wazee Supper Club and order pizza and beers and continue getting to know each other.

"What was your worst class in college?" he asks me.

"Hmm, I don't know." I think back for a second. "This one class—art history—I liked the subject matter, but the professor was this really uptight lady. She wore those shirts where the collar comes way up and it's so tight it looks like she shouldn't be able to breathe. She was just this very severe lady, the bun pulled back all tight, the whole deal. I had this class first thing in the morning, and she'd shut the lights off—a total recipe for disaster for a eight A.M. class, clearly—and then she'd talk in this monotone voice. The light from the projector kind of lit up her face in the dark in this really eerie way. Anyway, it was such a struggle staying awake in that class, I tell ya. I never signed up for an early morning class again, particularly not a class that required us to look at slides in the dark."

"I can top that. My freshman year I had geology at eight A.M. Every day the professor would turn out the lights so we could look at slides . . . *of rocks*. The professor would throw out pop quizzes at the end of class to make sure you'd been paying attention. He just asked questions from stuff he covered in lecture that day, so theoretically if you were in class, you'd be fine. Except I slept through every single minute of every single class. I'd just come to class, sit down next to my friend Bruce, and about four seconds after the lights went out, I was fast asleep. Then at the end of the class, Bruce would elbow me in the ribs. He'd be like, 'Dude! Wake up! We have a quiz!' I'd wake up all startled, 'Who? What? Where am I? What's going on?' Needless to say, my grade in that class wasn't among the finest of my college career."

I laugh. "Rocks at eight A.M. That is pretty brutal. You're right, you win; that's worse than my tale of collegiate woe. At least I got to look at pretty pictures."

After dinner, we walk a couple of blocks to a bar and get

a couple more beers, and before we know it it's after midnight and we're about a million miles away from the car.

"What are we going to do?" I ask. "It's too cold to walk all that . . ." I realize what I've just said, and I want to bludgeon myself with something heavy and painful. ". . . way."

"Why don't you call a taxi and we'll wait for it inside over another beer."

"That is a very good idea. You have some good critical thinking skills in that head of yours. It's just one of the many things I really like about you."

We exchange smiles and flirty glances, and I realize that even though we've only gone on one date (albeit a twelve-hour one), I'm falling hard for this guy.

CHAPTER SEVEN

After that first marathon date, Ryan and I see each other every chance we get, and when we don't get together in person, we talk on the phone.

Hanging out with someone in a wheelchair requires a lot of patience. Suddenly I have to wait for what feels like centuries for rickety old elevators to take us up a single flight of steps I would normally sprint up in seconds. Instead of being able to go through whatever door is closest to us, we often have to go around to some obscure back entrance that is wheelchair accessible. I never noticed any of this before because I never had to. But it could very easily have been me in that car accident. It could have been anyone. And now I notice this stuff.

Every time he smiles at me, I get this dizzy feeling in my chest—not in my head, but in my chest, an actual physical reaction of lightness and excitement and sheer happiness. I think about him constantly. I think about things he said or the way he made me laugh. I fantasize about kissing him, running my hands across his chest, waking up in bed in his arms, getting him out of his clothes and licking and kissing every part of his warm flesh. I am, in short, out of my head with desire for him.

I want to kiss him desperately, but it's awkward. I'll drive him home after we go on a date, and I'll walk him to the door, and because there is the height issue, I can't just lean in close and hope he takes the hint and kisses me. So we don't kiss, to my eternal sorrow.

One day we go to the Natural Science Museum, and as we're walking along, I put my hand over his. He envelopes my hand in his, and, as simple a gesture as it is, it thrills me. It's like when you go camping and have been denied luxuries like a comfortable place to sleep and something more gourmet to eat than trail mix, and suddenly the simplest things become intensely pleasurable. We hold hands for maybe fifteen minutes, and the entire time I'm hyperaware of the warmth of his large, soft hands. I'm aware of the little glitter-sized pools of sweat that form in the heat between our palms. Then he lets go of my hand to hit some button on his mechanized chair. For the rest of the time we're at the museum, all I can think about is holding his hand again, but maneuvering around the exhibits is tricky with his chair, and an opportunity to take his hand in mine never comes up again.

CHAPTER EIGHT

One night I invite Ryan over for a gourmet meal of French food and good but inexpensive French wine. The menu is carefully planned to ensure every dish offers intensely flavorful, sensual delights. We start with a rich lobster bisque. For dinner we have roast duck, topped with candied orange in a Grand Marnier sauce, accompanied by wild rice. For dessert, I make *la tarte d'eté,* which is an almond shortbread filled with custard and raspberries, topped with milk chocolate mousse.

It's a meal in which every bite demands to be savored slowly. Every time Ryan tastes a new item, he emits a low, sexual groan of pleasure.

We don't talk much over the course of the meal, except to discuss food.

"This food is absolutely spectacular," Ryan says for approximately the twentieth time this evening.

"Thank you. I love to cook, so I'd be happy to cook for you anytime."

"Where did you learn to cook like this?"

"Both my mother and grandmother are good cooks. My mother and sister are girly girls, into all the stereotypical stuff you associate women with, like cooking, being into clothes and shoes, doing their hair and makeup. I was always a jock and never really got into clothes and makeup, at least not like my mom did, but cooking was one area that Mom and I could really bond over. My sister, Bridgette, is a decent cook, but I don't think she was passionate about it like I was. So it was often Mom and me cooking dinners together. We just kind of worked quietly beside each other. I found cooking to be a good way to unwind after a long day, and, you know, you have to eat, so you might as well eat well if you can."

I watch him lick the custard and chocolate mousse from his spoon, his tongue and mouth closing over the creamy sweetness, and it's so damn sexy it's all I can do to keep myself from lunging across the table and ravaging him.

When we're done with dinner, I ask, "Would you like to go in the living room and watch a video?"

"Sure."

This, naturally, had been my plot all along—to get him alone in a darkened room. Insert a sound track of a sinister laugh here.

We go into the living room, and I let him select from my anemic DVD collection. I put the DVD in, and from the corner of my eye I see him swinging from his chair to my couch. I turn the movie on, dim the lights, and sit next to him.

The film starts, but I don't think either of us pay much attention to it. We keep stealing glances at each other. I love how he looks in the dimmed light, the whites of his eyes seeming to sparkle in the darkness. This goes on for several minutes until I finally say, "Can I kiss you?"

He pauses a moment and then nods.

I lean in, and we exchange a few polite, soft kisses. Then we pull away and pretend to watch the movie for a few minutes until we simultaneously practically leap on each other, our tongues exploring the other's mouth and lips hungrily. I sit on his lap to make it easier for us to kiss, and he wraps his arms around me.

Our kisses are passionate and intense, and we keep up the make-out session for hours. But that's it, that's all we do. He doesn't even feel me up. It's like being in secondary school again, but at least in secondary school, the guy *tried* to feel me up (and then had his hand firmly swatted away, but it's the thought that counts). I can feel his erection boring into my thigh. He allows me to grope at his chest to my heart's desire, but when I try to stroke his erection that is threatening to rip a hole through his jeans, he firmly takes me by the wrist and pulls my hand away.

I now know how all the rejected secondary school boys felt.

Phenomenally frustrated.

CHAPTER NINE

Several more times over the course of the next few weeks, Ryan and I do a repeat of our smooch fest. Because we're not having sex, I live my life in a constant state of sexual arousal. Although actually, I think even if we were having sex, I would be living my life in a constant state of sexual arousal. But at least I'd have some occasional release for my pent-up ardor.

I think about having sex with him more or less constantly. It really makes getting any work done at the office nearly impossible. As soon as I get focused on crunching numbers and filling out forms, my mind starts to wander. Then several minutes later I'll finally catch myself daydreaming, clear my head, try to work, and am productive for mere moments before my thoughts start drifting off again.

I want to be with him every possible moment. In the mornings when I wake up alone, I feel an actual physical ache that he's not there beside me. I want to be with him when I go to bed at night and when I wake up in the morning. I want to eat dinner with him every evening and snuggle next to him on the couch when I watch TV. I want to travel and see the world with him.

I'm afraid I may be falling in love with him.

And I have no idea how he feels about me.

He comes over to dinner fairly regularly. I still cook nice meals, but not the gourmet (and pricey) feast I prepared the first time he came over. It's become our pattern that when I cook, he brings over the wine. When I go to his place, we order out. I bring the beer.

One evening at my place over a meal of baked goat cheese salads and Provencal grilled chicken with vegetables and penne pasta, he says, "I've been thinking I'd go back to work."

"Yeah? Even though you can afford not to?"

"I'm bored. I've been doing a lot a charity work, and I feel like I've read every book at the library, but . . . it's not enough. I need to be challenged."

"I think that's great. Have you started looking yet?"

"I've been looking in the papers for openings, and I've sent out some e-mails to former colleagues asking them to let me know about any opportunities they hear about. But I'm not really sure whether I want to go back to what I was doing."

"Why not?"

"Oh . . . I don't know. I guess . . . I'm not sure if people would take me seriously with me in my chair. What I did for a living—I mean, I had to take on a real leadership role. I'd go into companies and make recommendations for how they could improve their business practices. I'm not sure if people could really . . . I don't know . . ."

"I can't even believe I'm hearing you say this. Look, I know it can be scary to get back to something when you haven't done it in a while. I'm going to give you some advice, okay? I'm sorry to use a cliché, but you really do need to just get back on the horse. I'm speaking from experience here. When I was in high school, I was on the swim team. I don't mean to brag, but I really was the best on the team. But then I got injured, and I was out of commission for several weeks. When I came back, I had really lost my edge. Girls who weren't that strong of swimmers were just leaving me in their wake, literally. It was so hard for my ego to take that ultimately I just told the coach I would never be back in shape in time, and I just quit. I gave up, just like that. I'm still mad at myself for doing that. I know I would have been a strong swimmer again if I'd just given it some time, but my ego clouded my judgment. Anything can be scary when you've stopped doing it for a long time. It's scary at first, but it does get easier."

"I know. You're right."

I take a bite out of my pasta and try to decide whether I have the courage to ask him about sex and about us. I don't have the courage, it turns out, but I do it anyway. "Ryan, since we're talking about, you know, getting back on the horse again and everything, going back to things you haven't done in a while . . . do you . . . think maybe we will ever have sex?"

He expels a loud breath of air and looks anywhere in the room except at me.

"Oh, Aimee, I don't know."

"Can we . . . talk about this? About what you're nervous about?"

"What makes you think I'm nervous?"

"I don't . . . maybe 'nervous' isn't the right word. But you seem uncomfortable about something."

"I'm not. I swear."

"Oh. Well, you know, if you ever want to talk about it . . ."

"Sure. Yeah. No problem."

I nod at him. But then I realize his nonanswer just made me have more questions. I'm no closer to having any answers—or getting any sex—so I say, "Ryan, are you not attracted to me in that way?"

"Aimee, don't be ridiculous. You're gorgeous. I just . . . look, I don't want to talk about this."

"Okay. That's fine."

But it's not fine. My question wasn't really about sex. That's not what I really wanted to know. What I really want to know is, how does he feel about me? Because I am in love with him. I love him so much it hurts. And if I'm just the transitional girl between his accident and the girl who turns out to be the love of his life, I don't think I could bear it.

CHAPTER TEN

I bemoan the cruel circumstances of my unfortunate celibacy to Olivia the moment she gets into work the next morning. I don't even look up from where I have my head lying on my desk, buried in my arms.

"We still haven't had sex. We've been going out for two months and no sex. Nothing."

"Have you talked to him about it?" she says.

"Noooo," I moan. "I tried to, but he says he doesn't want to talk about it." I sit there in a giant stew of self-pity for a moment. Then I lift my head up and look at Olivia. She's smiling so hard it looks like the muscles in her cheeks are going to snap from all the pressure. "What's up with you? Did you win the lottery or something?"

"In a way, yes."

"What's going on?"

"I went on a date last night!"

"A date?" She's got my full attention now. "You didn't tell me you had a date. Why didn't you tell me you had a date? Who'd you have a date with? How'd you meet him?"

"I didn't want to jinx it, that's why I didn't tell you. You know Suzy from accounting?"

"Yeah, I know Suzy."

"Well, I was telling her a week or so back how I hadn't been on a single date in nearly a year, and she said her husband had this friend, this great catch in his mid-thirties. She said he was funny and smart and had a good job, but he's kind of shy so he has trouble meeting women, but she said she'd tell him about me and see if he wanted to meet me. So she talked to her husband, and her husband talked to Russ, and Russ and I e-mailed each other back and forth for the last week, and then last night we met and, Aimee"—Olivia clasps her hand to her heart—"it was the best date of my life. We talked, we laughed . . . things were just so comfortable between us. And he already asked me out for another date! We're going out tomorrow night. I can't wait!"

I smile. Her excitement is such a wonderful thing to see.

"Good. Good for you, Olivia. I really hope this works out for you. He sounds great. Tell me about him."

Olivia fills me in on his vitals—what he does for a living, what he looks like, what his interests are. I smile and tell her repeatedly that he sounds great, which he does. And I'm happy for her, I really am, but my feelings of sorrow and confusion over Ryan are making it hard for me to pay attention.

And then the phone rings.

It's Ryan. And my world lights up again. "Hey, Ryan. What's up?"

"Aimee, I—"

"You what? Do you want to come over for dinner tonight? I wanted to try out this new recipe."

"I don't think so."

"Oh. Well, do you want to go out to eat? Or I can come over to your place."

"Aimee, I think we shouldn't see each other anymore."

"What? What are you talking about? Why?"

"I just think things are getting too serious between us."

"How can you possibly say that? We haven't even slept together."

"I know, I just think maybe this isn't a good time for me to be in a relationship."

I can't believe he's using the this-isn't-a-good-time-for-me tap dance routine on me.

"Ryan, I am so sick of you being so afraid. I can't believe you don't even have the courage to break up with me in person. You call me on the *phone?* When I'm at *work?* That is the lamest thing I've ever heard. You are such a chickenshit. I don't even know how I could ever have let myself fall in love with someone so spineless!"

"You love me?"

"Of course I love you, you jackass."

"Aimee, I didn't mean to hurt you. I didn't mean to string you along. I'm just not ready for this . . ."

"Well, don't call me when you are ready, because I'm not waiting around."

This time, it's my turn to slam the phone down on him.

I look at Olivia, and the look of pity on her face makes me burst into tears.

CHAPTER ELEVEN

I spend most of my day in the office bathroom crying.

I sit on the toilet in the closed stall with a wad of toilet paper that has been reduced to a soppy pulp from my snot and tears, and I think. I think maybe I should call Sean and see if we can get back together. At least with Sean I was safe, because even though I cared about him, my love for him was never as intense as the way I feel about Ryan. When you love someone this hard, there is so much more to lose, so much more hurt to feel when it doesn't work out.

At the end of the day, I stop on my way home from work and get an oversized jug of wine that I intend to sip every last drop of this very evening.

When I pull into my driveway, Ryan is sitting on my front porch. The front porch we'd fashioned a makeshift ramp on so he could get into and out of my house. "Makeshift." The word means something crude and temporary. Like our relationship.

"What are you doing here?" I say.

"I'm here to say I'm sorry."

I sigh. "Come in. Let's get out of the cold."

We go inside into the living room. He swings from his chair to the couch, and this strikes me because it suggests that he's settling in for a real conversation and not a quick blow-off where he can roar away in seconds. For a change.

"So. You're sorry," I say. "Sorry that you don't feel as strongly about me as I do about you? Sorry about breaking my heart? What is it that you're sorry about exactly?"

"Well, for a start, I'm sorry about the lame breakup over the phone."

"Yeah, that was a pretty feeble move."

"I just . . . I'm not sure I'm ready to get serious with someone right now."

"Serious? We weren't getting serious. It wasn't like I was demanding an engagement ring or something."

"I know, but the thing is, Aimee, with you . . . I could see an engagement ring in our future. I've never felt this way about anyone. It's a lot to get a handle on."

"I've got some good news for you. That's exactly how I feel about you."

"But what if you get bored? What if you decide you want a guy you can go skiing and running along the beach with?"

"Ryan, you are everything I want in a guy. I feel like one of the luckiest women in the world because I was able to find such a great man. Look, the guy of my dreams came to me in a package I wasn't quite expecting, but I think sometimes the best gifts come in unexpected packages. Nobody is perfect, but even us imperfect people have good sex and fall in love and lead happy lives, if we let ourselves. I think you need to get over your fears and take a risk with me."

"I'm not afraid."

"Yeah, Ryan, you are. If you weren't afraid, we wouldn't have been dating for two months with only a few chaste kisses between us."

"I'm not afraid," he says again, and I know he's trying to convince himself.

"Well, good, then can we finally have sex?"

He just looks at me, and I can see that he wants to, but he's nervous. He is, despite his protests, scared. I'm not quite sure what he's afraid of. That he'll disappoint himself? That I'll be disappointed? That I won't like his body? That he won't? Fortunately, I have more faith in what we have together and enough courage for us both. I sit in his lap on the couch, put my arms around his shoulders, and kiss him gently. Our kisses are tentative at first, but soon they become more urgent, more intense. I don't know about Ryan, but the overwhelming desire I've tried to hold at bay for the last two months rages within me. I tear off my blouse and my bra. Ryan moans and takes my breast in his hand and my nipple in his mouth. From there, any tentativeness is banished, and instinct takes over.

I won't go into all the carnal and salacious details, but I will say this: Santa was very, very good to me this year.

NOTES FROM THE GIRLS' GLOBAL GUIDE TO GUYS

1. Paris. City of Lights? Romantic. Heavily accented gropers? Not so much.

2. Venice. Pasta, wine, art, and men who tell you you're *bella* even when your hair hasn't been washed in three days. What's not to love?

3. Athens. Just remember: in the land of ouzo shots, everything is romantic.

4. Budapest. Even surrounded by castles, heartbreak bites.

5. Amsterdam. Tall, blond, smiley people. Sex shops. You do the math.

And that's just the beginning . . .

Best friends Jadie Peregrine and Tate Moran have had it with the dating life in Boulder, Colorado. Somewhere in the world there has to be a place where this whole romance thing is easier—a magical country where the men aren't commitment-phobes, cross-dressers, or just plain psychotic. That thought starts Jadie on an inspired plan: why not write a very different sort of travel guide, one that gives the 411 on what it's like to date men all over the world? Jadie and Tate: Love Anthropologists. From London to Amsterdam, Hungary to Greece and all points in between, they'll research the field of male dating patterns and report back to their sisters-in-arms. And if they happen to meet Mr. Right along the way, so much the better. Now, with their bags packed, passports ready, and their hearts on the line, two best friends are in for the adventure of a lifetime, because when it comes to travel, men, and love, nothing goes according to plan . . .

Here is an exciting sneak peek of Theresa Alan's
THE GIRLS' GLOBAL GUIDE TO GUYS
coming in April 2005!

CHAPTER ONE

Boulder, Colorado

"It couldn't possibly have been that bad."

"Oh, but it was. I saw his you-know-what within an hour of knowing him, totally against my will."

"He flashed you?"

"Not exactly. We stopped by my apartment after dinner before we went to the club because we'd gone for Italian, and I had garlic breath, and I wanted to brush my teeth before we went dancing, even though I knew within four seconds of meeting him that it could never go anywhere. I don't know *what* Sylvia was thinking setting us up. But to be polite I had to go through the charade of the date anyway, even though I wasn't remotely attracted to him. So I started brushing my teeth, but I wanted to check on him and make sure he was okay; so I came out from the bathroom into the living room, and he was just sitting there on the couch, naked."

"No!"

"Yes. Naked and, ah . . . you know, aroused." I'm stuck in traffic, story of my life, talking on my cell phone, which is paid for by the company I work for, making it one of the very, very few perks of being employed by Pinnacle Media. "I mean, I know it's been a while since I've dated anyone, but isn't the whole point of dating and sex to kind of, I don't know, enjoy this stuff *together?* Like getting turned on by the other person's touch, and not by the sound of someone brushing her teeth in the bathroom?"

"So what did you do?"

"Well, I looked at him like the maniac he was, and he realized that I was appalled and said that he'd assumed that when I said I was going to brush my teeth, that meant I was going to put my diaphragm in."

"I don't . . . is English his native language? I don't see how anyone could possibly come to that conclusion."

"Right, Tate, that's my point. The guy was a loon. So I reply, quite logically under the circumstances I think, my mouth foaming with toothpaste, 'No, I willy was bruffing my teef.' And this whole situation strikes me as so wildly funny. I mean, in the past six months, I've dated a bitter divorcé, been hit on by a string of lesbians, and now this. How did my dating life go so tragically wrong? Anyway, I just lost it. I crumpled to the ground in a fit of hysteria. I mean, I started laughing so hard I literally couldn't stand, and he looked all put out and confused. And out of the corner of my eye, as I was convulsing around like a fish out of water, I see him get dressed, and then *he stepped over* my writhing body and said, *'I don't know where things went wrong between us . . .'* "

"No!" Tate howls with laughter.

"Yes. He said some other stuff, but I was laughing too hard to hear him. I mean, hello, I can tell you *exactly* where you went wrong, buddy."

Tate and I laugh. Then Tate says, "Did you tell Sylvia about how the guy she set you up with is a kook?"

"Hell, yes. I called her up, and I was like, 'Um, thanks for setting me up with a sexual predator.' And you know what she said? She said, 'I knew it had been a long time for both of you, and I thought you might just enjoy each other's company, even if it never got serious.' I don't think you need to be an English lit major to read the hidden meaning in that sentence. I mean, obviously Sylvia thinks I'm such a sad schlub who is so desperate for sex I'll have a one-night stand with a scrawny, socially inept engineer."

"Jadie, look at it this way: you can put all these experiences into your writing. Maybe you'll write a book one day about all the hilarious dates you've been on."

I groan. "Oh, God, please don't tell me I'm going to go on enough bad dates to fill an entire book."

"There's a guy out there for you, I know there is."

"Maybe. I'm just pretty sure he's not in Boulder, Colorado."

"He's out there. I know he is. Somewhere. Look, I gotta go. I'm going to be late for my shift."

"Have fun slinging tofu."

"Oh, you know I always do."

I click the phone off, and now that I have nothing to occupy myself with I can focus completely on how annoyed I am at sacrificing yet another hour of my life to traffic. Why aren't we going anywhere, why?

I can't wait until the day I can work full-time as a writer and won't have to commute in highway traffic twice a day anymore.

I'm a travel writer, though most people call me a "creative project manager for a web design company." Personally I think this shows an appalling lack of imagination. I *have* published travel articles, after all. Several of them, in fact. Granted, all told, in my five years of freelancing I've only made a few hundred bucks on my writing, and my travel expenses have come to about ten times more than what I made from my articles, but it's a start. (By the way, in case you're wondering, "creative project manager" is a fancy title for "underpaid doormat who works too hard." Basically, Pinnacle Media's philosophy is to give their staff fancy titles instead of livable salaries, as if this were a fair exchange.) Essentially, my job is to manage people who do actual work. I make sure the copywriters, graphic designers, and programmers are getting their pieces of the puzzle done on time. Every now and then I get to brainstorm ideas for how to design a Web site, and those are the few moments when I actually like my job, when I get to be creative and use my brain, letting the ideas come tumbling out. But mostly my job feels ethereal and unsubstantial. The world of the Internet moves so quickly that by the time a Web site gets launched, the company we created the site for is already working on a redesign, and within months, any work I did on a site disappears. That's why I like writing for magazines. I do the work, it gets printed with my byline, and I have the satisfaction of having something tangible to show for my efforts.

Finally I see what has been holding traffic up—a car that's pulled over to the side of the road with a flat tire. Great. Forty extra minutes on my commute so people can slow down to see the very exciting sight of a car with a flat tire. I growl through gritted teeth at the sinister gods of traffic who are clearly intent on giving me an aneurism.

Eventually I make it home, grab the mail, unlock my door, and dump the mail on my kitchen table, my keys clattering down beside the stack of bills and catalogs advertising clothes I wouldn't wear under threat of torture. I sift through the pile; in it is the latest issue of the alumni magazine from the journalism school at the University of Colorado at Boulder, my alma matter. I flip idly through it until I see a classmate of mine, Brenda Amundson, who smiles up at me from the magazine's glossy pages in her fashionable haircut and trendy clothes. As I read the article, my mood sinks.

I know I'm not the first person who has struggled to make it as a writer, but sometimes, like, oh, say, when I get my alumni magazine and read that Brenda Amundson, who is my age— twenty-seven—and has the same degree I have, is making a trillion zillion dollars a year writing for a popular sitcom in

L.A., while I'm struggling to get a few bucks writing for magazines no one has ever heard of, my self-esteem wilts.

I change into a T-shirt and shorts to go for a run—I need to blow off steam. To warm up, I walk to a park, then start an easy jog along the path along Boulder Creek. It's 7:30 at night, but the sun is still out and the air is warm.

Boulder has its faults, but it's so gorgeous you forgive them. No matter how many years I've lived here, the scenery never stops being breathtaking. As I run, I take in the quiet elegance of the trees, the creek, the stunning architecture. The University of Colorado at Boulder is an intensely beautiful campus. Every building is made out of the red and pink colors of sandstone rocks and topped with barrel-tiled roofs. Behind them are the Flatirons, the jagged cliffs in the foothills of the Rocky Mountains that draw rock climbers from around the world and help routinely put Boulder on "best places to live" lists in magazines.

I jog for about half an hour, then walk and stretch until I've caught my breath. I sit down on the grass and watch three college students playing Frisbee in one corner of the field. Across the way, two young people with dreadlocks and brightly colored rags for clothes are playing catch with a puppy.

The puppy makes me smile, but I realize as I watch it that I still feel tense. My jaw muscles are sore from clenching them, a bad habit I have when I am stressed, which is most of the time these days it seems.

I need to get away, to relax. I long to hit the road.

I've always loved traveling. Since I was a little kid I always wanted to escape, to find a place I could comfortably call home and just be myself. In the small town where I grew up, life had been a daily exercise in not fitting in.

The fact that I was considered weird was mostly my parents' fault. They ran a health food store/new age shop where they tried to sell crystals to align chakras, tarot cards, incense, meditation music, that sort of thing. I'm fairly certain that no one ever bought a single sack of brown rice or bag of seaweed from their grocery store. They got by because of the side businesses they ran in the shop—Mom cut hair and Dad built and repaired furniture. Yes, I know, a health food/new age/hair salon/furniture shop is unusual, but when I was growing up, it was all I knew.

My mom was the kind to bake oatmeal cookies sweetened with apple juice and honey. You can imagine how popular the treats I brought to school for bake sales and holiday parties were. About as popular as me. Which is to say not at all.

I sat through years of school lunches all on my own, eating carob bran muffins and apples while every other kid had Ding-Dongs and Pop-Tarts. And I dreamed and dreamed of getting away and seeing the world. Going to places where I could be whoever I wanted to be and wouldn't be the weird kid in town.

I found that place in Boulder, Colorado. Boulder is a place where pot-smoking, dreadlocked eighteen-year-olds claim poverty yet wear Raybans. Boulderites believe themselves to be one with nature, but ironically own some of the most expensive homes in the country and drive CO_2-spewing SUVs. It's a place that manages to be somehow new age and old school. A place where yuppies and hippies collide and where, inexplicably, people think running in marathons is actually fun.

My life is equally mixed up. It feels like a pinball machine—I'm the ball, getting flung around in directions I couldn't foresee and never considered. Like how I ended up working for Pinnacle Media. I thought that after graduation I would become this world-renowned journalist covering coup attempts, international corruption and intrigue, the works. But after I got my degree, I couldn't get a job writing so much as obituaries for some small-town newspaper. Frustratingly, papers like the *New York Times* and *Washington Post* seemed to be doing okay even without my help, and nobody from these respective papers was banging down my door begging me to write for them. They didn't even glance at my resume, just like every other newspaper in America, no matter how small or inconsequential. So I took a job doing Web content at an Internet company during the height of Internet insanity, when every twenty-year-old kid with a computer was declaring himself a CEO and launching an on-line business determined to get rich quick. The company was living large for a while, but then the economy started to turn. I could tell we were going down, and I felt lucky when I landed the job at Pinnacle.

That feeling lasted, oh, twenty-eight seconds.

But whenever I complain about work, people tell me to get another job, like getting another job is easy, especially with the economy the way it is. My mantra is *Someday the economy will get better and I'll be able to find another job. Someday the economy will get better and I'll be able to find another job.*

Until that magical day, I travel to get away whenever possible, taking a handful of short trips each year to cities in the United States, Mexico, or Canada. I've been saving up money and vacation time to go on a real trip, something longer than a four-day weekend, but I keep waiting for some flash of insight that will tell me where the best place is to go, some location that will prove a treasure trove of sales to magazines.

Although maybe it doesn't really matter where I go, whether Barbados is the happening spot this year or if Madagascar is the place to be, whether the Faroe Islands are going to be the next big thing or if Malta will be all the rave. After all, the articles I have sold haven't come from the short trips I've taken but from living in the Denver/Boulder area—stuff about little known hot spots in Colorado and how to travel cheap in Denver. Mostly I write for small local newspapers and magazines. I've gotten a few pieces published in national magazines, but the biggies, the large circulation publications that pay livable wages like United Airlines' *Hemispheres* or Condé Nast *Traveler,* remain elusively, tantalizingly out of reach.

In the past year, depressed about my career, I decided I would try to get another area of my life in shape—my love life. It hasn't exactly gone according to plan.

First, there was the bitter divorcé. I didn't know he was bitter until we went out on our first date. I knew he was divorced; he'd told me. I just didn't know how frightening the depths of his contempt for his ex went.

I met Jeff at the Tofu Palace, the restaurant where I used to work when I was in college. My friend Tate still works there, and I was waiting for her to get finished with her shift when Jeff and I got to talking. I was sitting at the table next to him, and as another waitress, Sylvia, brought him his shot of wheat grass, he said something that made me laugh, and he kept on cracking me up with little quips and witty remarks. I don't even remember what we talked about, just that he seemed like a nice guy, and when he asked if he could have my number, I told him he could. I started to write it down, and he said abruptly, "Before you give me your number, there is something you should know."

I immediately thought he was going to say that he was out on bail for murder charges or something.

"I'm divorced and have two kids."

I waited a beat. "And?"

"And what? That's it."

"That's your big secret? You're divorced and have kids?"

"Yeah, that's it."

"I think I can handle it."

(Of course, that really wasn't his big secret. His real secret was that he was a complete psychopath whose rage toward his ex festered in a frightening and unseemly way.)

The fact that he had kids appealed to me. He told me he saw them—a three-year-old girl and two-year-old boy— every other weekend. I imagined Jeff and I getting married, and I would be able to help raise these kids and watch them grow, but on a convenient part-time basis without any of that painful pregnancy and birthing business.

But then I went out on my one and only date with Jeff, and that fantasy was blown to bits.

Things started well enough. Then in the middle of a nice meal after a couple of glasses of wine, I asked him something about his ex. Something like if they'd managed to stay friends or why they broke up, I can't remember exactly. Jeff got this maniacal look in his eyes and said, "That lying, money-grubbing bitch. I hate her. Women—all they want is your money. Lying . . . cheating . . . manipulative bitches. But sometimes you get sick of porn and want the real thing." He laughed about that last thing, as if it were a joke, but it very clearly wasn't. And when I looked at him wide-eyed and open-mouthed, he seemed to come out of his trance, and our gazes met. I was blinking in shock, and I think he realized that like an evil villain going around disguised as a good guy, he'd accidentally let the mask slip off and some serious damage control was in order. He smiled. "Just kidding. It was rough going there for a while, but we're friends again." He saw my incredulity. "No, really. I love women." *Yeah, to have sex with. "Sometimes you get sick of porn and want the real thing" . . . unbefuckinglievable.*

So that was the end of Jeff.

So now you'll want to know about the lesbians. Their names are Laura and Mai, and they live in my apartment building.

We'd always been polite when we'd met in the hallway or at the mailboxes over the years. Then a few months ago, as I held the front door to the building open for them, they asked me what I had going on that night. It was a Friday, yet I had a whopping nothing to do and no place to be. They said they were going dancing at a lesbian bar that night, did I want to go with them? I said sure, it sounded like fun.

Laura and Mai are both big girls and very pretty. Laura

looks like Mandy Moore would if Mandy were a size four-teen. And Mai has a build like Oprah—busty and curvy and strong. And they have the cutest style. Their outfits wouldn't be featured in *InStyle* or anything, but I think they have a certain bohemian charm, and can we talk accessories? Clunky, colorful jewelry to die for.

We hit the club a few hours later, dancing our little hearts out. For some reason I didn't think it was strange that they kept buying drinks for me and plying me with alcohol. After all, they knew I was straight, I knew they'd been dating each other forever, what was there to worry about?

It was late when we got back.

"Do you want to come to our place for a nightcap?" Mai asked.

"No. Can't drink no more. Alcohol . . . too much."

"Why don't you come inside and we'll give you some water so you won't have a hangover," Laura said.

I was too drunk to protest—or really even know what was happening. As I staggered into their apartment, I noticed that the hide-a-bed had been pulled out. I remember thinking, *I didn't know their couch had a hide-a-bed.*

We sat on the edge of the hide-a-bed, the two of them flanking me. In an instant, Laura was blowing in my ear and Mai was kissing my neck and stroking my breast. It took me a moment to process what was happening. My brain was working in slow motion. It was like I'd gotten stuck in a sand trap, and no matter how much I tried to accelerate, the wheels of my brain just went around and around and never got any-where. But eventually I realized that my breast was being stroked by a woman. I found this information to be very con-fusing.

Once I finally noticed what was going on, I seemed to sober up instantly. I sprang up off the couch. "I'm . . . I'm . . . I'm straight!" I yelped.

"There's no reason to be locked into these artificial con-structions . . . these meaningless boundaries . . ." Mai began.

"Like boundaries! Boundaries good!" My English skills, despite my degree in journalism, had been reduced to the level of a two-year-old. That's when I began backing up toward the door. In moments I was sprinting backward at Mach-10 speed, a blur of a human at break-the-sound-barrier velocity.

Unfortunately, I hadn't noticed that there was a coffee table between me and the door to freedom.

Another person would have stubbed her leg on it, or perchance been knocked sideways. Me? I was going so fast I became airborne and did a back flip—my head hit the corner of the table on my way down. I knocked myself semiunconscious.

They say there are two responses to fear: fight or flight. No one ever said that knocking yourself unconscious was an appropriate reaction to an uncomfortable situation. But there you have it. I'd turned myself into the perfect victim. I had no way to defend myself. I was at their mercy.

Fortunately, Laura and Mai weren't rapists. They'd put the moves on me, been rebuffed, and now they were a flurry of concern, hovering over me and wanting to know if I was okay.

In my half-conscious state, I was dimly aware that the two of them were dragging me over to the hide-a-bed and hoisting me onto it—managing to knock my head on the metal frame as they did. I quickly fell into a merciful sleep.

In the morning, I didn't remember where I was or what had happened. I just knew my head was in excruciating pain. In addition to a bruise the size of a plum on the back of my head from the coffee table, I had a searing pain just above my ear from where they'd knocked me against the bed frame. On top of all that, I had a blinding hangover.

I groaned in pain. Moments later I heard the patter of bare feet against the wood floor, and I opened my eyes in an attempt to figure out where I was and what was going on.

It was Mai and Laura, who'd run out to check on whether I was all right. They were naked, hovering over me like oversized Florence Nightingales so that when I opened my eyes, all I saw was tit. Four large, ponderous tits, encircling me in a mammary orbit.

I promptly shut my eyes and wondered, *How did my life start to read like a* Penthouse *letter?* Sure, some people—guys, no doubt—might like a life that read like a *Penthouse* letter. I was not one of those people.

A few weeks later I had yet another tangle with a lesbian—that night also involved alcohol and confusing and misguided tit groping, though thankfully no head trauma—but if you don't mind, it's still too painful and embarrassing to think about, so I'd rather not tell the story in all its gory detail.

Add on the sexual predator from last night, and you have the sum total of my love life in the last six months. And it was no romance novel before that, I can assure you.

I wonder if there is a place where this whole dating and romance thing is easier. Some country where the men aren't as psychotic as the men in America all seem to be. If so, I'm moving there posthaste. I just need to find this magical la-la land. I'll search the globe until I find it . . .

I smile at the idea. Then I think: *If I'm interested in how romance is different in other parts of the world, maybe other people would be, too. Maybe that could be my angle when I pitch stories; maybe it would be unique enough to get me in the door of the major magazines.*

The ideas zip through my head, and I have internal arguments with myself about where and when I should go. One part of me really wants to just take off. For months I've been fantasizing about how different my life will be if I can just get away for a while so I can recharge my brain by filling it with art and culture and recharge my body by having lavish amounts of salacious sex with a handsome, accented stranger. But the other part of me knows for a fact that I'll lose my job if I leave. There have already been numerous rounds of layoffs at my company. I'm the lucky one for still having a job.

Well, that's what I tell myself anyway. *I'm lucky to have my job, I'm lucky to have my job.* I know a lot of people who have been out of work for months. As a single woman with no more than a couple of months' worth of survival savings in the bank, I'd be in the poorhouse in no time if I got laid off, so I *am* lucky to have a job. But since the layoffs began, everyone at work is worried they'll be next, and they are resentful, tense, and hostile. Looking for other jobs while at the office is a generally accepted practice. The bitterness factor went through the roof when we survivors were doing our own jobs plus the jobs of the people who'd been let go. These days the opposite problem has hit—there's almost no work to go around, and somehow that's even worse, at least for me. The strain of trying to pretend to look busy is much worse than the strain of actually being busy. For one thing, I'm constantly bored, and for another thing, I live in constant terror that someone is going to figure out I don't have anything to do and that they could easily get along without me, and they're going to fire my ass.

But the thing of it is, I hate my job, and there is a part of me that would love to get fired despite the economic strain. I'd finally have the time I need to pursue my real dreams and goals. Anyway, I've been racking up vacation time for months—I should take it before the company goes under and I lose it all.

But taking a trip would be so impractical . . .

But is "practical" the kind of person I want to be? No! I want to be adventurous! I want to take risks and follow my dreams!

I jump up and run home. There, I strip out of my sweaty clothes, take a quick shower, throw some fresh clothes on, and sprint the four blocks from my apartment to the Tofu Palace where Tate is working tonight.

She has just finished taking an order from a table and is heading to the kitchen to give the cooks the order.

The Tofu Palace specializes in food for diners who have

wheat allergies, are lactose intolerant, and so on. Vegetarian, vegan, whatever your dietary oddity, the Tofu Palace is here to serve. The Palace does pretty well, what with it being located in Boulder, one of the most health-conscious cities in the universe. Boulder attracts skiers, hikers, mountain climbers, and marathon runners up the yin yang. A Boulderite is as likely to eat red meat as to stir-fry a hubcap for dinner.

The Palace is brightly painted. One wall is purple, one red, one deep blue. The ceiling is pale green, and the work of local artists decorates the walls.

When I worked here in college, I was the only member of the waitstaff without multiple body piercings or a single tattoo. Tate has several of both. Her belly button and nose are pierced, and her ears are studded with earrings. She has a tattoo of a thin blue-and-white ring encircling her upper right arm that looks like a wave, a rose on her ankle, and the Chinese symbol for harmony on her breast. (Only a special few have seen this one, and one drunken night she flashed me and I became one of them. It was a shining moment in an otherwise disappointing life.) Today she is wearing her long black hair in a loose bun that is held together by what looks like decorative chopsticks. She's petite, but so thin her limbs seem long and she looks taller than she is, with the graceful lithe muscles of a ballerina. It would be fair to call Tate's look exotic. My looks, with my honey-blond hair and dimples, would be best described as wholesome Iowa farm girl.

I follow her into the kitchen.

"Tate, you're a genius."

"What are you talking about? Lance, leave the onions out of this burrito."

"Just write it down," Lance booms.

"I did. I just don't want a repeat of last time. I lost that tip because of you."

Lance, the cook, just grunts.

"Your idea for the book," I continue. I follow her over to the refrigerator, where she pulls out a couple of cans of organic soda. "What I'll do is write a book about romance and dating around the globe. I'll interview women all over the world and find out their most hilarious dates ever. I'll find out about differences in dating and marriage in different cultures—the works. I'll be able to sell tons of articles based on my research to bridal magazines and women's rags. You know, stuff like, 'Looking to make your wedding original? Borrow from traditional Chinese or Turkish or Moroccan customs to make your wedding an international success.' Or for *Cosmo,* I can write about different sexual rituals around the world, or for *Glamour* I can write something like, 'You think the dating scene in America is grim? At least you don't have to do like the Muka-Muka do—they have to eat worms and beat each other up to see if they're compatible.'"

"Who the hell are the Muka-Muka?"

"Well, that's just to illustrate. I don't know the worst mating rituals in the world yet—that's why I need to write a book about it. I'll be like the John Gray of international relations between men and women. I'll be like an anthropologist studiously researching the most important issue known to humankind: love."

"And along the way, as you're doing all this important academic research, you might just happen to stumble on Mr. Right."

Damn. Sometimes it's a problem that this girl knows me so well. "Well, you know, if it just so happens that way . . . But you have to come with me. You have money saved."

She pushes the kitchen door open with her butt and delivers the sodas to her table. She drops off a bill at another, then clears off the plates at yet another. I hover at the doorway of the kitchen, waiting for her.

"How much do you have saved?" I ask her as soon as she gets back.

"Order up!" Lance says.

Tate checks the order and starts balancing the plates on her arms. "I'm not sure exactly. Maybe five thousand."

Five grand! And she makes a lot less money than I do. Granted, she doesn't need a car, she lives with four roommates, and she doesn't need to spend a dime on her wardrobe for work, but still, I'm impressed.

"What are you going to do with it? What could be better than traveling the world with your friend? Come on, Tate, we need some adventure. We need to shake things up a bit."

"Where were you thinking about going?"

"I don't know. I'd like to see the whole world, but I don't have quite enough vacation time saved up for that. How about Europe—the countries are small so we can knock out a bunch at once. Paris . . . Italy . . . Germany . . ."

"But we don't speak those languages."

"So? It'll be an adventure. You're not scared, are you?" Okay, I admit, I'm being manipulative. I know Tate well enough to know that the best way to get her to do something is to accuse her of being scared to do it.

"Of course I'm not scared!" She stamps out of the kitchen and delivers the order. When she returns, she pulls me aside conspiratorially. "What about our jobs?"

"I'll work it out with my boss, ask if they can hire a temp for a while or something. And Jack will understand. His waiters are always taking off on road trips for weeks at a time."

"That's true."

"So you're thinking about it?"

"When are you thinking of going?"

"As soon as possible."

"You'll plan everything?"

"Of course. Come on, it'll be the adventure of a lifetime. And maybe you'll find your soul mate. Another free spirit just like you."

She bites her lip. "It might be fun."

"It'll be a blast."

"Do you really think we could do this?"

"Of course we can."

She nods. "This is crazy."

"You love crazy."

She's still nodding. "Tell me when I should show up at the airport."

"Yes!" I give her an enormous hug. "It's going to be the experience of a lifetime," I assure her.

It's a big promise, but there is no doubt in mind that it's a promise I can keep.

MAYBE THIS CHRISTMAS

Jane Blackwood

CHAPTER ONE

Christmas Eve

Other than the elephant on her chest, Laura was just fine and dandy. The big, stinking, festering elephant. She could hear the heart monitor, knew the constant *beep beep* sounded normal, meant she was still alive. But this thing pressing down on her chest, that couldn't be normal. No way.

She took a deep, painful breath, bringing a shaking hand to her forehead, and stopped. Her hand was unusually clean, her fingernails clipped and nearly clean. It looked so normal it was startling. Because nothing about Laura's life had been normal in a long time.

"Are you all right?"

Laura moved her head, her dull brown eyes finally focusing on the old lady in the bed next to her. She knew her type. The kind of woman who belonged to a bridge club, who had relatives and children who loved her, who never had dirty fingernails or hid a bottle of Mad Dog in a paper bag. Bet she never had to squat behind a Dumpster in the middle of winter. Bet she . . .

The old lady shook her head, her mouth turning down at the corners, even though her eyes still twinkled. Laura had seen that look plenty of times at the Coolidge Street soup kitchen, all those goodie-goodies dishing out their food and their crap and smiling until they got hold of her stench. Stupid bleeding hearts.

"Should I ring the nurse for you?"

"No," Laura said, her voice roughened by years of smoking cheap cigarettes and drinking cheaper booze. After the musical sound of the old broad's voice, she sounded like a foghorn that needed some work.

The old lady sighed. "I'm Grace."

"No kidding."

"I was born on Christmas Day eighty-five years ago. At least my mother didn't name me Merry. Or Noel." Silence. "And you are?"

"Tired."

The old lady—Grace—had enough smarts to laugh. "Pleased to meet you, Laura." She leaned over conspiratorially and whispered, "I overheard the nurse."

Laura would have rolled over and turned her back to Grace if she had enough energy and if she thought such a movement wouldn't jostle that elephant into pressing down on her chest again.

"It's tough being in the hospital this time of year."

"Oh?" Laura asked, even though she knew what Grace meant. It was Christmas Eve, and Grace was probably lonely and wishing she was surrounded by her loving family. Ten kids and twenty grandchildren. Boo hoo.

"It's my birthday tomorrow, you know," she said, that twinkle in her eye growing so bright Laura had to squint her eyes else be blinded by it. Ugh.

"Happy birthday."

Grace was quiet for a blessed minute before she opened her yap again. "Do you have any family?"

"Sure. My daughter's a prostitute to feed her heroin addiction, my oldest son's in prison for vehicular homicide, and my youngest son is somewhere in the Mid East." That ought to shut her up. Old bag with her perfect life.

"Oh, Laura," she said with such honest sadness it almost made Laura feel guilty for bringing up her pitiful life. "I'm so sorry. I'm afraid I like to talk about other people's families because my own memories are so precious."

"Yeah, well, we all haven't had perfect lives." But it had been perfect once. It had been a wonderful life full of laughter and family and Christmases she could still remember if she was sober enough—or drunk enough. The Christmases before everything went to shit, they were something a person ought to remember. But sometimes it was better left part of a murky dream, a life that maybe never even existed.

"My life has been far from perfect. But I'm not going to complain," Grace said, moving her hands restlessly on her blanket. "I have four children, and I can still picture them coming down the stairs on Christmas Day. If I close my eyes, I can hear them. Sometimes I wish I could go back and watch it all over again. We didn't have those fancy videotape recorders like they have now. I wish we did. But I've still got a lot stored in here," she said, tapping her head. "You ever wish you could go back?"

Laura turned her head sharply away because for some damned reason her eyes started to burn, and if she wasn't real careful, she'd be crying. Hell, she couldn't remember the last time she'd cried over what she'd lost. Stupid tears. Go back, she asked. Oh, God above, if only that was possible. Go back before that Christmas, before everything spiraled down to hell, before she lost everything she loved. Go back? Just the thought was torture.

"I'm tired," she croaked out, her face still turned away from her pestering neighbor.

"Would you go back if you could?"

What is this, twenty questions? If you're that bored, read a book.

Laura closed her eyes and felt that elephant pressing down again, hard. Go back. Yes, yes, she'd go back to feel her daughter's silky hair, to hug her skinny little boys, to feel her husband wrap his body around hers while they slept. "I can't," she said as her chest sank beneath a horrible weight and the pain started.

Grace was saying something, but she couldn't quite make it out. Something about Christmas and wishes and things that were gone forever. She fought for a while against the pain, clutching her chest, holding her left arm rigid, fighting, fighting against the pain and a heart that had turned brittle long ago. And then, Laura stopped fighting. She let go, and the roaring in her ears stopped. Just like that.

"You can, Laura. Hold my hand. You can."

She heard Grace with such clarity, it was as if she was wearing headphones and those words were the only sound. Grace's hand was cool and strong in hers, and Laura knew the old lady was trying to give her comfort as she died. What a silly old woman, Laura thought, before everything went black.

CHAPTER TWO

December 15

Laura didn't dare open her eyes because she knew if she did, her head would explode off her shoulders. She lay there for ten minutes cursing her stupidity for letting Eddie give her his moonshine. Good ol' Eddie meant well, but he'd taken ten years off her life already. At least.

"It'll kill me before it kill you, Lorna Doon," he'd said a hundred times as he slugged back a long drink. It took a full five minutes before she remembered she shouldn't have a hangover, unless they had them in heaven. Or hell. She knew, without opening her eyes, that she was no longer in the hospital. It was too silent, smelled too good, to be the hospital. And it sure as hell wasn't the one-room dump she lived in over Coolidge Street.

That's when Laura finally opened her eyes. And closed them. And slowly opened them again.

"What the hell." Well, not hell. And not heaven either. Laura was home. Not the lousy one-room, rat-infested, piece-of-shit apartment she'd called home for the past five years. But home.

Home.

Laura looked down and laughed. That ugly old comforter that Brian hated was draped across the bed. Their bed, the sleigh bed they'd picked out two months before their wedding twenty-five years ago. She looked around the room in confusion. This room, this life, didn't exist anymore. She'd sold this house, the furniture, even the ugly comforter, years and years ago.

In some other room, Laura heard the familiar sounds of someone moving about a kitchen, the bang of a spoon against a bowl, water running.

Brian. The kids.

I'm either drunk or dead.

"Hello?" she called out, and smiled. She hadn't heard that voice in a long time, clear and uncluttered by twenty years of chain smoking.

"Mommmmyyy." In a flash, a little girl who bore a heart-ripping resemblance to her own daughter at that age flew into the room and onto the bed. The girl's dark blond hair was sticking up and matted from sleep.

Laura looked down at her face, perfect and sweet and smiling up at her, and her heart nearly stopped. "Mary," Laura whispered, hugging her little girl to her, afraid if she held too tightly, she'd disappear. This was a dream. No, this was where she'd gone when she'd died. God had decided to let her into heaven after all. She squeezed her eyes tightly, letting tears seep out and fall onto her daughter's head. She breathed in deeply of her strawberry-shampooed head, felt her soft hair against her cheek, the child's little hands trying to reach around her for a hug.

"Hey, you raining on me," Mary said, pretending to be cross. She looked as though she must be around three, adorable and chubby with a straight fringe of bangs over her dark eyes.

Laura laughed. "Yeah, I guess I am. I missed you."

"I missed you, too," Mary said, like she always had when she was little, even if Laura had only been in the other room.

Except the last time Laura had seen Mary she hadn't said anything, and Laura wasn't even certain her daughter had recognized her. Her twenty-year-old daughter had been waiting for a john, standing on a corner leaning against a telephone pole as if she'd fall if it wasn't there. Laura remembered thinking she ought to go to her daughter, talk to her, try to get her to straighten out her life. But as she walked toward her, Laura caught her reflection in a store window and flinched. She looked like shit, an old lady with greasy uncombed hair and a stained sweatshirt. Who was she to tell her daughter to straighten out her life? So she'd turned around and walked the other way, her heart hurting at the choice she'd made.

"I'm hungry. I want Dinosaur Eggs."

Laura slowly sat up, hoping her stomach would come with her. Her head pounded, and her vision blurred for an instant, but she stood up well enough. Mary tugged at her finger, pulling her toward the kitchen, toward her sons if this little fantasy was accurate. Toward Brian. *No way.*

"Mommy's got to use the bathroom. You go ahead. I'll be right there."

"Are you sick? You need aspin?"

"I just might take a couple aspirin."

Mary smiled as if reassured and ran off down the hall toward the kitchen.

"Holy shit," Laura whispered shakily. What the hell was happening? She looked around the room. It was exactly as she remembered. Messy and disorganized, with clothes strewn across a chair and papers piled high on her dresser. A dream was never this accurate. A dream didn't feel this real. She shuffled into the bathroom, her hands on either side of her head because it sure as heck felt as though it was about to roll off her shoulders. Hangovers were the devil. Were there hangovers in heaven?

She went to the sink and turned the water on, ice cold winter water, and splashed her face, already feeling slightly better. When she lifted her head, she saw her reflection and slowly smiled, amazed.

"Hello, Laura. Long time no see." There she was, the pretty young woman she'd been. Even with the circles beneath her eyes, the mascara smudges and the unkempt hair, she was a good-looking kid. Cinnamon brown hair, brown eyes, nice mouth. She peered into the mirror, touching her face, smiling, frowning, testing what it could do. Gone were the wrinkles, the bags, the look of a woman who had seen too much. Her hands were clean and soft, her nails neat and manicured, her neck smooth. "It's my face, all right," she said, then stuck out her tongue.

Then she lifted up her PJ top and really grinned. "Hot mama." Even after three kids, her breasts were still fairly perky, her stomach flat. She looked behind her at her ass, patting her bum, watching it bounce firmly up and down. The last time her butt had bounced attractively had been . . . about twenty years ago.

After popping two aspirin, washing her face, and brushing her hair she figured she still wasn't ready to face whatever it was she was experiencing. Maybe it was some drug-induced fantasy inspired by that old lady with all her talk about going back. Laura closed her eyes. Of course that was it. She was either dead or unconscious, and if this was all in her head, she might as well enjoy it.

Warily, she stepped back into the bedroom. Even if none of it was real, facing Brian again was enough to scare her to death. If she wasn't already there, that was.

She walked into the kitchen, her bare feet feeling the ice-cold tile she'd picked out. Crazy how real everything was. Laura stopped and nearly fainted at the sight of her little family sitting down to breakfast, Justin scooping up Cocoa Puffs and Zack chewing on a cinnamon raisin bagel. And Mary waiting for her to make Dinosaur Egg oatmeal, holding the packet in front of her, proud that she'd gotten it out of the box all by herself.

"Dinosaur Eggs."

"Okay." Laura grabbed the packet, blinking tears from her eyes, wondering whether to curse this fantasy or thank God for giving her this wonderful glimpse of how things used to be.

Laura was pouring the hot water onto the oatmeal when she heard his deep voice, filled with impatience. "You want coffee?"

Her entire body felt a jolt go through it. *Brian. My God, Brian.*

Slowly she turned around, willing her body not to collapse, willing herself to act as if she'd just seen him a few minutes ago in bed. She was afraid that if she did something unexpected, all this would end in a flash with a nurse jostling her awake, with the devil knocking on her soul.

"Sure. Coffee."

" 'Cause there's not much left. You can make more."

He looked . . . beautiful to her and so young. Hell, he was young enough to be her son, and it took a minute before she remembered in this drug-induced fantasy that *she* was young, too. She had to stop herself from throwing herself into his arms. So real. So damned real, even though she knew none of this was real, not her kids, not the smell of coffee, and certainly not her husband standing in front of her looking harassed and pissed off.

With a shaking hand, she poured the coffee into her mug, the one she'd broken years ago, the one Brian had given her for Valentine's when they were still dating. It was red with little boy and girl paper-doll cutouts in white holding hands, except two of the dolls were kissing. She looked at the mug, felt it cool in her hand. Cool and hard and smooth except for a small chip on the handle. Taking a deep breath, Laura put the mug against her lips and took a sip, and immediately put it back on the counter, spinning around in horror.

"Oh, God. Oh, God." She was hardly aware of the kids staring at her, spoons stopped in mid bite, of Brian's startled look. The coffee, spreading over her tongue, hot and good. And *real*. "No. It can't be," she said, breathing in gasps. Finally she took in her children's frightened faces and ran out the sliding glass door to the deck, mindless of the winter cold and her bare feet.

Behind her the door opened and slammed.

"What the hell is wrong with you? Do you have to throw up? Is that it?"

"Brian, please don't. You don't understand. I don't understand what is happening to me."

She stood there, arms wrapped around herself, staring blindly at the terrifyingly familiar yard with its cheap swing set and toys half-buried by a thin layer of old, crusty snow. She heard him swear beneath his breath, disgust and anger in every syllable. "You don't know what's happening? Yeah, well, that makes two of us."

Laura let out a laugh and turned to face him. He stood there, every pore filled with anger directed at her, and she didn't blame him. "I ruined your life, the kids'. And they're sitting in there eating cereal for God's sake. As if nothing happened, as if nothing bad in their lives ever happened. And you." She held up her hand in a futile gesture, drinking him in. She'd forgotten how handsome he was, how nice he'd kept his body, his beautiful, young body.

"What the hell are you talking about?" he said, but some of the anger had been replaced with concern.

Laura was looking at a man, a warm, breathing man, who had been dead for nearly twenty years. Who wanted to know what her problem was. "What's today's date?"

"What?" he asked, confused by her non sequitur.

"The date. Today's date." She knew she must sound insane. Heck, she felt pretty insane about now.

"December fifteenth."

"Two thousand four?"

"No," he said full of sarcasm. "Two thousand two."

Laura closed her eyes briefly as the significance of the date settled in. On December twenty-fourth two thousand four, at about five o'clock Christmas Eve, Brian had handed her divorce papers. She'd taken them with relish, the papers in one hand, a bottle of wine in the other. *Good riddance to bad rubbish. You think I need you? All you do is criticize. All you do is nag at me day and night. Screw you. You think you can do better than me?*

She'd gotten angry. He'd cried, probably wondering where the girl he'd married had gone.

She'd gone to hell, that's where.

"I've got to get to work. You okay?"

Laura looked at him, twenty years of living under her belt, and saw something she hadn't seen all those years ago. This man standing in the cold with her, looking at her with a potent mix of anger and frustration, didn't love her. She hadn't seen it then, had been blindsided by those divorce papers. She'd reacted angrily at first, then fell hard and long. It hurt, even with twenty years of distance between her real life and this moment she was living.

"You don't love me."

"Sure I do," he said quickly.

Laura shook her head and smiled. "You don't, Brian. It's okay, I really didn't deserve your love. I fucked everything up so badly it's a wonder you lasted this long."

"What are you talking about?"

She knew that somewhere in the house or maybe in his office those damning divorce papers were hidden somewhere. They'd been dated in November, and Brian had held on to them, waiting for some miracle to happen to make his wife change. She was tempted to let him know she knew about his secret, but stopped herself, some small goodness left in her heart.

She shook her head. "I'm cold. Let's go inside."

The kids looked up when they walked back in, Zack

pausing the longest to see if he could tell if the fight they were having was over. Laura gave him a smile, and the poor kid visibly relaxed. Hadn't she seen all those years ago what she was doing to him? She really couldn't remember. But now she was more an observer than a participant, seeing things she hadn't seen before: Brian's anger, Zack's fear. Brian's ambivalence.

Brian kissed the kids goodbye, pausing to give her a hard look before heading to the door. "You have to pick Zack up from school today."

"What time?"

"Four-thirty. Last time you were late," Zack said.

"I'll be there today," she said as cheerfully as she could, trying to ignore the hard glare from her husband.

"You goddamn better be," Brian said for her ears only as he opened the door and left.

She felt a tug on her PJs and looked down into Mary's serious face. "I have to go potty."

"Okay. Go ahead."

"You have to help."

Laura laughed aloud. She hadn't helped anyone go potty in decades. She hadn't sung nursery rhymes or picked up kids at school or cared in years about anything but herself and where her next meal and bottle were coming from. As she pulled down her little girl's pink Hello Kitty pajamas and helped her onto the potty she felt her eyes burn and her throat close. "Pat, pat, pat, you like that," Mary said, repeating the long-forgotten little rhyme she'd made up to teach her daughter how to wipe. Hearing it brought it all back, through the dark, rusty memories that she thought she'd long ago managed to finally, finally forget. Was that what all this was about, to force her to remember just how rotten she was? To make her see how beautiful her kids were before she'd ruined their lives? If so, this was a cruel, cruel way of doing it.

She accepted the blame. Guilty as charged, God. Wasn't

that enough? God didn't have to pull this Ebenezer Scrooge Christmas Carol crap to get her to realize she was solely responsible for ruining the lives of her three children. And for killing her husband. Let's not forget about that little fact.

Mary hopped off the toilet and pulled up her pants before running off to find her brothers. "Bye, Mommy."

The last thing Mary had said to her had been, "Fuck you, Mom." Then she'd viciously given her the bird. And Laura had yelled it right back at her. Mother of the year.

Laura didn't have to go to a shrink to find out when things had gone south; she knew. It was losing their fourth child, her stillborn baby, perfect but dead. No one blamed her for going a little crazy, for sinking into a dark hole. Therapy and Prozac did the trick—for a while. But she never got over it, and by the time she could have, she'd already messed things up so badly it was too late. Now the pain of losing that baby was so distant it didn't hurt anymore; it had become simply one more horrible thing in a series of horrible things that had happened since the day Brian handed over those divorce papers.

She'd spiraled out of control, he'd gotten custody of the kids, she'd failed to show up to pick Zack up from some school event, he'd driven like a maniac to get to his son, angry at her and afraid for Zack. And he'd died in a car crash, the man she still loved then with all her heart. Somehow Laura had convinced a judge she was a fit mother. She wasn't, of course, and the kids had gone from foster home to her and back and forth, so completely screwing them up that they hadn't a chance of living a normal life.

There it was, her miserable life in a nutshell. How different her life would have been if they'd somehow gotten through it, if she'd pulled it together. She could still picture the scene in her head, Brian wearing that ridiculous Santa suit, his hand outstretched, gripping the envelope from his lawyer so hard it folded in half. "I can't take any more," he'd said.

What would have happened if she'd fallen to her knees and begged his forgiveness? What if she could go back to that moment and make it disappear forever . . .

Laura let out a gasp. What if she could go back? She *was* back.

"Oh, my God," she whispered, looking in the bathroom mirror at her stunned expression. Suddenly everything was clear, as if she'd experienced an epiphany of sorts. She knew why she was here and what she had to do. Laura looked at her reflection, determined, young, and amazingly sincere.

"Okay, Brian Randall, you may not love me now, but I've got ten days to change your mind."

CHAPTER THREE

Brian sat in his Honda Accord in the driveway for a full minute before forcing himself into the house. He hated his life. No, he quickly amended, he hated his *wife*. And like always, when he allowed himself to actually think that way, he felt guilty. How many times had people said to give Laura time, that she'd been through an ordeal, that he should be more understanding. Well, he was done being understanding. He'd been through an ordeal, too. Sure, it wasn't the same for a man, he knew that. But he'd lost a child, too, and he hadn't gone off the deep end.

He let out a puff of frustration. Two years and she should be getting over it, shouldn't she? It wasn't just the drinking, though that was a big part of the problem. She'd become a bitch, a nasty, miserable bitch who only became more nasty after a couple of drinks. She lost it with the kids too easily; she screamed at him constantly. His life sucked, pure and simple.

He couldn't believe the girl he married had become the woman who was now his wife. The resemblance wasn't even close. God, he'd loved her, loved their life. It had been so damned good he couldn't wait to get home. She'd be there, looking showered and pretty, playing with the kids or making him dinner, glad to see him. It wasn't perfect, no life was. But he'd been happy. They'd been happy.

Now the only reason he hurried home was to act as a buffer between her and the kids. She couldn't take the whining, the fighting, the endless cleaning, and why couldn't he help more? He'd look around the house, see dirty clothes and dirty breakfast dishes and a wife who clearly hadn't showered, and wonder what the hell she was talking about.

"Shit," he said, finally opening the car door and heaving himself out. That's when he realized that someone had shoveled the driveway. He looked down at nearly bare asphalt, at the small piles on the side of the drive, and figured one of the neighborhood kids had come around. Then he saw the snowman, complete with hat and scarf and realized Jennifer, their baby-sitter, must have been watching the kids all afternoon. Sometimes Laura would call Jennifer "to get the hell away from the kids."

The Christmas tree was lit in the front window, and despite his foul mood, his spirits lifted a bit. Then he saw Mary and Justin waving wildly from the window, and a grin split his face. Despite everything, it was good to be home.

"Hey," he called out as his two youngest barreled into him.

"Mommy cooked 'sagna," Mary said. "Yummy."

"Yucky," Justin said.

"Lasagna. Really," he said, looking up as Laura entered the kitchen, a big smile on her face, and for a moment Brian forgot their lives had turned to shit.

"Hi. I figured I'd try to make it, though it's been a while. I think I got the sauce right."

"Smells good."

"You should see the tree Zack made at school. It's made from *TV Guides*. Did you ever do that when you were a kid?"

"Not that I remember," he said, staring at her, trying to gauge whether she was as sober as she sounded.

"You know, you fold the pages down, then you glue a couple together and spray paint it all. You never did that?"

He shook his head. "Who shoveled the driveway?"

"We all did," Laura said, smiling at him as if she hadn't been a basket case that morning, as if they hadn't had one of their worst fights the night before.

"And we all made the snowman," Justin said. "But Mommy wouldn't let us knock it down 'cause you didn't get a chance to see it. Can we knock it down after supper?"

"Nooo," Mary wailed. "I love the snowman. Daddy, don't let him knock it down."

Brian hunkered down to Mary's level. "Don't worry, we won't knock it down. If Justin wants to knock down a snowman, he can build his own and knock that down."

Once the kids were out of the kitchen, Brian turned to Laura, who stood there as if she hadn't a worry in the world. She was actually smiling at him and wearing an apron that hadn't seen the light of day since the day her mother gave it to her. As a joke.

"Don't think a snowman and some lasagna is going to make everything all right. It won't."

She looked as guilty as O.J. Simpson. "I thought it might be a start."

"I'm not really hungry anyway," he said, hating that he sounded like a jerk, even though he knew she deserved it. The things she'd said the night before, the way she'd looked at him, screaming in front of the kids, swearing. He couldn't forget that. He wouldn't.

Laura watched him walk out of the kitchen, only slightly amazed that he could reject a good lasagna. They must have had one hell of a fight recently. Man, they used to fight. "I'll save some for you," she said cheerfully. "The portion without the arsenic if you're nice."

"Don't bother," he yelled back.

It didn't bother her. She figured if he was mad at her, she deserved it, and she was so separated from whatever stupid thing they'd fought about, it didn't make a difference to her.

She'd married Brian because he'd been so kind, so mellow. It was only later she found out he could be tough and unforgiving.

She and the kids ate the lasagna pretending Brian's absence at the table was no big deal. It wasn't too bad; not as good as she remembered, but not bad. The kids ate it, even Justin, because she let them have chocolate milk with it mostly to satisfy her own strange craving for the stuff. Just to bug Brian, she made him a big plate and put it in the fridge for later with a note stuck to it with tape. "I promise it's not poisoned," she'd written. "Much." He just might smile, and Laura knew that if she could only get a smile out of him, she'd be halfway to getting him back. If she had a chance.

What if God was just giving her a glimpse of her life before sending her down to hell? What if her epiphany had merely been wishful thinking? What if she'd only been granted this single day to remind her of how blessed she'd been?

Bedtime was tough, those little kids in their jammies all scrubbed and sleepy. She didn't want to scare them, even though she was terrified inside that she'd never get the chance to hold them again. She might wake up dead in the morning, or worse, alive and in the hospital, so she held her kids as if it were the last time.

"Mom, you're choking me," Zack complained, but when she pulled back he was grinning.

"I just love you so much," she said, trying not to sound overly dramatic.

"Me, too?" Justin asked, even though she'd thought he was already asleep.

"Big time, buddy." She gave him a big kiss, swallowing

down a huge lump that had formed in her throat. "You guys are the best." She closed her eyes against the image of them as teenagers who were so lost to her, of the tattoos and piercings and the coldness in their eyes. She closed their door, praying to a God she'd forgotten existed that she'd wake up in the morning and she'd still be here.

Once the kids were in bed she went to find Brian, knowing he'd be in his office reading. Escaping. She'd never thought of it as that, but now she realized that was exactly what he'd been doing all those years.

"Hey."

He sat in his leather chair, his feet propped up on a matching ottoman, the glow of the nearby lamp softening his features. When he heard her voice, he straightened up, not bothering to hide his irritation at being interrupted.

"Whatcha reading?" It was one thing she remembered: how to bug him. She was an expert.

He let out a beleaguered sigh. "Laura, just go to bed."

"Not tired," she said, and plopped herself down on the love seat across from him. She watched him read for a good five minutes, his attention so completely on the pages in front of him Laura knew he was making a huge effort not to look up. "Good book?"

"The latest Grisham. It's okay." He didn't spare her a glance.

"I haven't read a book in ages," she said without thinking. About the only thing she had read was someone's discarded newspaper or the label on Mad Dog telling her that drinking alcohol could lead to health problems.

"You had your nose in a book the other night."

"I meant a good book."

She watched him try to ignore her and begin reading again and wondered if she should go to bed. The thing was, she wasn't tired, not a bit. She hadn't felt so energetic in years. Decades. It was that young blood pounding through her veins, blood that hadn't yet forgotten what it felt like to have the man in front of her naked next to her. In her. Laura let out a sigh.

"What." Pure impatience and anger was in that single syllable.

"I'm bored. You want to play chess?"

He stared at her a good long time before turning back to his book.

"When was the last time we played chess?" she persisted. She wasn't certain, but she thought she detected the tiniest quirk near his mouth. "I know I always lose, but maybe I'll get—" She stopped dead, a flash of memory hitting hard. Laura and Brian had played chess many times, with Laura losing nearly every match—until the day Laura decided to make things more interesting with a little game of strip chess. Every time Brian captured one of Laura's pieces, she had to remove an article of clothing. It didn't take long before she was sitting there with not much more than a big smile on her face—looking at a completely naked husband who'd just conceded the match. They'd made love right there on the floor amongst their scattered clothes.

"I don't think chess is a good idea," Brian said, his voice flat, and Laura knew she must have imagined that almost smile. He'd probably been irritated.

"Brian?"

He slammed his book down so forcefully, Laura let out a small squeak. "Jesus, Laura, go to bed."

It was strange, but Laura was oddly unfazed by his outburst, other than the surprise of it. "You're just scared you'll lose again. And what would you do then, huh, Brian?"

Other than the flare of his nostrils, he made no indication he'd heard her. But Laura knew he had, knew she just might be getting under his skin. She only hoped that was a good thing.

After Laura left, Brian put down the book he'd been pretending to read and let out a long breath. What the hell had gotten into his wife? Damn, he was tired. He never knew when he came home at night which Laura he'd find waiting there. Tonight was perhaps the cruelest of all, because Laura seemed so close to how she used to be. He couldn't let himself be drawn in by her; he refused to be taken in by a single day of sanity.

Brian pressed the heels of his hands hard against his eyes. "Don't do it, don't," he said fiercely to himself. How many times had he forgiven her only to have his heart ripped viciously out of his chest. Man, she could bring him down if he let her. But he wouldn't. Not this time. He might ride it out for as long as he could for the kids, but he'd be damned if he let himself fall again. No way.

He didn't love her anymore; she'd been right about that this morning. It was a good thing, too, because when she'd told him that, it was as if she didn't care one way or another. "You don't love me," she'd said, like some shrink making a clinical observation. It would have hurt not too long ago. But now he was over it. Over *her*.

He settled back into his chair and picked up his book, telling himself he was relieved this hell was almost over. And let his gaze drift up to the ceiling and follow her footsteps to bed.

CHAPTER FOUR

December 16

Laura slept alone and woke up alone. But she woke up young and to the sounds of her kids tramping down the stairs, her personal alarm clock. This, whatever *this* was, definitely was not a drug-induced hallucination, a thought that produced a wide grin.

"Still here," she said, squeezing her eyes shut, letting her face hurt from smiling so much. Laura gave herself a good ol' pinch for the fun of it, laughing aloud. She felt refreshed and remarkably happy for a woman whose husband had hidden divorce papers somewhere. It didn't matter: she was still here, she could hug her kids, see their smiles. Stretching and yawning she looked around her room, feeling something wonderful, something almost like contentment. And hope.

Then her eyes settled on an old mahogany cigar box her mother had given her when she was eight years old, a memory box. She hadn't seen it in years, couldn't recall what had happened to it. She'd lost it somewhere and hadn't cared at the time because it had become a mockery of sorts, a reminder of a woman who no longer existed. Her mother had given it to Laura six months before she died, and it was only when she was an adult that Laura realized her mother had known she was dying. When her mother had given it to Laura, it had been empty but for a picture of the two of them sitting on the front steps of their house, laughing as if they'd been tickling each other. That picture was as lost as the rest of her memories.

But there the box sat, as it always had, under her nightstand table. She hesitated a moment, afraid that this box somehow held the key to the reason she had been given this gift. She let out a small sound of surrender, then hoisted it up to her lap and opened the lid. What silly, stupid things to save: a poem she'd written when she was ten, a bottle cap, a theater ticket, a Red Sox rain ticket, a note from Brian that made her smile every time she read it because it was so damned unromantic. "I love you no shit."

She went through, her eyes burning, knowing that nothing in that box was really worth saving except the picture of her mother, and knowing she'd been a fool to lose it. Not that it would have made a difference in her real life. She closed the lid with a small click just as Mary burst through the door clutching her little bunny.

"I want Dinosaur Eggs," she said as she flung herself onto the bed.

"Me, too," Laura said, making Mary giggle. "I *am* going to have Dinosaur Eggs. Mmm." It was strange, but since she'd woken up back home she'd had the weirdest cravings for kid food, like chocolate milk and Dinosaur Eggs. For a snack the night before, she'd poured herself a bowl of Captain Crunch.

The two headed to the kitchen, surprising Brian, who was in the process of pouring cereal for the two boys. He was dressed in his "uniform": Dockers, white oxford cotton shirt, conservative striped tie. Once in a while he'd go a little crazy and wear a blue or yellow shirt. His brown hair was short, his face cleanly shaven. His hazel eyes . . . hostile.

"You're up early," he said, and Laura didn't miss the implied criticism that she usually slept late. Man, he was being a bastard. Maybe that's why she drank so much all those years ago, Laura thought.

She chose to ignore his jibe and gave him a brilliant smile instead, almost laughing at the stunned expression on his face. She knew he fully expected her to take the bait and be bitchy, but she was feeling much too happy to get into a fight. Besides, it was fun throwing him off balance. When she was through with him, he wouldn't know what hit him.

Laura looked at the calendar, noting with a small twinge of panic that she only had nine days to work her magic on Brian. "Hey, it's Tuesday. Family night at Sal's. Why don't we go out for dinner tonight. When was the last time we all went out?"

The kids all let out a cheer, and Brian looked as though he wanted to kill her, which made her smile even broader.

"I may have to work late," he said, his cheeks turning ruddy with the lie. The kids all booed, and Laura joined in, forcing a reluctant smile out of him. "Maybe tomorrow night."

"Tonight," Laura persisted. "Tonight. We'll save ten percent and get free ice cream."

The kids started chanting: "Tonight, tonight."

Brian gave her a hassled look before relenting as she knew he would. "Fine. Just have the kids ready. And if you're not ready," he said to Laura with a strange inflection and an icy look, "we'll go without you. Right?"

She knew exactly what that look meant, and for a minute it bothered her. A lot. He wanted her sober, and that was just fine by her. She hadn't had a drink yesterday, and she wouldn't today. This body, this Laura, was a light weight compared to the old lush she became. She hadn't even felt the smallest twinge yesterday, hadn't even given it a thought. Come to think of it, that *was* a bit odd, but she wasn't about to question why.

Sal's was a mediocre Italian restaurant people kept going to out of habit rather than any real desire for the food. Its high-backed booths formed a perimeter around a salad bar Sal had installed when they were the rage back in the eighties. It was the last cutting-edge thing Sal had ever done. Laura remembered going to the restaurant when she was a kid, and she was pretty certain that other than the prices, not a lot had changed.

The kids loved the place, though, because the booth tables were covered with blank newsprint and the waitress always gave them a handful of crayons.

Laura wanted to go to the restaurant for all those reasons, but especially because Sal's would close in a few years. She wanted to warn old Sal that his sons wouldn't keep his legacy but sell it to the highest bidder: a New Age holistic medical center.

When Laura walked in with her family, the old worn restaurant looked like a little bit of heaven. Gennaro, the oldest son, stood at the cash register, and Laura was about to give him a little talk about family and tradition, but stopped when she saw his face. He looked completely miserable with dark circles beneath his eyes and frown lines bracketing his mouth that even the most miraculous holistic medicine wouldn't touch. He looked like a man living a life sentence. Funny, in her memories, Sal's had always been such a happy place.

True enough, when Gennaro caught sight of the family, he beamed them a smile and welcomed them in a way that made them feel as if they'd been missed. That's what Laura had remembered; that's what she'd seen as a young woman. But now she saw a man made old before his time chained to a life he had no choice in making.

"It's good to be back," Laura said, and smiled at the truth of that statement.

Gennaro led them to a large booth, and they all slid in: Laura, Justin, and Mary on one side, Brian and Zack on the other. Brian hadn't looked at her all night, hadn't commented on the makeup she rarely wore and had carefully applied.

"I know what I want," Brian said, pushing the menu toward the center of the table.

"I want a hot dog," Justin said, a mutinous expression on his face.

"They don't have hot dogs," Zack said.

"They make the meatballs out of hotdogs," Laura said, giving Brian an exaggerated wink. "Why don't you get the spaghetti and hotdog meatballs."

Justin smiled because he knew his mother was being silly. "Okay."

Gennaro came back, pad in hand, and took everyone's order. "And to drink?"

All three kids called out, "Chocolate milk."

"That's four chocolate milks and a beer for him," Laura said, jerking her thumb at Brian. "Unless you want chocolate milk, too?"

Brian didn't look amused.

"I guess not. Four milks and a Bass Ale."

"You can have a glass of wine, Laura."

Laura blinked. "I want chocolate milk."

"Don't blame this one on me."

"I'm not. I really, really want chocolate milk."

" 'Cause I never said you couldn't have a glass of wine."

She propped her chin on her hand and narrowed her eyes. "I know." She gave him her most dazzling smile, which, of course, made him frown even more deeply.

"What the hell kind of game is this?" he asked, but Laura sensed he was getting less and less irritated by the second.

She leaned forward slightly. "It's the 'I want chocolate milk game.' "

"I wanna play," Mary said, and finally he smiled.

"When are you going to give me a smile like that?" Laura asked, and she could only laugh when he forced his smile away. "You're losing it, Brian."

"Losing what?"

"That hatin' feelin'," she said, breaking into the old Righteous Brothers' hit. "You lost that hatin' feeling. Oh-oh that hatin' feeling. You lost that hatin' feeling now it's gone, gone, gone."

"Will you quit it?" Brian asked almost good-naturedly. "You're ruining one of my favorite Hall and Oates' songs."

"Ugh! It's a Righteous Brothers' song."

"Hall and Oates did it better," he said, sounding so normal, so much like the man Laura fell in love with.

"You are so wrong." Those words hung there, suspended, until Brian looked down at his place setting.

"Brian?"

He looked up, and Laura thought, or maybe she imagined, something more than the indifference she saw there just a day ago. "You're not always wrong. Just mostly." She smiled and tilted her head, searching for something in those beautiful hazel eyes of his. Then he turned as Gennaro approached their table with a Bass Ale and four chocolate milks.

CHAPTER FIVE

December 17

Tammy Booker had been Laura's best friend until things had gone so wrong Laura hadn't even cared that Tammy was no longer there to cry with. And party with.

Tammy's life had been far shittier than Laura's. She'd gotten herself married to a big lunkhead who was cute and stupid in high school and turned out to be just plain stupid after his football muscle turned to couch-potato fat. But he didn't hit her and he didn't cheat on her and Tammy would sigh and say, "The kids love him at least."

Her hair unnaturally blond and longer than it should be, Tammy attracted all kinds of attention from all kinds of men—something she enjoyed. But as far as Laura knew, her friend had never cheated on her lunkhead, and Laura had the sneaking suspicion that despite all her complaining about her husband, Tammy just might love him a bit more than she was letting on. Either that or she truly was the most miserable person on earth.

The two would meet every Wednesday for a lunch that used to last until dinner and sometimes beyond that. They were good at complaining, and the more drinks they poured down their throats, the bigger the complaints got. The good thing about Tammy was that she never got too serious, because the last thing Laura had needed was someone psychoanalyzing her. Tammy made her laugh, made her forget about a life she'd thought had royally sucked.

Laura pulled into the nearly vacant parking lot of Ryan's Pub and parked next to Tammy's silver Honda minivan, feeling extremely nervous at the thought of seeing her friend again after all these years. The last time Laura had seen Tammy, she'd had a red minivan. "My life has become a series of minivans," she'd said once. Tammy was definitely good with the one-liners. They'd joked once that Laura was going to write down all Tammy's one-liners and create a bestseller.

It was going to be weird and wonderful seeing Tammy again. Of course, this woman wouldn't know what Laura had done. This Tammy was still her friend, her confidante. They'd never called an official end to their friendship, but after a while, Laura couldn't stand to keep in touch with anyone who knew her, never mind someone who knew her as well as Tammy had.

She walked into the pub, her eyes adjusting to the immediate gloom of the place to spot Tammy in their usual booth by the back wall. Laura didn't want to make an ass of herself, but the minute she saw Tammy's smiling face, her ridiculous bleach-blond hair, and her trademark long red fingernails, she started to cry.

"Hey, what's wrong?" Tammy said, standing up, concern and worry marring her pretty face.

Laura laughed, waved her friend off, and wiped the tears away. "I'm just . . ." She stopped and wondered whether or not she should tell Tammy exactly what was happening to her. "I'm fine. Just tired. Brian and I had a fight this week. It's okay now, but it's been a tough week. I'll tell you all about it after we eat."

"No gloom and doom allowed through those doors," Tammy said with a nod toward the entrance. "You know the rules, girly girl." Tammy lifted her martini in a toast and took a sip. "On second thought, a little gloom and doom feels about right. We should just leave 'em. Just take off and have a good ol' time somewhere warm and never come back. I swear, Laura, sometimes I think if I have to spend another minute with that man, I'll just die. Or kill him. Which do you think would be better, death or death row?"

Laura laughed. "I suppose it depends on what your concept of heaven is."

"Or hell."

Tammy looked miserable, and Laura really tried to feel sorry for her, but she found, to her amazement, her well had run dry. This girlfriend was talking to the wrong woman if she thought she was going to get any sympathy. So she had a big lunk for a husband, so he wasn't the smartest or most exciting guy in the world, he loved her. He was alive.

"I have something to tell you." Laura almost groaned aloud, for she hadn't realized she was going to talk about her fantastic journey until she opened her mouth.

Tammy's eyes widened, and she leaned forward to receive what she thought was going to be some juicy gossip. The bartender came over with her usual, a scotch on the rocks, but Laura waved him away. "I want to be stone cold sober for this."

"What? What? You're leaving him. You are."

"No," Laura said with a small amount of dismay. "I'm going to work harder than I ever had in my life to make that man love me again. I blew it, Tammy. I ruined everything in my life, and I'm not going to do it again."

"What are you talking about?" she said, waving a hand at

her and rolling her eyes. "That man's lucky to have you. Look at you, just as skinny and pretty as the day you two met."

Laura's eyes nearly crossed in disbelief. She'd forgotten that Tammy was about as deep as a puddle on a hot day. It had been one of the things she'd loved about her. Laura took a deep breath. "What I'm about to tell you is unbelievable. I don't mean that it's cool or crazy. Well, it is crazy. I mean it's completely *unbelievable*," she said, annunciating each syllable of the word.

Tammy looked as if she was going to kill her if she didn't spit it out in a second.

"I'm not me. I am me, but . . . Shit. I've come back to me, to this time." Laura squeezed her eyes shut. This was way more difficult to explain than she'd thought it would be. She opened her eyes and looked directly at her friend, willing her to believe. "Three days ago I was this old lady dying at West Valley Med Center, and now I'm back here, back with Brian and the kids."

The confusion on Tammy's face was almost comical. "West Valley Med isn't even open yet."

"I know it's unbelievable. Let me tell you my life story, and then maybe you'll get what I'm trying to say. In a few days, Brian is going to hand me divorce papers, and I'm going to lose it, go over the deep end. And if I remember correctly, you help me along the way, not that I blame you. I know this because I already lived it. Anyway, next year in May, Brian gets killed in a car accident and it's my fault. I was supposed to pick Zack up from some school thing, and I was here with you getting wasted and cursing Brian for leaving me. After that, things really went south and I ended up losing the kids. They ended up in foster care. Mary's a prostitute, Zack's in prison, Justin's in the army last I heard. And I'm close to living on the street, but I have this heart attack, and I end up back here."

Tammy pulled back, skepticism unmistakable in her contact-blue eyes. "Are you talking about a dream or something? A premonition?"

"No. This all really happened, and now I'm back. Like *Back to the Future* without the charm."

Tammy pushed away, shaking her head. "You're right. It's unbelievable. I don't understand why you're saying all these things." She narrowed her eyes. "Are you on something?"

Laura reached over the table and pulled Tammy closer. "I'm not on anything. I'm saying these things because they're true. Look at me, Tam," she said, shaking her friend's arms. "I'm telling the truth."

Tammy stared at Laura as if she really could see into her heart at the truth of what she was saying. Then she shook her head. "It doesn't make any sense. If you're back in your body, where's the original you."

"Here. She, I mean *I,* didn't go anywhere. I'm me but with all these horrible memories."

Tammy closed her eyes and smiled, sagging with relief. "You had a bad dream."

"No. I had a life, which I completely screwed up, and now I'm back here to fix it."

"Laura, that's impossible. Things like that don't happen. They don't. If things like that happened, why can't I be transported back to high school where I was dumb enough to fall in love with Ron so I could go out with Mark Rushton instead?"

Laura shrugged. "Who knows? Maybe if you screw up your life the way I did, you will."

Tammy rolled her eyes. "It was a dream."

"It wasn't. Tammy, I promise you I'm not insane. I did not dream all those horrible things; they really happened. There was this old lady in the bed next to me, and she asked me if I would go back if I could. She kept asking me that. And here I am. I destroyed every person I loved most in this world, and I'm not going to do it again," she said fiercely.

Tammy looked closely at her friend's face. "You really believe this, don't you?"

"With all my heart. And don't for a second think I don't know I sound crazy. I don't know if I would have believed you if you'd come to me with this kind of story. But I had to tell someone. I had to. Do you have any idea what it was like to see Brian alive again? And my kids? God, to have Mary be little and giving me hugs and telling me she loves me." She swallowed away the burning in her throat.

"Either this is really happening or you had the most fucked up dream I've ever heard of."

"I wish it had been a dream. Then I wouldn't feel so rotten."

Tammy gave Laura a weak smile. "So what do you have to do? I mean, did you get any instructions or anything?"

Laura laughed. "Yeah, God spelled it all out for me at the pearly gates." She shook her head. "I don't know what the hell I'm really doing here. All I know is that in eight days, Brian's going to hand me those divorce papers. I can't let that happen. He doesn't love me anymore, so I don't know if I can stop it all from happening again."

"Do you love him?"

Laura pulled her lips in. "I love him," she said with a big dose of uncertainty. "I love the memory of him. And of course I feel incredibly guilty. But I'm not *in* love with him. I hardly know him anymore. I haven't seen him in twenty years. He was dead."

Tammy put a hand over her mouth in horror. "This is too weird," she said. "I'm actually starting to believe you. I hope that doesn't make me crazy, too."

"Naw. Just a good friend. And maybe just drunk enough."

Tammy laughed. Then she put on a truly horrified expression. "Does this mean you're not drinking anymore?"

"I think so. For a while. To be honest, I don't even want to. I've been having these really weird cravings for chocolate milk and kid cereal."

Tammy shuddered. "Yuck."

"Yeah, I know. I swear, if Chuck hadn't taken that drink away, I wouldn't have touched it. And I wouldn't have wanted to."

"You're kidding."

Laura shook her head. "Maybe it was all part of the deal."

"You're not going to get all religious on me and put a fish on the back of your car, are you?" Tammy asked sternly.

"No. But I was thinking about starting up a cult. Want to join?"

Tammy took a big sip of her drink. "What if it's not permanent? What if you wake up tomorrow and you're an old hag again?"

"I didn't say I was an old hag."

Tammy grinned. "Laura, what if it's only for a couple of days?"

She shrugged, pressing down the sense of panic she felt. "I got to see my kids again. And Brian. And you. I haven't seen you in years, you know. That's why I started to cry. If I wake up tomorrow in that hospital, I'll still think I was so completely lucky." Even as she said it, she didn't believe it. If she woke up tomorrow in that hospital, she'd want to die.

"Promise to look me up." A thought suddenly struck Tammy. "Am I still alive? Oh, God, am I still married to Ron?"

Laura laughed. She'd forgotten how much fun Tammy had been. "I don't know. We lost touch after Brian died. I really don't know where you are. But if I go back, I'll find you. Promise."

CHAPTER SIX

Brian looked at the clock. Four-thirty. On a normal day, he wouldn't even be thinking of going home. But Wednesdays were never normal. Wednesdays Laura went to "lunch" with Tammy and sometimes didn't come home until well after he'd been home. If he was honest, he was glad to beat Laura home because he was the one who drove Jennifer, their baby-sitter, home.

He let the thought in, that nasty bit of hope that had flared despite his best efforts to keep it at bay: maybe things would be different now. Laura sure as hell was acting differently. As far as he could tell, she'd gone three days without drinking a drop, and she was acting . . . strangely. Something had happened, jarred her, ripped her out of whatever dark place she'd been in for the past two years.

He looked at the clock again, squeezing his fist until it hurt before grabbing up the phone. "Hey, Mac, I'm heading out now. I'm going to bring some work home. Yeah. I'll see you tomorrow." He stuffed his briefcase with papers he knew in his heart he wouldn't look at until the next morning and headed out the door.

When he walked in his own door twenty minutes later he knew instantly that something had happened. Something bad. It was obvious that his kids had been crying, and Laura sat on the couch clutching Mary to her, tears streaming down her face.

"What happened?" he asked, trying to tamp down the anger, the fear that clutched at him.

"Mary almost got died," Justin said.

"Killed. Mary almost got killed," Zack corrected.

"What happened?" he asked, all control nearly gone.

Laura looked up at him, and the despair in her eyes nearly floored him. "She wanted a book from the bookcase, so she climbed up to get it, and the bookcase fell on top of her. She didn't even get hurt," she said, her voice filled with pain and disbelief.

Brian rushed over to Mary and lifted her into his arms. The little girl buried her head against his shoulder.

"I was downstairs in the kitchen. The kids were upstairs playing. I heard a huge crash, and then Justin started screaming that something horrible had happened to Mary. I could tell from his voice. And then I ran up and all I saw was the bookcase and her little pink sweater under it. I didn't hear anything. She wasn't crying. She wasn't moving. And, God, Brian, I thought she was . . ."

"She thought she was dead," Zack supplied, filled with his importance of relaying the story.

"I wanted my Pooh book," Mary said, lifting her head off his shoulder.

"It was horrible. She wasn't moving and she wasn't crying. Why wouldn't she cry?" Laura said, her voice, her entire body, shaking. "This didn't happen the first time. I would have remembered this. This didn't happen. I don't understand."

"What are you talking about?" Brian demanded.

But Laura just kept shaking her head, tears streaming down her face.

Laura felt as if she were tottering on the edge of a high cliff with nothing but blackness below her. Mary had not climbed a bookcase and nearly died the first time around. She knew she hadn't. The only difference between now and then was that this time she'd been home. This time she'd done the right thing, and Mary had almost died. All those years ago, she would have still been at the bar with Tammy, and Jennifer would have been with the kids. Maybe Jennifer had been playing a game with Mary, or maybe she'd given her too much juice and she'd been on the potty instead of climbing up that bookcase. Whatever happened all those years ago hadn't happened this time. That told Laura two things: she could change the future, and it might not be as wonderful as she wanted it to be.

What if Mary had died? What if a miracle hadn't happened and she was sitting on this couch gazing up at Brian begging him to forgive her for not being there to catch that bookcase before it crushed their baby?

"I was making supper," she said softly, staring blindly in front of her. "Mexican casserole."

"She's okay," Brian said, and his tone drew her eyes up to his. She saw no blame, no condemnation, only gratitude that Mary was okay.

And then the words screamed in her head so loudly she winced. *It wasn't your fault. It wasn't your fault. It wasn't your fault.*

"It wasn't my fault," she said aloud.

"No. It wasn't," he said softly. "I never thought it was."

And Laura wondered if he realized she wasn't talking about Mary at all.

CHAPTER SEVEN

December 18

Every once in a while, Brian would take out the papers he'd had his divorce lawyer draw up and read them, words that would dissolve a marriage. Cold, factual, unemotional words that would end something that once had been wonderful and he'd thought was now over.

They'd been young when they'd married, though at the time neither thought so. They were ready to take on the world, to have babies, to be a family. They'd been so truly happy for so long, the couple other couples pointed to with envy. Brian and Laura, they always seemed to have such fun together. At parties, he preferred his wife's company, and she his. They weren't clingy or overtly public with their love, but they always had fun. They felt lucky to have found each other.

He missed that. He missed her. It wasn't only the physical part of their marriage, which had virtually ended two years before, but the emotional part as well. He hadn't heard Laura laugh in so long—at least not with him.

It was two o'clock in the morning, and he was sitting up

in bed in their guest room, divorce papers on his lap. For the first time in a very long time he wished he was sleeping with his wife. That thought pissed him off and was making him crazy. The thing was that he missed her, and unless he was a sucker for the Christmas spirit, the woman he'd seen tonight was the woman he'd married.

It wasn't my fault.

No kidding. He'd been telling Laura that for two years, and every time she'd say, "I know it wasn't." Tonight, for the first time, she said it, and he was pretty sure she'd believed it. Those first weeks after they lost the baby had been hellish. They'd walked around in a daze, too wrapped up in their own misery to help each other. Gradually, things got better for Brian. He'd never forget that little baby girl, the unfathomable sadness he'd felt when she died. But with each week that passed, he got a little better, came back to himself a little bit more. Laura couldn't. Nothing helped, not therapy or antidepressants or his love. He'd lost his wife that day, and it killed him to watch her self-destruct. But when it started affecting the kids, that's when his concern and love started turning. That's when he began to lose his patience. That's when his love started to die as well.

"Working?" her voice, soft and achingly familiar, washed over him. She stood in the doorway, her dark hair curling around her head as if she'd been sleeping. She wore blue-and-red-plaid flannel pajamas, and damn if he didn't think she looked sexy as hell. She was being incredible, and he was looking over divorce papers. He put the papers into his briefcase, hoping she didn't notice his guilt-flushed cheeks.

"How long are you going to stay in here?" she asked. Normally, that question was laced with sarcasm and scathing disinterest. Tonight, it was simply a question. And he wasn't certain if that bothered him even more.

She looked around the room. "I think we should turn this into a playroom. If memory serves, we've never had a guest stay in here. Except for you."

"I like having my own space."

"It could be an office. Or a den. We could put a big screen TV in here. Surround sound. A media room or something. Or I could make this a sewing room."

"You don't sew."

"I could start."

"Laura, you can hardly sew on a button."

She folded her arms under her breasts, and damn if he didn't notice how nice and full they looked. He'd always loved her body, even when he wasn't sure if he loved her. "We could knock down that wall and make the kitchen bigger."

He tried not to smile and tried even harder to stop himself from wanting her.

"Let me be frank, here," she said, her voice tinged with amusement and impatience.

"Okay, you're Frank."

Her face lit up, and she gave him such a brilliant smile he couldn't help but smile back. "Brian. I'd forgotten how funny you are."

"Yeah, Letterman called the other night. Laura, just say what you came to say."

Well, Laura thought, he asked for it. "I'm horny." She covered her mouth with a hand in mock horror. "Did I say horny? I meant to say lonely."

Brian laughed, his good ol' belly laugh that she hadn't heard in decades. He had such a goofy-sounding laugh, unmistakable, full of abandon, so *Brian*.

"Come on, we can ruin our marriage another day. How about you taking care of your husbandly duties. Hmmm?"

He looked tempted, she had to give him credit for that. But the fact he was able to slowly shake his head was pretty disheartening, in more ways than one. Because a funny thing was starting to happen to her old, damaged heart. It was beginning to remember why she'd fallen in love with Brian all those years ago. It was beginning to fall in love all over again.

The ache inside had nothing to do with her libido—well, not entirely—but with a stunning and disquieting need to be held. She couldn't remember the last time a man, any man, had held her, had wrapped his big body around hers, had nestled against her back, had pulled her close. She only knew that it had been Brian, and she wanted that again.

"Brian," she said, and watched as he stiffened slightly. "I want to sleep with you tonight. Just sleep." She could feel her eyes begin to burn, and his image blurred slightly. She wouldn't beg. Or maybe she would.

"Laura."

"It's been so long, Bri. You can't imagine. Just hold me tonight." *Before I go, before I die, before you die, I need for you to hold me against you.* "Think of it as an early Christmas present."

He stared at her, hard and cold, with a fury that almost frightened her. "Why are you doing this to me?" he demanded.

"Because I'm not giving up. I am not going to let us go."

"Maybe we're already gone."

Laura ducked her head so he wouldn't see how much those weary words hurt—and they hurt way more than she would have thought possible just a few days ago. Her throat was so tight, she wasn't sure she'd be able to talk, so she remained silent, staring at his slippers neatly placed by the bed.

He sighed. "Okay. I guess it won't kill me."

Laura gave him a watery smile. "The night's half gone anyway, so it hardly counts."

"It counts," he said, but he sounded less hostile now, less forced.

He followed her into their room, his bare feet padding lightly on the hardwood floor. Laura climbed into bed and held back the covers for him. He lay down beside her on his back, not touching her, his hands folded across his stomach. She laughed.

"What."

"This does not count. The coffin thing you've got going there isn't going to cut it, buddy. You've got to spoon."

He groaned, but turned to his side and pulled her close. God he felt good, all warm and strong. And safe. She hugged his arm across her and smiled.

Brian frowned. He did not want to be in this bed holding a woman he'd convinced himself he didn't love and certainly didn't want. But here he was, holding her to him, trying not to become aroused by her soft round bum, breathing in her clean shampoo smell. This sucked. Big time. Why the hell was she doing this to him? And why was he letting her? He'd told himself a hundred times that he was through, that he didn't love her.

But he did. Damn if his heart wasn't swelling inside his chest, making him feel like the biggest fool God created. He ought to go on *Dr. Phil* as a loser husband who got walked over time and time again by his wife only to take her back if she smiled at him. Or started to cry.

Laura's angry, hysterical tears annoyed him. But those unshed tears tonight, the ones that never fell but just made her eyes look luminous and so sad he'd wanted to drag her into his arms and never let go, they got to him.

Almost against his will, he pulled her even closer, squeezing his eyes tight when she let out a soft sound and he could feel the blood rush almost painfully to his groin. She moved her bum slightly against his erection, and he clenched his jaw.

"Brian."

"I'm sleeping."

"Not all of you," she said in a sing-song.

He let out an exaggerated snore and felt more than heard

her chuckle. His arousal didn't mean anything other than the fact that he was a man who hadn't had sex in way too long. Man with woman, erection. Anyone could do the math.

Just why his heart was as swollen as his dick, now that was another thing entirely.

Laura woke up to the sound of the shower and Brian's soft humming. She felt incredibly rested. Sublime. Almost as if they'd had a nice night of satisfying marital sex.

Now, that was a thought. If she and Brian ever decided to get around to getting naked, it sure as heck wouldn't be marital sex. She'd never been a sex-crazed person. She'd enjoyed sex, had her share of blissful moments, but it had been years years since she'd been with a man. And now she was old-lady horny in a young woman's body. A dangerous combination given that a young, extremely hot male was just a few feet away. Naked. Soapy. Wet.

Laura bit her lip, then slipped out of bed and tiptoed across the cold wood floor toward the bathroom. The master bedroom bath was one of the nicest rooms in their small Cape Cod-style house. They'd taken away a closet to enlarge the master suite's bathroom, putting in a big claw-foot tub and a separate glass-lined shower. Clear glass.

Laura eased the door open and took her first fully naked peek at her husband in more than twenty years. And forgot to breathe.

"Holy shit," she whispered. Her memories of Brian were foggy indeed if she didn't remember this beautiful male bod in front of her. She probably just hadn't appreciated his beauty back then, his youth, his unbelievable maleness. Brian wasn't exactly sculpted, he was too beefy for that. But he was—exquisite. His broad shoulders narrowed down to his nicely defined waist that led to a set of muscled buns that were finer than fine.

"That's it, soap up." She licked her lips, feeling things her body hadn't felt in a very long time, letting her eyes trail down the length of him.

"Getting a good look?"

Her eyes shot up to find him staring at her but with far less ardor than she was staring at him. "I was . . ."

"You were . . ." he led.

"I was . . . Have you been working out?"

He narrowed his eyes and turned to face her, his hands on his hips.

"The view's pretty good from that side, too."

"Get out," he growled, but it was a good-natured growl.

CHAPTER EIGHT

December 19

Heather Harlow's well-toned, well-dressed body thrummed with excitement. He'd asked her out to lunch, a public lunch.

"This is it," Heather said, leaning over to her best friend and fellow secretary, Janice. "He asked me out."

Heather didn't work directly for Brian, so she figured it was okay to have an affair with him. They'd been flirting for months, but lately things were getting much more intense. He was the first guy who really listened to her as if what she was saying was interesting. It wasn't an act, she knew that. And the way he looked at her made her melt inside, his eyes piercing through her, doing more than any other man's caress. If he didn't kiss her soon, she was going to die.

They hadn't even touched in more than the most casual of ways. And yet, she loved him. She loved the way he cared so much about his family, even the way he was willing to try so hard with his loser wife. This guy knew the meaning of commitment. She knew he never would have an affair unless he'd made the decision to file for divorce. He'd shared everything with her, all his pain, his strength. Everything but his body.

"You're a damned fool if you think he's going to leave that wife of his for you," Janice said with an irritatingly knowing shake of her head.

"He's meeting me for lunch today."

"Honey, when a man meets you for drinks after work, that's something to get excited about. When he asks you for lunch, it's a brush-off."

Heather shook her head. "Brian's got class. He'd never ask me for drinks after work."

Janice rolled her eyes. "I like Brian. I think he's a good man. In fact, I think he deserves better than that wife he's got. But I don't think he's ever going to divorce her."

Heather leaned in closer. "He went to a lawyer. He's got the papers. All he needs to do is file."

Janice's eyebrows shot up. "Really. And you know this for a fact?"

"He showed them to me. Janice, this isn't a fling. I'm in love with him," she said, her eyes watering. "And I'm pretty sure he feels the same way. We've talked about this, about being together."

Janice blew out a breath. "I didn't know things had gone so far."

"We haven't . . . you know." Heather felt her fair skin blush. "We haven't even kissed. Or touched. Not really. Not the way I want to. He's so lonely and . . ."

"Gorgeous. A gorgeous, lonely man. God save us from them."

Heather laughed. "In a few days, I've got a feeling he's going to be a very happy gorgeous man."

Laura looked down at her daughter's mulish expression and couldn't help but smile.

"My legs don't work," she said, pretending to collapse to the sidewalk.

Laura heaved her up easily and propped her on her hip, surprised how strong this young body of hers was. "Mary, you're getting to be too big a girl for me to carry around," she admonished, but she didn't mean it, and Mary probably could tell.

"I'm a baby."

Mary was a baby when it suited her, Laura thought, yet couldn't help but be impressed by her daughter's manipulative powers. She'd have to pull on the reins a bit in the future . . .

Her heart fell, as it always did, when she thought that there might not be a future. But every morning she woke up and found herself at home, she let herself believe that maybe this was a permanent assignment.

She'd gone into Southerton, a neat little New England village just south of Boston, to shop for Christmas outfits for the kids. That morning she'd looked in their closets and found nothing remotely appropriate for church. Laura remembered that she'd stopped going when the kids were little, but since she figured God gave her this second chance, the least she could do was go to church on Christmas Day.

She bought the boys little versions of what their dad wore to work every day: khakis, conservative tie, button-down shirt. Justin's was blue pin-stripe and Zack's white. For Mary she found a pretty little blue-and-maroon-plaid dress and hat set. They would all look adorable, and she could look up at God in church and say, *See? I'm doing something right here. Can I please stay?*

Laura walked down Lincoln Street, Mary on one hip, her shopping bags banging against the other, and headed toward the street's few restaurants. Brian worked at a computer software company not far away, and she'd thought about dropping in and inviting him for lunch but had chickened out.

Instead, she'd decided on a girls' day out with clothes shopping and lunch at Friendly's, a local ice cream chain with the best grilled cheese sandwiches on the planet. She had a major craving for a grilled cheese, and it had been years since she'd been in a Friendly's restaurant for one.

"You hungry, squirt? Want a grilled cheese?"

"And French fries?"

Laura smiled down at her. "We'll share an order. With vinegar." Mary wrinkled her nose. "You've got to put vinegar on 'em."

"Yuck."

Laura was still smiling when she opened the doors, but stopped dead in her tracks when her eyes focused on the couple in front of them sitting in a booth, holding hands.

"Daddy!"

Daddy didn't seem all that happy to see them. And neither did his redheaded girlfriend. He sat there, holding this woman's hands across the table, staring at her all mooneyed. Cheating on her with a woman who had a bad dye job and too much makeup. A man magnet if she'd ever seen one, with big boobs and a tiny waist. Even if she hadn't been sitting there holding her husband's hands, Laura would have hated her on sight.

"Laura. Hey."

Not a bad recovery, but she'd have to be an idiot to not know what she was looking at. Girlfriend immediately tucked her hands onto her lap and looked defiant and guilty. Just like the girlfriend of a married man would look when confronted by the wife.

"Mommy, let me down. I want to see Daddy."

Her arms suddenly turning to rubber, Laura let Mary slide out of her arms and to the floor where she took off running into her father's arms while Laura stood there stupidly holding onto the bags of Christmas clothes. Brian looked at her over Mary's head, and Laura couldn't begin to know what his expression meant, whether it was regret, guilt or anger, or a sickening combination of all three.

"Mary, we have to go," she said woodenly.

"Laura, don't go. Wait," he said, standing up with Mary in his arms. His wife-cheating, two-timing arms.

Rage, hot-spitting and explosive, nearly erupted, and if it hadn't been for Mary clutching her little arms around his neck, Laura's hands would have been wringing that same neck. It shouldn't surprise her to find him with another woman. But it did. Big time. All those years ago, and now, she'd never suspected he'd been cheating on her. Brian, good, solid, dependable Brian did not cheat.

Well, apparently he did.

"Brian, don't go." That from the skinny redheaded menace.

"You," Laura said, pointing a finger at her, "have nothing to say about whether he stays or goes."

The woman lurched back as if she was in danger of being assaulted, which, honestly, she was. "My God, I think she's drunk. She's drunk, Brian."

Laura felt the world drop from beneath her feet and her anger turn to humiliation. She felt more betrayed now than when she'd walked in on them so cozily holding hands across the table. He'd talked about her. Complained about her. To this nobody, this woman who didn't know anything about them or what they'd been through or who Brian was. She hadn't been there when he was a student without a dime to his name, when going out for pizza was something he saved all week to do. She hadn't been there when he'd cried when Zack had gotten so sick that time and they'd had to bring him to the hospital.

"I've got to go," Laura said, looking around her blindly. "You take Mary home." She started backing out the door, knocking into a customer who entered the restaurant.

"Mommy, I want to go with you."

"I have to go." And she turned and ran out the door and kept running until her lungs burned from the cold December air. She stopped at the corner where a bundled-up African-American man was waving a bell looking for donations for the Salvation Army. She leaned up against the building, the cold brick holding her up, and stared at him for a while, listened to that bell clang and clang, and closed her eyes.

"You okay, miss?"

Laura opened her eyes to see the man's concern, his genuine distress for another human in pain. She smiled and nodded. "I'm okay. Thanks." *I'm just about to lose it. I'm thinking that I don't know what the hell is going on and what I'm doing breaking a heart over a man who's been dead for two decades. Sure, I'm just dandy.*

He looked at her a bit longer, as if he could read the crazy, frantic thoughts in her head, before nodding and going back to his bell clanging.

"Laura."

She sagged against the building and looked up first at Brian, then at Mary, who seemed blissfully unaware that anything out of the ordinary had occurred.

"Nothing happened."

She let out a watery laugh.

"You've got to believe me."

"Do you think I'm stupid? Or drunk."

He actually looked contrite. "I'm sorry she said that. I'm sorry you walked in there because nothing happened."

She turned to face him. "Brian, what if you walked in on me holding some guy's hands and looking dreamily into his eyes? Huh? Would you believe me if I told you that nothing was going on?"

"No."

Laura tilted her head, her stance belligerent. "Then why do you expect me to believe you now?"

"Because I don't lie."

"Yeah. You and George Washington." She held out her

hands to take Mary, and he transferred their daughter to her without a word. "All this time I thought our marriage fell apart because of me. I was ready and willing to take full blame. But it wasn't just me. You gave up, Brian. You left me out to dry. You failed our marriage and you failed me. Maybe if you'd just given me more time. Maybe if you hadn't been so busy setting up your next girlfriend, we could have saved our marriage."

He looked completely stricken by her words. "Our marriage hasn't failed."

"Then why do you have divorce papers all ready to whip out? Huh?"

He looked so stunned Laura almost laughed.

"No answer? The man who doesn't lie has no answer?"

"Mommy," Mary said, nestling her head against her neck. "I'm cold."

"Okay, sweetie," Laura said, feeling guilty about fighting in front of her. She glared at Brian. "I'm through talking for now."

She walked away and he let her. Brian watched until she was out of sight before hanging his head and staring at the sidewalk as if it might give him some sort of wisdom. Laura would never believe that he'd been calling off an almost affair. One week ago his lunch with Heather might have ended differently — like in a hotel room. But today he told Heather he would never leave his wife, never tear apart his family. He couldn't do it, not when Laura had given him so much hope in the past few days, not when it was so damned obvious that she was trying her best to make things right.

The truth was, Laura was right. He had given up on her, their marriage. And now he had to find a way to win her back.

It was after nine o'clock by the time Brian pulled his Honda into the driveway. He was reluctant to open his door to the frigid air outside—and the frigid air he was almost certain to encounter inside. The house looked normal; the Christmas tree still sparkled in the front window, and the outside lights were on. Still, he didn't know what he'd find when he opened that door. He knew what he should expect: an empty bottle of something and soft snores coming from the sofa. Maybe he was as dumb as a brick, but he didn't think Laura would be comatose on wine.

"Only one way to find out," he said aloud before pushing open his door. He'd rehearsed in his head what he'd say, the denials, the explanations. The fact was, he had cheated on Laura a hundred times, if only in his heart. He'd had himself convinced that Heather was what he needed, someone light and airy and low maintenance. A quick fix to what was ailin' him. It was hard to resist a woman who loved you, and Heather loved him. He'd thought he'd had strong feelings for her, too—until Laura walked in and he saw that look on her face. She'd been devastated, hurt, angry, and he couldn't believe he'd been a big enough prick to do that to her. In that moment, Heather became what she really was—a rebound girl, someone to make him feel good, someone who made him feel as if he mattered. Now he'd not only broken his wife's heart; he'd broken Heather's. She didn't deserve that, and neither did Laura.

He could tell himself a hundred times that Laura had hurt him, that she deserved whatever she got. But when he saw her looking at him as if he'd just taken her sunshine away—and holding Mary in one arm and Christmas packages in the other—he'd felt like a jerk. Hell, a guy couldn't sink much lower than he'd sunk, getting caught holding hands with another women in front of his wife and baby girl.

Brian opened the door, almost hoping she'd be in the living room asleep, hoping he'd get some kind of reprieve before encountering her, hoping she'd give him an excuse to be angry with her. But she was right there, sitting at the kitchen table with a half-full glass of chocolate milk in front of her, staring at it the way she used to stare at an empty gin and tonic. In that moment, he realized he would always love her, was amazed he'd thought he'd ever completely lost his love for her. She didn't look up when he entered, and she looked so damned vulnerable all he wanted to do was pull her close and hold her until she forgave him.

"I don't know if you'll believe me, but I was telling Heather that we could never have an affair. I was planning to, I won't lie about that. But I swear we never even kissed."

She swallowed but still kept her eyes on that chocolate milk as if it was the only thing keeping her sane.

"Do you love her?"

"No."

Finally she looked up at him, her eyes dry but filled with so much hurt, his heart squeezed painfully in his chest.

"She loves you," she said.

He nodded.

"When were you planning to give me those papers? After you two screwed?"

He pressed his jaw together. "Something like that."

"Always honorable."

He didn't want to, but anger started bubbling in his gut. "Listen, you put me through hell for months. I never knew if you'd be home when I got home or if you'd be passed out on the couch with the kids staring at the television. I didn't have an affair, but I know plenty of guys who would have."

"Oh, well, let's just give you a medal for not cheating on your wife," she said, finally looking as angry as he knew she must feel.

"You're right, I do deserve a medal." She let out a snort. "Have you been living in this house for the past two years or not? Or do you just not remember how miserable we've both been?"

To his surprise, she started laughing.

Laura shook her head, laughing at herself, at her predicament, at her reaction to what she'd seen. She'd been here for only a handful of days; she couldn't know how miserable they'd both been. Her memories of those months leading up to that fateful Christmas Eve were hazy at best, overshadowed by years of suffering and drinking, of simply surviving. But she couldn't explain that to Brian.

"I'm not proud of myself, Laura. But these past months, I needed someone to care whether I lived or died. You didn't."

She didn't argue because she didn't have a single thing she could say in her defense. Sure, he wasn't the angel she'd thought he'd been. But he wasn't a complete bastard—if she believed him about how far his relationship had gone.

"How did she take it?"

"What?"

"Your girlfriend."

She could almost hear him grinding his teeth together. "She's not my girlfriend."

She gave him a look of exasperation. "Fine. How did she take the news that you were not going to consummate her love?"

"Not well."

Laura smiled. "Could you explain to me why you broke it off?"

His gaze slid away from her. "It was what you said about not giving up on us. I guess I figured it was too soon to completely give up on us."

"You really think so?"

"I don't trust you," he said, and his words hit her like soft blows to her heart. He had no business trusting her, she knew that, but still it hurt. "But we did have a life together. We were happy."

"We were. I remember that," she said, sounding slightly desperate to her own ears. "We got married because we were madly in love and thought it would last forever."

"We were just kids."

Laura lowered her gaze once again to her chocolaty glass. "I still feel like a kid. I've lived a whole life, and in my heart,

I still feel like a kid. I want someone to take care of me. To kiss me when I'm hurt, to make bad things go away. But they don't go away. They stay there and haunt you and slowly kill you."

"You're only a kid if you believe someone can make everything better for you. Wishing for it doesn't make you a child. Wishing for it and knowing you can't have it is what makes you an adult."

Laura felt a wave of despair because she knew he was right. She couldn't have what she wanted simply by wishing it. "I have things I want so badly," she said, but couldn't finish for the tears clogging her throat.

Brian moved to the table and sat down. His hand moved toward hers; then he stopped. "Like what?"

"Like I want to be here forever. I want things to be better. I want all the bad things in my head to go away. I don't want you to . . ." The tears overflowed. *Die. I don't want you to die.*

He grabbed her hand then, a convulsive gesture that almost seemed against his will. "I won't hurt you."

"Can we try, Brian?"

He gave her hand a squeeze, then let go. "We can try."

CHAPTER NINE

December 23

Laura looked out the window at the large fluffy snowflakes falling from a gray-white sky. It was supposed to rain tomorrow, ruining what would have been a white Christmas. She couldn't remember that Christmas, what her kids had wanted from Santa, what the weather had been like. Her only memories had been of those divorce papers and getting very drunk alone in a hotel until Tammy showed up to help her drown her sorrows.

With all her power she was going to make sure that no matter what happened tomorrow, she would remember this Christmas and smile. She would remember her children's faces when they came down the stairs and saw those presents; she would remember what their jammies looked like, their favorite gift, their mussed-up hair. She'd remember it sweetly, even if it ended badly, even if she woke up in hell or heaven. *God, please let me remember these days.*

Yesterday was Zack's Christmas pageant. She couldn't remember going to it those years before. This time, she'd walked into that auditorium and listened to those Christmas carols, her little boy's short solo, as if it were all the first time. This time she would remember. This time, this time. God, her heart was breaking, because she felt this looming sense that it was all going to end. People didn't go back in time, they didn't change the past. The feeling of unreality was growing the closer she got to Christmas Eve. She found herself praying to a God that not too long ago she would have sworn didn't exist. She wondered if He was up there having a good laugh or crying for all that could have been.

It was Saturday morning, and the kids were still in their PJs and watching Sponge Bob on TV. Brian was in the basement trying to put together Mary's spring horse. She was pretty certain Mary hadn't gotten a spring horse that last Christmas, but this year she would. Mary, when she was all grown up, would remember getting a spring horse, something she'd wanted with all her heart, something her mommy hadn't known the first time around.

Laura poked her head down the stairs and heard Brian swearing softly. Tiptoeing down, she spied him lying beneath the toy on the concrete floor and pulling at the horse with all this strength, trying to get a spring in a tiny little hole in the horse's frame and missing time after time.

"God *dammit*," he said, letting the whole thing go.

"Need some help?"

"Yes. Hell yes. How the heck do they expect someone to put this thing together alone? What if some single parent buys this thing? They'd have to give it to the kid like this." The pink and white horse hung awkwardly from three springs.

"You got three in," Laura said, trying to make him feel better. Nothing could be more endearing than seeing him struggle with his daughter's pink and white horsy. He looked ridiculous and wonderful.

"Okay, you guide the spring end thing into the hole while I pull it. Ready?"

"Ready."

He pulled, his entire body straining, while she tried to put the damn spring in the damn hole. "Stop moving so much," she said, getting frustrated. Then it slipped in, and Laura let out a whoop.

"I've been down here more than an hour with this thing," he said, leaning back and placing his hands on the cold floor.

"You're my hero," Laura said, planting a quick kiss on his lips. She went to straighten, but he grabbed her arm and pulled her back for another kiss. Heat, like Laura hadn't felt in a lifetime, coursed through, slow, hot, and thick. She let out a small sound, and suddenly she found herself on the floor lying on top of her husband making out like a teenager. He felt so good, so solid and strong and warm. So much like Brian. Those memories, of how he felt, smelled, sounded, came roaring back. He kissed her the way he had when they'd been dating, all wet and sexy and slow. Her body, her young body, sang with need and want, and she pressed herself against his fast-growing erection.

His hands went down her pants and squeezed her butt, and he moved against her, a desperate man, breathing hard, pressing her close, moving rhythmically against her.

"You feel so good," she said, pushing herself against him. And when his hand went lower and moved between her legs and entered her, she nearly came. "Oh, Brian, Brian." He moved his finger in an out once, twice, and she convulsed around him.

He chuckled, surprised, pleased. "Damn, Laura, that was fast."

Her body was on fire, singing with pleasure, wanting more. Incredible. She'd always just sort of drooped and sighed after an orgasm. She'd never asked for more. But this time, she couldn't help herself.

"I want you inside me," she said, pressing against his erection, forcing a groan out of him.

"Mmoommmyy."

Brian groaned again, but this time not in ecstasy. "Shit. Whose idea was it to have kids?"

"Both of ours, if I remember correctly."

Again came the wail, as if she didn't answer at that very second, Mary's life would end.

"Coming," she called.

"You sure were."

"Ha ha."

It *had* been a long time since she'd had sex, but her physical reaction to his touch was—mind-blowing. They'd had a fairly active, normal sex life. Satisfying. Maybe a little boring, like any couple who had been married for years and had a bunch of kids ready to ruin the moment. But Laura was fairly certain, even though it had been a long, long time since she'd gotten lucky, that she'd never quite felt so turned on in her life.

Maybe it was a little fringe benefit of this strange excursion of hers.

That night they all went out for a walk in the snow. It was warm after the five-inch snowfall, and a surreal fog lifted off the snow. The neighborhood was quiet, the lights from the houses twinkling in the odd light of the foggy darkness.

Brian held Mary—her legs weren't working again, apparently—and Zack and Justin had run up ahead with a well-known top secret plan to ambush their parents with snowballs. As they went around a corner, two snowballs plopped by harmlessly, followed by groans of disappointment from the two boys.

"Better luck next time," Laura said, laughing.

She laughed, but her heart was slowly breaking. This was too perfect; it couldn't last. The sense of foreboding was growing, but all Laura could do was try to enjoy each moment she could. Maybe she was wrong. Maybe she had been given a gift and she was home for good.

But maybe she'd wake up tomorrow and it would all be gone.

"Brian," she said, her throat clogged with tears. "I love you." He could never know how big an admission this was. She'd fallen in love with him all over again.

Brian stopped and looked at her, his eyes moving over her face. "I thought I'd never say this to you again, but I love you, too."

"Too left-handed."

Brian dropped Mary down, and she thankfully ran after her two big brothers. "I can't believe I'm saying this. Two weeks ago I thought I wouldn't care if you dropped off the face of the Earth, and right now I'm looking at you thinking I'd die if you did."

Laura grinned. "A little better."

"I thought that was kind of good."

"It sounded sincere, but you could drop the whole not caring bit the next time," she said, sounding put off.

He growled and pulled her close. "You know I love you."

"I know. And I'm amazed."

Zack let out a whoop as he pummeled Justin with a snowball to the back. Mary, noticing her parents were no longer engrossed with each other, walked over and held her arms up. Brian scooped her up, and Laura had to look away. At that moment, she hated herself with a renewed sense of loathing. How had she given this all up. How?

"I want to make love tonight," she whispered. *One last time.*

Brian smiled. "I think that's a plan."

She wanted to remember this night, how Brian felt beneath her hands, how his eyes looked at her as if she were beautiful. Three kids had done a number on her body, she knew that, but he still looked at her as if she were twenty years old with a flat stomach and high firm breasts.

When he came to bed that night, she was naked beneath the covers, a little surprise for her husband and one that was met with a grunt of satisfaction.

"God, it's been so long," he said.

"You ain't kidding."

He ran a hand down her body, and she closed her eyes. *My husband is going to make love to me. A man who died twenty years ago, a man I destroyed.*

"Brian," she said, feeling panic grow. "Make love to me."

"I thought that's what I was doing."

"No. Make love as if it's the last time. As if . . ."

He kissed her, and she knew it was to shut her up. She let him. She welcomed his mouth, his tongue, his body pressing hotly against hers. She ran her hands through his thick, soft hair; she pressed herself against his erection. She felt electrified, magnified. When he pulled hard on her nipple, when he moved his hand down between her legs, when he touched her and entered her and moved inside her, she wanted to scream out her pleasure.

"Inside me," she panted, and wrapped her hand around his penis.

"We don't have to hurry."

"Yes, we do. Next time we can go slow, but right now, Brian, I want you inside me. I'm going to . . . God, Brian." She came, her breasts hot, her entire body on fire. He chuckled, all proud, as if he'd invented a woman's orgasm.

"I told you so," she said when she could talk.

"Why don't we just go for two?" he said, so smugly she had to laugh.

She'd never had more than one orgasm. That night she learned to never say never.

CHAPTER TEN

Christmas Eve

Laura hadn't felt so happy in a lifetime. Corny as it was, she actually looked up at the incredible winter sky and made a wish on the brightest star. "I wish," she said, tears burning her eyes and squeezing at her throat, "that Brian and the kids will always remember this Christmas as the happiest in their lives." *Because it's my happiest. By far.*

She closed her eyes and breathed in the sharp, crisp air, feeling ridiculously content for someone who was on the verge of tears. Inside, Brian and the kids were gathering around the Christmas tree to open the Christmas Eve presents—special presents given to the kids from Mom and Dad instead of from Santa. Christmas music was playing on the TV's cable—Perry Como singing about chestnuts roasting on an open fire.

"Hey, are you going to join the rest of us?" Brian called softly from the door. He was wearing a thick gray sweater that made his changeable eyes look gray-green. He'd been a little put out by her insistence he not wear the Santa suit this year, but he let her have her way. It was silly, but Laura thought she'd have a better chance of changing the future if she changed as many little details as she could.

"You okay?"

"I've never been better. Brian, I love you."

He came up behind her and wrapped his arms across her, pulling her close. "It's freezing out here."

"I know. But it's beautiful."

He looked up, and she could feel the rumble of his agreement. An *mmmm* that went right through her and warmed her better than a fur coat.

"Mommy, the presents," Zack called out.

"What presents?"

"Very funny," he said, but Laura thought she heard just the slightest bit of worry in his tone.

They opened their presents, a book light that attached to their beds and books.

"Awesome," Zack said. "All the Goosebumps I haven't read." So Laura had gone a little nuts, buying fifteen of the things; she didn't know if she'd be around to buy the whole set one at a time. The awful foreboding she'd been feeling was almost gone, and Laura chalked it up to so desperately wanting to stay. Tomorrow she'd wake up to the sounds of the kids' squealing because Santa had come. She'd go downstairs and *oooh* and *aahh* and act as surprised as the kids that Santa had somehow been able to give them exactly what they wanted. She'd make coffee and breakfast while Brian put everything together. Then they'd all get in their Christmas outfits and go to church, and she'd thank God for letting her see Christmas morning and apologize for thinking He didn't exist for so long.

After the kids went to bed, Laura and Brian stuck the presents beneath the tree, then sat on the couch and stared at the fire. "You went a little nuts this year. I don't think I want to see the Visa bill, do I?"

"Nope." She snuggled closer to him and kissed his cheek. "You smell good," she said, nuzzling his neck.

To her surprise, he moved away from her. "I have something I want to show you," he said, and her stomach dropped so fast she thought she might vomit. Things had been going so well, she'd almost forgotten what had happened all those years ago. It didn't feel real; it was as if she was watching a home movie in slow motion. He bent to his briefcase, just as he had all those years ago, and shuffled through some papers before bringing out a thick manila envelop.

She knew what he'd do next; she could see it in her mind, her terrifyingly clear mind. He straightened, tapped the envelop in his hand twice, then turned, his handsome face grim.

"Brian," she choked out.

And then he threw it in the fire.

"You know what that was?"

She nodded, her eyes brimming with tears.

"I never want to think about doing something like that again. Promise me I'll never have to," he said, his voice rough.

"I promise." Her tears spilled over as she stood and rushed into his arms. "I promise," she said, over and over.

He pushed her back and held her head between his hands. "And I promise you that I'll never do anything to make you want to leave me."

Laura let out a watery laugh. "Do you know what this means?"

"It means we're going to grow old and gray together."

She pulled him tight, resting her head against his chest. *I did it, Brian. I saved us. I did it.*

They went up to bed together, holding hands. Laura couldn't remember ever holding hands with Brian as they went to bed, not even when they were dating. As she walked, feeling the strength of his grasp, she had a brief and wonderful image of them, both slightly bent and gray, their movements slightly slower, their steps a bit more tentative as they went up the stairs together, holding hands.

CHAPTER ELEVEN

Christmas Day

Laura woke to the sound of a steady beeping noise. At first, she thought it was the alarm, and she wondered why Brian had set the alarm on Christmas morning. Except Brian wasn't shutting the damn thing off and . . . it smelled funny.

Her entire body froze except for the painful beating of her heart. "No," she whispered, clutching at her blanket that didn't feel anything like her ugly old quilt. Her eyes still closed, she willed everything to stop, to go away. She willed Brian to be sleeping next to her in their bed, for her kids to be waking up excited because it was Christmas morning and Santa had come.

Please, God, please. This wasn't a dream. Tell me it wasn't.

"Are you all right, Laura?"

Grace. It was the old lady's voice. She remembered it because she sounded so calm, so goddamn *nice* when everything in her life had just gone to shit.

"Should I ring the nurse for you?"

Laura managed to shake her head. She couldn't speak; she was still too paralyzed for that. Still too scared.

I'm going to open my eyes and see my room. I'm going to turn my head and see Brian. She breathed in and out, short of breath, terrified, wrapped in an anguish so immobilizing she wondered if she could will herself to die.

"Grace?" *Don't answer. Be Brian, all confused about why the hell I'm calling him Grace.*

"Yes?"

She opened her eyes and saw acoustic tile and a bag of fluids. She looked down at the white hospital blanket, at her hands, her old hands. "No." She whispered it, then screamed that same denial. "It's not fair," she said, bringing those old hands up and burying her face against them. "It wasn't a dream. It wasn't."

"Of course it wasn't," Grace said in the same soothing tones Laura had used with Mary when her little girl had a bad dream. She'd say anything to calm her down. Anything.

"But it was," Laura said, sobbing, her heart ripping slowly in half.

"What's wrong? Honey, what's wrong?"

She heard Brian's voice and thought she must be going crazy. "What happened?" he demanded.

"I don't know. I think she had a bad dream," came Grace's calm reply.

Laura jerked her hands down and looked up at the beloved face of her husband. "Brian?"

"The one and only," he said with that grin she fell in love with all those years ago. It was Brian, an older, slightly heavier version perhaps, but it was him. It was. Alive and well and looking at her as if she'd just gone a little crazy.

"It can't be," she said finally, then looked over to Grace. "Tell me what's happening."

Grace smiled and tilted her head. "Sometimes," she said, "we get an unexpected gift. If I were you, I'd just say thank you."

Laura smiled through her tears. "Thank you," she said.

Grace nodded. "You're very welcome. Now, if you don't mind, I'm going to take a little walk down the hall. The doctor said it's good for the circulation." She gave Laura a little wink before heading out of the room.

"She seems nice."

"You don't know the half of it," Laura said, laughing. "Come here, let me take a look at you."

Brian sat on the edge of the bed, indulging his wife. She held his face between her hands and smiled. He had a few more lines than he'd had the last time she'd seen him, and the few wrinkles he had were deeper. His hair was slightly thinner and much more gray, but he was still the most handsome man she knew. "You've aged well."

He laughed. "You, too. Though I could do without this heart thing of yours. Thank God it wasn't anything more serious."

"You're telling me," a young man said from the door. "We just about had a heart attack last night when you passed out."

"Zachary," Laura breathed. He was clean-cut, clean-shaven, and she was pretty certain he hadn't just been let out of prison for visitation rights.

"Justin and Mary are right behind me. Mary caught sight of someone she knows, and Justin's in the can."

Laura watched, amazed, as her daughter and son walked through the door. She knew what they looked like as adults, that wasn't the shocker, but they looked so normal. So happy and healthy, so different than the adults she'd seen last.

And they were all grown. All those years, missed again. She supposed she should be grateful, but Laura mourned those years she'd never know, those Christmases she had no memories of. She hardly knew these young people smiling down at her. It was as frightening as it was gratifying.

"Mom, I brought your memory box. I thought since you couldn't be home for Christmas I could bring some of home to you."

Laura smiled up at her daughter, this beautiful girl with the shining long, light brown hair and sharp brown eyes. She was amazing. She was a stranger. Laura took the box and put it aside, almost afraid to open it up to see what was inside. She would see things in that box that would have no meaning to her, items from a life she hadn't lived.

After her family had gone, Laura took the box, heavier than she remembered, and put it on her lap. She traced a finger along the edge, prolonging the moment when she would open a stranger's life.

She shook her head at her fear and opened the lid, pulling out the top paper. It was a graduation program for Mary, and she smiled because Mary had been so nervous that day about making her salutatorian speech. Laura blinked.

How had she known that? She hadn't been there, and yet she could remember the bright pink strand of hair on her artistic daughter's head, the way Mary had cried when they'd hugged, how worried she'd been thinking about all those graduation parties she planned to attend.

She held the paper in a shaking hand as memory after memory came forward, until she lived that day. With a growing sense of excitement, she picked up a bit of green felt cut out like a clover with gold glitter still clinging to it. It was Justin's St. Patrick's Day kindergarten project. She'd kept it because he'd cried so hard when he noticed the gold glitter was falling off and she'd promised she'd keep it forever because she liked it so much. Next was what looked like a wedding invitation. She let out a laugh as memories flooded her. Tammy and Ron had renewed their vows five years before. Ron had been in a serious car accident and was in a coma for two days. Tammy had been frantic, terrified that he'd die and even more terrified by just how much she really did love her lunkhead husband. She quit drinking and devoted her life to making her husband well again. Laura shook her head. Tammy had become insufferably in love with her husband.

Item after item fit together like puzzle pieces, putting together a life she'd thought was gone. When she was finished going through each item in the memory box, it was as if she'd lived the years she'd lost. Everything was there, stored away, safe. A life she'd made all those years ago when she'd been given an unexpected gift.

STOP THE PRESS . . .

Here's the front page story: Pulitzer Prize-winning, buttoned-up journalist, Harry Crandall, becomes publisher of small-town newspaper. Firing reporters left and right, he makes no friends in the newsroom, especially not with the cute, rough-around-the-edges editor, Jamie McLane. She's got a pool going—first reporter who can find out why the cold-hearted-but-extremely gorgeous taskmaster had to leave New York takes the jackpot. And she plans to be the winner . . . if she can keep from falling for the jerk.

ARE YOU GETTING THIS ALL DOWN?

Here's the curve ball: Turns out Crandall thinks McLane's one of the best natural reporters he's ever met. Sure, she needs practice—some late nights; a little field work; a lot of arguing behind closed doors that leaves him ready for a cold shower. His reporter's instincts tell him she's working hard to get the story on him, but if she wants him to reveal his sources, she'll have to be willing to give him something of hers in return . . .

Please turn the page for an exciting sneak peek of
Jane Blackwood's
A HARD MAN IS GOOD TO FIND
coming in December 2004!

CHAPTER ONE

Jaimie McLane stared at the headline—"Man Loses Cock"—for the tenth time wishing somehow it would disappear and wishing just as hard no one would notice it.

"Did you see this?" Nate Baxter asked, handing her that day's edition of the *Nortown Journal* and trying not to grin. The assistant editor had thought the headline was a real hoot the night before when Jaimie had gleefully typed it over the story about a local farmer who had lost his prize Rhode Island Red rooster. It had been a joke; it was not, obviously, meant to run over the story.

"I'm screwed. I can't believe we let this through. Harry's going be shitting bricks over this." Jaimie buried her head in her hands. "I'm so dead. Dead, dead, dead," she moaned, beating her head against her fists.

"He won't fire you," Nate said.

He being Harry, her new boss and the man she was quickly growing to dislike intensely. She knew herself well enough to know she could never fully hate something as beautiful as Harry Crandall. Perhaps she could loathe him instead. When he'd walked in two months ago her heart had actually done the oddest thumpety-thump, something that hadn't happened in . . . well, it had never happened quite that way. Her cheeks had flamed, her ears turned red, and the neon sign on her forehead that flashed "hottie alert" whenever she saw a man who made her lungs compress buzzed on. He was a juicy combination of Matthew McConaughey and Paul Newman in his prime with a bit of a young Cary Grant thrown into the mix to give him that standoffish better-than-you air she found so unpleasant in Harry and so pleasing in Cary. Except he didn't have any of their boyish charm or lazy smiles. Jaimie grimaced at her thoughts. That's what came from watching too many movies late at night—most of them black-and-white relics in which every star was either now dead or suffering from Alzheimer's.

He might be eye-candy, but Harry had managed to throw a big ol' bucket of cold water over her head after he fired three reporters the first week. Fine, they were dead wood, but they were *her* dead wood. Everyone in the newsroom was walking around as if the slightest mistake would end with him or her out on the street. And now she had the awful feeling he was about to turn his ax on her.

"He should fire me. I would." Jaimie peered up through her fingers. "I'm not sure I should tell him I don't get the sexual connotation or admit to fooling around on deadline and being too stupid to remember to change it. I can't believe it got through."

Nate skittered away suddenly, moving so fast his skimpy combover blew in the breeze, and slinked around to his desk that sat opposite Jaimie's.

He had arrived. Mr. Pulitzer-prize-winning Harry Crandall. Mr. *GQ New York Times*. As he had done since he took over the paper precisely sixty days ago—Jaimie had the date marked with a black X on her calendar at home—Harry walked in without looking at a single person in the newsroom, went straight to his office, and shut the door. Mr. Personality. If the guy smiled, his face would probably crack, Jaimie thought grumpily.

"How long before he sees it?" Nate whispered.

"Five minutes." Jaimie glanced nervously at the clock before booting up her computer and pretending to work. "I'm so dead." Far sooner than five minutes, she saw his office door open but didn't look up as she stared intensely and blindly at the screen in front of her.

"McLane. Get in here."

"Shit," she whispered, feeling the noose tighten around her neck.

She walks toward the door, her heels clicking on the hardwood floor. Right before she enters, she smoothes her skirt and checks her lipstick on the doorknob. "Don't tell me to apologize, chief, 'cause I won't. You and I both know that was the best story this paper has ever seen." He stands and glares; smoke from his cigar swirls around his head. "I oughta fire you, but I got a thing about firing dames." He throws down his cigar in disgust. "Especially dames that look like you," he says so she can't hear.

"Jaimie, you going in or what?" Nate asked.

Jaimie closed her eyes briefly, wishing her life were really a black-and-white movie instead of this very sucky reality. "Oh, God. I'm dead," she croaked. And Nate, supportive friend as always, began to whistle "Taps." Jaimie gave him the bird behind her back right before walking into Harry's sparsely furnished office. It held only a large antique oak desk and a water bottle that chose that moment to burp up a bubble. And it was so cold Jaimie wondered if she'd be able to see her breath, so she hugged her brown sweater more tightly around her. Other than his irascible nature, the only thing she'd noticed about her new boss was that he kept the air-conditioning in his office so high, his windows fogged up. *The Ice Man Cometh.*

Harry's desk was clean but for that day's edition of the *Nortown Journal,* folded in half, front page showing. He looked at her with an unyielding gaze, his dark gray eyes boring into her, making Jaimie want to squirm. He didn't look exactly angry, more . . . impatient. He had been pushed back in his chair, but he moved slowly forward until he was standing and leaning over his desk, his large hands lying on either side of the paper, the tips of his fingers pressing into the wood. And now, to Jaimie's growing fear, he did look angry. She watched, in curious fascination, as a bead of sweat moved down his lean face, over his hard jaw, and dropped silently onto his well-starched white dress shirt. How on earth could the man be sweating in air this frigid? Unless he was so angry he'd broken out into a cold sweat.

Jaimie swallowed and tried not to look as terrified as she felt. "Before you say anything, would you rather I be stupid or incompetent?" *Please, please laugh.*

"I'd rather you not be here at all," he said with horrible calmness.

Oh, shit. "Are you firing me?" she choked out. She kept waiting for the ax to fall, an ax wielded grimly by a stone-faced man in a perfectly tailored suit.

"I'm putting you on probation." He sat down, looking remarkably less angry than when he'd stood up, his movements slow and measured.

Somehow, probation was worse, far more humiliating, than being fired. If she'd been fired, she could have gotten all indignant, vowed to find a better job at a better paper for more money. Seasoned journalists got fired; greenhorns got probation. It would have been difficult to decide which burned brighter, the red on her cheeks or the anger in her eyes. Jaimie took a breath to calm down. "I understand you are angry, but . . ."

"I'm not angry and there are no 'buts,' no excuse for what happened. And you know it. For the sake of clearing the air, let me tell you what happened. It was late, near deadline, and you and your pal Nate came up with this very funny headline. It wasn't meant to run, am I right?"

"Yes," she ground out.

"And yet it ran anyway." He looked at her expectantly.

"Obviously, yes." *You arrogant son of a . . .*

"I can tell you one thing. I bet it was the most well read story in the paper today." His eyes flickered down to the paper and Jaimie thought she detected the slightest bit of humor in their cold depths. He gave her an assessing look, a completely asexual look, and Jaimie curled her fingers around the cuffs of her too-long sweater as she fought a shiver.

"You're a damned good editor, Jaimie, and I'm certain something like this won't happen again."

She could almost hear the unspoken *or else* in his tone. While she knew she deserved more than he'd given, Jaimie couldn't stop the deep resentment churning in her gut. Maybe it would be better if she did leave. That thought left her colder than Harry's office. "I've been editor here for five years, and there's never been this kind of screwup. It won't happen again."

He nodded, an agreement and a dismissal, and Jaimie left the office feeling relief and slightly less loathing. She was at her desk for two seconds before Kath Kopf came over, a wide grin on her face.

"So, are you fired?"

"Don't sound so hopeful," Jaimie grumbled. "No, I'm not fired."

"Did he ask you out?"

"No, we just had sex on his desk. He's got a small dick."

"Really?" Kath asked in mock dismay. "When I had sex with him on my desk, I thought it was rather large."

"We all have different standards," she said dryly. "He put me on probation. All in all, I got off easy."

Kath's smile disappeared. "Probation? I didn't think we had anything like that here." She gave Harry's office a worried look. "Do you think he's done firing people?"

Jaimie was startled by the real concern in Kath's voice. Kath, short for Katherine, had been at the *Nortown Journal* nearly as long as Jaimie. She was a hard-working, fast-writing, tough-as-nails reporter who should have moved on to another, better paper years ago. "Kath, you have nothing to worry about. You're safer than I am."

"But I heard he's hiring a couple of Columbia University hotshots."

Jaimie hadn't even heard that—something that made her feel even more impotent. "You're not seriously worried, are you?"

"We all are," Nate said, unabashedly eavesdropping on their conversation. "He fired three reporters already."

"I'm pretty certain he's all done firing." Her two friends looked uncertain, which made her unsure about Harry's plans as well. "Do you want me to talk to him?" she asked, praying hard and fast they'd say no.

"We want you to sleep with him, then use your body to gain favors for us," Nate said, as Kath nodded.

Jaimie gave them a withering look. "Thanks for the vote of confidence, guys, but I really don't plan to use this body as an instrument of extortion. Anyway, sexual harassment is illegal."

"When did you get all politically correct?" Nate said, smiling evilly.

Jaimie let out a beleaguered sigh so her friends would know exactly how much she hated to confront Harry with their concerns. "I'll talk to him, but I really doubt I'll find anything out. And I'm not going to talk to him today. I'm already on his shit list."

Kath gave Nate a look. "We think you should, um, make friends," she said.

"I am not sleeping with that man," Jaimie said, blown

away by her friends' suggestion and the fact they'd met and discussed this at length, coming to the astounding conclusion she'd have any influence over Harry.

"Who said you should sleep with him?" Kath said. "We just want him to get to know us, like us. It's easy to fire people when you don't know them. He won't be able to fire people he likes."

Jaimie shook her head in confusion. "What are you suggesting, then?"

"For starters, you could invite him to the softball game. Have him join the dead pool. Tell him about Duffy's Bar. Use your imagination."

Jaimie gave her friends a sick look. "Why me? Ted's way more friendly with him than I am."

Nate rolled his eyes. "Ted's sports editor. He doesn't have anything to do with the newsroom," he said as if talking to a simpleton. "It's got to come from you, our hallowed leader. Otherwise, he's going to slowly and methodically replace us with new college grads. They get paid less, they're eager, and they'll kiss his ass."

"So you are making me the official ass kisser? Is that it?"

Kath grinned and gave Nate a nudge with her elbow. "Finally she gets it."

Jaimie made a sick face. "You do realize what you're asking me to do. Play nice with a guy I can't stand."

"He's not that bad," Kath said. "Plus, I wouldn't kick him out of bed. Wink wink."

"You still think Ted Bundy's innocent," Jaimie said, dismissing Kath's assessment of Attila the Hun. "Just because he's okay-looking . . ."

"Okay-looking?"

Jaimie narrowed her eyes. "Just because Harry's . . ."

"Gorgeous."

"Is he?" Nate asked, looking over at Harry's office with pure puzzlement.

"Yes. He is. But he's a jackass," Jaimie said with force.

"And you're going to invite that jackass to the softball game, right?"

Jaimie looked Nate in the eye. "To save the newsroom, I'd do just about anything."

THE 24 DAYS OF CHRISTMAS

LINDA LAEL MILLER

CHAPTER ONE

The snow, as much a Thanksgiving leftover as the cold turkey in the sandwich Frank Raynor had packed for lunch, lay in tattered, dirty patches on the frozen ground. Surveying the leaden sky through the window of the apartment over his garage, Frank sighed and wondered if he'd done the right thing, renting the place to Addie Hutton. She'd grown up in the big house, on the other side of the lawn. How would she feel about taking up residence in what, in her mind, probably amounted to the servants' quarters?

"Daddy?"

He turned to see his seven-year-old daughter, Lissie, framed in the doorway. She was wearing a golden halo of her own design, constructed from a coat hanger and an old tinsel garland filched from the boxes of Christmas decorations downstairs.

"Does this make me look like an angel?"

Frank felt a squeeze in his chest as he made a show of assessing the rest of the outfit—jeans, snow boots, and a pink T-shirt that said "Brat Princess" on the front. "Yeah, Lisser," he said. "You've got it going on."

Lissie was the picture of her late mother, with her short, dark and impossibly thick hair, bright hazel eyes, and all those pesky freckles. Frank loved those freckles, just as he'd loved Maggie's, though she'd hated them, and so did Lissie. "So you think I have a shot at the part, right?"

The kid had her heart set on playing an angel in the annual Christmas pageant at St. Mary's Episcopal School. Privately, Frank didn't hold out much hope, since he'd just given the school's drama teacher, Miss Pidgett, a speeding ticket two weeks before, and she was still steamed about it. She'd gone so far as to complain to the city council, claiming police harassment, but Frank had stood up and said she'd been doing fifty-five in a thirty, and the citation had stuck. The old biddy had barely spoken to him before that; now she was crossing the street to avoid saying hello.

He would have liked to think Almira Pidgett wasn't the type to take a grown-up grudge out on a seven-year-old, but, unfortunately, he knew from experience that she was. She'd been *his* teacher, when he first arrived in Pine Crossing, and she'd disliked him from day one.

"What's so bad about playing a shepherd?" he hedged, and took a sip from his favorite coffee mug. Maggie had made it for him, in the ceramics class she'd taken to keep her mind off the chemo, and he carried it most everywhere he went. Folks probably thought he had one hell of an addiction to caffeine; in truth, he kept the cup within reach because it was the last gift Maggie ever gave him. It was a talisman; he felt closer to her when he could touch it.

Lissie folded her arms and set her jaw, Maggie-style. "It's dumb for a girl to be a shepherd. Girls are supposed to be angels."

He hid a grin behind the rim of the mug. "Your mother would have said girls could herd sheep as well as boys," he replied. "And I've known more than one female who wouldn't qualify as an angel, no matter what kind of getup she was wearing."

A wistful expression crossed Lissie's face. "I miss Mommy so much," she said, very softly. Maggie had been gone two years, come June, and Frank kept expecting to get used to it, but it hadn't happened, for him *or* for Lissie.

I want you to mourn me for a while, Maggie had told him, toward the end, *but when it's time to let go, I'll find a way to tell you.*

"I know," he said gruffly. "Me, too."

"Mommy's an angel now, isn't she?"

Frank couldn't speak. He managed a nod.

"Miss Pidgett says people don't turn into angels when they die. She says they're still just people."

"Miss Pidgett," Frank said, "is a—stickler for detail."

"A what?"

Frank looked pointedly at his watch. "You're going to be late for school if we don't get a move on," he said.

"Angels," Lissie said importantly, straightening her halo, "are always on time."

Frank grinned. "Did you feed Floyd?"

Floyd was the overweight beagle he and Lissie had rescued from the pound a month after Maggie died. In retrospect, it seemed to Frank that *Floyd* had been the one doing the rescuing—he'd made a man and a little girl laugh, when they'd both thought nothing would ever be funny again.

"Of course I did," Lissie said. "Angels always feed their dogs."

Frank chuckled, but that hollow place was still there, huddled in a corner of his ticker. "Get your coat," he said.

"It's in the car," Lissie replied, and her gaze strayed to the Advent calendar taped across the bottom of the cupboards. Fashioned of matchboxes, artfully painted and glued to a length of red velvet ribbon, now as scruffy as the snow outside, the thing was an institution in the Raynor family. Had been since Frank was seven himself. "How come you put that up here?" she asked, with good reason. Every Christmas of her short life, her great-aunt Eliza's calendar had hung in the living room of the main house, fixed to the mantelpiece. It was a family tradition to open one box each day and admire the small treasure glued inside.

Frank crossed the worn linoleum floor, intending to steer his quizzical daughter in the direction of the front door, but she didn't budge. She was like Maggie that way, too—stubborn as a mule up to its belly in molasses.

"I thought it might make Miss Hutton feel welcome," he said.

"The lady who lived in our house when she was a kid?"

Frank nodded. Addie, the daughter of a widowed judge, had been a lonely little girl. She'd made a point of being around every single morning, from the first of December to the twenty-fourth, for the opening of that day's matchbox. This old kitchen had been a warm, joyous place in those days—Aunt Eliza, the Huttons' housekeeper, had made sure of that. Putting up the Advent calendar was Frank's way of offering Addie a pleasant memory. "You don't mind, do you?"

Lissie considered the question. "I guess not," she said. "You think she'll let me stop by before school, so I can look inside, too?"

That Frank couldn't promise. He hadn't seen Addie in more than ten years, and he had no idea what kind of woman she'd turned into. She'd come back for Aunt Eliza's funeral, and sent a card when Maggie died, but she'd left Pine Crossing, Colorado, behind when she went off to college, and, as far as he knew, she'd never looked back.

He ruffled Lissie's curls, careful not to displace the halo. "Don't know, Beans," he said. The leather of his service belt creaked as he crouched to look into the child's small, earnest face, balancing the coffee mug deftly as he did so. "It's almost Christmas. The lady's had a rough time over the last little while. Maybe this will bring back some happy memories."

Lissie beamed. "Okay," she chimed. She was missing one of her front teeth, and her smile touched a bruised place in

Frank, though it was a sweet ache. Not much scared him, but the depth and breadth of the love he bore this little girl cut a chasm in his very soul.

Frank straightened. "School," he said with mock sternness.

Lissie fairly skipped out of the apartment and down the stairs to the side of the garage. "I know what's in the first box anyway," she sang. "A teeny, tiny teddy bear."

"Yup," Frank agreed, following at a more sedate pace, lifting his collar against the cold. Thirty years ago, on his first night in town, he and his aunt Eliza had selected that bear from a shoebox full of dime-store geegaws she'd collected, and he'd personally glued it in place. That was when he'd begun to think his life might turn out all right after all.

Addie Hutton slowed her secondhand Buick as she turned onto Fifth Street. Her most important possessions, a computer and printer, four boxes of books, a few photo albums, and a couple of suitcases full of clothes, were in the backseat—and her heart was in her throat.

Her father's house loomed just ahead, a two-story saltbox, white with green shutters. The ornate mailbox, once labeled "Hutton," now read "Raynor," but the big maple tree was still in the front yard, and the tire swing, now old and weatherworn, dangled from the sturdiest branch.

She smiled, albeit a little sadly. Her father hadn't wanted that swing—said it would be an eyesore, more suited to the other side of the tracks than to their neighborhood—but Eliza, the housekeeper and the only mother Addie had ever really known, since her own had died when she was three, had stood firm on the matter. Finally defeated, the judge had sent his secretary's husband, Charlie, over to hang the tire.

She pulled into the driveway and looked up at the apartment over the garage. A month before, when the last pillar of her life had finally collapsed, she'd called Frank Raynor and asked if the place was rented. She'd known it was available, having maintained her subscription to the hometown newspaper and seen the ad in the classifieds, but the truth was, she hadn't been sure Frank would want her living in such close proximity. He'd seemed surprised by the inquiry, and, after some throat clearing, he'd said the last tenant had just given notice, and if she wanted it, she could move in any time.

She'd asked about the rent, since that little detail wasn't listed—for the first time in her life, money was an issue—and he'd said they could talk about that later.

Now she put the car into park and turned off the engine with a resolute motion of her right hand. She pushed open the door, jumped out, and marched toward the outside stairs. During their telephone conversation, Frank had offered to leave the key under the doormat, and Addie had asked if it was still safe to leave doors unlocked in Pine Crossing. He'd chuckled and said it was. All right, then, she'd said. It was decided. No need for a key.

A little breathless from dashing up the steps, Addie stopped on the familiar welcome mat and drew a deep breath, bracing herself for the flood of memories that were bound to wash over her the moment she stepped over that worn threshold.

A brisk winter wind bit through her lightweight winter coat, bought for southern California, and she turned the knob.

Eliza's furniture was still there, at least in the living room. Every stick of it.

Tears burned Addie's eyes as she took it all in—the old blue sofa, the secondhand coffee table, the ancient piano, always out of tune. She almost expected to hear Eliza call out the old familiar greeting. "Adelaide Hutton, is that you? You get yourself into this kitchen and have a glass of milk and a cookie or two."

Frank's high school graduation picture still occupied the

place of honor on top of the piano, and next to it was Addie's own.

Addie crossed the room, touched Frank's square-jawed face, and smiled. He wasn't handsome, in the classic sense of the word—his features were too rough cut for that, his brown eyes too earnest, and too wary. She wondered if, at thirty-seven, he still had all that dark, unruly hair.

She turned her head, by force of will, to face her younger self. Brown hair, not as thick as she would have liked, blue eyes, good skin. Lord, she looked so innocent in that photograph, so painfully hopeful. By the time she graduated, two years after Frank, he was already working his way through college in Boulder, with a major in criminal justice. They were engaged, and he'd intended to come back to Pine Crossing, as soon as he'd completed his studies, and join the three-man police force. With Chief Potter about to retire, and Ben Mead ready to step into the top job, there would be a place waiting for Frank the day he got his degree.

Addie had loved Frank, but she'd dreamed of going to a university and majoring in journalism; Frank, older, and with his career already mapped out, had wanted her to stay in Pine Crossing and study at the local junior college. He'd reluctantly agreed to delay the marriage, and she'd gone off to Denver to study. There had been no terrible crisis, no confrontation—they had simply grown apart.

Midway through her sophomore year, when he'd just pinned on his shiny new badge, she'd sent his ring back, by Federal Express, with a brief letter.

Though it was painful, Addie had kept up on Frank's life, through the pages of the Pine Crossing *Statesman*. In the intervening years, he'd married, fathered a child, and been tragically widowed. He'd worked his way up through the ranks, and now he was head man.

Addie tore herself away from the pictures and checked out the kitchen. Same ancient oak table, chairs with hand-sewn cushions, and avocado green appliances. Even Eliza's antique percolator was in its customary place on the counter. It was almost as if the apartment had been preserved as a sort of memorial, yet the effect was heart-warming.

Suspended above the counter was Eliza's matchbox Advent calendar, the fraying ends and middle of the supporting ribbon carefully taped into place.

A powerful yearning swept through Addie. She approached the calendar, ran her fingers lightly from one box to another. Her throat closed, and the tears she'd blinked away earlier came back with a vengeance.

"Oh, Eliza," she whispered, "I'd give anything to see you again."

Pulling on the tiny ribbon tab at the top, she tugged open the first box, labeled, like the others, with a brass numeral. The miniature teddy bear was still inside.

She'd been five the night Frank came to live with his aunt, a somber, quiet little boy, arriving on the four o'clock bus from Denver, clutching a threadbare panda in one hand and a beat-up suitcase in the other.

Needing a distraction, Addie opened the cupboard where Eliza had kept her coffee in a square glass jar with a red lid. Bless Frank, he'd replenished the supply.

Addie started a pot brewing, and while the percolator was chortling and chugging away, she went downstairs to bring in her things. By the time she'd lugged up the various computer components and the books, the coffee was ready.

She set the computer up in the smaller of the two bedrooms, the one that had been Frank's. Other memories awaited her there, but she managed to hold them at bay while she hooked everything up and plugged into the telephone line.

In her old life, she'd been a reporter. She had done a lot of her research on-line, and kept up with her various sources via e-mail. Now, the Internet was her primary way of staying in touch with her six-year-old stepson, Henry.

The system booted up and—bless Frank again—she heard

the rhythmic blipping sound of a dial tone. Evidently, he hadn't had the phone service shut off after the last renter moved out.

She was into her e-mail within seconds, and her first reaction was disappointment. Nothing from Henry.

Perched on the chair at the secondhand desk where Frank had worked so diligently at his homework, when they were both kids, she scrolled through the usual forwards and spam.

At the very end was a message with the subject line, THIS IS FROM TOBY.

Addie's fingers froze over the keyboard. Toby was her ex-husband. They'd been divorced for two years, but they'd stayed in contact because of Henry. She'd had no legal claim to the child—in the darkest hours of the night she still kicked herself for not adopting him while she and Toby were still married—but Toby had a busy social life, and she'd been a free baby-sitter. Until the debacle that brought her career down around her ears, that was. After that, Toby's live-in girlfriend, Elle, had decided Addie was a bad influence, and the visits had all but stopped.

Trembling slightly, she opened the e-mail.

MEET THE FOUR O'CLOCK BUS, Toby had written. That was all. No explanations, no smart remarks, no signature.

"Damn you, Toby," she muttered, and scrabbled in the depths of her purse for her cell phone. His number was on speed dial, from the old days, before she'd become a *persona non grata*.

His voice mail picked up. "This is Toby Springer," he said. "Elle and I are on our honeymoon. Be home around the end of January. Leave a message, and we'll get back to you then."

Addie jammed the disconnect button with her thumb, checked her watch.

Three-ten.

She fired back an e-mail, just in case Toby, true to form, was shallow enough to take a laptop on his honeymoon. He was irresponsible in just about every area of his life, but when it came to his loan-brokering business, he kept up.

WHERE IS HENRY? Addie typed furiously, and hit Send.

After that, she drank coffee and paced, watching the screen for an answer that never came.

At five minutes to four, she was waiting at the Texaco station, in the center of town. The bus rolled in right on time and stopped with a squeak of air brakes.

The hydraulic door whooshed open.

A middle-aged woman descended the steps, then an old man in corduroy pants, a plaid flannel shirt and a quilted vest, then a teenage girl with pink hair and a silver ring at the base of her right eyebrow.

Addie crammed her hands into the pockets of her coat and paced some more.

At last, she saw him. A bespectacled little boy, standing tentatively in the doorway of the bus, clutching a teddy bear under one arm.

Henry.

She'd been afraid to hope. Now, overjoyed, Addie ran past the gas pumps to gather him close.

CHAPTER TWO

Henry sat at Eliza's table, huddled in his favorite pajamas, his brown hair rumpled, his horn-rimmed glasses slightly askew. "So anyway," he explained, sounding mildly congested, "Elle said I was incrudgible and Dad had better deal with me or she'd be out of there."

Addie seethed. She hadn't pressed for details the afternoon before, after his arrival, and Henry hadn't volunteered any. They'd stopped at the supermarket on the way home from the Texaco station, stocked up on fish sticks and French fries, and come back to the apartment for supper. After the meal, Henry had submitted sturdily to a bath, a dose of children's aspirin, and the smearing on of mentholated rub. Then, exhausted, he'd donned his pajamas and fallen asleep in Frank's childhood bed.

Addie had spent half the night trying to track Toby down, but he might as well have moved to Argentina and taken on a new identity. It seemed he'd dropped off the face of the earth.

Now, in the chilly glare of a winter morning, Henry was more forthcoming with details. "Dad and me flew to Denver together; then he put me on the bus and said he'd call you when he'd worked things out with Elle."

Addie gritted her teeth and turned her back, fiddling with the cord on the percolator. The Advent calendar dangled in front of her, a tattered, colorful reminder that there was joy in the world, and that it was often simple and homemade.

"Hey," she said brightly, turning around again, "it's the second of December. Want to see what's in the box?"

Henry adjusted his glasses and examined the length of ribbon, with its twenty-four colorful matchboxes. Before he could reply, a firm knock sounded at the front door.

"Come in!" Addie called, because you could do that in Pine Crossing, without fear of admitting an ax murderer.

A little girl dashed into the kitchen, wearing everyday clothes and a tinsel halo. Addie was struck dumb, momentarily at least. *Frank's child,* she thought, amazed to find herself shaken. *This is Frank's child.*

Addie had barely had time to recover from that realization when Frank himself loomed in the doorway. His badge twinkled on the front of his brown uniform jacket.

One of her questions was put to rest, at least. Frank still had all his hair.

He smiled that slow, sparing smile of his. "Hello, Addie," he said.

"Frank," she managed to croak, with a nod.

He put a hand on the girl's shoulder. "This is my daughter, Lissie," he said. "She's impersonating an angel."

The brief, strange tension was broken, and Addie laughed. Approaching Lissie, she put out a hand. "How do you do?" she said. "My name is Addie. I don't believe I've ever had the pleasure of meeting an angel before." She peered over Lissie's small shoulders, pretending to be puzzled. "Where are your wings?"

The child sighed, a little deflated. "You don't get those unless you're actually in the play," she said. "Shepherds aren't allowed to have wings."

Addie gave Frank a quizzical look. He responded with a half smile and a you've-got-me shake of his head.

"I made the halo myself," Lissie said, squaring her shoulders. She'd been sneaking looks at Henry the whole time; now she addressed him directly. "Who are you?"

"Henry," he replied solemnly, and pushed at the nose-piece of his glasses.

"My dad got married, and his wife says I'm incrudgible."

"Oh," Lissie said with a knowing air.

Frank and Addie exchanged glances.

"Sorry to bother you," Frank said, nodding toward the Advent calendar. A smile lit his eyes. "Lissie was hoping she could be around for the opening of Box Number 2."

Addie's throat tightened. Those memories again, all of them sweet. "You do the honors, Miss Lissie," she said with a grand gesture of one arm.

Lissie started toward the calendar, and once again Frank's hand came to rest on her small shoulder. Although they didn't look at each other, some silent message traveled between father and daughter.

"I think Henry should open the box," Lissie said. "Unless being incrudgible means he'll mess it up."

Henry hesitated, probably wondering if incrudgibility was, indeed, a factor in the enterprise. Then, very carefully, he dragged his chair over to the counter, climbed up on it, and pulled open the second box. Lissie looked on eagerly.

Henry turned his head, his nose wrinkled. "It's a ballerina," he said with little-boy disdain.

Addie had known what was inside, of course, knew what was tucked into all the boxes. She'd been through the ritual every Christmas of her childhood, from the time she was five. Eliza had let her choose that tiny doll from a shoe box full of small toys, the very first year, dab glue onto its back, and press it into place.

She looked at Frank, looked away again, quickly. She'd been so jealous of him, those first few weeks after his arrival, afraid he'd take her place in Eliza's affections. Instead, Eliza had made room in her heart for both children, each lost and unwanted in their own way, and let Addie take part in the tradition, right from the first.

"We'd better be on our way," Frank said, somewhat gruffly. "Lissie's got school."

Addie touched Henry's forehead reflexively, before helping him down from the chair. Despite the aspirin and other stock remedies, he still had a slight fever, and that worried her.

"Are you going to go to my school?" Lissie asked Henry. "Or are you just here for a vacation?"

"I don't know," Henry said, and he sounded so bereft that the insides of Addie's sinuses burned. Damn Toby, she thought bitterly. Damn him for being selfish and shallow enough to put a small boy on a bus and leave him to his fate. Did the man have so much as a clue how many things could have gone horribly wrong along the way?

Frank caught her eye. "Everything all right, Addie?" he asked quietly.

She bit her lower lip. Nodded. Frank didn't keep up with gossip; he never had. It followed, then, that he didn't know what she'd been accused of, that she'd staked her whole career on a big story, that she'd almost gone to jail for protecting her source, that that source, as it turned out, had been lying through his capped and gleaming teeth.

Frank looked good-naturedly skeptical of her answer. He shrugged and raised a coffee mug to his lips. It was white, chipped here and there, with an oversized handle and Frank's name emblazoned in gold letters across the front, inside a large red heart.

"Thanks," he said.

Addie had lost track of the conversation, and it must have shown in her face, because Frank grinned, inclined his head toward the Advent calendar, and said, "It means a lot to Lissie, to open those boxes."

"Maybe you should take it back to your place," she said. Henry and Lissie were in the living room by then; one of them was plunking out a single-finger version of "Jingle Bells" on Eliza's ancient piano. "After all, it's a family heirloom."

"It seems fitting to me, having it here," Frank reasoned, watching her intently, "but if you'd rather we didn't come stomping into your kitchen every morning, I'd understand. So would Lissie."

"It isn't that," Addie protested, laying a hand to her heart. "Honestly. It was so sweet of you to remember, but—" Her voice fell away, and she struggled to get hold of it again. "Frank, about the rent—you didn't say how much—"

"Let's not worry about that right now," Frank interrupted. "It's almost Christmas, and, besides, this is your home."

Addie opened her mouth, closed it again. Her father, the judge, had quietly waited out her ill-fated engagement to Frank, but he'd been unhappy with her decision to go into journalism instead of law. When she refused to change her major, he'd changed his will, leaving the main house and property to Eliza. A year later, he'd died of a heart attack.

Addie had never been close to her father, but she'd grieved all right. She hadn't needed the inheritance. She'd buckled down, gotten her degree, and landed a promising job with a California newspaper. She'd been the golden girl—until she'd trusted the wrong people, and written a story that nearly brought down an entire chain of newspapers.

Frank raised his free hand, as though he might touch the tip of her nose, the way he'd done when they were young, and thought they were in love. Then, apparently having second thoughts, he let it fall back to his side.

"See you tomorrow," he said.

CHAPTER THREE

Addie awoke to silvery light and the sort of muffled sounds that always meant snow. She lay perfectly still, for a long time, hands cupped behind her head, grinning like a delighted fool. Snow. Oh, how she had missed the snow, in the land of palm trees and almost constant sunshine.

Henry was trying to make a phone call when she got to the kitchen. After a moment's pause, she started the coffee.

"I hate my dad," he said, hanging up the receiver with a slight slam. "I hate Elle, too."

Addie wanted to wrap the child in her arms and hold him close, but she sensed that he wouldn't welcome the gesture at this delicate point. He was barely keeping himself together as it was. "No, sweetie," she said softly. "You don't hate either of them. You're just angry, and that's understandable. And for the record, you're not incorrigible, either. You are a *very* good boy."

He stared at her in that owlish way of his. "I don't want to go back there. Not ever. I want to stay here, with you."

Addie's heart ached. *You have no rights,* she reminded herself. *Not where this child is concerned.* "You know I'd love to have you live with me for always," she said carefully, "but that might not be possible. Your dad—"

Suddenly, Henry hurled himself at her. She dropped to her knees and pulled him into her arms.

There was a rap at the front door.

"Addie?" Frank called.

Henry pulled back and rubbed furiously at his eyes, then straightened his glasses.

"Come in," Addie said.

Frank appeared in the doorway, carrying his coffee cup and a bakery box. He paused on the threshold, watching as Addie got to her feet.

"Do you sleep in that stupid halo?" Henry asked, gazing balefully at Lissie, who pressed past her father to bounce into the kitchen.

"Henry," Addie said in soft reprimand. He wasn't usually a difficult child, but under the present circumstances . . .

"You're just jealous," Lissie said with cheerful confidence, striking a pose.

Frank set his coffee mug on the counter with an authoritative thump. "Lissandra," he said. "Be nice."

"Well, he is," Lissie countered.

"Am not," Henry insisted, digging in his heels and folding his arms. "And your hair is poofy."

"Somebody open the box," Frank put in.

"My turn," Lissie announced, and dragged over the same chair Henry had used the day before. With appropriate ceremony, she tugged at the little ribbon-pull at the top of the matchbox and revealed the cotton-ball snowman inside. He still had his black top hat and bead eyes.

"We could build a snowman, after school," Lissie told Henry, inspired. "And my hair is not *either* poofy." She paused. "You *are* going to school, aren't you?"

Henry looked up at Addie. "Do I have to?"

She ruffled his hair, resisted an impulse to adjust his glasses. He hated it when she did that, and, anyway, it might call attention to the fact that he'd been crying. "I think you should," she said. She'd had him checked out at the Main Street Clinic the day before, and physically, he was fine. She had explained his situation to the doctor, and they'd agreed that the best thing to do was keep his life as normal as possible.

Henry sighed heavily. "Okay, I'll go. As long as I get to help build the snow-dude afterwards."

Frank refilled his coffee mug at the percolator and helped himself to a pastry. "Sounds like a fair deal to me," he said, munching. He looked at Addie over the top of Lissie's head. "You going to help? With the snowman, I mean?"

Addie flushed and rubbed her hands down the thighs of her jeans. "I really should look for a job."

"School doesn't get out until three," Lissie reasoned, climbing down from the chair. "That gives you plenty of time."

"I'll take a late lunch hour," Frank put in, offering Addie a bear claw. Her all-time favorite. Had he remembered that, or was it just coincidence? "I heard there was an opening over at the *Wooden Nickel*. Receptionist and classified ad sales."

Addie lowered the bear claw.

"Kind of a comedown from big-city journalism," Frank said. "But other than waitressing at the Lumberjack Diner, that's about all Pine Crossing has to offer in the way of employment."

She studied his face. So he did know, then—about what had happened in California. She wished she dared ask him how *much* he knew, but she didn't. Not with Lissie there, and Henry already so upset.

"I'll take the kids to school," Frank went on, raising Addie's hand, pastry and all, back to her mouth even as he turned to the kids. "Hey, Hank," he said. "How'd you like a ride in a squad car?"

* * *

The snow was still drifting down, in big, fat, pristine flakes, when Addie set out for the *Wooden Nickel,* armed with a truthful resumé and high hopes. The *Nickel* wasn't really a newspaper, just a supermarket giveaway, but that didn't mean the editor wouldn't have heard about her exploits in California. Even though the job probably didn't involve writing anything but copy for classified ads, she might be considered a bad risk.

The wheels of the Buick crunched in the mounting snow as she pulled up in front of the small storefront where the *Wooden Nickel* was published. Like most of the businesses in town, it faced the square, where a large, bare evergreen tree had been erected.

She smiled. The lighting of the tree was a big deal in Pine Crossing, right up there with the pageant at St. Mary's. Henry would probably enjoy it, and the festivities might even take his mind off his father's disinterest, if only for an evening.

Her smile faded. *Call him, Toby,* she pleaded silently. *Please call him.*

Mr. Renfrew was the editor of the *Wooden Nickel,* just as he had been when Addie was a child. He beamed as she stepped into the office, brushing snow from the sleeves of her coat.

"Addie Hutton!" he cried, looking like Santa, even in his flannel shirt and woolen trousers, as he came out from behind the counter. "It's wonderful to see you again!"

He hugged her, and she hugged him back. "Thanks," she said after swallowing.

"Frank was by a little while ago. Said you might be in the market for a job."

It was just like Frank to try and pave the way. Addie didn't know whether to be annoyed or appreciative, and decided she was both. "I brought a resumé," she said. She had only a few hundred dollars in her checking account, until the money from the sale of her furniture and other personal belongings came through from the auction house in California, and now there was Henry to think about.

She needed work.

"No need for anything like that," Mr. Renfrew said with a wave of his plump, age-spotted hand. "I've known you all your life, Addie. Knew your father for most of his." He paused, frowned. "I can't pay you much, though. You realize that, don't you?"

Addie smiled, nodded. Her eyes were burning again.

"Then it's settled. You can start tomorrow. Nine o'clock sharp."

"Thank you," Addie said, almost overcome. Her salary at the *Wooden Nickel* probably wouldn't have covered her gym membership back home, but she blessed every penny of it.

Mr. Renfrew gave her a tour of the small operation and showed her which of the three desks was hers.

When she stepped back out into the cold, Frank just happened to be loitering on the sidewalk, watching as members of the volunteer fire department strung lights on the community tree from various rungs of the truck ladder.

Addie poked him good-naturedly in the back. "You put in a good word for me, didn't you?" she accused. "With Mr. Renfrew, I mean."

Frank grinned down at her. "Maybe I did," he admitted. "Truth is, he didn't need much persuading. How about a cup of coffee over at the Lumberjack?"

She looked pointedly at the mug in his right hand. "Looks as if you carry your own," she teased.

Something changed in his face, something so subtle that she might have missed it if she hadn't been looking so closely, trying to read him. Then his grin broadened, and he upended the cup, dumping the dregs of his coffee into a snowbank. "I guess I need a refill," he said.

They walked to the diner, on the opposite side of the square, Frank exchanging gruff male greetings with the light-stringing firemen as they passed.

Inside the diner, they took seats in a booth, and the waitress filled Frank's mug automatically, before turning over the clean cup in front of Addie and pouring a serving for her.

"What happened in California?" Frank asked bluntly, when they were alone.

Addie looked out into the square, watching the firemen and the passersby, and her hand trembled a little as she raised the cup to her mouth. "I made a mistake," she said, after a long time, when she could meet his eyes again. "A really stupid one."

"You've never done anything stupid in your life," Frank said.

Except when I gave back your engagement ring, Addie thought, and immediately backed away from that memory. "That's debatable." She sighed. "I got a tip on a big scandal brewing in the city attorney's office," she said miserably. "I checked and rechecked the facts, but I should have *triple*-checked them. I wrote an article that shook the courthouse from top to bottom. I was nearly jailed when I wouldn't reveal my source—and then that source turned out to be a master liar. People's reputations and careers were damaged. My newspaper was sued, and I was fired."

Frank shook his head. "Must have been rough."

Addie bit her lower lip, then squared her shoulders. "It was," she admitted solemnly. "Thanks to you, I have a job and a place to live." She leaned forward. "We have to talk about rent, Frank."

He leaned forward, too. "That whole place should have been yours. I'm not going to charge you rent."

"It should have been Eliza's, and she left it to you," Addie insisted. "And I *am* going to pay rent. If you refuse, I'll move."

He grinned. "Good luck finding anything in Pine Crossing," he said.

She slumped back in her seat. "I'm paying. You need the money. You can't possibly be making very much."

He lifted his cup to his mouth, chuckled. "Still stubborn

as hell, I see," he observed. "And it just so happens that I do all right, from a financial standpoint anyway." He set the mug down again, regarded her thoughtfully. "Tell me about the boy," he said.

She smiled at the mention of Henry. For all the problems, it was a blessing having him with her, a gift. She loved him desperately—he was the child she might never have. She was thirty-five, after all, and her life was a train wreck. "Henry is my stepson. His father and I were badly matched, and the marriage came crashing down under its own weight a couple of years ago. I fell out of love with Toby, but Henry is still my man."

"He seems troubled," Frank remarked. The diner's overhead lights shimmered in his dark hair and on the broad shoulders of his jacket. Danced along the upper half of his badge.

"My ex-husband isn't the most responsible father in the world. He remarried recently, and evidently, the new Mrs. Springer is not inclined to raise another woman's child. Toby brought him as far as Denver by plane, then put him on a bus, like so much freight. Henry came all that way alone. He must have been so scared."

Frank's jawline tightened, and a flush climbed his neck. "Tell your ex-husband," he muttered, "never to break the speed limit in my town."

While Floyd the beagle galloped around the snowman in ever-widening circles, barking joyously at falling flakes, Henry and Lissie pressed small stones into Frosty's chest, and Addie added the finishing touch: one of Frank's old baseball caps.

The moment was so perfect that it worried Frank a little.

He was telling himself not to be a fool when Almira Pidgett's vintage Desoto ground up to the curb. She leaned across the seat, rolled down the passenger window, and glowered through the snowfall.

"Well," she called, raising her voice several decibels above shrill to be heard over the happy beagle, "it's nice to see our chief of police hard at work, making our community safe from crime."

Lissie and Henry went still, and some of the delight drained from Addie's face. Out of the corner of his eye, Frank saw Lissie straighten her halo.

You old bat, Frank thought, but he smiled as he strolled toward the Desoto, his hands in the pockets of his uniform jacket. "Hello, Miss Pidgett," he said affably, bending to look through the open window. "Care to help us finish our snowman?"

"Hmmph," she said. "Is that Addie Hutton over there? I must say, she doesn't look much the worse for wear, for someone who almost went to prison."

Frank's smile didn't waver, even though he would have liked to reach across that seat and close both hands around Almira's neck. "You ought to work up a little Christmas spirit, Miss Pidgett," he said. "If you don't, you might just be visited by three spirits one of these nights, like old Ebenezer Scrooge."

CHAPTER FOUR

"It's a Christmas tree," Henry announced importantly, the following morning, after opening the fourth box. Frank had lifted him onto the counter for the unveiling. "Are *we* going to get a Christmas tree, Addie?"

"Sure," Addie said, a little too quickly. Her smile felt wobbly on her face. There had still been no call from Toby, no response to her barrage of e-mails and phone messages. And every day that Henry stayed with her would make it that much more difficult, when the time came, to give him up.

"It's too early for a tree," Lissie said practically, watching as Henry scrambled down off the counter with no help from Frank. She looked especially festive that day, having replaced the snow-soaked gold tinsel in her halo with bright silver. "The needles will fall off."

"We had a fake one in California," Henry said. "It was made of the same stuff as that thing on your head, so the needles *never* fell off. We could have left it up till the Fourth of July."

"That's stupid," Lissie responded. "Who wants a Christmas tree on the Fourth of July?"

"Liss," Frank said. "Throwing the word 'stupid' around is conduct unbecoming to an angel."

The little girl sighed hugely. "It's useless trying to be an angel anyway," she said. "I guess I'm going to be a shepherd for the rest of my life."

Addie straightened Lissie's halo. "Nonsense," she said, suppressing a smile. "I think it's safe to say that you most certainly will not be a shepherd three weeks from now."

Outside, in the driveway, a horn bleated out one cheery little honk.

"Car pool," Frank explained when Addie lifted her eyebrows in question.

She hastened to zip Henry into his coat. He endured this fussing with characteristic stoicism, and when he and Lissie had gone, Frank lingered to refill his cup at the percolator.

"No word from Wonder Dad, huh?" he asked.

Addie shook her head. "How can he do this, Frank?" she muttered miserably. "How can he just *not call?* For all he knows, Henry never arrived, or I wasn't here when he did."

"He knows," Frank said easily. "You've been calling and e-mailing, haven't you?"

Addie nodded, pulling on her coat and reaching for her purse. She wanted to get to work early, show Mr. Renfrew she was dependable. "But he hasn't answered."

"And you think that means he didn't get the messages?"

Addie paused in the act of unplugging the coffeepot. Frank had a point. Toby was a master at avoiding confrontation, not to mention personal responsibility. He wouldn't call, or even respond to her e-mails, until he was sure she'd had time enough to cool off.

She sighed. "You're right," she said.

Frank gave her a crooked grin and spread his hands. "Are we still on for the tree-lighting ceremony tonight?" he asked.

Addie nodded, glanced at the Advent calendar, with its four open boxes. Twenty to go. "Have you noticed a pattern?" she asked. "I mean, maybe I'm being fanciful here, but the first day, there was a teddy bear. Henry was carrying a bear when he got off the bus. Then—okay, the ballerina doesn't fit the theory—but yesterday was the snowman. We built one. And today, it's the Christmas tree, and the shindig at the square just happens to be tonight. "

Frank put a hand to the small of her back and gently propelled her toward the doorway. "The bear," he said, "was pure coincidence. The snowman gave the kids the idea to build one. And the fire department always lights the tree three weeks before Christmas."

They'd crossed the living room, and Frank opened the front door to a gust of dry, biting wind. Addie pulled her coat more tightly around her. "All very practical," she said with a tentative smile, "but I heard you tell Miss Pidgett she might be visited by three spirits some night soon. If that's not fanciful, I don't know what is."

They descended the steps, and Frank didn't smile at her remark. He seemed distracted. "Lissie really wants that part," he fretted. "The one in the pageant at St. Mary's, I mean. And Almira isn't going to give it to her, not because the kid couldn't pull it off, but because she doesn't like me."

Addie thought of Lissie's tinsel halo and felt a pinch of sorrow in the deepest region of her heart. "Maybe if you talked to Miss Pidgett, explained—"

Frank stopped beside his squad car, which was parked in the driveway, beside Addie's station wagon. "I can't do that, Addie," he said quietly. "I'm the chief of police. I can't ask the woman to do my kid a favor."

She touched his arm. Started to say that *she* could speak to Miss Pidgett, and promptly closed her mouth. She knew how Frank would react to that suggestion; he'd say she was over the line, and he'd be right.

Frank surprised her. He leaned forward and kissed her lightly on the forehead. "Thanks, Addie," he said.

"For what?"

"For coming home."

CHAPTER FIVE

Addie stopped on the sidewalk outside the *Wooden Nickel,* at eight forty-five A.M. precisely, to admire the glowing tree in the center of the square. She hoped she would never forget the reflection of those colored lights shining on Henry and Lissie's upturned faces the night before. After the celebration, they'd all gone back to Frank's place for spaghetti and hot cocoa, and Addie had been amazed that she didn't so much as hesitate on the threshold.

When she and her father had lived there, the very walls had seemed to echo with loneliness, except when Eliza or Frank were around.

Now another father and daughter occupied the space. The furniture was different, of course, but so was the atmosphere. Sorrow had visited those rooms, leaving its mark, but despite that, the house seemed to exude warmth, stability—love.

A rush of cold wind brought Addie abruptly back to the present moment. She shivered and pushed open the front door of the *Wooden Nickel,* and very nearly sent Mr. Renfrew sprawling.

He was teetering on top of a foot ladder, affixing a silver bell above the door.

Addie gasped and reached out to steady her employer. "I'm sorry!" she cried.

Mr. Renfrew grinned down at her. "What do you think of the bell?" he asked proudly. "It belonged to my grandmother."

Addie put a hand to her heart. The bell was silver, with a loop of red ribbon attached to the top.

"What's the matter?" Mr. Renfrew asked, getting down from the ladder.

In her mind's eye, Addie was seeing the little bell in the Christmas box Lissie had opened that morning. Silver, with red thread.

She smiled. "Nothing at all," she said happily, unbuttoning her coat. "It looks wonderful."

"There's a phone message for you, Addie," put in Stella Dorrity, who worked part-time helping Mr. Renfrew with the ad layouts. "He left a number."

Addie felt her smile fade. "Thank you," she said, reaching out for the sticky note Stella offered.

Toby. Where on earth had he gotten her work number? She'd only been hired the day before.

Shakily, she hung up her coat and fished her cell phone out of her purse. "Do you mind if I return the call before I start work?" she asked Mr. Renfrew.

"You go right ahead," he said, still admiring his bell.

"You'd better move that ladder," Stella told him, arms folded, "before somebody breaks their neck."

Addie slipped into the cramped little room behind the reception desk, where the copy machine, lunch table, and a small refrigerator stood shoulder to shoulder.

She punched in the number Stella had taken down, not recognizing the area code.

Toby answered on the third ring. "Yo," he said.

"It's about time you bothered to check up on your son!" Addie whispered.

A sigh. "I knew you'd take care of him."

"He's scared to death," Addie sputtered. "When I saw him get off that bus, all alone—"

"You were there," Toby broke in. "That's what matters."

"What if I hadn't been, Toby? Did you ever think of that?"

"Listen to me, Addie. I know you're furious, and I guess you have a right to be. But I had to do something. The blended-family thing isn't working for Elle."

Addie closed her eyes, counted to ten, then to fifteen, for good measure. Even then, she wanted to take Toby's head off at the shoulders. "Isn't *that* a pity? Tell me, Tobe, did you think about any of this before you decided to tie the knot?"

"It's love, babe," Toby said lightly. "Will you keep him— just until Elle and I get settled in?"

"He's a little boy, not a goldfish!"

"I know, I know. He wants to be with you, anyway. Do this for me, Addie—please. I'm out of options, here. I'll straighten everything out with him when we get back from—when we get back."

"What am I supposed to tell Henry in the meantime? He needs to talk to you. Damn it, *you're his father.*"

"I'll send him a postcard."

"A postcard? Well, that's generous of you. It's almost Christmas, you've just shipped him almost two hundred miles on a Greyhound, all by himself, and you're going to *send a postcard?*"

Another sigh. Toby, the martyred saint. "Add, what do you want me to do?"

"I want you to call him. *Tonight,* Toby. Not when you get back from your stupid honeymoon. I want you to tell Henry you love him, and that everything will be all right."

"I do love him."

"Your idea of love differs significantly from mine," Addie snapped.

"Don't I know it," Toby replied. "All right. Let's have the number. I'll give the kid a ring around six, your time."

"You'd better, Toby."

She knew he wanted to ask what she would do about it if he didn't. She also knew he wouldn't dare.

"Six o'clock," he said with resignation, and hung up in her ear.

"I think Lissie sleeps in that dumb halo," Henry observed that night as he sat coloring at the kitchen table. Addie was at the stove, whipping up a stir-fry, and even though she had one ear tuned to the phone, she was startled when it actually rang. She glanced at the clock on the opposite wall.

Six o'clock, straight up.

"Could you get that, please?" she asked.

Henry gave her a curious look and stalwartly complied. "Hello?"

Watching the boy out of the corner of her eye, Addie saw him stiffen.

"Hi, Dad."

Addie bit her lip and concentrated on the stir-fry, but she couldn't help listening to Henry's end of the conversation. Toby, she could tell, was making his stock excuses. Henry, playing his own customary role, made it easy.

"Sure," he finished. "I'll tell her. See you."

"Everything cool?" she asked carefully.

Henry adjusted his glasses. "I might get to stay till February. Maybe even until school lets out for the summer."

Addie dealt with a tangle of feelings—exhilaration, annoyance, dread and more annoyance—before assembling a smile and turning to face the little boy. "Is that okay with you?"

Henry grinned, nodded. "Yeah," he said. "Maybe he'll forget where he put me, and I'll get to stay forever."

Although she wanted to keep Henry for good, Addie felt a stab at his words. He was so young, and the concept that his own father might misplace him, like a set of keys or a store receipt, was already a part of his thought system.

She dished up two platefuls of stir fry and set them on the table. "We have to take this one step at a time," she warned. Toby was a creature of moods, changeable and impulsive. If things went badly with Elle, or if the new wife was struck by a sudden maternal desire, Toby might swoop down at any moment and whisk Henry away, once and for all.

"Do you think she sleeps in it?" Henry asked, settling himself at the table.

Addie was a few beats behind. "What?"

"Lissie," Henry said patiently, reaching for his fork. "Do you think she sleeps in that halo?"

CHAPTER SIX

Seated at her desk, the telephone receiver propped between her left shoulder and her ear, Addie doodled as she waited for her sales prospect, Jackie McCall, of McCall Real Estate, to come back on the line. A holly wreath, like the one in that morning's matchbox, took shape at the point of her pencil.

The bell over the front door jingled, and Almira Pidgett blew into the *Wooden Nickel*, red-cheeked and rushed. Her hat, with its fur earflaps, made her look as though she should have arrived in a motorcycle sidecar or a Model T—all she lacked was goggles.

Alone in the office, Addie put down her pencil, cupped a hand over the receiver and summoned up a smile. "Good morning," she said. "May I help you?"

"Where," demanded Miss Pidgett, "is Arthur?"

Addie held on to the smile with deliberation. "Mr. Renfrew had a Rotary meeting this morning. He's in the banquet room at the Lumberjack."

Miss Pidgett, plump and white-haired, had been an institution in Pine Crossing for as long as Addie could remember.

She had been Addie's teacher, in both the first and second grades, but, unlike Lissie, and Frank, for that matter, Addie had always enjoyed the woman's favor. She'd played an angel three years in a row, at the Christmas pageant, and graduated to the starring role, that of Mary, before going on to high school.

Now Miss Pidgett sighed and tugged off her knit gloves. "I wish to place an advertisement," she announced.

Jackie McCall came back on the line. "Sorry to keep you waiting, Addie," she said. "It's crazy over here. Would you mind if I called you back?"

"That would be convenient," Addie replied.

Miss Pidgett waited, none too patiently, at the counter, while Addie and Jackie exchanged good-byes and hung up.

"I don't think it's proper for you to spend so much time with Frank Raynor," the older woman blurted out, her expression grim.

Addie took a deep breath. Smiled harder. "Frank is an old friend of mine," she said. "Now, about that advertisement—"

"He's an outsider," Miss Pidgett insisted.

"He's lived in Pine Crossing for thirty years," Addie pointed out.

"His mother was the town tramp," Miss Pidgett went on, lowering her voice to a stage whisper. "God knows who his father was. Anybody but Eliza Raynor would have refused to take him in, after all that happened."

Addie felt a flush climb her neck. She couldn't afford to tell Miss Pidgett off, but she wanted to. "I don't know what you're talking about," she said, approaching the counter. "Were you interested in a classified ad, or something larger?"

"Full page," Miss Pidgett said, almost as an aside. "Don't tell me you didn't know that Janet Raynor ran away with Eliza's husband. That's why they have the same last name."

"I *didn't* know," Addie said carefully, feeling bereft. "And I don't think—"

Miss Pidgett cut her off. "Your father hired Eliza out of

the goodness of his heart. She was destitute, after her Jim and that trollop ran off to Mexico together. They got a quickie divorce, and Jim actually *married* the woman, if you can believe it. A few years later, he ditched her, and Janet had the nerve to send that boy to live with Eliza."

Addie's face warmed. Oh, well, she thought. She could always apply for a waitress job at the Lumberjack. "I didn't know any of those things," she reiterated quietly, "but it doesn't surprise me to learn that Eliza took in a lonely, frightened little boy and loved him like her own. After all, none of what happened was Frank's fault, was it?"

Miss Pidgett reddened. "Eliza was a fool."

"Eliza," Addie corrected, "was the kindest and most generous woman I have ever known. You, on the other hand, are an insufferable gossip." She paused, drew another deep breath. "If I were you, I'd keep a sharp eye out for the ghosts of Christmas past, present, and future!"

"Well!" Miss Pidgett cried, and turned on the heel of one snow boot to stomp out the door.

The bell over the door jangled frantically at her indignant departure.

Mr. Renfrew, just returning from his Rotary breakfast, nearly collided with Miss Pidgett on the sidewalk. Through the glass, Addie saw the old woman shake a finger under his nose, her breath coming in visible puffs as she ranted, then stormed off.

"I'll be darned if I could make heads or tails of what *that* was all about," Mr. Renfrew observed when he came inside. He looked affably baffled, and his ears were crimson from the cold. "Something about taking her business to the *Statesman*."

"I'm afraid I told her off," Addie confessed. "I'll understand if you fire me."

"The old bat," Frank said at six o'clock that evening as he hung a fragrant evergreen wreath on Addie's front door, after listening to her account of Miss Pidgett's visit to the *Wooden Nickel*. The children were in the yard below, running in wild, noisy, arm-waving circles around the snowman, joyously pursued by Floyd the beagle.

Addie hugged herself against the chill of a winter night and gazed up at Frank, perplexed. "No one ever told me," she said. "About your mother and Eliza's husband, I mean."

Frank gave her a sidelong glance. "Old news, kid," he said. "Not the kind of experience Aunt Eliza would have shared with her employer's little girl."

"There must have been so much gossip. How could I have missed hearing it?"

He touched the tip of her nose, and Addie felt a jolt of sensation, right down to her heels. "You were Judge Hutton's daughter. That shielded you from a lot."

Addie bit her lower lip. "I'm so sorry, Frank."

He frowned, taking an unlikely interest in the wreath. "About what?"

"About all you must have gone through. When you were little, I mean."

He turned to face her, spread his hands, and spared her a crooked grin. "Do I look traumatized?" he asked. "Believe me, after five years of sitting outside bars, waiting for my mother, the gossips of Pine Crossing were nothing. Aunt Eliza loved me. She made sure I had three square meals a day, sent me to school with decent clothes on my back, and taught me to believe in myself. I'd say I was pretty lucky."

Addie looked away, blinked, and looked back. "I was so jealous of you," she said.

He touched her again, laying his hand to the side of her face, and the same shock went through her. The wheels and gears of time itself seemed to grind to a halt, and he bent his head toward hers.

"Daddy!"

They froze.

"Damn," Frank said, his breath tingling against Addie's mouth.

She laughed, and they both looked down to see Lissie gazing up at them from the yard, hands on her hips, tinsel halo picking up the last glimmers of daylight. Henry was beside Lissie, the lenses of his glasses opaque with steam.

"You can't kiss unless there's mistletoe!" Lissie called.

"Says who?" Frank called back. Then, to everyone's surprise, he took Addie's face in his hands, tilted her head back, and kissed her soundly.

Afterward, she stared up at him, speechless.

CHAPTER SEVEN

"A shepherd," Henry said when the matchbox was opened the next morning. Lissie peered in, as if doubting his word. Frank had brought the child to Addie's door before dawn that morning, haloed, still in her pajamas and wrapped in a blanket. There had been an automobile accident out on the state highway, and he had to go.

"Hurry up, both of you," Addie replied with an anxious glance at the clock. "I don't want to be late for work." To her way of thinking, she was lucky she still had a job, after the scene with Miss Pidgett the day before.

An hour later, Frank showed up at the *Wooden Nickel*, looking tired and gaunt. He filled his coffee mug from the pot in the small break room. "Where is everybody?" he asked, scanning the office, which was empty except for him and Addie.

"Mr. Renfrew had a doctor's appointment, and Stella went to Denver with her sister to shop for Christmas presents," Addie said. The office, never spacious to begin with, seemed to shrink to the size of a broom closet, with Frank taking up more than his share of space.

Frank rubbed the back of his neck with one hand and sighed before taking a sip of his coffee. "Hope she's careful," he said. "The roads are covered with black ice."

Addie waited.

"The accident was bad," he told her grimly. "Four people airlifted to Denver. One of them died on the way."

"Oh, Frank." Addie wanted to round the counter and put her arms around him, but she hesitated. Sure, he'd kissed her the evening before, but now he had the look of a man who didn't want to be touched. "Was it anyone you know?"

He shook his head. "Thanks for taking care of Lissie," he said after a long silence. He was staring into his coffee cup now, as though seeing an uncertain future take shape there.

"Anytime," Addie replied gently. "You okay?"

He made an attempt at a smile. "I will be," he said gruffly. "It just takes a while to get the images out of my head."

Addie nodded.

"Have supper with us tonight?" Frank asked. He sounded shy, the way he had when he asked her to his senior prom, all those eventful years ago. "Miss Pidgett is casting the play today. I figure Lissie is going to need some diversion."

Addie ached for the little girl, and for the good man who loved her so much. "My turn to cook," she said softly. "I'll stop by St. Mary's and pick up the kids on my way home." There was no daycare center in Pine Crossing, so the children of working parents gathered in either the library or the gym until someone came to collect them.

"Thanks," Frank said. He was on the verge of saying something else when Mr. Renfrew came in.

The two men exchanged greetings, and the telephone rang. Addie took down an order for a classified ad, and when she looked up from her notes, Frank was gone.

"Nice guy, that Frank," Mr. Renfrew said, shrugging off his overcoat.

"Yes," Addie agreed, hoping she sounded more casual than she felt.

"Miss Pidgett been back to place her ad?"

Addie felt a rush of guilt. "No," she said. "Mr. Renfrew, I'm—"

He held up a hand to silence her. "Don't say you're sorry, Addie. It was about time somebody put that old grump in her place."

With that, the subject of Almira Pidgett was dropped.

Henry raced toward the car when Addie pulled up outside the elementary school that afternoon, waving what looked like a brown bathrobe over his head. Lissie followed at a slower pace, head down, scuffing her feet in the dried snow. Even her tinsel halo seemed to sag a little.

Addie's heart went out to the child. She pushed open the car door and stood in the road.

"I'm a shepherd!" Henry shouted jubilantly.

Addie ruffled his hair. "Good job," she said, pleased because he was so excited. She watched Lissie's slow approach.

"I'm the innkeeper's wife," the little girl said, looking wretched. "I don't even get to say anything. My *whole part* is to stand there and look mean and shake my head 'no' when Mary and Joseph ask for a room."

Addie crouched, took Lissie's cold little hands in hers. "I'm so sorry, sweetie. You would have made a perfect angel."

A tear slipped down Lissie's right cheek, quivered on the shoulder of her pink nylon jacket. It was all Addie could do in that moment not to storm into the school and give Miss Pidgett a piece of her mind.

"Tiffany Baker gets to be the most important angel," Lissie said. "She has a whole bunch of lines about good tidings and stuff, and her mother is making her wings out of *real* feathers."

Addie stood up, steered the children toward the car.

"That sucks," Henry said. "Tiffany Baker sucks."

"Henry," Addie said.

"Last year she got to go to Denver and be in a TV commercial," Lissie said as she and Henry got into the backseat and fastened their seat belts. In the rearview mirror, Addie saw Lissie's lower lip wobble.

"There are six other angels," the little girl whispered. "I wouldn't have minded being one of them."

Addie had to fight hard not to cry herself. The child had been wearing a tinsel halo for days. Didn't Almira Pidgett have a heart?

"Maybe we could rent some Christmas movies," she suggested in deliberately cheerful tones.

Lissie pulled off her halo, held it for a moment, then set it aside. "Okay," she said with a complete lack of spirit.

CHAPTER EIGHT

Frank shoved a hand through his hair. "It's been nine days," he whispered to Addie in her kitchen that snowy Saturday morning. "I thought Lissie would be over this play thing by now. Is it really such a bad thing to play the innkeeper's wife?"

Addie glanced sadly at the Advent calendar, still taped to the bottom of the cupboard. Lissie hadn't shown much interest in the daily ritual of opening a new matchbox since the angel disappointment, and that morning was no exception. The tiny sleigh glued inside looked oddly forlorn. "It is if you wanted to be an angel," she said.

"I haven't seen her like this since Maggie died."

Addie sank into a chair at the table. Frank, leaning one shoulder against the refrigerator and sipping coffee, sighed.

"I wish there was something I could do," Addie said.

"Join the club," Frank replied, glancing toward the living room. Henry and Lissie were there, with the ever-faithful Floyd, watching Saturday morning cartoons.

"Sit down, Frank," Addie urged quietly.

He didn't seem to hear her. He was staring out the window at the fat, drifting flakes of snow that had been falling since the night before. "This isn't about Lissie," he said. "That's what makes it so hard. It's about me, and all the times I've butted heads with Almira Pidgett over the years."

Addie's mouth tightened at the mention of the woman, and she consciously relaxed it. "It's not your fault, Frank," she said, and closed her hands around her own coffee cup, grown cold since the pancake breakfast the four of them had shared half an hour before. "Miss Pidgett is a Grinch, plain and simple."

Just then, Addie thought she heard sleigh bells, and she was just shaking her head when a whoop of delight sounded from the living room. Henry. Henry, who was wary of joy, already knowing, young as he was, how easily it could be taken away.

"There's a man down there, driving a sleigh!" Henry shouted, almost breathless with glee. "He's got horses pulling it, instead of reindeer, but he sure looks like Santa!"

"Who?" Frank asked, pleasantly bemused.

Addie was already on her way to investigate. Henry was bounding down the outside stairs, followed by Floyd, and, at a more sedate pace, Lissie. Frank brought up the rear.

Mr. Renfrew, bundled in a stocking cap, ski jacket, and quilted trousers, all the same shade of red, waved cheerfully from the seat of a horse-drawn sleigh.

"Merry Christmas!" he called. "Anybody want a ride?"

Henry was jumping up and down. "I do!" he shouted. "I do!"

"Can Floyd come, too?" Lissie asked cautiously.

Mr. Renfrew's eyes twinkled as he looked over the children's heads to Frank and Addie. "Of course," he answered. Then, in a booming voice, he added, "Don't just stand there! Go put on your cold-weather gear and jump in!"

CHAPTER NINE

There were two bench seats in the back of that old-fashioned sleigh, upholstered in patched leather and facing each other.

"Want to ride up here with me, boy?" Mr. Renfrew asked Henry, his eyes twinkling.

Henry needed no persuading. He scrambled onto the high seat, fairly quivering with excitement. "Can Lissie have a turn, too?" he asked, his breath forming a thin, shifting aura of white around his head.

A sweet, almost painful, warmth settled over Addie's heart. She glanced at Frank, who hoisted the overweight beagle into the sleigh to join Lissie, who was already seated, facing backward.

"Sure, Lissie can have a turn," Mr. Renfrew said, turning to smile down at the child.

Lissie, who had been subdued since putting away her tinsel halo, perked up a little, grinning back at him. Floyd, perched beside her, gave her an exuberant lick on the cheek.

Frank helped Addie up into the sleigh, then sat down beside her, stretching his arm out along the back of the seat, the way a shy teenage boy might do on a movie date. He wasn't quite touching her, but she felt the strength and substance and warmth of him just the same, a powerful tingle along her nape and the length of her shoulders. The energy danced down her spine and arched between her pelvic bones.

It was all she could do not to squirm.

Mr. Renfrew set the sleigh in motion, bells jingling. There was a jerk, but then they glided, as though the whole earth had suddenly turned smooth as a skating rink. Addie bit down on her lower lip and tried to focus on the ride, wincing a little as Lissie turned to kneel in the seat, her back to them, ready to climb up front when she got the nod.

"Addie." Frank's voice. Very close to her ear. Fat snowflakes drifted down, making silent music.

She made herself look at him, not in spite of her reluctance, but *because* of it. The decision was a ripple on the surface of something much deeper, churning far down in the whorls and currents of her mind.

"Relax," he said. "You think too much."

Some reckless sprite rose up out of that emotional sea to put words in Addie's mouth. "You might not say that if you knew what I was thinking *about.*"

Frank lowered his arm, let it rest lightly around her shoulders. "Who says I don't?" he countered, with a half grin and laughter in his eyes. But there was sadness there, too, and something that might have been caution. Perhaps, like Henry, Frank was a little afraid to trust in good things.

Addie blushed and looked away.

They rode over side streets and back roads, and finally left Pine Crossing behind, entering the open countryside. After getting permission from both Addie and Frank, Mr. Renfrew let Henry drive the team, then Lissie. The snow came down harder, and the wind grew colder, and Floyd alternately barked and howled in canine celebration.

Addie had a wonderful time. Something had changed between her and Frank, a subtle, indefinable shift that gave her an odd thrill, a feeling both festive and frightening. She decided to think about it later, when Frank and Lissie weren't around, and Henry had gone to bed.

After an hour or so, they returned to Pine Crossing, traveling down the middle of the main street, between parked cars. Frank sat up very straight, looking imperious and waving in the stiff-handed way of royalty as various friends called amused greetings from the sidewalks.

Lissie climbed back down into the seat beside Floyd as they passed the school, and Addie noticed the deflation in the child's mood. Her small shoulders sagged as she looked at the reader board in front of St. Mary's.

PLAY REHEARSAL TONIGHT, 6 PM
MARY, JOSEPH AND ANGELS ONLY.

Addie bristled inwardly. The sign was obviously Almira's handiwork, and it might as well have said, *Innkeeper's wife will be turned away at the door.*

"No room at the inn," she murmured angrily.

Frank squeezed her hand, so she knew he'd heard, but he was watching Lissie, who sat with her head down, obviously fighting tears, while Floyd nibbled tentatively at the pompom on top of her pink knitted cap.

"Life is hard sometimes, Liss," Frank said quietly. "It's okay to feel bad for a while, but sooner or later, you've got to let go and move on."

Addie's throat tightened. She wanted to take the child in her arms, hold her, tell her everything would be all right, but it wasn't her place. Frank was Lissie's father. She, on the other hand, was little more than an acquaintance.

They passed Pine Crossing General Hospital, then the Sweet Haven Nursing Home. An idea rapped at the backdoor of Addie's brain; she let it in and looked it over.

She barely noticed when they pulled up in front of the house.

Frank got out of the sleigh first, helped Addie, Lissie, and the dog down, then reached up to claim Henry from the driver's seat. Everyone thanked Mr. Renfrew profusely, and Frank invited him in for coffee, but he declined, saying he had things to do at home. Almost Christmas, you know.

"Better get Floyd inside and give him some kibble," Frank told his daughter, laying a hand on her shoulder. "All those snowflakes he ate probably won't hold him long."

Lissie smiled a little, nodded, and grabbed Henry by the arm. "Come on and help me," she said. "I'll show you where we're going to put up the Christmas tree."

Addie thrust her hands into the pockets of her coat and waited until the children were out of earshot. "What if there were more than one way to be an angel?" she asked.

Frank pulled his jacket collar up a little higher, squinted at her. "Huh?"

"You kept so many of Eliza's things," Addie said, looking up at him. If they'd had any sense, they'd have gone in out of the cold. "Do you still have her sewing machine?"

"Maggie used it for mending," Frank answered with a slight nod, and then looked as though he regretted mentioning his late wife's name. "Why?"

"I'd like to borrow it, please."

Frank looked at his watch. "Okay," he said. "What's this about?"

Having noted the time-checking, Addie answered with a question. "Do you have to work tonight, Frank?"

"Town council meeting," he said. "That's why I didn't suggest dinner."

"I'll be happy to look after Lissie and Floyd until you get home," she told him, so he wouldn't have to ask. But she was already on her way to the steps leading up to her over-the-garage apartment.

Frank caught up with her, looking benignly curious. "Wait a second," he said. "There's something brewing, and I'd like to know what it is."

"Maybe you'll just have to be surprised," Addie responded, watching as snowflakes landed in Frank's dark hair and on his long eyelashes. "Right along with Miss Almira Pidgett."

Frank searched her face, looking cautiously amused. "Tell me you're not planning to whip up a trio of spirit costumes and pay her a midnight visit," he said. "Much as I love the idea, it would be trespassing, and breaking and entering, too. Not to mention harassment, stalking, and maybe even reckless endangerment."

Addie laughed, starting up the steps. "You have quite an imagination," she said. "Drop off the sewing machine before you leave for the meeting if you have time, okay?"

He spread his hands and then let them flop against his sides. "So much for my investigative skills," he said. "You're not going to tell me anything, are you?"

Addie paused, smiled, and batted her lashes. "No," she said. "I'm not."

CHAPTER TEN

"Why are we going to a thrift store?" Henry asked reasonably. He blinked behind his glasses, in that owlish way he had. He and Lissie were buckled in, in the back of Addie's station wagon, with Floyd panting between them, delighted to be included in the outing. Lissie was still very quiet; in the rearview mirror, Addie saw her staring forlornly out the window.

She flipped on the windshield wipers and peered through the increasing snowfall. The storm had been picking up speed since they got home from the sleigh ride with Mr. Renfrew, and now that dusk had fallen, visibility wasn't the best. "I plan to do some sewing, and I need material," Addie answered belatedly, wondering if they shouldn't just stay home.

Lissie showed some interest, at last. "Mom used to make my Halloween costumes out of stuff from the Goodwill," she said.

"I was Harry Potter Halloween before last," Henry said sadly, as Addie drew a deep breath, offered a silent prayer, and pulled out onto the road. "This year, Dad and Elle went to a costume party, but I didn't get to dress up."

Addie felt a pang of guilt, bit her lower lip. She'd thought of calling, inviting Henry to come trick-or-treating in her apartment complex, but she'd overruled the urge. After all, Toby and Elle had made it pretty clear, following all the publicity, that they didn't want her around Henry.

"With those glasses," Lissie remarked, perking up, "you wouldn't even need a costume to look like Harry Potter."

"I had a cape, too," Henry told her in a lofty tone. "Didn't I, Addie?"

Addie gazed intently over the top of the steering wheel. "Yes," she answered. Toby had dropped him off at her apartment that Halloween afternoon, a few months after their divorce became final, without calling first, flustered over some emergency at work. She'd fashioned the cape from an old shower curtain and taken him around the neighborhood with high hopes and a paper sack. They'd both had a great time.

"I was a hobo once," Lissie said. "When Mom was still alive, I mean. She bought an old suit and sewed patches on it and stuff. I had a broom handle with a bundle tied to the end, and I won a prize."

"Big deal," Henry said.

Addie pulled up to a stop sign intersecting the main street through town, and sighed with relief. The blacktop, though dusted with a thin coating of snow, had recently been plowed. She signaled and made a cautious left turn toward the center of Pine Crossing.

The lights of St. Mary's shimmered golden through the falling snow. Addie would have preferred not to pass the school, with the rehearsal going on and Lissie in the car, but it didn't make sense to risk the children's safety by taking unplowed side streets.

When they rolled up in front of the thrift store, at the opposite end of town, Lissie hooked a leash to Floyd's collar.

She and Henry walked him in the parking lot while Addie hurried inside.

An artificial Christmas tree stood just inside the door, offering a cheerful if somewhat bedraggled welcome. Chipped ornaments hung from its crooked boughs, and a plastic star glowed with dim determination at its top.

I know just how you feel, Addie thought, as she passed the tree, scanning the store and zeroing in on the women's dresses.

She selected an old formal, a musty relic of some long-forgotten prom. The voluminous, floor-length underskirt was satin or taffeta, with the blue iridescence of a peacock feather.

"I don't think that will fit you," said a voice beside Addie, startling her a little. "It's a fourteen-sixteen, and you can't be bigger than an eight. But you can try it on if you want to."

Addie turned and smiled at the young girl standing beside her. Her name tag read, "Barbara," and she was chubby, with bad skin and stringy hair. "I just want the fabric," Addie said. "Is there anything here with pearl buttons? Or crystal beads?"

Barbara brightened a little. "Jessie Corcoran donated her wedding gown last week," she said. "It's real pretty. Her mom told my mom she ordered it special off the Internet." She paused, blushed. "I guess things didn't work out with that guy from Denver. For Jessie, I mean. Since she came back home to Pine Crossing one day and chucked the dress the next—"

"She might want it back," Addie mused.

Barbara shook her head, and her eyes widened behind the smudged lenses of her glasses. "She stuffed it right into the donation box, out there by the highway—my friend Becky saw her do it. Didn't even care if it got dirty, I guess. People dumped other stuff right in on top of it, too. A pair of old boots and a couple of puzzles with a lot of pieces missing."

"My goodness," Addie said.

Barbara produced the dress, ran a plump, reverent hand over the skirt. The bodice gleamed bravely with pearls and tiny glass beads. In its own way, the discarded wedding gown looked as forlorn as the Christmas tree at the front of the store.

"How much?" Addie asked.

Barbara didn't even have to look at the tag. "Twenty-five dollars," she said. "Are you getting married?"

Addie was taken aback, as much by the price as by the question. "Ordered special" or not, the dress was hardly haute couture.

Barbara smiled. "It's a small town," she said. "I guess you used to live in Frank Raynor's house. Now you're staying in the apartment over his garage and working at the *Wooden Nickel*. Down at the bowling alley—my mom plays on a league—they're saying Frank's been alone long enough. He needs a wife, and Lissie needs a mother."

Addie opened her mouth, closed it again. Shook her head. "No," she said.

"You don't want the dress?"

"No—I mean, yes. I *do* want the dress. I'll give you ten dollars for it. But there isn't going to be a wedding." She wanted to make sure this news got to the bowling league, from whence it would spread all over the county.

Barbara looked disappointed. "That's too bad," she said. "Everybody got their hopes up, for a while there. Fifteen dollars, and the dress is yours."

"I'm sorry," Addie said. She glanced toward the front windows bedecked in wilting garland, and thought of Lissie's halo, now a castoff, like Jessie Corcoran's wedding gown and the peacock-blue prom dress. "Fifteen dollars it is," she told Barbara. "I'd better hurry—the roads are probably getting worse by the moment."

Five minutes later, she was out the door, her purchases carefully folded and wrapped in a salvaged dry cleaner's bag. Henry, Lissie and Floyd were already in the backseat of the station wagon.

"Buckle up," she told them, starting the engine.

"What did you buy in there?" Henry wanted to know.

"Secondhand dreams," Addie said. "With a little creativity, they can be good as new."

"How can dreams be secondhand?" Lissie asked, sounding both skeptical and intrigued.

Addie flipped on the headlights, watched the snowflakes dancing in the beams. "Sometimes people give up on them, because they don't fit anymore. Or they just leave them behind, for one reason or another. Then someone else comes along, finds them, and believes they might be worth something after all."

"That's really confusing," Henry said. "Can we stop for pizza?"

"No," Addie replied. "We've got beans and weenies at home."

"I wanted to be an angel," Lissie said, very softly. "That was my dream."

"I know," Addie answered.

It was after ten when Frank climbed the stairs to Addie's front door, listened for a moment to the faint whirring of his aunt's old sewing machine inside, and knocked lightly. Floyd let out a welcoming yelp, the machine stopped humming, and Frank heard Addie shushing the dog good-naturedly as she crossed the living room and peered out at him through the side window.

Her smile, blurred by the steamy glass, tugged at his heart.

"Shhh," she said, putting a finger to her lips as she opened the door. He wasn't sure if she was addressing him or Floyd. "Lissie's asleep in my room."

Frank stepped over the threshold, settled the dog with a few pats on the head and some ear ruffling, and eyed the sewing setup in the middle of the living room. Bright blue cloth billowed over the top of an old card table like a trapped cloud, the light from Eliza's machine shimmering along its folds.

He set Maggie's coffee mug aside, on the plant stand next to the door, and stuffed his hands into the pockets of his jacket. "Are you going to tell me what you're making, or is it still a secret?"

"It's still a secret," Addie answered with a grin. Her gaze flicked to the cup, then back to his face. "Do you want some coffee? I just brewed a pot of decaf a few minutes ago."

He hesitated. "Sure," he said.

"How did the meeting go?" Addie started toward the mug, then stopped. Frank handed it to her.

"Fine," he said.

"You look tired." Carrying the mug, she headed for the kitchen. "Long night?"

He stood on the threshold between the living room and the kitchen, gripping the doorframe, watching her pour the coffee. For an instant, he flashed back to that afternoon's sleigh ride, and the way it felt to put his arm around her shoulders. He shook off the memory, reached for the cup as she approached, holding it out. "Yeah," he said.

Hot coffee sloshed over his hand, and the mug slipped, tumbling end over end, shattering on the floor. The whole thing was over in seconds, but Frank would always remember it in slow motion.

Addie gasped, put one hand over her mouth.

Frank stared at the shards of Maggie's last gift, disbelieving.

"I'm sorry," Addie said. She grabbed a roll of paper towels.

He was already crouching, gathering the pieces. "It wasn't your fault, Addie." He couldn't look at her.

She squatted, a wad of towels in her hand, blotting up the flow of coffee. He stopped her gently, took over the job. When he stole a glance at her face, there were tears standing in her eyes.

"Maggie's cup," she whispered. He didn't remember telling her his wife had made the mug; maybe Lissie had.

"Don't," he said.

She nodded.

Floyd tried to lick up some of the spilled coffee, and Frank nudged him away with a slight motion of his elbow. He put the pieces of the cup into his pocket, straightened, and disposed of the paper towels in the trash can under the sink.

"Shall I wake Lissie up?" Addie asked tentatively, from somewhere at the periphery of Frank's vision.

He shook his head. "I'll do it," he said.

Lissie didn't awaken when he lifted her off Addie's bed, or even when he eased her into her coat.

"Thanks for taking care of her," he told Addie as he carried his sleeping daughter across the living room, Floyd scampering at his heels.

Addie nodded and opened the door for him, and a rush of cold air struck his face. Lissie shifted, opened her eyes, and yawned, and the fragments of Maggie's cup tinkled faintly in his pocket, like the sound of faraway bells.

An hour later, with Lissie settled in her own bed and Floyd curled up at her feet, Frank went into the kitchen and laid the shards of broken china out on the counter, in a jagged row. There was no hope of gluing the cup back together, but most of the bright red heart was there, chipped and cracked.

"Maggie," he whispered.

There was no answer, of course. She was gone.

He took the wastebasket from the cupboard under the sink, held it to the edge of the counter, and slowly swept the pieces into it. A crazy urge possessed him, an unreasonable desire to fish the bits out of the garbage, try to reassemble them after all. He shook his head, put the bin away, and left the kitchen, turning out the lights as he passed the switch next to the door.

The house was dark as he climbed the stairs. For the first six months after Maggie died, he hadn't been able to sleep in their room, in their bed. He'd camped out in the den, downstairs, on the fold-out couch, until the night Lissie had a walking nightmare. Hearing his daughter's screams, he'd rushed upstairs to find her in the master bedroom, clawing at the covers, as if searching, wildly, desperately, for something she'd lost.

"I can't find my mommy!" she'd sobbed. "I can't find my daddy!"

"I'm here," he'd said, taking her into his arms, holding her tightly as she struggled awake. "Daddy's here."

Now Frank paused at the door of his and Maggie's room. *Daddy's here,* he thought, *but Mommy's gone. She's really, truly gone.*

He went inside, closed the door, stripped off his jacket, shoes and uniform, and stretched out on the bed, staring up at the ceiling. His throat felt tight, and his eyes burned.

Maggie's words came back to him, echoing in his mind. *I want you to mourn me for a while, but when it's time to let go, I'll find a way to tell you.*

A single tear slipped from the corner of his right eye and trickled over his temple. "It's time, isn't it?" he asked in a hoarse whisper.

Once again, he heard the cup smashing on Addie's kitchen floor.

It was answer enough.

CHAPTER ELEVEN

Addie didn't even try to go to sleep that night. She brewed another pot of coffee—no decaf this time—and sewed like a madwoman until the sun came up.

It was still snowing, and she was glad it was Sunday as she stared blearily out the front window at a white-blanketed, sound-muffled world.

"Can I open the calendar box," Henry asked from behind her, "or do we have to wait for Lissie?"

Addie took a moment to steel herself, then turned to smile at her stepson. Still in his pajamas, he wasn't wearing his glasses, and his dark hair was sleep-rumpled. Blinking at her, he rubbed his eyes with the backs of his hands.

"We'd better wait," she said. Lissie might show up for the ritual, but she wondered about Frank. The look on his face, when that cup tumbled to the floor and splintered into bits, was still all too fresh in her mind.

Of course it had been an accident. Addie understood that, and she knew Frank did, too. Just the same, she'd glimpsed the expression of startled sorrow in his eyes, seen the slow, almost reverent way he'd gathered up the pieces. . . .

Something a lot more important than a ceramic coffee mug had been broken.

"Couldn't I peek?" Henry persisted, still focused on the matchbox calendar. In a way, Addie was pleased; he was feeling more secure with the new living arrangement, letting down his guard a little. In another way, she was unsettled. For all his promises that Henry could stay until February, or even until school was out for the summer, Toby might appear at any moment, filled with sudden fatherly concern, and whisk the child away.

"I guess," she said, just as a firm rap sounded at the front door.

"They're here!" Henry shouted, bounding across the linoleum kitchen floor and into the living room.

Frank stepped over the threshold, looking grimly pleasant, and Addie knew by the shadows in and beneath his eyes that he hadn't had much more sleep than she had, if any. There was no sign of Lissie.

"Where's Halo Woman?" Henry asked, taking his glasses from the pocket of his pajama top and jamming them onto his face.

Frank smiled at the new nickname. "Lissie's got a fever this morning," he said. "The doctor's been by. Said she needs to stay in bed, keep warm, and take plenty of fluids."

"And you have to work," Addie guessed aloud, folding her arms and leaning against the framework of the kitchen door because she wanted to cross the room and embrace Frank. She sensed that he wouldn't welcome a show of sympathy just then.

He nodded. "The roads are wicked, thanks to all this new snow. I've got every man I could call in out there patrolling, but we're still shorthanded."

"We could baby-sit her," Henry announced. He grinned. "And dog-sit Floyd."

Addie watched Frank's face closely. He didn't like asking for help, she could see that. "Mrs. Jarvis usually watches her when there's a crisis," he said, "but her sister just moved into the nursing home, and she's been spending a lot of time there, trying to help her adjust."

"What's easier, Frank?" Addie said gently. "For Henry and me to come down to your place, or for you to bring Lissie and Floyd up here?"

He thrust a hand through his snow-sprinkled hair, glanced at the sewing machine and billows of blue fabric. "You've got a project going here," he reflected. "And Lissie would probably enjoy a visit. I'll wrap her up in a quilt and bring her up." He was quiet for a long moment. "If it's really all right with you."

"Frank," Addie told him, feeling affectionately impatient, "of *course* it is."

"I better get dressed!" Henry decided, and dashed off to his room.

"About the cup," Frank began, looking miserable. He'd closed the door against the cold and the blowing snow, but he didn't move any closer. The gap between them, though only a matter of a dozen feet, felt unaccountably wide. "I guess I overreacted. I'm sorry, Addie."

She still wanted to touch him, still wouldn't let herself do it. "It meant a lot to you," she said gently.

He nodded. "Just the same," he reasoned in a gruff voice, "it was only a coffee mug."

Addie knew it was much more, but it wasn't her place to say so. "Go and get Lissie," she told him. "I'll bring out some pillows and a blanket, make up the couch." She paused, then went on, very carefully, "Have you eaten? I'm going to make breakfast in a few minutes."

"No time," he said with a shake of his head. "I'll hit the drive-through or something." He hesitated, as if he wanted to say something else, opened the door again, and went out.

Because she felt a need to move and be busy, exhausted as she was, Addie went into her room and grabbed the pillows off the bed. She was plumping them on one end of the couch when Frank returned, carrying Lissie. Floyd trailed after them, snowflakes melting on his floppy ears, wagging not just his tail, but his whole substantial hind end. Addie would have sworn that dog was grinning.

Henry, dressed and hastily groomed, waited impatiently until Lissie was settled. "What about the calendar box?" he blurted. "Can we look now?"

"I know what it is anyway," Lissie said with a congested sniff. She was still in her flannel nightgown and smelled pleasantly of mentholated rub.

Henry looked imploringly up at Addie.

"Go ahead." She smiled.

Frank wrote down his cell phone number, handed it to Addie, kissed his daughter on top of the head, and left the apartment. The place seemed to deflate a little when he was gone.

"It's a dog!" Henry announced, returning to the living room. He'd dragged a chair over to the cupboards to peer inside that day's matchbox. "Brown and white, like Floyd. But a lot littler."

"It's snowing really hard," Lissie fretted, turning to look out the front window. "Dad said the roads are slick. Do you think he'll be okay?"

Addie sat down on the edge of the couch, giving Lissie as much room as she could, and touched the child's forehead with the back of her hand. "Sure he will," she said quietly. "What would you like for breakfast? Scrambled eggs, or oatmeal?"

"Oatmeal," Lissie answered.

"Scrambled eggs," Henry chimed in at the same moment.

Addie laughed. "I'll make both," she said.

The kids ate in the living room, watching a holiday movie marathon on television, while Addie washed the dishes. The phone rang just as she was putting the last of the silverware away.

"Hello?" she said cheerfully, expecting the caller to be Frank checking up on his daughter.

"I'm in Denver," Toby said.

Addie stretched the phone cord to its limits, hooked one foot around a chair leg, and dragged it close enough to collapse onto. *"What?"*

"I can't believe this snow."

Addie closed her eyes. Waited.

Toby spoke into the silence. "How's Henry? Can I talk to him?"

She couldn't very well refuse, but stalling was another matter. Her stomach felt like a clenched fist, and her heart skittered with dread. "What are you doing in Denver?"

"Put Henry on, will you?"

Addie turned to call the boy, and was startled to find him standing only a few feet away, watching. She held out the receiver. "It's your dad," she said.

Henry didn't move. She couldn't see his eyes, because of the way the light hit the lenses of his glasses, but his chin quivered a little, and his freckles seemed to stand out.

"I can't leave," he said. "I'm a shepherd."

Addie blinked back tears. "You've got to talk to him, buddy," she said very gently.

He crossed to her, took the phone.

"I can't leave, Dad," he said. "I'm a shepherd."

Addie started to rise out of her chair, meaning to leave the room, but Henry laid a small hand on her arm and looked at her pleadingly.

"In the play at school," he went on, after listening to whatever Toby said in the interim. "Yeah, I like it here. I like it a lot."

Addie rubbed her temples with the fingertips of both hands.

"No, it didn't come yet." Henry put a hand over the receiver. "Dad sent a box," he said to Addie. "Christmas presents."

Addie's spirits rose a little. If Toby had mailed Henry's gifts, he probably intended to leave the boy with her at least through the holidays. On the other hand, Toby was nothing if not a creature of quicksilver moods. And he was in Denver, after all, which might mean he'd changed his mind. . . .

"I understand," Henry said. "You're stuck because of the snow. You shouldn't try to drive here. The roads are really bad—Lissie's dad says so, and he's the chief of police."

More verbiage from Toby's end. Addie didn't catch the words, but the tone was upbeat, thrumming with good cheer.

"Right." Henry nodded somberly. "Sure, Dad." He swallowed visibly, then thrust the phone at Addie. "He wants to talk to you again."

Addie bit her lower lip, nodded for no particular reason, and took the receiver.

"Addie?" Toby prompted, when she was silent too long. "Are you there?"

"Yes," she said, sitting up very straight on her chair, which seemed to be teetering on the edge of some invisible abyss. One false move and she'd never stop falling.

"Look, I was planning to rent a car, drive down there, and surprise Henry with a visit. But it looks like that won't be possible, because of the weather. I'll be lucky to get out of here between storm fronts, according to the airline people."

Addie let out her breath, but inaudibly. She didn't want Toby to guess how scared she'd been when she'd thought he was coming to take Henry away, or how relieved she was now that she knew he wasn't. "Okay," she said.

Toby chuckled uncomfortably. "You know, I remember you as being more communicative, Addie. Cat got your tongue?"

She glanced sideways, saw that Henry was still standing close by, listening intently. Floyd had joined him, leaning heavily against the boy's side as if to offer forlorn support. "I guess I'm just surprised. I thought you were on your honeymoon."

"Elle got bored with the tropics. She's in Manhattan, doing some Christmas shopping. Her folks live in Connecticut, so we're spending the holidays with them. I decided I wanted to see the kid, and picked up a standby seat out of LaGuardia—"

The trip was a whim, to Toby. *Henry* was a whim.

Don't say it, Addie told herself. *Don't make him angry, because then he'll come here, if he has to hitch a ride on a snowplow, and when he leaves, Henry will go with him.* "I'm sorry it didn't work out," she said instead. It wasn't a complete lie. As much as Henry wanted to stay in Pine Crossing with her, he was a normal little boy. He loved his father and craved his attention. A visit would have delighted him.

"Tell Dad you'll take a picture of me being a shepherd," Henry prompted.

Addie dutifully repeated the information.

"A what?" Toby asked, sounding distracted. Maybe they **were** announcing his flight back to New York, and maybe he had simply lost interest.

"Henry's playing a shepherd in the Christmas play," Addie said moderately and, for her stepson's sake, with a note of perky enthusiasm. "I'll take some pictures."

"Oh, right," Toby answered. "Okay. Look, Addie—I appreciate this. My dad sent you a check." He lowered his voice. "You know, for the kid's expenses."

Henry and Floyd returned to the living room, summoned by Lissie, who called out that they were about to miss the part where Chevy Chase got tangled in the Christmas lights and fell off the roof.

"Your dad?" Addie asked, very carefully.

Toby thrust out a sigh. "Look, we're kind of living on Elle's money right now. The mortgage business isn't so great at this time of year. And since Henry isn't hers—"

Chevy Chase must have taken his header into the shrubbery, because Henry and Lissie hooted with delighted laughter.

"Henry can stay with me as long as necessary," Addie said, again with great care, framing it as a favor Toby was doing for her, and not the reverse. "Try not to worry, okay? I'll take very good care of him."

Toby was quiet for so long that Addie got nervous. "Thanks, Add," he said. "Listen, it's time to board."

"Where can I get in touch with you, Toby? In case there's an emergency, I mean?"

"Send me an e-mail," Toby said hurriedly. "I check every few days." With that, he rang off.

They were all asleep when Frank let himself into the apartment at six-fifteen that evening, even the dog. Lissie snoozed at one end of the couch, Henry at the other. Addie had curled up in the easy chair, her brown hair tumbling over her face.

Frank felt a bittersweet squeeze behind his heart as he switched on a lamp, turned off the TV, and put the pizza boxes he was carrying down on the coffee table.

Floyd woke up first, beagle nose in overdrive, and yelped happily at the prospect of pepperoni and cheese. The sound stirred Lissie and Henry awake, and, finally, Addie opened her eyes.

"Pizza!" Henry whooped.

Frank laughed, though his gaze seemed stuck on Addie. The situation was innocent, but there was something intimate about watching this particular woman wake up. Her tentative, sleepy smile made him ache, and if she asked how his day had gone, he didn't know what he'd do.

"How was your day?" she inquired, standing up and stretching both arms above her head. Making those perfect breasts rise.

"Good," he managed, figuring he sounded like a caveman, barely past the grunt stage. He averted his gaze to Lissie, who was off the couch and lifting one of the pizza box lids to peer inside. "Feeling better?" he asked.

Lissie nodded, somewhat reluctantly. "I'll probably have to go to school tomorrow and listen to Tiffany Baker bragging about being an angel in the Christmas play," she said, but with some spirit.

"Probably," Frank agreed.

Floyd put both paws up on the edge of the coffee table and all but stuck his nose into the pizza. Grinning, Frank took him gently by the collar and pulled him back.

"I'll get some plates," Addie said, heading for the kitchen.

"Bring one for Floyd," Henry suggested.

Addie laughed, and Frank unzipped his uniform jacket and shrugged it off, thinking how good it was to be home.

CHAPTER TWELVE

Much to Lissie's annoyance, and Frank's relief, the child was well enough to go to school the next morning. The snow had stopped, and though the ground was covered in glittering white, there was a springlike energy in the air.

Addie was in a cheerful mood, humming along with the kitchen radio while she supervised the opening—with a suitable flourish on Lissie's part—of that day's calendar box. Inside was a miniature gift, wrapped in shiny paper and tied in a bow.

Henry scrunched up his face, intrigued. "Is there anything inside it?"

"No, silly," Lissie responded. "It's supposed to represent a Christmas present."

"I'm getting presents," Henry said. "From my dad. He sent a box."

"You need a Christmas tree if you're going to get presents," Lissie reasoned. "Dad's getting ours tonight, after work."

Henry looked questioningly at Addie. "Are we getting one, too?"

"Sure are," Frank put in, before Addie could answer.

"A real one?" Henry asked hopefully.

"The genuine article," Frank promised, hoping he wasn't stepping on Addie's toes in some way. Maybe she wanted buying the tree to be a family thing, just her and Henry. It took some nerve, but he made himself meet her eyes.

She looked uncertain.

"You two put on your coats and head for the car," Frank told the kids. "I'll drop you off at school on my way to work."

They dashed off.

"Everything okay, Addie?" Frank asked quietly, when the two of them were alone in the apartment kitchen. She was dressed for another day at the *Wooden Nickel*.

She hugged herself. "I wasn't really planning on Christmas," she said. "And I've been so busy since Henry got here, I haven't really thought about it."

He wanted to cross the room, maybe touch her hair, but things were still a little awkward between them. Had been since Maggie's mug had struck the floor. "I shouldn't have said anything about the tree."

"It's okay," she said. "I don't have ornaments, though, or lights."

"A lot of your father's stuff is still in the storeroom," he reminded her. "I'm pretty sure there are some decorations." He paused, shoved a hand through his hair. "Damn, Addie, I'm sorry. I wish I'd kept my mouth shut."

Her smile faltered a little. "I vaguely remember strings and strings of those old-fashioned bubble lights," she said wistfully. "And lots of shiny ornaments. They must have been packed away when Mom died—Dad didn't care much about Christmas. Said it was a lot of sentimental slop, and way too commercial. He used to give me money and tell me to buy what I wanted."

Frank's spirits plunged like an elevator after the cable breaks. *Way to go, Raynor,* he thought. *First, you put Addie on the spot in front of the kids, and now you remind her that her childhood Christmases wouldn't exactly inspire nostalgia.*

He found his voice. "Look, you helped me out yesterday when I needed somebody to look after Lissie. I'll spring for an extra evergreen. We could make a night of it—hit the tree lot, then have supper at the Lumberjack, afterward. The kids would like that."

She grabbed her coat off the back of a chair and shrugged into it. "Sure," she said, but she sounded sad. "Thanks, Frank."

He spent the rest of the day kicking himself.

The box from Toby was waiting on the doorstep when Addie arrived home from work late that afternoon. She'd picked Henry and Lissie up at school, and Henry was beside himself with excitement.

"Can I open it?" he asked, peeling off his coat. Lissie had gone to let Floyd out, but she'd be joining them in a few minutes for hot cocoa.

Addie's mood, bordering on glum ever since morning, lifted a little. She smiled as she hung up her own coat. "Let me peek inside first," she suggested. "Just in case the stuff isn't wrapped."

"Okay," Henry said. The two of them had wrestled the large box over the threshold, and it was sitting on the living room floor, looking mysterious. "I didn't think he'd really send it," he confided. "Sometimes Dad says he's going to do stuff, and he forgets."

Addie ruffled his hair. "Well, he didn't forget this time," she said. She got a knife from the silverware drawer and advanced on the box. Henry was fairly jumping up and down while she carefully cut the packing tape.

"I know about Santa Claus," Henry announced, out of the blue. "So you don't have to worry about filling my stocking or anything like that."

Addie stiffened slightly and busied herself with the box. She didn't want Henry to see her face. She pulled back the flaps and looked inside, relieved to find packages wrapped in shiny, festive paper and tied with curling ribbon. "It's okay to look," she said.

Henry let out a whoop of glee and started hauling out the loot. He had the packages piled around the living room in an impressive circle when Lissie and Floyd came in. Lissie was carrying her tinsel halo in one hand.

"Whoa," she said, beaming. "You really cleaned up!"

Floyd made the rounds, sniffing every box.

"I wish today was Christmas," Henry said.

Lissie sagged a little. "Me, too," she confessed. "Then that stupid play would be over, and I wouldn't have to feel bad about not being an angel."

Addie brought out the cocoa she'd been brewing in the kitchen, the old-fashioned kind, like Eliza used to make for her and Frank on cold winter afternoons. "Feeling bad is a choice, Lissie," she said. She'd made a few calls that day, when things were slow at the *Wooden Nickel;* her plan was coming together. "You could just as easily choose to feel good."

Lissie frowned. "About what?"

"About the fact that there are other ways to be an angel," Addie said.

The kids zeroed in on the hot chocolate and looked up at her curiously, with brown foamy mustaches.

"What other way is there," Lissie inquired, "besides getting hit by a truck or something?"

"That would be a radical method," Addie allowed, eyeing the sewing machine and her thrift-store creation of peacock blue taffeta. "I spoke to someone at the hospital today. At the nursing home, too. There are some people there who would really like a visit from an angel, especially at Christmas."

Lissie's gaze strayed to the sewing project, and the light dawned in her eyes. "You made me an angel dress?"

Addie nodded. "It's pretty fancy, too, if I do say so myself."

Lissie crossed to the card table, where the sewing machine was set up, and laid a tentative hand on the small, shimmering gown. Except for the hem, a few nips and tucks to make it fit perfectly, and some beads and sequins rescued from the scorned wedding dress, it was complete.

"Would I have to sing?" Lissie asked in a voice small with wonder.

Addie laughed. "No," she said. "Not if you didn't want to."

"There aren't any wings," Henry pointed out, ever practical. "You can't be an angel without wings."

"I think I could rig something up," Addie said. The wings wouldn't be as fancy as Tiffany Baker's feathered flying apparatus, but the skirt of Jessie's wedding dress would serve if she bent some coat hangers into the proper shape.

"Do they need a shepherd, too?" Henry asked hopefully.

"A shepherd would be the perfect touch," Addie decided.

Lissie was standing on the coffee table, halo askew but on, looking resplendent in her blue angel duds, when Frank rapped at the door, let himself in, and whistled in exclamation. Addie, with a mouthful of pins, offered a careful smile.

"I get to be an angel after all," Lissie told her father.

Frank looked confused. "Don't tell me. Tiffany Baker has been abducted by space aliens. Shall I put out an all-points bulletin?"

Lissie giggled, though whether it was Frank's expression or the concept of her rival being carried off to another planet that amused her was anybody's guess. "I'm going to visit people in the hospital, and the nursing home. Addie's making my wings out of coat hangers."

Frank smiled. "Great idea," he said, looking at Addie. He took in the array of Christmas presents lying all over the room. "Looks like Santa crashed his sleigh in here."

Addie, who had been kneeling to pin up Lissie's hem, finished the job and got to her feet. "Want some coffee?" she asked Frank, and then wished she hadn't. Now he'd be thinking about the broken mug again, missing Maggie. She blushed and looked away.

He made a show of consulting his watch, shook his head. "We'd better get to the tree lot," he said. "Everybody ready?"

Floyd yelped with excitement.

Addie's gaze flew to Frank's face. So did Henry's and Lissie's.

"Can Floyd go, too?" Lissie asked.

Frank sighed. "Sure," he said, after a few moments of deliberation. "He can sniff out the perfect tree and wait in the car while we're in the Lumberjack having supper. We'll bring him a doggy bag."

How many men would include a beagle on such an expedition? Unexpected tears burned in Addie's eyes. That was the moment she realized the awful, wonderful truth. She'd fallen in love with Frank Raynor—assuming that she'd ever fallen out in the first place. The downside was, he still cared deeply for his late wife. She'd seen his stricken expression when the cup was broken.

The children, naturally oblivious to the nuances, shouted with joy, and Floyd barked all the harder. Addie's hands trembled a little as she helped Lissie out of the gown.

"You're an amazing woman," Frank said quietly, standing very close to Addie, while the kids scrambled to get into their coats. "Thank you."

Addie didn't dare look at him. The revelation she'd just undergone was too fresh—she was afraid he'd see it in her eyes. "We'd better take my station wagon," she said. "It probably wouldn't be kosher to tie a couple of Christmas trees to the top of your squad car."

He didn't answer.

A light snow began as they drove to the lot, Frank at the wheel. From the backseat, the kids sang "Jingle Bells," with Floyd howling an accompaniment.

Within half an hour, they'd selected two lusciously fragrant evergreen trees, and Frank had secured them in the back of the station wagon. When they pulled up in front of the Lumberjack Diner, Floyd sighed with patient resignation, settled his bulk on the seat, and went to sleep.

"This feels almost like being a family," Frank said quietly, as the four of them trooped into the restaurant. "I like it."

The waitresses wore all wearing felt reindeer antlers bedecked in tiny blinking lights. "Blue Christmas" wailed from the jukebox, and various customers called out cheerful greetings to the newcomers. There were a couple of low-key whistles, too, and when Addie stole a look at Frank, she was amazed to see that he was blushing.

"About time you hooked up with a woman, Chief," an old man said, patting Frank on the shoulder as he passed the booth where they were seated. "Good to see you back in Pine Crossing, Addie."

She felt warm inside, but it was a bruised and wary warmth. *Don't get your hopes up,* Addie warned herself in the silence of her mind. When she sneaked a look at Frank, unable to resist, she saw that he was blushing again. And grinning a little.

The meal was delicious, and when it was over, there were plenty of scraps for Floyd. He gobbled cheerfully while they drove home, the car full of merriment and the distinctive scents of fresh pine and leftover meatloaf.

Frank sent Lissie and Floyd into the house when they arrived, and Henry plodded up the apartment stairs, worn out by a jolly evening. He didn't even protest when Addie called after him to start his bath.

She hesitated, watching as Frank unloaded the trees. The snow was falling faster, stinging her cheeks.

"It'll need to settle, and dry out a little," Frank said, setting the tree Addie had chosen upright on the sidewalk, stirring that lovely fragrance again.

Addie laid a hand on his arm. "Thank you, Frank," she said very softly. "For the tree, for the meal at the Lumberjack, and for caring about a dog's feelings."

He looked surprised. "I'm the one who should be doing the thanking around here," he said, and when she started to protest, he raised a hand to silence her. "Lissie's wearing her halo again. For one night, she gets to be an angel. I can't begin to tell you what that means to me, Addie."

Addie's throat tightened. If she stayed one moment longer, she'd tell Frank Raynor straight out that she loved him, and ruin everything. "I'd better make sure Henry doesn't get to looking at his presents, forget to turn off the tap, and flood the bathroom," she said, and hurried away.

She felt Frank watching her and would have given anything for the courage to look straight at him and see what was in his face, but she couldn't take the risk.

The stakes were suddenly too high.

CHAPTER THIRTEEN

"It's an angel," Lissie said dismally, before Henry got that day's matchbox open. The day of the pageant had come, and while the little girl was ready to play the innkeeper's wife to the best of her ability, Addie knew it wouldn't be any fun for her.

She glanced at Frank, then laid a hand on Lissie's shoulder. "We're booked at the hospital and the Sweet Haven Nursing Home," she reminded the child. She'd found an old white boa, on a second trip to the Goodwill, and planned to glue the feathers onto the clothes-hanger wings on her breaks and during her lunch hour. Lissie's wings wouldn't be as glorious as Tiffany's, but they would be pretty and, Addie hoped, a nice surprise. "Tomorrow night, six o'clock. The patients are looking forward to it."

Lissie nodded.

Frank took the kids to school that morning. Addie had an extra cup of coffee, then set out for work in the station wagon.

At three-ten that afternoon, Lissie burst into the *Wooden Nickel,* setting the silver bell jingling above the door. Addie, taking her break at her desk, quickly shoved the half-feathered wing she'd been working on out of sight.

"Is everything all right?" she asked.

Lissie beamed. "Tiffany got another commercial," she blurted. "She had to be in Denver *today,* and there's no way she can get back in time for the pageant. Miss Pidgett got so upset, she had to go lie down in the principal's office, and Mr. Walker, the teacher's aide, said *I* could take Tiffany's place!"

Stella and Mr. Renfrew applauded, and Addie rounded the counter to hug Lissie. "It's a miracle," she said.

"How come your fingers are sticky?" Lissie wanted to know.

Addie ignored the question. "Do you know the angel's lines?"

" 'Be not afraid,' " Lissie spouted proudly, " 'for behold, I bring you tidings of great joy!' "

"Guess you've got it," Addie said, her arm around Lissie's shoulders. "Have you told your dad?"

Lissie shook her head. "He's on patrol," she replied, and suddenly, her brow furrowed with worry. "Tiffany took her costume with her. I've got my dress—the one you made—but the wings—"

"There will be wings," Addie promised, though she didn't know how she was going to pull that off. There were still two hours left in the workday, and the pageant was due to start at six-thirty.

"Great!" Lissie cried. "Henry's over at the library. Are you going to pick us up, or is Dad?"

"Whoever gets there first," Addie said, her mind going into overdrive.

Lissie nodded and went out, setting the bell over the door to ringing again.

"Another angel gets its wings," Stella said with a smile.

"We'd better get to gluing," Mr. Renfrew added, eyes sparkling.

"Do you suppose there's anything seriously wrong with Miss Pidgett?" Addie fretted, gratefully parceling out feathers stripped from the thrift-store boa and handing Arthur Renfrew the second wing, which was made from the skirt of Jessie Corcoran's wedding gown.

"She's run every pageant since 1962," Stella put in. "Maybe she's just worn out."

"More likely, it's a case of the 'means,'" Mr. Renfrew said, opening a pot of rubber cement and gingerly gluing a feather onto an angel's wing.

Frank arrived at St. Mary's at six-thirty sharp, fresh from the office, where he'd filled out a lengthy report on a no-injury accident out on the state highway, and scanned the crowd. Miss Pidgett, sitting in a folding chair toward the front of the small auditorium, fanned herself with a program and favored him with a poisonous look.

He smiled and nodded, just as though they were on cordial terms, and she blushed and fanned harder.

A small hand tugged at his jacket sleeve, and he looked down to see Lissie standing beside him, resplendent in her peacock blue angel gown and a pair of feathered wings.

"I thought you were the innkeeper's wife," he said stupidly. The fact was, he couldn't quite believe his eyes, and he was afraid to hope she'd landed the coveted role of lead angel. He checked his watch, wondering if he'd somehow missed the pageant, and Lissie had already changed clothes to make an unscheduled visit to Sweet Haven.

"Tiffany's in a toilet paper commercial, up in Denver," Lissie said, glowing. "She took her wings with her, but Addie made me these, so I'm good to go."

Addie. Frank felt as though the breath had just been knocked out of his lungs. He crouched, so he could look straight into his daughter's eyes. "Honey, that's great," he said, and the words came out sounding husky.

"Did you bring a camera? Henry promised his dad some pictures."

Just then, Addie arrived, looking pretty angelic herself in a kelly green suit. Her hair was pinned up, with a sprig of mistletoe for pizzazz. "I've got one," she said, waving one of those yellow throwaway numbers. "Hi, Frank."

"I'd better go," Lissie told them. "Maybe angels are like brides. Maybe people aren't supposed to see them before it's time!"

"Maybe not," Addie told her.

Lissie put up her hand, and the two of them did a high five.

The audience, mostly consisting of parents, grandparents, aunts, uncles and siblings, shifted and murmured in their folding chairs, smiling holiday smiles.

Frank made a point of looking at Addie's back.

"What?" she asked, fumbling to see if her label was sticking out.

"I was looking for wings," Frank said. "It seems some angels don't have them."

Her eyes glistened, and the junior high school band struck up the first strains of "Silent Night." "We'd better sit down," she whispered, and they took chairs next to Mr. Renfrew and Stella.

The lights went down, and the volume of the music went up. The stage curtains creaked and shivered apart. A small door stood on stage right, with a stable opposite. A kid in a donkey suit brayed, raising a communal chuckle from the audience.

Mary and Joseph shuffled on stage, looking suitably weary. Joseph knocked at the door, and it nearly toppled over backward. Henry peered out of the opening, blinking behind his glasses, and started shaking his head before Joseph could ask for a room. Addie took a picture with the throwaway, and the flash almost blinded Frank.

Henry, taking the innkeeper thing to heart, shook his head again. "No!" he shouted. "I said *no!*"

"Oh, dear," Addie whispered. "He's ad-libbing."

Frank laughed, which earned him a glower from Miss Pidgett, who turned in her seat and homed in on him like a heat-seeking missile.

"You can have the barn!" Henry went on. He was a born actor.

Joseph and Mary drooped and consigned themselves to the stable. Henry slammed the door so hard that the whole thing teetered. Addie gripped Frank's arm, and they both held their breathes, but the efforts of the eighth-grade shop class held.

The donkey brayed again, but he'd already been upstaged by the innkeeper.

Shepherds meandered onto the stage, in brown robes, each with a staff in hand. One carried a stuffed lamb under one arm. They all searched the sky, looking baffled. Henry, bringing up the rear, shoved at the middle of his glasses and wrote himself another line.

"What are all those things in the sky? Angels?"

The other shepherds gave him quelling looks, but Henry was undaunted.

"It's not every night you see a bunch of angels hanging around," he said.

In what he hoped was a subtle move, Frank took Addie's hand.

Miss Pidgett rose out of her seat, then sat down again.

There was a cranking sound, and Lissie descended from the rigging on a rope, wings spread almost as wide as her grin. Less splendid angels inched in from either side of the stage, gazing up at her in bemusement.

"Now *there's* an angel!" Henry boomed, looking up, too.

A ripple of laughter moved through the crowd, and Addie covered her face with her free hand, but only for a moment. She was smiling.

Lissie shouted out her lines, and the unseen stagehands cranked her down. Somebody made a sound like a baby crying, and attention shifted to Mary and Joseph. Darned if there hadn't been a blessed event.

After the pageant, refreshments were served in the cafeteria, and Addie took at least twenty pictures of Henry and Lissie. Practically everybody in town, with the noticeable exception of Miss Pidgett, stopped to compliment both kids on their innovative performances.

They glowed with pride, but the angel and the shepherd were soon yawning, like the rest of the cast.

"I'll take them home in the station wagon," Addie said.

"Meet you there in a couple of minutes," Frank replied, feeling oddly tender. "I just want to say hello to the mayor."

Addie nodded, gathered up the kids and their gear, and left.

Frank completed his social obligation and was just turning to go when there was a scuffle in a far corner of the room. Instinctively, he headed in that direction.

Miss Almira Pidgett lay unconscious on the floor.

CHAPTER FOURTEEN

It was after ten when Addie saw the lights of Frank's squad car sweep into the driveway. Lissie was asleep on the couch, still wearing her costume and covered in a quilt, and Henry had long since fallen into bed. Neither of them had wanted to leave the twinkling Christmas tree, standing fragrant in front of the window.

Addie pulled on her coat and went out onto the stairs. Frank had called her from the hospital earlier, where Almira Pidgett was admitted for observation, and she'd been waiting for news ever since. It had been difficult, pretending nothing was wrong while Lissie and Henry celebrated their theatrical debuts, but she hadn't wanted to ruin their evening, so she'd kept the old woman's illness to herself.

Frank appeared at the bottom of the stairs, paused, rested one hand on the railing, and looked up.

"Is she all right?" Addie asked.

Frank's shoulders moved in a weary sigh, but he nodded. "Looks like Miss Pidgett will be in the hospital for a few days. The doctor said it was diabetic shock. Good thing she wasn't home alone."

Addie sagged with relief. She might not have been Miss Pidgett's greatest fan, but she'd been desperately worried, just the same.

"Come upstairs and have some coffee," she said.

Frank grinned, started the climb. "You looked pretty good in that green outfit tonight," he told her.

She'd exchanged her good suit for jeans, sneakers, and a flannel shirt. "Lissie stole the whole show," she said with a laugh. The wind was cold, and it was snowing a little, but the closer Frank got, the warmer she felt. Go figure, she thought.

He ushered her inside, paused to admire the Christmas tree. They'd decorated it together, and it had been a sentimental journey for Addie. She'd been surprised to realize how many memories those old ornaments stirred in her. They hadn't been able to use the bubble lights—they were ancient, and the wires were frayed—but Frank had anted up some spares, and the whole thing looked spectacular, especially with Henry's much-handled presents wedged underneath.

Floyd, lying in the kitchen doorway, got up to waddle across the linoleum and greet his master. Frank closed the door, ruffled the dog's ears, and then went to stand next to the couch, looking down at his sleeping daughter.

"They were something, weren't they?" he asked quietly.

Addie smiled. "Oh, yeah," she said. "What a pair of hams."

They went into the kitchen, and Addie put on the coffee. Frank sat down at the table and rubbed his face with both hands. It was a weary gesture that made Addie want to stand behind him and squeeze his shoulders, maybe even let her chin rest on top of his head for a moment or two, but she refrained.

"The last thing I need," Frank muttered, "is a shot of caffeine."

"I've got decaf," Addie said.

"Perish the thought," Frank replied.

She laughed. "You're a hard man to please, Frank Raynor."

She moved toward cupboards next to the stove, meaning to get out a bag of cookies, but Frank caught her hand as she passed.

"No, actually," he said, "I'm not." And he pulled her onto his lap.

She should have resisted him, but she didn't. Her heart shimmied up into her throat.

For a moment, it seemed he might kiss her, but he frowned, and touched the tip of her nose instead. "How come you gave back my engagement ring, Addie Hutton?" he asked, very quietly.

Tears burned behind her eyes. "I was young and stupid."

He moved his finger and planted a kiss where it had been. "Young, yes. Stupid, never. I should have waited for you, Addie. I should have known you needed an education of your own."

She touched his mouth very lightly. "You wouldn't have met Maggie," she reminded him. "And you wouldn't have had Lissie."

He sighed. "You're right," he said. "But you wouldn't have met Bozo the Mortgage Broker, either. And you wouldn't have gotten into all that trouble in California."

She couldn't speak.

"What are you going to do now?" Frank asked, his arms still tight around her. "You can't work at the *Wooden Nickel* for the rest of your life, selling classified ads. You're a journalist. You'll go crazy."

"I've been thinking about writing a book," Addie admitted.

Frank's eyes lit up. "Well, now," he said. "Fiction or nonfiction?"

"A romance novel," Addie said, and blushed.

He raised one eyebrow, still grinning. "Is that so?"

Just then, the phone rang.

Because it was late, which might mean the call was important, and maybe because the atmosphere was getting intense in that kitchen, Addie jumped off Frank's lap and rushed to answer it with a breathless, "Hello?"

"Addie," Toby said. "I hope you weren't in bed."

Addie blushed again. "No—no, I was up. Is everything okay? Where are you?"

"Connecticut," Toby answered. "Addie, I have news. Really big news."

Addie closed her eyes, tried to brace herself. He was coming to get Henry. She'd known it was going to happen. "What?" she croaked.

"Elle and I are going to have a baby," Toby blurted. "Isn't that great?"

Addie's eyes flew open. Frank was setting the cups on the counter.

"Great," she said.

"I guess you're wondering why I'd call you to make the announcement," Toby said, sounding more circumspect.

Actually, she hadn't gotten that far. She was still trying to work out what this meant to Henry, and to her. "Right," she said.

Frank raised his eyebrows, thrumming the fingers of one hand on the countertop while he waited for the coffee to finish brewing.

"The pregnancy will be stressful," Toby went on. "For Elle, I mean. That's why I was wondering—"

Addie held her breath.

"That's why *we* were wondering if you'd keep Henry for a while longer."

Addie straightened. "You'll have to grant me temporary custody, Toby," she said. "I won't have you jerking Henry back and forth across the country every time it strikes your fancy."

"Is that what you think of me? That I'd do something like that?"

What *was* the man's home planet? "Yes," she said. "That's what I think."

Toby got defensive. "I could send Henry to stay with my dad and stepmother, you know."

"But you won't," Addie said. She'd received a check from Toby's father in that day's mail. It would pay some bills, and provide a Christmas for Henry, and she was very grateful. According to the enclosed note, Mr. Springer and his third trophy wife were spending what remained of the winter in Tahiti.

"All right," Toby admitted. "I won't."

"Ground rules, Toby," Addie said, as Frank gave her a chipper salute. "I want legal custody, signed, sealed and delivered. And you will call this child once a week, without fail."

"You got it," Toby agreed with a sigh.

"One more thing," Addie said.

"What?" Toby asked sheepishly.

"Congratulations," Addie told him.

Frank poured the coffee, carried the cups to the table. He'd taken off his uniform jacket, hung it over the back of a chair. His shoulders strained at the fabric of his crisply pressed shirt.

"Thanks," Toby said, and the conversation was over.

"I take it a celebration is in order?" Frank asked.

Addie jumped, kicked her heels together, and punched one fist in the air.

"Not much gets past a Sherlock Holmes like me," Frank said.

CHAPTER
FIFTEEN

Frank's tree glittered, and a Christmas Eve fire flickered merrily in the hearth. Three stockings hung from the mantelpiece—Lissie's, Henry's, and Floyd's. Nat King Cole crooned about merry little Christmases.

"They're asleep," Frank said from the stairway. "I guess that second gig at the hospital and the nursing home did them in. Who'd have thought Almira Pidgett would turn out to be a fan of the angel-and-shepherd road show?"

Addie smiled, cup of eggnog in hand, and turned to watch him approach. Miss Pidgett had warmed to Lissie and Henry's impromptu performance when they shyly entered her hospital room the night after the pageant, and tonight, she'd welcomed them with a twinkly smile. "Christmas is a time for miracles," she said.

Frank took the cup out of her hand, set it aside, and pulled her close. "You think it's too soon?" he asked.

"Too soon for what?" she countered, but she knew. A smile quirked at the corner of her mouth.

"You and me to take up where we left off, back in the day," Frank prompted, kissing her lightly. "I love you, Addie."

She traced the outline of his lips. "And I love you, Frank Raynor."

"But you still haven't answered my question."

She smiled. "I don't think it's too soon," she said. "I think it's *about time.*"

"Do I get to be in your romance novel?"

"You already are."

He gave a wicked chuckle. "Maybe we'd better do a little research," he teased, and tasted her mouth again. Then, suddenly, he straightened, squinted at the Christmas tree behind her. "But wait. What's that?"

Addie turned to look, confused.

Eliza's Advent calendar was draped, garland-style, across the front of the tree.

"Why, it's Aunt Eliza's Advent calendar!" Frank said, and twiddled at a nonexistent mustache.

"You might make it in a romance novel," Addie said, "but if you're thinking of going into acting, don't give up your day job."

"We forgot to check the twenty-fourth box," Frank said, recovering quickly from the loss of a career behind the footlights.

"We did not forget," Addie said. "It was a little crèche. The kids looked this morning, before breakfast."

"I think we should look again," Frank insisted. "Specifically, I think *you* should look again."

She moved slowly toward the tree, confused. They'd agreed not to give each other gifts this year, though she'd bought a present for Lissie, and he'd gotten one for Henry.

The twenty-fourth box, unlike the other twenty-three, was closed. Addie slid it open slowly, and gasped.

"My engagement ring," she said. The modest diamond was wedged in between the crèche and the side of the matchbox. "You kept it?"

Frank stood beside her, slipped an arm around her waist. "Eliza kept it," he said. "Will you marry me, Addie?"

She turned to look up into his eyes. "Oh, Frank."

"I'll get you a better ring, if you want one."

She shook her head. "No," she said. "I want this one."

"Then, you will? Marry me, I mean?"

"Yes."

He pulled her into his arms, kissed her. "When?" he breathed when it was over.

Addie was breathless. "Next summer?"

"Good enough." He laughed, then kissed her again. "In the meantime, we can work on that research."

A BRIGHT RED RIBBON

Fern Michaels

Even in her dream, Morgan Ames knew she was dreaming, knew she was going to wake with tears on her pillow and reality slapping her in the face. She cried out, the way she always did, just at the moment Keith was about to slip the ring on her finger. That's how she knew it was a dream. She never got beyond this point. She woke now, and looked at the bedside clock; it was 4:10. She wiped at the tears on her cheeks, but this time she smiled. Today was the day. Today was Christmas Eve, the day Keith was going to slip the ring on her finger and they would finally set the wedding date. The big event, in her mind, was scheduled to take place in front of her parents' Christmas tree. She and Keith would stand in exactly the same position they stood in two years ago today, at the very same hour. Romance was alive and well.

She dropped her legs over the side of the bed, slid into a daffodil-colored robe that was snugly warm, and pulled on thick wool socks. She padded out to the miniature kitchen to make coffee.

Christmas Eve. To her, Christmas Eve was the most wonderful day of the year. Years ago, when she'd turned into a teenager, her parents had switched the big dinner and gift opening to Christmas Eve so they could sleep late on Christmas morning. The dinner was huge; friends dropped by before evening services, and then they opened their presents, sang carols, and drank spiked eggnog afterward.

Mo knew a watched kettle never boiled so she made herself some toast while the kettle hummed on the stove. She was so excited her hands shook as she spread butter and jam on the toast. The kettle whistled. The water sputtered over the counter as she poured it into the cup with the black rum tea bag.

In about sixteen hours, she was going to see Keith. At last. Two years ago he had led her by the hand over to the twelve-foot Christmas tree and said he wanted to talk to her about something. He'd been so nervous, but she'd been more nervous, certain the something he wanted to talk about was the engagement ring he was going to give her. She'd been expecting it, her parents had been expecting it, all her friends had been expecting it. Instead, Keith had taken both her hands in his and said, "Mo, I need to talk to you about something. I need you to understand. This is my problem. You didn't do anything to make me . . . what I'm trying to say is, I need more time. I'm not ready to commit. I think we both need to experience a little more of life's challenges. We both have good jobs, and I just got a promotion that will take effect the first of the year. I'll be working in the New York office. It's a great opportunity, but the hours are long. I'm going to get an apartment in the city. What I would like is for us to . . . to take a hiatus from each other. I think two years will be good. I'll be thirty and you'll be twenty-nine. We'll be more mature, more ready for that momentous step."

The hot tea scalded her tongue. She yelped. She'd yelped that night, too. She'd wanted to be sophisticated, blasé, to say, okay, sure, no big deal. She hadn't said any of those things. Instead she'd cried, hanging on to his arm, begging to know if what he was proposing meant he was going to date others. His answer had crushed her and she'd sobbed then. He'd said things like, "Ssshhh, it's going to be all right. Two years isn't all that long. Maybe we aren't meant to be with each other for the rest of our lives. We'll find out. Yes, it's going to be hard on me, too. Look, I know this is a surprise . . . I didn't want . . . I was going to call . . . This is what I propose. Two years from tonight, I'll meet you right here, in front of the tree. Do we have a date, Mo?" She nodded miserably. Then he'd added, "Look, I have to leave, Mo. My boss is having a party in his townhouse in Princeton. It won't look good if I'm late. Christmas parties are a good way to network. Here, I got you a little something for Christmas." Before she could dry her eyes, blow her nose, or tell him she had a ton of presents for him under the tree, he was gone.

It had been the worst Christmas of her life. The worst New Year's, too. The next Christmas and New Year's had been just as bad because her parents had looked at her with pity and then anger. Just last week they had called and said, "Get on with your life, Morgan. You've already wasted two years. In that whole time, Keith hasn't called you once or even dropped you a post card." She'd been stubborn, though, because she loved Keith. Sharp words had ensued, and she'd broken the connection and cried.

Tonight she had a date.

Life was going to be so wonderful. The strain between her and her parents would ease when they saw how happy she was.

Mo looked at the clock. Five-thirty. Time to shower, dress, pack up the Cherokee for her two-week vacation. Oh, life was good. She had it all planned. They'd go skiing, but first she'd go to Keith's apartment in New York, stay over, make him breakfast. They'd make slow, lazy love and if the mood called for it, they'd make wild, animal love.

Two years was a long time to be celibate—and she'd been celibate. She winced when she thought about Keith in bed with other women. He loved sex more than she did. There was no way he'd been faithful to her. She felt it in her heart. Every chance her mother got, she drove home her point. Her parents didn't like Keith. Her father was fond of saying, "I know his type—he's no good. Get a life, Morgan."

Tonight her new life would begin. Unless . . . unless Keith was a no show. Unless Keith decided the single life was better than a married life and responsibilities. God in heaven, what would she do if that happened? Well, it wasn't going to happen. She'd always been a positive person and she saw no reason to change now.

It wasn't going to happen because when Keith saw her he was going to go out of his mind. She'd changed in the two years. She'd dropped twelve pounds in all the right places. She was fit and toned because she worked out daily at a gym and ran for five miles every evening after work. She'd gotten a new hair style in New York. And, while she was there she'd gone to a color specialist who helped her with her hair and makeup. She was every bit as professional looking as some of the ad executives she saw walking up and down Madison Avenue. She'd shed her scrubbed girl-next-door image. S.K., which stood for Since Keith, she'd learned to shop in the outlet stores for designer fashions at half the cost. She looked down now at her sporty Calvin Klein outfit, at the Ferragamo boots and the Chanel handbag she'd picked up at a flea market. Inside her French luggage were other outfits by Donna Karan and Carolyn Roehm.

Like Keith, she had gotten a promotion with a hefty salary increase. If things worked out, she was going to think about opening her own architectural office by early summer. She'd hire people, oversee them. Clients she worked with told her she should open her own office, go it alone. One in particular had offered to back her after he'd seen the plans she'd drawn up for his beach house in Cape May. Her father, himself an architect, had offered to help out and had gone so far as to get all the paperwork from the Small Business

Administration. She could do it now if she wanted to. But, did she want to make that kind of commitment? What would Keith think?

What she wanted, really wanted, was to get married and have a baby. She could always do consulting work, take on a few private clients to keep her hand in. All she needed was a husband to make it perfect.

Keith.

The phone rang. Mo frowned. No one ever called her this early in the morning. Her heart skipped a beat as she picked up the phone. "Hello," she said warily.

"Morgan?" Her mother. She always made her name sound like a question.

"What's wrong, Mom?"

"When are you leaving, Morgan? I wish you'd left last night like Dad and I asked you to do. You should have listened to us, Morgan."

"Why? What's wrong? I told you why I couldn't leave. I'm about ready to go out the door as we speak."

"Have you looked outside?"

"No. It's still dark, Mom."

"Open your blinds, Morgan, and look at the parking lot lights. It's snowing!"

"Mom, it snows every year. So what? It's only a two-hour drive, maybe three if there's a lot of snow. I have the Cherokee. Four-wheel drive, Mom." She pulled up the blind in the bedroom to stare out at the parking lot. She swallowed hard. So, it would be a challenge. The world was white as far as the eye could see. She raised her eyes to the parking lights. The bright light that usually greeted her early in the morning was dim as the sodium vapor fought with the early light of dawn and the swirling snow. "It's snowing, Mom."

"That's what I'm trying to tell you. It started here around midnight, I guess. It was just flurries when Dad and I went to bed but now we have about four inches. Since this storm seems to be coming from the south where you are, you probably have more. Dad and I have been talking and we won't be upset if you wait till the storm is over. Christmas morning is just as good as Christmas Eve. Just how much snow do you have, Morgan?"

"It looks like a lot, but it's drifting in the parking lot. I can't see the front, Mom. Look, don't worry about me. I have to be home this evening. I've waited two long years for this. Please, Mom, you understand, don't you?"

"What I understand, Morgan, is that you're being foolhardy. I saw Keith's mother the other day and she said he hasn't been home in ten months. He just lives across the river, for heaven's sake. She also said she didn't expect him for Christmas, so what does that tell you? I don't want you risking your life for some foolish promise."

Mo's physical being trembled. The words she dreaded, the words she didn't ever want to hear, had just been uttered: Keith wasn't coming home for Christmas. She perked up almost immediately. Keith loved surprises. It would be just like him to tell his mother he wasn't coming home and then show up and yell, "Surprise!" If he had no intention of honoring the promise they'd made to each other, he would have sent a note or called her. Keith wasn't that callous. Or was he? She didn't know anything anymore.

She thought about the awful feelings that had attacked her over the past two years, feelings she'd pushed away. Had she buried her head in the sand? Was it possible that Keith had used the two-year hiatus to soften the blow of parting, thinking that she'd transfer her feelings to someone else and let him off the hook? Instead she'd trenched in and convinced herself that by being faithful to her feelings, tonight would be her reward. Was she a fool? According to her mother she was. Tonight would tell the tale.

What she did know for certain was, nothing was going to stop her from going home. Not her mother's dire words, and certainly not a snowstorm. If she was a fool, she deserved to have her snoot rubbed in it.

Just a few short hours ago she'd stacked up her shopping bags by the front door, colorful Christmas bags loaded with presents for everyone. Five oversize bags for Keith. She wondered what happened to the presents she'd bought two years ago. Did her mother take them over to Keith's mother's house or were they in the downstairs closet? She'd never asked.

She'd spent a sinful amount of money on him this year. She'd even knitted a stocking for him and filled it with all kinds of goodies and gadgets. She'd stitched his name on the cuff of the bright red stocking in bright green thread. Was she a fool?

Mo pulled on her fleece-lined parka. Bundled up, she carried as many of the bags downstairs to the lobby as she could handle. She made three trips before she braved the outdoors. She needed to shovel and heat the car up.

She was exhausted when she tossed the fold-up shovel into the back of the Jeep. The heater and defroster worked furiously, but she still had to scrape the ice from the windshield and driver's side window. She checked the flashlight in the glove compartment. She rummaged inside the small opening, certain she had extra batteries, but couldn't find any. She glanced at the gas gauge. Three-quarters full, enough to get her home. She'd meant to top off last night on her way home from work, but she'd been in a hurry to get home to finish wrapping Keith's presents. God, she'd spent hours making intricate, one-of-a-kind bows and decorations for the gold-wrapped packages. A three-quarter tank would get her home for sure. The Cherokee gave her good mileage. If memory served her right, the trip never took more than a quarter of a tank. Well, she couldn't worry about that now. If road conditions permitted, she could stop on 95 or when she got onto the Jersey Turnpike.

Mo was numb with cold when she shrugged out of her parka and boots. She debated having a cup of tea to warm her up. Maybe she should wait for rush hour traffic to be over. Maybe a lot of things.

Maybe she should call Keith and ask him point blank if he was going to meet her in front of the Christmas tree. If she did that, she might spoil things. Still, why take her life in her hands and drive through what looked like a terrible storm, for nothing. She'd just as soon avoid her parents' pitying gaze and make the trip tomorrow morning and return in the evening to lick her wounds. If he was really going to be a no show, that would be the way to go. Since there were no guarantees, she didn't see any choice but to brave the storm.

She wished she had a dog or a cat to nuzzle, a warm body that loved unconditionally. She'd wanted to get an animal at least a hundred times these past two years, but she couldn't bring herself to admit that she needed someone. What did it matter if that someone had four legs and a furry body?

Her address book was in her hand, but she knew Keith's New York phone number by heart. It was unlisted, but she'd managed to get it from the brokerage house Keith worked for. So she'd used trickery. So what? She hadn't broken the rules and called the number. It was just comforting to know she could call if she absolutely had to. She squared her shoulders as she reached for the portable phone on the kitchen counter. She looked at the range-top clock. Seven forty-five. He should still be home. She punched out the area code and number, her shoulders still stiff. The phone rang five times before the answering machine came on. Maybe he was still in the shower. He always did cut it close to the edge, leaving in the morning with his hair still damp from the shower.

"C'mon, now, you know what to do if I don't answer. I'm either catching some z's or I'm out and about. Leave me a message, but be careful not to give away any secrets. Wait for the beep." Z's? It must be fast track New York talk. The deep, husky chuckle coming over the wire made Mo's face burn with shame. She broke the connection.

A moment later she was zipping up her parka and pulling on thin leather gloves. She turned down the heat in her cozy apartment, stared at her small Christmas tree on the coffee table, and made a silly wish.

The moment she stepped outside, grainy snow assaulted her as the wind tried to drive her backward. She made it to the Cherokee, climbed inside, and slammed the door. She shifted into four-wheel drive, then turned on the front and back wipers. The Cherokee inched forward, its wheels finding the traction to get her to the access road to I-95. It took her all of forty minutes to steer the Jeep to the ramp that led onto the Interstate. At that precise moment she knew she was making a mistake, but it was too late and there was no way now to get off and head back to the apartment. As far as she could see, it was bumper-to-bumper traffic. Visibility was almost zero. She knew there was a huge green directional sign overhead, but she couldn't see it.

"Oh, shit!"

Mo's hands gripped the wheel as the car in front of her slid to the right, going off the road completely. She muttered her favorite expletive again. God, what would she do if the wipers iced up? From the sound they were making on the windshield, she didn't think she'd have to wait long to find out.

The radio crackled with static, making it impossible to hear what was being said. Winter advisory. She already knew that. Not only did she know it, she was participating in it. She turned it off. The dashboard clock said she'd been on the road for well over an hour and she was nowhere near the Jersey Turnpike. At least she didn't think so. It was impossible to read the signs with the snow sticking to everything.

A white Christmas. The most wonderful time of the year. That thought alone had sustained her these past two years. Nothing bad ever happened on Christmas. Liar! Keith dumped you on Christmas Eve, right there in front of the tree. Don't lie to yourself!

"Okay, okay," she muttered. "But this Christmas will be different, this Christmas it will work out." Keith will make it up to you, she thought. Believe. Sure, and Santa is going to slip down the chimney one minute after midnight.

Mo risked a glance at the gas gauge. Half. She turned the heater down. Heaters added to the fuel consumption, didn't they? She thought about the Ferragamo boots she was wearing. Damn, she'd set her rubber boots by the front door so she wouldn't forget to bring them. They were still sitting by the front door. She wished now for her warm ski suit and wool cap, but she'd left them at her mother's last year when she went skiing for the last time.

She tried the radio again. The static was worse than before. So was the snow and ice caking her windshield. She had to stop and clean the blades or she was going to have an accident. With the faint glow of the taillights in front of her, Mo steered the Cherokee to the right. She pressed her flasher button, then waited to see if a car would pass her on the left and how much room she had to exit the car. The parka hood flew backward, exposing her head and face to the snowy onslaught. She fumbled with the wipers and the scraper. The swath they cleared was almost minuscule. God, what was she to do? Get off the damn road at the very next exit and see if she could find shelter? There was always a gas station or truck stop. The problem was, how would she know when she came to an exit?

Panic rivered through her when she got back into the Jeep. Her leather gloves were soaking wet. She peeled them off, then tossed them onto the backseat. She longed for her padded ski gloves and a cup of hot tea.

Mo drove for another forty minutes, stopping again to scrape her wipers and windshield. She was fighting a losing battle and she knew it. The wind was razor sharp, the snow coming down harder. This wasn't just a winter storm, it was a blizzard. People died in blizzards. Some fool had even made a movie about people eating other people when a plane crashed during a blizzard. She let the panic engulf her again. What was going to happen to her? Would she run out of gas and freeze to death? Who would find her? When would they find her? On Christmas Day? She imagined her parents' tears, their recriminations.

All of a sudden she realized there were no lights in front of her. She'd been so careful to stay a car length and a half behind the car in front. She pressed the accelerator, hoping desperately to keep up. God in heaven, was she off the road? Had she crossed the Delaware Bridge? Was she on the Jersey side? She simply didn't know. She tried the radio again and was rewarded with squawking static. She turned it off quickly. She risked a glance in her rearview mirror. There were no faint lights. There was nothing behind her. She moaned in fear. Time to stop, get out and see what she could see.

Before she climbed from the car, she unzipped her duffel bag sitting on the passenger side. She groped for a tee shirt and wrapped it around her head. Maybe the parka hood would stay on with something besides her silky hair to cling to. Her hands touched a pair of rolled-up sleep sox. She pulled them on. Almost as good as mittens. Did she have two pairs? She found a second pair and pulled them on. She flexed her fingers. No thumb holes. Damn. She remembered the manicure scissors she kept in her purse. A minute later she had thumb holes and was able to hold the steering wheel tightly. Get out, see what you can see. Clean the wipers, use that flashlight. Try your high beams.

Mo did all of the above. Uncharted snow. No one had gone before her. The snow was almost up to her knees. If she walked around, the snow would go down between her boots and stirrup pants. Knee-highs. Oh, God! Her feet would freeze in minutes. They might not find her until the spring thaw. Where was she? A field? The only thing she knew for certain was, she wasn't on any kind of a road.

"I hate you, Keith Mitchell. I mean, I really hate you. This is all your fault! No, it isn't," she sobbed. "It's my fault for being so damn stupid. If you loved me, you'd wait for me. Tonight was just a time. My mother would tell you I was delayed because of the storm. You could stay at my mother's or go to your mother's. If you loved me. I'm sitting here now, my life in danger, because . . . I wanted to believe you loved me. The way I love you. Christmas miracles, my ass!"

Mo shifted gears, inching the Cherokee forward.

How was it possible, Mo wondered, to be so cold and yet be sweating? She swiped at the perspiration on her forehead with the sleeve of her parka. In her whole life she'd never been this scared. If only she knew where she was. For all she knew, she could be driving into a pond or a lake. She shivered. Maybe she should get out and walk. Take her chances in the snow. She was in a no-win situation and she knew it. Stupid, stupid, stupid.

Maybe the snow wasn't as deep as she thought it was. Maybe it was just drifting in places. She was saved from further speculation when the Cherokee bucked, sputtered, slugged forward, and then came to a coughing stop. Mo cut the engine, fear choking off her breathing. She waited a second before she turned the ignition key. She still had a gas reserve. The engine refused to catch and turn over. She turned off the heater and the wipers, then tried again with the same results. The decision to get out of the car and walk was made for her.

Mo scrambled over the backseat to the cargo area. With cold, shaking fingers she worked the zippers on her suitcases. She pulled thin, sequined sweaters—that would probably give her absolutely no warmth—out of the bag. She shrugged from the parka and pulled on as many of the decorative designer sweaters as she could. Back in her parka, she pulled knee-hi stockings and her last two pairs of socks over her hands. It was better than nothing. As if she had choices. The keys to the Jeep went into her pocket. The strap of her purse was looped around her neck. She was ready. Her sigh was as mighty as the wind howling about her as she climbed out of the Cherokee.

The wind was sharper than a butcher knife. Eight steps in

the mid-thigh snow and she was exhausted. The silk scarf she'd tied around her mouth was frozen to her face in the time it took to take those eight steps. Her eyelashes were caked with ice as were her eyebrows. She wanted to close her eyes, to sleep. How in the hell did Eskimos do it? A gurgle of hysterical laughter erupted in her throat.

The laughter died in her throat when she found herself facedown in a deep pile of snow. She crawled forward. It seemed like the wise thing to do. Getting to her feet was the equivalent of climbing Mt. Rushmore. She crab-walked until her arms gave out on her, then she struggled to her feet and tried to walk again. She repeated the process over and over until she was so exhausted she simply couldn't move. "Help me, someone. Please, God, don't let me die out here like this. I'll be a better person, I promise. I'll go to church more often. I'll practice my faith more diligently. I'll try to do more good deeds. I won't be selfish. I swear to You, I will. I'm not just saying this, either. I mean every word." She didn't know if she was saying the words or thinking them.

A violent gust of wind rocked her backward. Her back thumped into a tree, knocking the breath out of her. She cried then, her tears melting the crystals on her lashes.

"Help!" she bellowed. She shouted until she was hoarse.

Time lost all meaning as she crawled along. There were longer pauses now between the time she crawled on all fours and the time she struggled to her feet. She tried shouting again, her cries feeble at best. The only person who could hear her was God, and He seemed to be otherwise occupied.

Mo stumbled and went down. She struggled to get up, but her legs wouldn't move. In her life she'd never felt the pain that was tearing away at her joints. She lifted her head and for one brief second she thought she saw a feeble light. In the time it took her heart to beat once, the light was gone. She was probably hallucinating. Move! her mind shrieked. Get up! They won't find you till the daffodils come up.

They'll bury you when the lilacs bloom. That's how they'll remember you. They might even print that on your tombstone. "Help me. Please, somebody help me!"

She needed to sleep. More than anything in the world she wanted sleep. She was so groggy. And her heart seemed to be beating as fast as a racehorse's at the finish line. How was that possible? Her heart should barely be beating. Get the hell up, Morgan. Now! Move, damn you!

She was up. She was so cold. She knew her body heat was leaving her. Her clothes were frozen to her body. She couldn't see at all. Move, damn you! You can do it. You were never a quitter, Morgan. Well, maybe where Keith was concerned. You always managed, somehow, to see things through to a satisfactory conclusion. She stumbled and fell, picked herself up with all the willpower left in her numb body, fell again. This time she couldn't get up.

A vision of her parents standing over her closed coffin, the room filled with lilacs, appeared behind her closed lids. Her stomach rumbled fiercely and then she was on her feet, her lungs about to burst with her effort.

The snow and wind lashed at her like a tidal wave. It slammed her backward and beat at her face and body. Move! Don't stop now! Go, go, go, go.

"Help!" she cried. She was down again, on all fours. She shook her head to clear it.

She sensed movement. "Please," she whimpered, "help me." She felt warm breath, something touched her cheek. God. He was getting ready to take her. She cried.

"Woof!"

A dog! Man's best friend. *Her* best friend now. "You aren't better than God, but you'll damn well do," Mo gasped. "Do you understand? I need help. Can you fetch help?" Mo's hands reached out to the dog, but he backed away, woofing softly. Maybe he was barking louder and she couldn't hear it over the sound of the storm. "I'll try and follow you, but I don't think I'll make it." The dog barked again and as suddenly as he appeared, he was gone.

Mo howled her despair. She knew she had to move. The dog must live close by. Maybe the light she'd seen earlier was a house and this dog lived there. Again, she lost track of time as she crawled forward.

"Woof, woof, woof."

"You came back!" She felt her face being licked, nudged. There was something in the dog's mouth. Maybe something he'd killed. He licked her. He put something down, picked it up and was trying to give it to her. "What?"

The dog barked, louder, backing up, then lunging at her, thrusting whatever he had in his mouth at her. She reached for it. A ribbon. And then she understood. She did her best to loop it around her wrist, crawling on her hands and knees after the huge dog.

Time passed—she didn't know how much. Once, twice, three times, the dog had to get down on all fours and nudge her, the frozen ribbon tickling her face. At one point when she was down and didn't think she would ever get up, the dog nipped her nose, barking in her ear. She obeyed and moved.

And then she saw the windows full of bright yellow light. She thought she saw a Christmas tree through the window. The dog was barking, urging her to follow him. She snaked after him on her belly, praying, thanking God, as she went along.

A doggie door. A large doggie door. The dog went through it, barking on the other side. Maybe no one was home to open the door to her. Obviously, the dog intended her to follow. When in Rome . . . She pushed her way through.

The heat from the huge, blazing fire in the kitchen slammed into her. Nothing in the world ever felt this good. Her entire body started to tingle. She rolled over, closer to the fire. It smelled of pine and something else, maybe cinnamon. The dog barked furiously as he circled the rolling girl. He wanted something, but she didn't know what. She saw it out of the corner of her eye—a large, yellow towel. But she couldn't reach it. "Push it here," she said hoarsely. The dog obliged.

"Well, Merry Christmas," a voice said behind her. "I'm sorry I wasn't here to welcome you, but I was showering and dressing at the back end of the house. I just assumed Murphy was barking at some wild animal. Do you always make this kind of entrance? Mind you, I'm not complaining. Actually, I'm delighted that I'll have someone to share Christmas Eve with. I'm sorry I can't help you, but I think you should get up. Murphy will show you the way to the bedroom and bath. You'll find a warm robe. Just rummage for whatever you want. I'll have some warm food for you when you get back. You are okay, aren't you? You need to move, get your circulation going again. Frostbite can be serious."

"I got lost and your dog found me," Mo whispered.

"I pretty much figured that out," the voice chuckled.

"You have a nice voice," Mo said sleepily. "I really need to sleep. Can't I just sleep here in front of this fire?"

"No, you cannot." The voice was sharp, authoritative. Mo's eyes snapped open. "You need to get out of those wet clothes. Now!"

"Yes, sir!" Mo said smartly. "I don't think much of your hospitality. You could help me, you know. I'm almost half-dead. I might still die. Right here on your kitchen floor. How's that going to look?" She rolled over, struggling to a sitting position. Murphy got behind her so she wouldn't topple over.

She saw her host, saw the wheelchair, then the anger and frustration in his face. "I've never been known for my tact. I apologize. I appreciate your help and you're right, I need to get out of these wet clothes. I can make it. I got this far. I would appreciate some food though if it isn't too much trouble . . . Or, I can make it myself if you . . ."

"I'm very self-sufficient. I think I can rustle up something that doesn't come in a bag. You know, real food. It's time for Murphy's supper, too."

His voice was cool and impersonal. He was handsome, probably well over six feet if he'd been standing. Muscular. "It can't be suppertime already. What time is it?"

"A little after three. Murphy eats early. I don't know why that is, he just does."

She was standing—a feat in itself. She did her best to marshal her dignity as Murphy started out of the kitchen. "I'm sorry I didn't bring a present. It was rude of me to show up like this with nothing in hand. My mother taught me better, but circumstances . . ."

"Go!"

Murphy bounded down the hall. Mo lurched against the wall again and again, until she made it to the bathroom. It was a pretty room for a bathroom, all powdery blue and white with matching towels and carpet. And it was toasty warm. The shower was obviously for the handicapped with a special seat and grab bars. She shed her clothes, layer by layer, until she was naked. She turned on the shower and was rewarded with instant steaming water. Nothing in the world had ever looked this good. Or felt this good, she thought as she stepped into the spray. She let the water pelt her and made a mental note to ask her host where he got the shower head that massaged her aching body. The soap was Ivory, clean and sweet-smelling. The shampoo was something in a black bottle, something manly. She didn't care. She lathered up her dark, wet curls and then rinsed off. She decided she liked the smell and made another mental note to look closely at the bottle for the name.

When the water cooled, she stepped out and would have laughed if she hadn't been so tired. Murphy was holding a towel. A large one, the mate to the yellow one in the kitchen. He trotted over to the linen closet, inched it open. She watched him as he made his selection, a smaller towel obviously for her hair. "You're one smart dog, I can say that for you. I owe you my life, big guy. Let's see, I'd wager you're a golden retriever. My hair should be half as silky as yours. I'm going to send you a dozen porterhouse steaks when I get home. Now, let's see, he said there was a robe in here. Ah, here it is. Now, why did I know it was going to be dark green?" She slipped into it, the smaller towel still wrapped around her head. The robe smelled like the shampoo. Maybe the stuff came in a set.

He had said to rummage for what she wanted. She did, for socks and a pair of long underwear. She pulled on both, the waistband going all the way up to her underarms. As if she cared. All she wanted was the welcome warmth.

She looked around his bedroom. His. Him. God, she didn't even know his name, but she knew his dog's name. How strange. She wanted to do something. The thought had come to her in the shower, but now it eluded her. She saw the phone and the fireplace at the same time. She knew there would be no dial tone, and she was right. She sat down by the fire in the nest of cushions, motioning wearily for the dog to come closer. "I wish you were mine, I really do. Thank you for saving me. Now, one last favor—find that Christmas ribbon and save it for me. I want to have something to remember you by. Not now, the next time you go outside. Will you do that for . . . ?" A moment later she was asleep in the mound of pillows.

Murphy sat back on his haunches to stare at the sleeping girl in his master's room. He walked around her several times, sniffing as he did so. When he was satisfied that all was well, he trotted over to the bed and tugged at the comforter until he had it on the floor. Then he dragged it over to the sleeping girl. He pulled, dragged, and tugged until he had it snugly up around her chin. The moment he was finished, he beelined down the hall, through the living room, past his master, out to the kitchen where he slowed just enough to go through his door. He was back in ten minutes with the red ribbon.

"So that's where it is. Hand it over, Murphy. It's supposed to go on the tree." The golden dog stopped in his tracks, woofed, backed up several steps, but he didn't drop the ribbon. Instead, he raced down the hall to the bedroom, his master behind him, his chair whirring softly. He watched as the dog placed the ribbon on the coverlet next to Mo's face. He continued to watch as the huge dog gently tugged the small yellow towel from her wet head. With his snout, he nudged the dark ringlets, then he gently pawed at them.

"I see," Marcus Bishop said sadly. "She does look a little like Marcey with that dark hair. Now that you have the situation under control, I guess it's time for your dinner. She wanted the ribbon, is that it? That's how you got her here? Good boy, Murphy. Let's let our guest sleep. Maybe she'll wake up in time to sing some carols with us. You did good, Murph. Real good. Marcey would be so proud of you. Hell, I'm proud of you and if we don't watch it, I have a feeling this girl is going to try and snatch you away from me."

Marcus could feel his eyes start to burn when Murphy bent over the sleeping girl to lick her cheek. He swore then that the big dog cried, but he couldn't be certain because his own eyes were full of tears.

Back in the kitchen, Marcus threw Mo's clothes in the dryer. He spooned out wet dog food and kibble into Murphy's bowl. The dog looked at it and walked away. "Yeah, I know. So, it's a little setback. We'll recover and get on with it. If we can just get through this first Christmas, we'll be on the road to recovery, but you gotta help me out here. I can't do it alone." The dog buried his head in his paws, but made no sign that he either cared or understood what his master was saying. Marcus felt his shoulders slump.

It was exactly one year ago to the day that the fatal accident had happened. Marsha, his twin sister, had been driving when the head-on collision occurred. He'd been wearing his seat belt; she wasn't wearing hers. It took the wrecking crew four hours to get him out of the car. He'd had six operations and one more loomed on the horizon. This one, the orthopedic specialists said, was almost guaranteed to make him walk again.

This little cottage had been Marcey's. She'd moved down here after her husband died of leukemia, just five short years after her marriage. Murphy had been her only companion during those tragic years. Marcus had done all he could for her, but she'd kept him at a distance. She painted, wrote an art column for the *Philadelphia Democrat,* took long walks, and watched a lot of television. To say she withdrew from life was putting it mildly. After the accident, it was simpler to convert this space to his needs than the main house. A ramp and an oversized bathroom were all he needed. Murphy was happier here, too.

Murphy belonged to both of them, but he'd been partial to Marcey because she always kept licorice squares in her pocket for him.

He and Murphy had grieved together, going to Marcey's gravesite weekly with fresh flowers. At those times, he always made sure he had licorice in his pocket. More often than not, though, Murphy wouldn't touch the little black squares. It was something to do, a memory Marcus tried to keep intact.

It was going to be nice to have someone to share Christmas with. A time of miracles, the Good Book said. Murphy finding this girl in all that snow had to constitute a miracle of some kind. He didn't even know her name. He felt cheated. Time enough for that later. Time. That was all he had of late.

Marcus checked the turkey in the oven. Maybe he should just make a sandwich and save the turkey until tomorrow when the girl would be up to a full sit-down dinner.

He stared at the Christmas tree in the center of the room and wondered if anyone else ever put their tree there. It was the only way he could string the lights. He knew he could have asked one of the servants from the main house to come down and do it just the way he could have asked them to cook him a holiday dinner. But he needed to do these things, needed the responsibility of taking care of himself. In case this next operation didn't work.

He prided himself on being a realist. If he didn't, he'd be sitting in this chair sucking his thumb and watching the boob tube. Life was just too goddamn precious to waste even one minute. He finished decorating the tree, plugged in the lights, and whistled at his marvelous creation. He felt his eyes mist up when he looked at the one-of-a-kind ornaments that had belonged to Marcey and John. He wished for children, a houseful. More puppies. He wished for love, for sound, for music, for sunshine and laughter. Someday.

Damn, he wished he was married with little ones calling him Daddy. Daddy, fix this; Daddy, help me. And some pretty woman standing in the kitchen smiling, the smile just for him. Marcey had said he was a fusspot and that's why no girl would marry him. She had said he needed to be more outgoing, needed to smile more. Stop taking yourself so seriously, she would say. Who said you have to be a better engineer than Dad? And then she'd said, *If you can't whistle when you work you don't belong in that job.* He'd become a whistling fool after that little talk because he loved what he did, loved managing the family firm, the largest engineering outfit in the state of New Jersey. Hell, he'd been called to Kuwait after the Gulf War. That had to mean something in terms of prestige. As if he cared about that.

His chair whirred to life. Within seconds he was sitting in the doorway, watching the sleeping girl. He felt drawn to her for some reason. He snapped his fingers for Murphy. The dog nuzzled his leg. "Check on her, Murph—make sure she's breathing. She should be okay, but do it anyway. Good thing that fireplace is gas—she'll stay warm if she sleeps through the night. Guess I get the couch." He watched as the retriever circled the sleeping girl, nudging the quilt that had slipped from her shoulders. As before, he sniffed her dark hair, stopping long enough to lick her cheek and check on the red ribbon. Marcus motioned for him. Together, they made their way down the hall to the living room and the festive Christmas tree.

It was only six o'clock. The evening loomed ahead of him. He fixed two large ham sandwiches, one cut into four neat squares, then arranged them on two plates along with pickles and potato chips. A beer for him and grape soda for Murphy. He placed them on the fold-up tray attached to his chair. He whirred into the room, then lifted himself out of the chair and onto the couch. He pressed a button and the wide screen television in the corner came to life. He flipped channels until he came to the Weather Channel. "Pay attention, Murph, this is what you saved our guest from. They're calling it The Blizzard. Hell, I could have told them that at ten o'clock this morning. You know what I never figured out, Murph? How Santa is supposed to come down the chimney on Christmas Eve with a fire going. Everyone lights their fireplaces on Christmas Eve. Do you think I'm the only one who's ever asked this question?" He continued to talk to the dog at his feet, feeding him potato chips. For a year now, Murphy was the only one he talked to, with the exception of his doctors and the household help. The business ran itself with capable people standing in for him. He was more than fortunate in that respect. "Did you hear that, Murph? Fourteen inches of snow. We're marooned. They won't even be able to get down here from the big house to check on us. We might have our guest for a few days. Company." He grinned from ear to ear and wasn't sure why. Eventually he dozed, as did Murphy.

Mo opened one eye, instantly aware of where she was and what had happened to her. She tried to stretch her arms and legs. She bit down on her lower lip so she wouldn't cry out in pain. A hot shower, four or five aspirin, and some liniment might make things bearable. She closed her eyes, wondering what time it was. She offered up a prayer, thanking God that she was alive and as well as could be expected under the circumstances.

Where was her host? Her savior? She supposed she would have to get up to find out. She tried again to boost herself to a sitting position. With the quilt wrapped around her, she stared at the furnishings. It seemed feminine to her with the priscilla curtains, the pretty pale blue carpet, and satin-striped chaise longue. There was also a faint powdery scent to the room. A leftover scent as though the occupant no longer lived here. She stared at the large louvered closet that took up one entire wall. Maybe that's where the powdery smell was coming from. Closets tended to hold scents. She looked down at the purple and white flowers adorning the quilt. It matched the drapes. Did men use fluffy yellow towels? If they were leftovers, they did. Her host seemed like the green, brown, and beige type to her.

She saw the clock, directly in her line of vision, sitting next to the phone that was dead.

The time was 3:15. Good Lord, she'd slept the clock around. It was Christmas Day. Her parents must be worried sick. Where was Keith? She played with the fantasy that he was out with the state troopers looking for her, but only for a minute. Keith didn't like the cold. He only pretended to like skiing because it was the trendy thing to do.

She got up, tightened the belt on the oversize robe, and hobbled around the room, searching for the scent that was so familiar. One side of the closet held women's clothes, the other side, men's. So, there was a Mrs. Host. On the dresser, next to the chaise longue, was a picture of a pretty, dark-haired woman and her host. Both were smiling, the man's arm around the woman's shoulders. They were staring directly at the camera. A beautiful couple. A friend must have taken the picture. She didn't have any pictures like this of her and Keith. She felt cheated.

Mo parted the curtains and gasped. In her life she'd never

seen this much snow. She knew in her gut the Jeep was buried. How would she ever find it? Maybe the dog would know where it was.

Mo shed her clothes in the bathroom and showered again. She turned the nozzle a little at a time, trying to get the water as hot as she could stand it. She moved, jiggled, and danced under the spray as it pelted her sore, aching muscles. She put the same long underwear and socks back on and rolled up the sleeves of the robe four times. She was warm, that was all that mattered. Her skin was chafed and wind-burned. She needed cream of some kind, lanolin. Did her host keep things like that here in the bathroom? She looked under the sink. In two shoeboxes she found everything she needed. Expensive cosmetics, pricey perfume. Mrs. Host must have left in a hurry or a huff. Women simply didn't leave a fortune in cosmetics behind.

She was ready now to introduce herself to her host and sit down to food. She realized she was ravenous.

He was in the kitchen mashing potatoes. The table was set for two and one more plate was on the floor. A large turkey sat in the middle of the table.

"Can I do anything?" Her voice was raspy, throaty.

The chair moved and he was facing her.

"You can sit down. I waited to mash the potatoes until I heard the shower going. I'm Marcus Bishop. Merry Christmas."

"I'm Morgan Ames. Merry Christmas to you and Murphy. I can't thank you enough for taking me in. I looked outside and there's a lot of snow out there. I don't think I've ever seen this much snow. Even in Colorado. Everything looks wonderful. It smells wonderful, and I know it's going to taste wonderful, too." She was babbling like a schoolgirl. She clamped her lips shut and folded her hands in her lap.

He seemed amused. "I tried. Most of the time I just grill something out on the deck. This was my first try at a big meal. I don't guarantee anything. Would you like to say grace?"

Would she? Absolutely she would. She had much to be thankful for. She said so, in great detail, head bowed. A smile tugged at the corners of Bishop's mouth. Murphy panted, shifting position twice, as much as to say, let's get on with it.

Mo flushed. "I'm sorry, I did go on there a bit, didn't I? You see, I promised . . . I said . . ."

"You made a bargain with God," Marcus said.

"How did you know?" God, he was handsome. The picture in the bedroom didn't do him justice at all.

"When it's down to the wire and there's no one else, we all depend on that Supreme Being to help us out. Most times we forget about Him. The hard part is going to be living up to all those promises."

"I never did that before. Even when things were bad, I didn't ask. This was different. I stared at my mortality. Are you saying you think I was wrong?"

"Not at all. It's as natural as breathing. Life is precious. No one wants to lose it." His voice faltered, then grew stronger.

Mo stared across the table at her host. She'd caught a glimpse of the pain in his eyes before he lowered his head. Maybe Mrs. Bishop was . . . not of this earth. She felt flustered, sought to change the subject. "Where is this place, Mr. Bishop? Am I in a town or is this the country? I only saw one house up on the hill when I looked out the window."

"The outskirts of Cherry Hill."

She was gobbling her food, then stopped chewing long enough to say, "This is absolutely delicious. I didn't realize I had driven this far. There was absolutely no visibility. I didn't know if I'd gone over the Delaware Bridge or not. I followed the car's lights in front of me and then suddenly the lights were gone and I was on my own. The car just gave out even though I still had some gas left."

"Where were you going? Where did you leave from?"

"I live in Delaware. My parents live in Woodbridge, New Jersey. I was going home for Christmas like thousands of other people. My mother called and told me how bad the snow was. Because I have a four-wheel drive Cherokee, I felt confident I could make it. There was one moment there before I started out when I almost went back. I wish now I had listened to my instincts. It's probably the second most stupid thing I've ever done. Again, I'm very grateful. I could have died out there and all because I had to get home. I just had to get home. I tried the telephone in the bedroom but the line was dead. How long do you think it will take before it comes back on?" How anxious her voice sounded. She cleared her throat.

"A day or so. It stopped snowing about an hour ago. I heard a bulletin that said all the work crews are out. Power is the first thing that has to be restored. I'm fortunate in the sense that I have gas heat and a backup generator in case power goes out. When you live in the country these things are mandatory."

"Do you think the phone is out in the big house on the hill?"

"If mine is out, so is theirs," Marcus said quietly. "This is Christmas, you know."

"I know," Mo said, her eyes misting over.

"Eat!" Marcus said in the same authoritative tone he'd used the day before.

"My mother always puts marshmallow in her sweet potatoes. You might want to try that sometime. She sprinkles sesame seeds in her chopped broccoli. It gives it a whole different taste." She held out her plate for a second helping of turkey.

"I like the taste as it is, but I'll keep it in mind and give it a try someday."

"No, you won't. You shouldn't say things unless you mean them. You strike me as a person who does things one way and is not open to anything but your own way. That's okay, too, but you shouldn't humor me. I happen to like marshmallows in my sweet potatoes and sesame seeds in my broccoli."

"You don't know me at all so why would you make such an assumption?"

"I know that you're bossy. You're used to getting things done your way. You ordered me to take a shower and get out of my wet clothes. You just now, a minute ago, ordered me to eat."

"That was for your own good. You are opinionated, aren't you?"

"Yep. I feel this need to tell you your long underwear scratches. You should use fabric softener in the final rinse water."

Marcus banged his fist on the table. "Aha!" he roared. "That just goes to show how much you really know. Fabric softener does something to the fibers and when you sweat the material won't absorb it. So there!"

"Makes sense. I merely said it would help the scratching. If you plan on climbing a mountain . . . I'm sorry. I talk too much sometimes. What do you have for dessert? Are we having coffee? Can I get it or would you rather I just sit here and eat."

"You're my guest. You sit and eat. We're having plum pudding, and of course we're having coffee. What kind of Christmas dinner do you think this is?" His voice was so huffy that Murphy got up, meandered over to Mo, and sat down by her chair.

"The kind of dinner where the vegetables come in frozen boil bags, the sweet potatoes in boxes, and the turkey stuffing in cellophane bags. I know for a fact that plum pudding can be bought frozen. I'm sure dessert will be just as delicious as the main course. Actually, I don't know when anything tasted half as good. Most men can't cook at all. At least the men I know." She was babbling again. "You can call me Mo. Everyone else does, even my dad."

"Don't get sweet on my dog, either," Marcus said, slopping the plum pudding onto a plate.

"I think your dog is sweet on me, Mr. Bishop. You should put that pudding in a little dessert dish. See, it spilled on the floor. I'll clean it up for you." She was half out of her chair when the iron command knifed through the air.

"Sit!" Mo lowered herself into her chair. Her eyes started to burn.

"I'm not a dog, Mr. Bishop. I only wanted to help. I'm sorry if my offer offended you. I don't think I care for dessert or coffee." Her voice was stiff, her shoulders stiff, too. She had to leave the table or she was going to burst into tears. What was wrong with her?

"I'm the one who should be apologizing. I've had to learn to do for myself. Spills were a problem for a while. I have it down pat now. I just wet a cloth and use the broom handle to move it around. It took me a while to figure it out. You're right about the frozen stuff. I haven't had many guests lately to impress. And you can call me Marcus."

"Were you trying to impress me? How sweet, Marcus. I accept your apology and please accept mine. Let's pretend I stopped by to wish you a Merry Christmas and got caught in the snowstorm. Because you're a nice man, you offered me your hospitality. See, we've established that you're a nice man and I want you to take my word for it that I'm a nice person. Your dog likes me. That has to count."

Marcus chuckled. "Well said."

Mo cupped her chin in her hands. "This is a charming little house. I bet you get the sun all day long. Sun's important. When the sun's out you just naturally feel better, don't you think? Do you have flowers in the spring and summer?"

"You name it, I've got it. Murphy digs up the bulbs sometimes. You should see the tulips in the spring. I spent a lot of time outdoors last spring after my accident. I didn't want to come in the house because that meant I was cooped up. I'm an engineer by profession so I came up with some long-handled tools that allowed me to garden. We pretty much look like a rainbow around April and May. If you're driving this way around that time, stop and see for yourself."

"I'd like that. I'm almost afraid to ask this, but I'm going to ask anyway. Will it offend you if I clean up and do the dishes?"

"Hell, no! I hate doing dishes. I use paper plates whenever possible. Murphy eats off paper plates, too."

Mo burst out laughing. Murphy's tail thumped on the floor.

Mo filled the sink with hot, soapy water. Marcus handed her the plates. They were finished in twenty minutes.

"How about a Christmas drink? I have some really good wine. Christmas will be over before you know it."

"This is good wine," Mo said.

"I don't believe it. You mean you can't find anything wrong with it?" There was a chuckle in Marcus's voice so Mo didn't take offense. "What do you do for a living, Morgan Ames?"

"I'm an architect. I design shopping malls—big ones, small ones, strip malls. My biggest ambition is to have someone hire me to design a bridge. I don't know what it is, but I have this . . . this thing about bridges. I work for a firm, but I'm thinking about going out on my own next year. It's a scary thought, but if I'm going to do it, now is the time. I don't know why I feel that way, I just do. Do you work here at home or at an office?"

"Ninety percent at home, ten percent at the office. I have a specially equipped van. I can't get up on girders, obviously. I have several employees who are my legs. It's another way of saying I manage very well."

"It occurs to me to wonder, Marcus, where you slept last night. I didn't realize until a short while ago that there's only one bedroom."

"Here on the couch. It wasn't a problem. As you can see, it's quite wide and deep—the cushions are extra thick.

"So, what do you think of my tree?" he asked proudly.

"I love the bottom half. I even like the top half. The scent is so heady. I've always loved Christmas. It must be the kid in me. My mother said I used to make myself sick on Christmas

Eve because I couldn't wait for Santa." She wanted to stand by the tree and pretend she was home waiting for Keith to show up and put the ring on her finger, wanted it so bad she could feel the prick of tears. It wasn't going to happen. Still, she felt driven to stand in front of the tree and . . . pretend. She fought the burning behind her eyelids by rubbing them and pretending it was the wood smoke from the fireplace that was causing the stinging. Then she remembered the fireplace held gas logs.

"Me, too. I was always so sure he was going to miss our chimney or his sleigh would break down. I was so damn good during the month of December my dad called me a saint. I have some very nice childhood memories. Are you okay? Is something wrong? You look like you lost your last friend suddenly. I'm a good listener if you want to talk."

Did she? She looked around at the peaceful cottage, the man in the wheelchair, and the dog sitting at his feet. She belonged in a scene like this one. The only problem was, the occupants were all wrong. She was never going to see this man again, so why not talk to him? Maybe he'd give her some male input where Keith was concerned. If he offered advice, she could take it or ignore it. She nodded, and held out her wineglass for a refill.

It wasn't until she was finished with her sad tale that she realized she was still standing in front of the Christmas tree. She sat down with a thump, knowing full well she'd had too much wine. She wanted to cry again when she saw the helpless look on Marcus's face. "So, everyone is entitled to make a fool of themselves at least once in their life. This is . . . was my time." She held out her glass again, but had to wait while Marcus uncorked a fresh bottle of wine. She thought his movements sluggish. Maybe he wasn't used to so much wine. "I don't think I'd make a very good drunk. I never had this much wine in my whole life."

"Me either." The wine sloshed over the side of the glass. Murphy licked it up.

"I don't want to get sick. Keith used to drink too much and get sick. It made me sick just watching him. That's sad, isn't it?"

"I never could stand a man who couldn't hold his liquor," Marcus said.

"You sound funny," Mo said as she realized her voice was taking on a sing-song quality.

"You sound like you're getting ready to sing. Are you? I hope you aren't one of those off-key singers." He leered down at her from the chair.

"So what if I am? Isn't singing good for the soul or something? It's the feeling, the thought. You said we were going to sing carols for Murphy. Why aren't we doing that?"

"Because you aren't ready," Marcus said smartly. He lowered the footrests and slid out of the chair. "We need to sit together in front of the tree. Sitting is as good as standing . . . I think. C'mere, Murphy, you belong to this group."

"Sitting is good." Mo hiccupped. Marcus thumped her on the back and then kept his arm around her shoulder. Murphy wiggled around until he was on both their laps.

"Just what exactly is wrong with you? Or is that impolite of me to . . . ask?" She swigged from the bottle Marcus handed her. "This is good—who needs a glass?"

"I hate doing dishes. The bottle is good. What was the question?"

"Huh?"

"What was the question?"

"The question is . . . was . . . do all your parts . . . work?"

"That wasn't the question. I'd remember if that was the question. Why do you want to know if my . . . parts work? Do you find yourself attracted to me? Or is this a sneaky way to try and get my dog? Get your own damn dog. And my parts work just fine."

"You sound defensive. When was the last time you tried them out . . . what I mean is . . . how do you know?" Mo asked craftily.

"I know! Are you planning on taking advantage of me? I might allow it. Then again, I might not."

"You're drunk," Mo said.

"Yep, and it's all your fault. You're drunk, too."

"What'd you expect? You keep filling my glass. You know what, I don't care. Do you care, Marcus?"

"Nope. So, what are you going to do about that jerk who's waiting by your Christmas tree? Christmas is almost over. D'ya think he's still waiting?"

Mo started to cry. Murphy wiggled around and licked at her tears. She shook her head.

"Don't cry. That jerk isn't worth your little finger. Murphy wouldn't like him. Dogs are keen judges of character."

"Keith doesn't like dogs."

Marcus threw his hands in the air. "There you go! I rest my case." His voice sounded so dramatic, Mo started to giggle.

It wasn't much in the way of a kiss because she was giggling, Murphy was in the way, and Marcus's position and clumsy hands couldn't seem to coordinate with her. "That was sweet," Mo said.

"Sweet! Sweet!" Marcus bellowed in mock outrage.

"Nice?"

"*Nice* is better than *sweet*. No one ever said that to me before."

"How many were there . . . before?"

"None of your business."

"That's true, it isn't any of my business. Let's sing. 'Jingle Bells.' We're both too snookered to know the words to anything else. How many hours till Christmas is over?"

Marcus peered at his watch. "A few." He kissed her again, his hands less clumsy. Murphy cooperated by wiggling off both their laps.

"I liked that!"

"And well you should. You're very pretty, Mo. That's an awful name for a girl. I like Morgan, though. I'll call you Morgan."

"My father wanted a boy. He got me. It's sad. Do you know how many times I used that phrase in the past few hours? A lot." Her head bobbed up and down for no good reason. "Jingle Bells . . ." Marcus joined in, his voice as off-key as hers. They collapsed against each other, laughing like lunatics.

"Tell me about you. Do you have any more wine?"

Marcus pointed to the wine rack in the kitchen. Mo struggled to her feet, tottered to the kitchen, uncorked the bottle, and carried it back to the living room. "I didn't see any munchies in the kitchen so I brought us each a turkey leg."

"I like a woman who thinks ahead." He gnawed on the leg, his eyes assessing the girl next to him. He wasn't the least bit drunk, but he was pretending he was. Why? She was pretty, and she was nice. So what if she had a few hangups. She liked him, too, he could tell. The chair didn't intimidate her the way it did other women. She was feisty, with a mind of her own. She'd been willing to share her private agonies with him, a stranger. Murphy liked her. He liked her, too. Hell, he'd given up his room to her. Now, she was staring at him expectantly, waiting for him to talk about himself. What to tell her? What to gloss over? Why couldn't he be as open as she was?

"I'm thirty-five. I own and manage the family engineering firm. I have good job security and a great pension plan. I own this little house outright. No mortgages. I love dogs and horses. I even like cats. I've almost grown accustomed to this chair. I am self-sufficient. I treat my elders with respect. I was a hell of a Boy Scout, got lots of medals to prove it. I used to ski. I go to church, not a lot, but I do go. I believe in God. I don't have any . . . sisters or brothers. I try not to think too far ahead and I do my best not to look back. That's not to say I don't think and plan for the future, but in my position, I take it one day at a time. That pretty much sums it up as far as my life goes."

"It sounds like a good life. I think you'll manage just fine. We all have to make concessions . . . the chair . . . it's not the end of the world. I can tell you don't like talking about it, so, let's talk about something else."

"How would you feel if you went home this Christmas Eve and there in your living room was Keith in a wheelchair? What if he told you the reason he hadn't been in touch was because he didn't want to see pity in your eyes. How would you feel if he told you he wasn't going to walk again? What if he said you might eventually be the sole support?" He waited for her to digest the questions, aware that her intoxicated state might interfere with her answers.

"You shouldn't ask me something like that in my . . . condition. I'm not thinking real clear. I want to sing some more. I didn't sing last year because I was too sad. Are you asking about this year or last year?"

"What difference does it make?" Marcus asked coolly.

"It makes a difference. Last year I would have . . . would have . . . said it didn't matter because I loved him . . . Do all his parts . . . work?"

"I don't know. This is hypothetical." Marcus turned to hide his smile.

"I wouldn't pity him. Maybe I would at first. Keith is very active. I could handle it, but Keith couldn't. He'd get depressed and give up. What was that other part?"

"Supporting him."

"Oh, yeah. I could do that. I have a profession, good health insurance. I might start up my own business. I'll probably make more money than he ever did. Knowing Keith, I think he would resent me after awhile. Maybe he wouldn't. I'd try harder and harder to make it all work because that's the way I am. I'm not a quitter. I never was. Why do you want to know all this?"

Marcus shrugged. "Insight, maybe. In case I ever find myself attracted to a woman, it would be good to know how she'd react. You surprised me—you didn't react to the chair."

"I'm not in love with you," Mo said sourly.

"What's wrong with me?"

"There's nothing wrong with you. I'm not that drunk that I don't know what you're saying. I'm in love with someone else. I don't care about that chair. That chair wouldn't bother me at all if I loved you. You said your parts work. Or, was that a lie? I like sex. Sex is wonderful when two people . . . you know . . . I like it!"

"Guess what? I do, too."

"You see, it's not a problem at all," Mo said happily. "Maybe I should just lie down on the couch and go to sleep."

"You didn't answer the second part of my question."

"Which was?"

"What if you had made it home this Christmas and the same scenario happened. After two long years. What would be your feeling?"

"I don't know. Keith whines. Did I tell you that? It's not manly at all."

"Really."

"Yep. I have to go to the bathroom. Do you want me to get you anything on my way back? I'll be on my feet. I take these feet for granted. They get me places. I love shoes. Well, what's your answer? Remember, you don't have any munchies. Why is that?"

"I have Orville Redenbacher popcorn. The colored kind. Very festive."

"No! You're turning into a barrel of fun, Marcus Bishop. You were a bossy, domineering person when I arrived through your doggie door. Look at you now! You're skunked, you ate a turkey leg, and now you tell me you have colored popcorn. I'll be right back unless I get sick. Maybe we should have coffee with our popcorn. God, I can't wait for this day to be over."

"Follow her, Murph. If she gets sick, come and get me," Marcus said. "You know," he said, making a gagging sound. The retriever sprinted down the hall.

A few minutes later, Mo was back in the living room. She dusted her hands together as she swayed back and forth. "Let's do the popcorn in the fireplace! I'll bring your coffeepot in here and plug it in. That way we won't have to get up and down."

"Commendable idea. It's ten-thirty."

"An hour and a half to go. I'm going to kiss you at twelve o'clock. Well, maybe one minute afterward. Your socks will come right off when I get done kissing you! So there!"

"I don't like to be used."

"Me either. I'll be kissing you because I want to kiss you. So there yourself!"

"What will Keith think?"

"Keith who?" Mo laughed so hard she slapped her thighs before she toppled over onto the couch. Murphy howled. Marcus laughed outright.

On her feet again, Mo said, "I like you, you're nice. You have a nice laugh. I haven't had this much fun in a long time. Life is such a serious business. Sometimes you need to stand back and get . . . what's that word . . . perspective? I like amusement parks. I like acting like a kid sometimes. There's this water park I like to go to and I love Great Adventure. Keith would never go so I went with my friends. It wasn't the same as sharing it with your lover. Would you like to go and . . . and . . . watch the other people? I'd take you if you would."

"Maybe."

"I hate that word. Keith always said that. That's just another way of saying no. You men are all alike."

"You're wrong, Morgan. No two people are alike. If you judge other men by Keith you're going to miss out on a lot. I told you, he's a jerk."

"Okayyyy. Popcorn and coffee, right?"

"Right."

Marcus fondled Murphy's ears as he listened to his guest bang pots and pans in his neat kitchen. Cabinet doors opened and shut, then opened and shut again. More pots and pans rattled. He smelled coffee and wondered if she'd spilled it. He looked at his watch. In a few short hours she'd be leaving him. How was it possible to feel so close to someone he'd just met? He didn't want her to leave. He hated, with a passion, the faceless Keith.

"I think you need to swing around so we can watch the popcorn pop. I thought everyone in the world had a popcorn popper. I'm improvising with this pot. It's going to turn black, but I'll clean it in the morning. You might have to throw it out. I like strong black coffee. How about you?"

"Bootblack for me."

"Oh, me, too. Really gives you a kick in the morning."

"I don't think that's the right lid for that pot," Marcus said.

"It'll do—I told you I had to improvise."

"Tell me how you're going to improvise this!" Marcus said as the popping corn blew the lid off the pot. Popcorn flew in every direction. Murphy leaped up to catch the kernels, nailing the fallen ones with his paws. Marcus rolled on the floor as Mo wailed her dismay. The corn continued to pop and sail about the room. "I'm not cleaning this up."

"Don't worry, Murphy will eat it all. He loves popcorn. How much did you put in the pot?" Marcus gasped. "Coffee's done."

"A cup full. Too much, huh? I thought it would pop colored. I'm disappointed. There were a lot of fluffies—you know, the ones that pop first."

"I can't tell you how disappointed I am," Marcus said, his expression solemn.

Mo poured the coffee into two mugs.

"It looks kind of . . . syrupy."

"It does, doesn't it? Drink up! What'ya think?"

"I can truthfully say I've never had coffee like this," Marcus responded.

Mo settled herself next to Marcus. "What time is it?"

"It's late. I'm sure by tomorrow the roads will be cleared. The phones will be working and you can call home. I'll try and find someone to drive you. I have a good mechanic I'll call to work on your Jeep. How long were you planning on staying with your parents?"

"It was . . . vague . . . depending . . . I don't know. What will you do?"

"Work. The office has a lot of projects going on. I'm going to be pretty busy."

"Me, too. I like the way you smell," Mo blurted. "Where'd you get that shampoo in the black bottle?"

"Someone gave it to me in a set for my birthday."

"When's your birthday?" Mo asked.

"April tenth. When's yours?"

"April ninth. How about that? We're both Aries."

"Imagine that," Marcus said as he wrapped his arm around her shoulder.

"This is nice," Mo sighed. "I'm a home and hearth person. I like things cozy and warm with lots and lots of green plants. I have little treasures I've picked up over the years that I try to put in just the right place. It tells anyone who comes into my apartment who I am. I guess that's why I like this cottage. It's cozy, warm, and comfortable. A big house can be like that, too, but a big house needs kids, dogs, gerbils, rabbits, and lots of junk."

He should tell her now about the big house on the hill being his. He should tell her about Marcey and about his upcoming operation. He bit down on his lip. Not now—he didn't want to spoil the moment. He liked what they were doing. He liked sitting here with her, liked the feel of her. He risked a glance at his watch. A quarter to twelve. He felt like his eyeballs were standing at attention from the coffee he'd just finished. He announced the time in a quiet voice.

"Do you think he showed up, Marcus?"

He didn't think any such thing, but he couldn't say that. "He's a fool if he didn't."

"His mother told my mother he wasn't coming home for the holidays."

"Ah. Well, maybe he was going to surprise her. Maybe his plans changed. Anything is possible, Morgan."

"No, it isn't. You're playing devil's advocate. It's all right. Really it is. I'll just switch to Plan B and get on with my life."

He wanted that life to include him. He almost said so, but she interrupted him by poking his arm and pointing to his watch.

"Get ready. Remember, I said I was going to kiss you and blow your socks off."

"You did say that. I'm ready."

"That's it, you're ready. It would be nice if you showed some enthusiasm."

"I don't want my blood pressure to go up," Marcus grinned. "What if . . ."

"There is no *what if*. It's a kiss."

"There are kisses and then there are kisses. Sometimes . . ."

"Not this time. I know all about kisses. Jackie Bristol told me about kissing when I was six years old. He was ten and he knew *everything*. He liked to play doctor. He learned all that stuff by watching his older sister and her boyfriend."

She was *that* close to him. She could see a faint freckle on the bridge of his nose. She just knew he thought she was all talk and no action. Well, she'd show him and Keith, too. A kiss was . . . it was . . . what it was was . . .

It wasn't one of those warm, fuzzy kisses and it wasn't one of those feathery light kind, either. This kiss was reckless and passionate. Her senses reeled and her body tingled from head to toe. Maybe it was all the wine she'd consumed. She decided she didn't care what the reason was as she pressed not only her lips, but her body, against his. He responded, his tongue spearing into her mouth. She tasted the wine on his tongue and lips, wondered if she tasted the same way to him. A slow moan began in her belly and rose up to her throat. It escaped the moment she pulled away. His name was on her lips, her eyes sleepy and yet restless. She wanted more. So much more.

This was where she was supposed to say, *Okay, I kept my promise, I kissed you like I said.* Now she should get up and go to bed. But she didn't want to go to bed. Ever. She wanted . . . needed . . .

"I'm still wearing my socks," Marcus said. "Maybe you need to try again. Or, how about I try blowing *your* socks off?"

"Go for it," Mo said as she ran her tongue over her bruised and swollen lips.

He did all the things she'd done, and more. She felt his hands all over her body—soft, searching. Finding. Her own hands started a search of their own. She felt as warm and damp as he felt to her probing fingers. She continued to tingle with anticipation. The heavy robe was suddenly open, the band of the underwear down around her waist, exposing her breasts. He was stroking one with the tip of his tongue. When the hard pink bud was in his mouth she thought she'd never felt such exquisite pleasure.

One minute she had clothes on and the next she was as naked as he was. She had a vague sense of ripping at his clothes as he did the same with hers. They were by the fire now, warm and sweaty.

She was on top of him with no memory of getting there. She slid over him, gasped at his hardness. Her dark hair fanned out like a waterfall. She bent her head and kissed him again. A sound of exquisite pleasure escaped her lips when he cupped both her breasts in his hands.

"Ride me," he said hoarsely. He bucked against her as she rode him, this wild stallion inside her. She milked his body, gave a mighty heave, and fell against him. It was a long time before either of them moved, and when they did, it was together. She wanted to look at him, wanted to say something. Instead, she nuzzled into the crook of his arm. The oversized robe covered them in a steamy warmth. Her hair felt as damp as his. She waited for him to say something, but he lay quietly, his hand caressing her shoulder beneath the robe. Why wasn't he saying something?

Her active imagination took over. One-night stand. Girl lost in snowstorm. Man gives her shelter and food. Was this her payback? Would he respect her in the morning? Damn, it was already morning. What in the world possessed her to make love to this man? She was in love with Keith. *Was. Was* in love. At this precise moment she couldn't remember what Keith looked like. She'd cheated on Keith. But, had she really? *No,* her mind shrieked. She felt like crying, felt her shoulders start to shake. They calmed immediately as Marcus drew her closer.

"I . . . I never had a one-night stand. I would hate . . . I don't want you to think . . . I don't hop in and out of bed . . . this was the first time in two years . . . I . . ."

"Shhh, it's okay. It was what it was—warm, wonderful, and meaningful. Neither one of us owes anything to the other. Sleep, Morgan," he whispered.

"You'll stay here, won't you?" she said sleepily. "I think I'd like to wake up next to you."

"I won't move. I'm going to sleep, too."

"Okay."

It was a lie, albeit a little one. As if he could sleep. Always the last one out of the gate, Bishop. She belongs to someone else, so don't get carried away. How right it had all felt. How right it still felt. What had he just said to her? Oh yeah—*it was what it was.* Oh yeah, well, fuck you, Keith whatever-your-name-is. You don't deserve this girl. I hope your damn dick falls off. You weren't faithful to this girl. I know that as sure as I know the sun is going to rise in the morning. She knows it, too—she just won't admit it.

Marcus stared at the fire, his eyes full of pain and sadness. Tomorrow she'd be gone. He'd never see her again. He'd go on with his life, with his therapy, his job, his next operation. It would be just him and Murphy.

It was four o'clock when Marcus motioned for the retriever to take his place under the robe. The dog would keep her warm while he showered and got ready for the day. He rolled over, grabbed the arm of the sofa and struggled to his feet. Pain ripped up and down his legs as he made his way to the bathroom with the aid of the two canes he kept under the sofa cushions. This was his daily walk, the walk the therapists said was mandatory. Tears rolled down his cheeks as he gritted his teeth. Inside the shower, he lowered himself to the tile seat, turned on the water and let it beat at his legs and body. He stayed there until the water turned cool.

It took him twenty minutes to dress. He was stepping into his loafers when he heard the snowplow. He struggled, with his canes, out to the living room and his chair. His lips were white with the effort. It took every bit of fifteen minutes for the pain to subside. He bent over, picked up the coffeepot, and carried it to the kitchen where he rinsed it and made fresh coffee. While he waited for it to perk he stared out the window. Mr. Drizzoli and his two sons were maneuvering the plows so he could get his van out of the driveway. The younger boy was shoveling out his van. He turned on the outside lights, opened the door, and motioned to the youngster to come closer. He asked about road conditions, the road leading to the main house, and the weather in general. He explained about the Cherokee. The boy promised to speak with his father. They'd search it out and if it was driveable, they'd bring it to the cottage. "There's a five gallon tank of gas in the garage," Marcus said. From the leather pouch attached to his chair, he withdrew a square white envelope: Mr. Drizzoli's Christmas present. Cash.

"The phones are back on, Mr. Bishop," the boy volunteered.

Marcus felt his heart thump in his chest. He could unplug it. If he did that, he'd be no better than Keith what's-his-name. Then he thought about Morgan's anxious parents. Two cups of coffee on his little pull-out tray, Marcus maneuvered the chair into the living room. "Morgan, wake up. Wake her up, Murphy."

She looked so pretty, her hair tousled and curling about her face. He watched as she stretched luxuriously beneath his robe, watched the realization strike her that she was naked. He watched as she stared around her.

"Good morning. It will be daylight in a few minutes. My road is being plowed as we speak and I'm told the phone is working. You might want to get up and call your parents. Your clothes are in the dryer. My maintenance man is checking on your Jeep. If it's driveable, he'll bring it here. If not, they'll tow it to a garage."

Mo wrapped the robe around her and got to her feet. Talk about the bum's rush. She swallowed hard. Well, what had she expected? One-night stands usually ended like this. Why had she expected anything different? She needed to say something. "If you don't mind, I'll take a shower and get dressed. Is it all right if I use the phone in the bedroom?"

"Of course." He'd hoped against hope that she'd call from the living room so he could hear the conversation. He watched as she made her way to the laundry room, coffee cup in hand. Watched as she juggled cup, clothing, and the robe. Murphy sat back on his haunches and howled. Marcus felt the fine hairs on the back of his neck stand on end. Murphy hadn't howled like this since the day of Marcey's funeral. He had to know Morgan was going away. He felt like howling himself.

Marcus watched the clock, watched the progress of the men outside the window. Thirty minutes passed and then thirty-five and forty.

Murphy barked wildly when he saw Drizzoli come to what he thought was too close to his master's property.

Inside the bedroom, with the door closed, Morgan sat down, fully dressed, on the bed. She dialed her parents' number, nibbling on her thumbnail as she waited for the phone to be picked up. "Mom, it's me."

"Thank God. We were worried sick about you, honey. Good Lord, where are you?"

"Someplace in Cherry Hill. The Jeep gave out and I had to walk. You won't believe this, but a dog found me. I'll tell you all about it when I get home. My host tells me the roads are cleared and they're checking my car now. I should be ready to leave momentarily. Did you have a nice Christmas?" She wasn't going to ask about Keith. She wasn't going to ask because suddenly she no longer cared if he showed up in front of the tree or not.

"Yes and no. It wasn't the same without you. Dad and I had our eggnog. We sang 'Silent Night', off-key of course, and then we just sat and stared at the tree and worried about you. It was a terrible storm. I don't think I ever saw so much snow. Dad is whispering to me that he'll come and get you if the Jeep isn't working. How was your first Christmas away from home?"

"Actually, Mom, it was kind of nice. My host is a very nice man. He has this wonderful dog who found me. We had a turkey dinner that was pretty good. We even sang 'Jingle Bells'."

"Well, honey, we aren't going anywhere so call us either way. I'm so relieved that you're okay. We called the state troopers, the police, everyone we could think of."

"I'm sorry, Mom. I should have listened to you and stayed put until the snow let up. I was just so anxious to get home." Now, *now* she'll say if Keith was there.

"Keith was here. He came by around eleven. He said it took him seven hours to drive from Manhattan to his mother's. He was terribly upset that you weren't here. This is just my opinion, but I don't think he was upset that you were stuck in the snow—it was more that he was here and where were you? I'm sorry, Morgan, I am just never going to like that young man. That's all I'm going to say on the matter. Dad feels the same way. Drive carefully, honey. Call us, okay?"

"Okay, Mom."

Morgan had to use her left hand to pry her right hand off the phone. She felt sick to her stomach suddenly. She dropped her head into her hands. What she had wanted for two long years, what she'd hoped and prayed for, had happened. She thought about the old adage: Be careful what you wish for because you might just get it. Now, she didn't want what she had wished for.

It was light out now, the young sun creeping into the room. The silver-framed photograph twinkled as the sun hit it full force. Who was she? She should have asked Marcus. Did he still love the dark-haired woman? He must have loved her a lot to keep her things out in the open, a constant reminder.

She'd felt such strange things last night. Sex with Keith had never been like it was with Marcus. Still, there were other things that went into making a relationship work. Then there was Marcus in his wheelchair. It surprised her that the wheelchair didn't bother her. What did surprise her was what she was feeling. And now it was time to leave. How was she supposed to handle that?

Her heart thumped again when she saw a flash of red go by the bedroom window. Her Jeep. It was running. She stood up, saluted the room, turned, and left.

Good-byes are hard, she thought. Especially this one. She felt shy, schoolgirlish, when she said, "Thanks for everything. I mean to keep my promise and send Murphy some steaks. Would you mind giving me your address? If you're ever in Wilmington, stop . . . you know, stop and . . . we can have a . . . reunion . . . I'm not good at this."

"I'm not, either. Here's my card. My phone number is on it. Call me anytime if you . . . if you want to talk. I listen real good."

Mo handed over her own card. "Same goes for me."

"You just needed some antifreeze. We put five gallons of gas in the tank. Drive carefully. I'm going to worry so call me when you get home."

"I'll do that. Thanks again, Marcus. If you ever want a building or a bridge designed, I'm yours for free. I mean that."

"I know you do. I'll remember."

Mo cringed. How polite they were, how stiff and formal. She couldn't walk away like this. She leaned over, her eyes meeting his, and kissed him lightly on the lips. "I don't think I'll ever forget my visit." *Tell me now, before I leave, about the dark-haired, smiling woman in the picture. Tell me you want me to come back for a visit. Tell me not to go. I'll stay. I swear to God, I'll stay. I'll never think about Keith, never mention his name. Say something.*

"It was a nice Christmas. I enjoyed spending it with you. I know Murphy enjoyed having you here with us. Drive carefully, and remember to call when you get home."

His voice was flat, cool. Last night was just what he'd said: *it was what it was.* Nothing more. She felt like wailing her despair, but she damn well wasn't going to give him the satisfaction. "I will," Mo said cheerfully. She frolicked with Murphy for a few minutes, whispering in his ear, "You take care of him, you hear? I think he tends to be a little stubborn. I have my ribbon and I'll keep it safe, always. I'll send those steaks Fed Ex." Because her tears were blinding her, Mo turned and didn't look at Marcus again. A second later she was outside in the cold, bracing air.

The Cherokee was warm, purring like a kitten. She tapped the horn, two light taps, before she slipped the gear into four-wheel drive. She didn't look back.

It was an interlude.

One of those rare happenings that occur once in a life-time.

A moment in time.

In a little more than twenty-four hours, she'd managed to fall in love with a man in a wheelchair—and his dog.

She cried because she didn't know what else to do.

Mo's homecoming was everything she had imagined it would be. Her parents hugged her. Her mother wiped at her tears with the hem of an apron that smelled of cinnamon and vanilla. Her father acted gruff, but she could see the moist-ness in his eyes.

"How about some breakfast, honey?"

"Bacon and eggs sounds real good. Make sure the . . ."

"The yolk is soft and the white has brown lace around the edges. Snap-in-two bacon, three pieces of toast for dunking, and a small glass of juice. I know, Morgan. Lord, I'm just so glad you're home safe and sound. Dad's going to carry in your bags. Why don't you run upstairs and take a nice hot bath and put on some clothes that don't look like they belong in a thrift store."

"Good idea, Mom."

In the privacy of her room, she looked at the phone that had, as a teenager, been her lifeline to the outside world. All she had to do was pick it up, and she'd hear Marcus's voice. Should she do it now or wait till after her bath when she was decked out in clean clothes and makeup? She decided to wait. Marcus didn't seem the type to sit by the phone and wait for a call from a woman.

The only word she could think of to describe her bath was *delicious*. The silky feel of the water was full of Wild Jasmine bath oil, her favorite scent in the whole world. As she relaxed in the steamy wetness, she forced herself to think about Keith.

She knew without asking that her mother had called Keith's mother after the phone call. Right now, she was so happy to be safe, she would force herself to tolerate Keith. All those presents she'd wrapped so lovingly. All that money she'd spent. Well, she was taking it all back when she returned to Delaware.

Mo heard her father open the bedroom door, heard the sound of her suitcases being set down, heard the rustle of the shopping bags. The tenseness left her shoulders when the door closed softly. She was alone with her thoughts. She wished for a portable phone so she could call Marcus. The thought of talking to him while she was in the bathtub sent shivers up and down her spine.

A long time later, Mo climbed from the tub. She dressed, blow-dried her hair, and applied makeup, ever so sparingly, remembering that less is better. She pulled on a pair of Levi's and a sweater that showed off her slim figure. She spritzed herself lightly with perfume, added pearl studs to her ears. She had to rummage in the drawer for thick wool socks. The closet yielded a pair of Nike Air sneakers she'd left behind on one of her visits.

In the kitchen her mother looked at her with dismay. "Is that what you're wearing?"

"Is something wrong with my sweater?"

"Well, no. I just thought . . . I assumed . . . you'd want to spiff up for . . . Keith. I imagine he'll be here pretty soon."

"Well, it better be pretty quick because I have an errand to do when I finish this scrumptious breakfast. I guess you can tell him to wait or tell him to come back some other time. Let's open our presents after supper tonight. Can we pretend it's Christmas Eve?"

"That's what Dad said we should do."

"Then we'll do it. Listen, don't tell Keith. I want it to be just us."

"If that's what you want, honey. You be careful when you're

out. Just because the roads are plowed, it doesn't mean there won't be accidents. The weatherman said the highways were still treacherous."

"I'll be careful. Can I get anything for you when I'm out?"

"We stocked up on everything before the snow came. We're okay. Bundle up—it's real cold."

Mo's first stop was the butcher on Main Street. She ordered twelve porterhouse steaks and asked to have them sent Federal Express. She paid with her credit card. Her next stop was the mall in Menlo Park where she went directly to Gloria Jean's Coffee Shop. She ordered twelve pounds of flavored coffees and a mug with a painted picture of a golden retriever on the side, asking to have her order shipped Federal Express and paying again with her credit card.

She spent the balance of the afternoon browsing through Nordstrom's department store—it was so full of people she felt claustrophobic. Still, she didn't leave.

At four o'clock she retraced her steps, stopped by Gloria Jean's for a takeout coffee, and drank it sitting on a bench. She didn't want to go home. Didn't want to face Keith. What she wanted to do was call Marcus. *And that's exactly what I'm going to do. I'm tired of doing what other people want me to do. I want to call him and I'm going to call him.* She went in search of a phone the minute she finished her coffee.

Credit card in one hand, Marcus's business card in the other, Mo placed her call. A wave of dizziness washed over her the minute she heard his voice. "It's Morgan Ames, Marcus. I said I'd call you when I got home. Well, I'm home. Actually, I'm in a shopping mall. Ah . . . my mother sent me out to . . . to return some things . . . my dad was on the phone, I couldn't call earlier."

"I was worried when I didn't hear from you. It only takes a minute to make a phone call."

He was worried and he was chastising her. Well, she deserved it. She liked the part that he was worried. "What are you doing?" she blurted.

"I'm thinking about dinner. Leftovers or Spam. Something simple. I'm sort of watching a football game. I think Murphy misses you. I had to go looking for him twice. He was back in my room lying in the pillows where you slept."

"Ah, that's nice. I Federal Expressed his steaks. They should get there tomorrow. I tied the red ribbon on the post of my bed. I'm taking it back to Wilmington with me. Will you tell him that?" Damn, how stupid could one person be?

"I'll tell him. How were the roads?"

"Bad, but driveable. My dad taught me to drive defensively. It paid off." This had to be the most inane conversation she'd ever had in her life. Why was her heart beating so fast? "Marcus, this is none of my business. I meant to ask you yesterday, but I forgot. Who is that lovely woman in the photograph in your room? If it's something you don't care to talk about, it's okay with me. It was just that she sort of looked like me a little. I was curious." She was babbling again.

"Her name was Marcey. She died in the accident I was in. I was wearing my seat belt, she wasn't. I'd rather not talk about it. You're right, though—you do resemble her a little. Murph picked up on that right away. He pulled the towel off your head and kind of sniffed your hair. He wanted me to . . . to see the resemblance, I guess. He took her death real hard."

She was sorry she'd asked. "I'm sorry. I didn't mean to . . . I'm so sorry." She was going to cry now, any second. "I have to go now. Thank you again. Take care of yourself." The tears fell then, and she made no move to stop them. She was like a robot as she walked to the exit and the parking lot. Don't think about the phone call. Don't think about Marcus and his dog. Think about tomorrow when you're going to leave here. Shift into neutral.

* * *

She saw his car and winced. Only a teenager would drive a canary yellow Camaro. She swerved into the driveway. Here it was, the day she'd dreamed of for two long years.

"I'm home!"

"Look who's here, Mo," her mother said. That said, she tactfully withdrew, her father following close behind.

"Keith, it's nice to see you," Mo said stiffly. Who was this person standing in front of her, wearing sunglasses and a houndstooth cap? He reeked of Polo.

"I was here—where were you? I thought we had a date in front of your Christmas tree on Christmas Eve. Your parents were so worried. You look different, Mo," he said, trying to take her into his arms. She deftly sidestepped him and sat down.

"I didn't think you'd show," she said flatly.

"Why would you think a thing like that?" He seemed genuinely puzzled at her question.

"Better yet," Mo said, ignoring his question, "what have you been doing these past two years? I need to know, Keith?"

His face took on a wary expression. "A little of this, a little of that. Work, eat, sleep, play a little. Probably the same things you did. I thought about you a lot. Often. Every day."

"But you never called. You never wrote."

"That was part of the deal. Marriage is a big commitment. People need to be sure before they take that step. I don't believe in divorce."

How virtuous his voice sounded. She watched, fascinated, as he fished around in his pockets until he found what he was looking for. He held the small box with a tiny red bow on it in the palm of his hand. "I'm sure now. I know you wanted to get engaged two years ago. I wasn't ready. I'm ready now." He held the box toward her, smiling broadly.

He got his teeth capped, Mo thought in amazement. She made no move to reach for the silver box.

"Aren't you excited? Don't you want to open it?"

"No."

"No *what?*"

"No, I'm not excited; no, I don't want the box. No, I don't want to get engaged and no, I don't want to get married. To you."

"Huh?" He seemed genuinely perplexed.

"What part of *no* didn't you understand?"

"But . . ."

"But *what,* Keith?"

"I thought . . . we agreed . . . it was a break for both of us. Why are you spoiling things like this? You always have such a negative attitude, Mo. What are you saying here?"

"I'm saying I had two long years to think about us. You and me. Until just a few days ago I thought . . . it would work out. Now, I know it won't. I'm not the same person and you certainly aren't the same person. Another thing, I wouldn't ride in that pimpmobile parked out front if you paid me. You smell like a pimp, too. I'm sorry. I'm grateful to you for this . . . whatever it was . . . hiatus. It was your idea, Keith. I want you to know, I was faithful to you." And she had been. She didn't make love with Marcus until Christmas Day, at which point she already knew it wasn't going to work out between her and Keith. "Look me in the eye, Keith, and tell me you were faithful to me. I knew it! You have a good life. Send me a Christmas card and I'll do the same."

"You're dumping me!" There was such outrage in Keith's voice, Mo burst out laughing.

"That's exactly what you did to me two years ago, but I was too dumb to see it. All those women you had, they wouldn't put up with your bullshit. That's why you're here now. No one else wanted you. I know you, Keith, better than I thought I did. I don't like the word *dump.* I'm breaking off our relationship because I don't love you anymore. Right now, for whatever it's worth, I wouldn't have time to work at a relationship anyway. I've decided to go into business for myself. Can we shake hands and promise to be friends?"

"Like hell! It took me seven goddamn hours to drive here from New York just so I could keep my promise. You weren't even here. At least I tried. I could have gone to Vail with my friends. You can take the responsibility for the termination of this relationship." He stomped from the room, the silver box secure in his pocket.

Mo sat down on the sofa. She felt lighter, buoyant somehow. "I feel, Mom, like someone just took fifty pounds off my shoulders. I wish I'd listened to you and Dad. You'd think at my age I'd have more sense. Did you see him? Is it me or was he always like that?"

"He was always like that, honey. I wasn't going to tell you, but under the circumstances, I think I will. I really don't think he would have come home this Christmas except for one thing. His mother always gives him a handsome check early in the month. This year she wanted him home for the holidays so she said she wasn't giving it to him until Christmas morning. If he'd gotten it ahead of time I think he would have gone to Vail. We weren't eavesdropping—he said it loud enough so his voice carried to the kitchen. Don't feel bad, Mo."

"Mom, I don't. That dinner you're making smells soooo good. Let's eat, open our presents, thank God for our wonderful family, and go to bed."

"Sounds good to me."

"I'm leaving in the morning, Mom. I have some things I need to . . . take care of."

"I understand."

"Merry Christmas, Mom."

Mo set out the following morning with a full gas tank, an extra set of warm clothes on the front seat, a brand new flashlight with six new batteries, a real shovel, foot warmers, a basket lunch that would feed her for a week, two pairs of mittens, a pair of fleece-lined boots, and the firm resolve never to take a trip without preparing for it. In the cargo area there were five shopping bags of presents that she would be returning to Wanamaker's over the weekend.

She kissed and hugged her parents, accepted change from her father for the tolls, honked her horn, and was off. Her plan was to stop in Cherry Hill. Why, she didn't know. Probably to make a fool out of herself again. Just the thought of seeing Marcus and Murphy made her blood sing.

She had a speech all worked out in her head, words she'd probably never say. She'd say, *Hi, I was on my way home and thought I'd stop for coffee.* After all, she'd just sent a dozen different kinds. She could help cook a steak for Murphy. Maybe Marcus would kiss her hello. Maybe he'd ask her to stay.

It wasn't until she was almost to the Cherry Hill exit that she realized Marcus hadn't asked if Keith had shown up. That had to mean he wasn't interested in her. *It was what it was.* She passed the exit sign with tears in her eyes.

She tormented herself all of January and February. She picked up the phone a thousand times, and always put it back down. Phones worked two ways. He could call her. All she'd gotten from him was a scrawled note thanking her for the coffee and steaks. He did say Murphy was burying the bones under the pillows and that he'd become a coffee addict. The last sentence was personal. *I hope your delayed Christmas was everything you wanted it to be.* A large scrawled "M." finished off the note.

She must have written five hundred letters in response to that little note. None of which she mailed.

She was in love. Really in love. For the first time in her life.

And there wasn't a damn thing she could do about it. Unless she wanted to make a fool of herself again, which she had no intention of doing.

She threw herself into all the details it took to open a new business. She had the storefront, she'd ordered the vertical blinds, helped her father lay the carpet and tile. Her father had made three easels and three desks, in case she wanted to expand and hire help. Her mother wallpapered the kitchen, scrubbed the ancient appliances, and decorated the bathroom while she went out on foot and solicited business. Her grand opening was scheduled for April first.

She had two new clients and the promise of two more. If she was lucky, she might be able to repay her father's loan in three years instead of five.

On the other side of the bridge, Marcus Bishop wheeled his chair out onto his patio, Murphy alongside him. On the pull-out tray were two beers and the portable phone. He was restless, irritable. In just two weeks he was heading back to the hospital. The do-or-die operation he'd been living for, yet dreading. There were no guarantees, but the surgeon had said he was confident he'd be walking in six months. With extensive, intensive therapy. Well, he could handle that. Pain was his middle name. Maybe then . . . maybe then, he'd get up the nerve to call Morgan Ames and . . . and chat. He wondered if he dared intrude on her life with Keith. Still, there was nothing wrong with calling her, chatting about Murphy. He'd be careful not to mention Christmas night and their lovemaking. "The best sex I ever had, Murph. You know me—too much too little too late or whatever that saying is. What'd she see in that jerk? He is a jerk, she as much as said so. You're a good listener, Murph. Hell, let's call her and say . . . we'll say . . . what we'll do is . . . *hello* is good. Her birthday is coming up—so is mine. Maybe I should wait till then and send a card. Or, I could send flowers or a present. The thing is, I want to talk to her now. Here comes the mailman, Murph. Get the bag!"

Murphy ran to the doggie door and was back in a minute with a small burlap sack the mailman put the mail in. Murphy then dragged it to Marcus on the deck. He loved racing to the mailman, who always had dog biscuits as well as Mace in his pockets.

"Whoaoooo, would you look at this, Murph? It's a letter or a card from you know who. Jesus, here I am, thinking about her and suddenly I get mail from her. That must mean something. Here goes. Ah, she opened her own business. The big opening day is April first. No April Fool's joke, she says. She hopes I'm fine, hopes you're fine, and isn't this spring weather gorgeous? She has five clients now, but had to borrow money from her father. She's not holding her breath waiting for someone to ask her to design a bridge. If we're ever in Wilmington we should stop and see her new office. That's it, Murph. What I could do is send her a tree. Everyone has a tree when they open a new office. Maybe some yellow roses. It's ten o'clock in the morning. They can have the stuff there by eleven. I can call at twelve and talk to her. That's it, that's what we'll do." Murphy's tail swished back and forth in agreement.

Marcus ordered the ficus tree and a dozen yellow roses. He was assured delivery would be made by twelve-thirty. He passed the time by speaking with his office help, sipping coffee, and throwing a cut-off broom handle for Murphy to fetch. At precisely 12:30, his heart started to hammer in his chest.

"Morgan Ames. Can I help you?"

"Morgan, it's Marcus Bishop. I called to congratulate you. I got your card today."

"Oh, Marcus, how nice of you to call. The tree is just what this office needed and the flowers are beautiful. That was so kind of you. How are you? How's Murphy?"

"We're fine. You must be delirious with all that's happening. How did Keith react to you opening your own business? For some reason I thought . . . assumed . . . that opening the business wasn't something you were planning on doing right away. Summer . . . or did I misunderstand?"

"No, you didn't misunderstand. I talked it over with my father and he couldn't find any reason why I shouldn't go for it now. I couldn't have done it without my parents' help. As for Keith . . . it didn't work out. He did show up. It was my decision. He just . . . wasn't the person I thought he was. I don't know if you'll believe or even understand this, but all I felt was an overwhelming sense of relief."

"Really? If it's what you want, then I'm happy for you. You know what they say, if it's meant to be, it will be." He felt dizzy from her news.

"So, when do you think you can take a spin down here to see my new digs?"

"Soon. Do you serve refreshments?"

"I can and will. We have birthdays coming up. I'd be more than happy to take you out to dinner by way of celebration. If you have the time."

"I'll make the time. Let me clear my dock and get back to you. The only thing that will hinder me is my scheduled operation. There's every possibility it will be later this week."

"I'm not going anywhere, Marcus. Whenever is good for you will be good for me. I wish you the best. If there's anything I can do . . . now, that's foolish, isn't it? Like I can really do something. Sometimes I get carried away. I meant . . ."

"I know what you meant, Morgan, and I appreciate it. Murphy is . . . he misses you."

"I miss both of you. Thanks again for the tree and the flowers."

"Enjoy them. We'll talk again, Morgan."

The moment Marcus broke the connection his clenched fist shot in the air. "Yessss!" Murphy reacted to this strange display by leaping onto Marcus's lap. "She loves the tree and the flowers. She blew off what's-his-name. What that means to you and me, Murph, is maybe we still have a shot. If only this damn operation wasn't looming. I need to think, to plan. I'm gonna work this out. Maybe, just maybe we can turn things around. She invited me to dinner. Hell, she offered to pay for it. That has to mean something. I take it to mean she's interested. In *us,* because we're a package deal." The retriever squirmed and wiggled, his long tail lolling happily.

"I feel good, Murph. Real good."

Mo hung up the phone, her eyes starry. Sending the office announcement had been a good idea after all. She stared at the flowers and at the huge ficus tree sitting in the corner. They made all the difference in the world. He'd asked about Keith and she'd responded by telling him the truth. It had come out just right. She wished now that she had asked about the operation, asked why he was having it. Probably to alleviate the pain he always seemed to be in. At what point would referring to his condition, or his operation, be stepping over the line? She didn't know, didn't know anyone she could ask. Also, it was none of her business, just like Marcey wasn't any of her business. If he wanted her to know, if he wanted to talk about it, he would have said something, opened up the subject.

It didn't matter. He'd called and they sort of had a date planned. She was going to have to get a new outfit, get her hair and nails done. Ohhhhh, she was going to sleep so good tonight. Maybe she'd even dream about Marcus Bishop.

Her thoughts sustained her for the rest of the day and into the evening.

Two days later, Marcus Bishop grabbed the phone on the third ring. He announced himself in a sleepy voice, then waited. He jerked upright a second later. "Jesus, Stewart, what time is it? Five o'clock! You want me there at eleven? Yeah, yeah, sure. I just have to make arrangements for Murphy. No, no, I won't eat or drink anything. Don't tell me not to worry, Stewart. I'm already sweating. I guess I'll see you later."

"C'mon, Murph, we're going to see your girlfriend. Morgan. We're going to see Morgan and ask her if she'll take care of you until I get on my feet or . . . we aren't going to think about . . . we're going to think positive. Get your leash, your brush, and all that other junk you take with you. Put it by the front door in the basket. Go on."

He whistled. He sang. He would have danced a jig if it was possible. He didn't bother with a shower—they did that for him at the hospital. He did shave, though. After all, he was going to see Morgan. She might even give him a good luck kiss. One of those blow-your-socks-off kisses.

At the front door he stared at the array Murphy had stacked up. The plastic laundry basket was filled to overflowing. Curious, Marcus leaned over and poked among the contents. His leash, his brush, his bag of vitamins, his three favorite toys, his blanket, his pillow, one of his old slippers and one of Marcey's that he liked to sleep with, the mesh bag that contained his shampoo and flea powder.

"She's probably going to give us the boot when she sees all of this. You sure you want to take all this stuff?" Murphy backed up, barking the three short sounds that Marcus took for affirmation. He barked again and again, backing up, running forward, a sign that Marcus was supposed to follow him. In the laundry room, Murphy pawed the dryer door. Marcus opened it and watched as the dog dragged out the large yellow towel and took it to the front door.

"I'll be damned. Okay, just add it to the pile. I'm sure it will clinch the deal."

Ten minutes later they were barreling down I-95. Forty minutes after that, with barely any traffic on the highway, Marcus located the apartment complex where Morgan lived.

He used up another ten minutes finding the entrance to her building. Thank God for the handicapped ramp and door. Inside the lobby, his eyes scanned the row of mailboxes and buzzers. He pressed down on the button and held his finger steady. When he heard her voice through the speaker he grinned.

"I'm in your lobby and I need you to come down. Now! Don't worry about fixing up. Remember, I've seen you at your worst."

"What's wrong?" she said, stepping from the elevator.

"Nothing. Everything. Can you keep Murphy for me? My surgeon called me an hour ago and he wants to do the operation this afternoon. The man scheduled for today came down with the flu. I have all Murphy's gear. I don't know what else to do. Can you do it?"

"Of course. Is this his stuff?"

"Believe it or not, he packed himself. He couldn't wait to get here. I can't thank you enough. The guy that usually keeps him is off in Peru on a job. I wouldn't dream of putting him in a kennel. I'd cancel my operation first."

"It's not a problem. Good luck. Is there anything else I can do?"

"Say a prayer. Well, thanks again. He likes real food. When you go through his stuff you'll see he didn't pack any."

"Okay."

"What do you call that thing you're wearing?" Marcus asked curiously.

"It's my bathrobe. It used to be my grandfather's. It's old, soft as silk. It's like an old friend. But better yet, it's warm. These are slippers on my feet even though they look like fur muffs. Again, they keep my feet warm. These things in my hair are curlers. It's who I am," Mo said huffily.

"I wasn't complaining. I was just curious. I bet you're a

knockout when you're wearing makeup. Do you wear make-up?"

Mo's insecurities took over. She must look like she just got off the boat. She could feel a flush working its way up to her neck and face. She didn't mean to say it, didn't think she'd said it until she saw the look on Marcus's face. "Why, did Marcey wear lots of makeup? Well, I'm sorry to disappoint you, but I wear very little. I can't afford the pricey stuff she used. What you see is what you get. In other words, take it or leave it and don't ever again compare me to your wife or your girlfriend." She turned on her heel, the laundry basket in her arms, Murphy behind her.

"Hold on! What wife? What girlfriend? What pricey makeup are you talking about? Marcey was my twin sister. I thought I told you that."

"No, you didn't tell me that," Mo called over her shoulder. Her back to him, she grinned from ear to ear. Ahhh, life was lookin' good. "Good luck," she said, as the elevator door swished shut.

In her apartment with the door closed and bolted, Mo sat down on the living room floor with the big, silky dog. "Let's see what we have here," she said, checking the laundry basket. "Hmmm, I see your grooming is going to take a lot of time. I need to tell you that we have a slight problem. Actually, it's a large, as in *very large,* problem. No pets are allowed in this apartment complex. Oh, you brought the yellow towel. That was sweet, Murphy," she said, hugging the retriever. "I hung the red ribbon on my bed." She was talking to this dog like he was a person and was going to respond any minute. "It's not just a little problem, it's a big problem. I guess we sleep at the office. I can buy a sleeping bag and bring your gear there. There's a kitchen and a bathroom. Maybe my dad can come down and rig up a shower. Then again, maybe not. I can always come back to the apartment and shower. We can cook in the office or we can eat out. I missed you. I think about you and Marcus a lot. I thought I would never hear from him again. I thought he was married. Can you beat that?

"Okay, I'm going to take my shower, make some coffee, and then we'll head to my new office. I'm sure it's nothing like Marcus's office and I know he takes you there with him. It's a me office, if you know what I mean. It's so good to have someone to talk to. I wish you could talk back."

Mo marched into the kitchen to look in the refrigerator. Leftover Chinese that should have been thrown out a week ago, leftover Italian that should have been thrown out two weeks ago, and last night's pepper steak that she'd cooked herself. She warmed it in the microwave and set it down for Murphy, who lapped it up within seconds. "Guess that will hold you till this evening."

Dressed in a professional, spring-like suit, Mo gathered her briefcase and all the stuff she carried home each evening into a plastic shopping bag. Murphy's leash and his toys went into a second bag. At the last moment she rummaged in the cabinet for a water bowl. "Guess we need to take your bed and blanket, too." Two trips later, the only thing left to do was call her mother.

"Mo, what's wrong? Why are you calling this early in the morning?"

"Mom, I need your help. If Dad isn't swamped, do you think you guys could come down here?" She related the events of the past hours. "I can't live in the office—health codes and all that. I need you to find me an apartment that will take a dog. I know this sounds stupid, but is it possible, do you think, to find a house that will double as an office? If I have to suck up the money I put into the storefront, I will. I might be able to sublease it, but I don't have the time to look around. I have so much work, Mom. All of a sudden it happened. It almost seems like the day the sign went up, everybody who's ever thought about hiring an architect chose me. I'm not complaining. Can you help me?"

"Of course. Dad's at loose ends this week. It's that retirement thing. He doesn't want to travel, he doesn't want to garden, he doesn't know what he wants. Just last night he was talking about taking a Julia Child cooking course. We'll get ready and leave within the hour." Her voice dropped to a whisper. "You should see the sparkle in his eyes—he's ready now. We'll see you in a bit."

Once they reached the office, Murphy settled in within seconds. A square patch of sun under the front window became his. His red ball, a rubber cat with a hoarse squeak, and his latex candy cane were next to him. He nibbled on a soup bone that was almost as big as his head.

Mo worked steadily without a break until her parents walked through the door at ten minutes past noon. Murphy eyed them warily until he saw Mo's enthusiastic greeting, at which point he joined in, licking her mother's outstretched hand and offering his paw to her father.

"Now, that's what I call a real gentleman. I feel a lot better about you being here alone now that you have this dog," her father said.

"It's just temporary, Dad. Marcus will take him back as soon as . . . well, I don't know exactly. Dad, I am so swamped. I'm also having a problem with this . . . take a look, give me your honest opinion. The client is coming in at four and I'm befuddled. The heating system doesn't work the way he wants it installed. I have to cut out walls, move windows—and he won't want to pay for the changes."

"In a minute. Your mother and I decided that I will stay here and help you. She's going out with a realtor at twelve-thirty. We called from the car phone and set it all up. We were specific with your requirements so she won't be taking your mother around to things that aren't appropriate. Knowing your mother, I'm confident she'll have the perfect location by five o'clock this evening. Why don't you and your mother visit for a few minutes while I take a look at these blueprints?"

"I think you should hire him, Mo," her mother stage-whispered. "He'd probably work for nothing. A couple of days a week would be great. I could stay down here with him and cook for you, walk your dog. We'd be more than glad to do it, Mo, if you think it would work and we wouldn't be infringing on your privacy."

"I'd love it, Mom. Murphy isn't my dog. I wish he was. He saved my life. What can I say?"

"You can tell me about Marcus Bishop. The real skinny, and don't tell me there isn't a skinny to tell. I see that sparkle in your eyes and it isn't coming from this dog."

"Later, okay? I think your real estate person is here. Go get 'em, Mom. Remember, I need a place as soon as possible. Otherwise I sleep here in the office in a sleeping bag. If I break my lease by having a pet, I don't get my security deposit back and it was a hefty one. If you can find something for me it will work out perfectly since my current lease is up the first of May. I'm all paid up. I appreciate it, Mom."

"That's what parents are for, sweetie. See you. John . . . did you hear me?"

"Hmmmnn."

Mo winked at her mother.

Father and daughter worked steadily, stopping just long enough to walk Murphy and eat a small pizza they'd had delivered. When Mo's client walked through the door at four o'clock, Mo introduced her father as her associate, John Ames.

"Now, Mr. Caruthers, this is what Morgan and I came up with. You get everything you want with the heating system. See this wall? What we did was . . ."

Knowing her client was in good hands, Mo retired to the kitchen to make coffee. She added some cookies to a colorful tray at the last moment. When she entered the office, tray in hand, her father was shaking hands and smiling. "Mr. Caruthers liked your idea. He gets what he wants plus the atrium. He's willing to absorb the extra three hundred."

"I'm going to be relocating sometime in the next few weeks, Mr. Caruthers. Since I've taken on an associate, I need more room. I'll notify you of my new address and phone number. If you happen to know anyone who would be interested in a sublease, call me."

Caruthers was gone less than five minutes when Helen Ames bustled through the door, the realtor in tow. "I found it! The perfect place! An insurance agent who had his office in his home is renting it. It's empty. You can move in tonight or tomorrow. The utilities are on, and he pays for them. It was part of the deal. It's wonderful, Mo—there's even a fenced yard for Murphy. I took the liberty of okaying your move. Miss Oliver has a client who does odd jobs and has his own truck. He's moving your furniture as we speak. All we have to do is pack up your personal belongings and Dad and I can do that with your help. You can be settled by tonight. The house is in move-in condition. That's a term real estate people use," she said knowledgeably. "Miss Oliver has agreed to see if she can sublease this place. Tomorrow, her man will move the office. At the most, Mo, you'll lose half a day's work. With Dad helping you, you'll get caught up in no time. There's a really nice garden on the side of the house and a magnificent wisteria bush you're going to love. Plus twelve tomato plants. The insurance man who owns the house is just glad that someone like us is renting. It's a three-year lease with an option to buy. His wife's mother lives in Florida and she wants to be near her since she's in failing health. I just love it when things work out for all parties involved. He didn't have one bit of a problem with the dog after I told him Murphy's story."

Everything worked out just the way her mother said it would.

The April showers gave way to May flowers. June sailed

in with warm temperatures and bright sunshine. The only flaw in Mo's life was the lack of communication where Marcus was concerned.

Shortly after the Fourth of July, Mo piled Murphy into the Cherokee on a bright sunshiny Sunday and headed for Cherry Hill. "Something's wrong—I just feel it," she muttered to the dog all the way up the New Jersey Turnpike.

Murphy was ecstatic when the Jeep came to a stop outside his old home. He raced around the side of the house, barking and growling, before he slithered through his doggie door. On the other side, he continued to bark and then he howled. With all the doors locked, Mo had no choice but to go in the same way she'd gone through on Christmas Eve.

Inside, things were neat and tidy, but there was a thick layer of dust over everything. Obviously Marcus had not been here for a very long time.

"I don't even know what hospital he went to. Where is he, Murphy? He wouldn't give you up, even to me. I know he wouldn't." She wondered if she had the right to go through Marcus's desk. Out of concern. She sat down and thought about her birthday. She'd been so certain that he'd send a card, one of those silly cards that left the real meaning up in the air, but her birthday had gone by without any kind of acknowledgment from him.

"Maybe he did give you up, Murphy. I guess he isn't interested in me." She choked back a sob as she buried her head in the retriever's silky fur. "Okay, come on, time to leave. I know you want to stay and wait, but we can't. We'll come back again. We'll come back as often as we have to. That's a promise, Murphy."

On the way back to her house, Mo passed her old office and was surprised to see that it had been turned into a Korean vegetable stand. She'd known Miss Oliver had subleased it with the rent going directly to the management company, but that was all she knew.

"Life goes on, Murphy. What's that old saying, time waits for no man? Something like that anyway."

Summer moved into autumn and before Mo knew it, her parents had sold their house and rented a condo on the outskirts of Wilmington. Her father worked full-time in her office while her mother joined every woman's group in the state of Delaware. It was the best of all solutions.

Thanksgiving was spent in her parents' condo with her mother doing all the cooking. The day was uneventful, with both Mo and her father falling asleep in the living room after dinner. Later, when she was attaching Murphy's leash, her mother said, quite forcefully, "You two need to get some help in that office. I'm appointing myself your new secretary and first thing Monday morning you're going to start accepting applications for associates. It's almost Christmas and none of us has done any shopping. It's the most wonderful time of the year and last year convinced us that . . . time is precious. We all need to enjoy life more. Dad and I are going to take a trip the day after Christmas. We're going to drive to Florida. I don't want to hear a word, John. And you, Mo, when was the last time you had a vacation? You can't even remember. Well, we're closing your office on the twentieth of December and we aren't reopening until January second. That's the final word. If your clients object, let them go somewhere else."

"Okay, Mom," Mo said meekly.

"As usual, you're right, Helen," John said just as meekly.

"I knew you two would see it my way. We're going to take up golf when we get to Florida."

"Helen, for God's sake. I hate golf. I refuse to hit a silly little ball with a stick and there's no way I'm going to wear plaid pants and one of those damn hats with a pom-pom on it."

"We'll see," Helen sniffed.

"On that thought, I'll leave you."

At home, curled up in bed with Murphy alongside her, Mo turned on the television that would eventually lull her to sleep. She felt wired up, antsy for some reason. Here it was, almost Christmas, and Marcus Bishop was still absent from her life. She thought about the many times she'd called Bishop Engineering, only to be told Mr. Bishop was out of town and couldn't be reached. "The hell with you, Mr. Marcus Bishop. You gotta be a real low-life to stick me with your dog and then forget about him. What kind of man does that make you? What was all that talk about loving him? He misses you." Damn, she was losing it. She had to stop talking to herself or she was going to go over the edge.

Sensing her mood, Murphy snuggled closer. He licked at her cheeks, pawed her chest. "Forget what I just said, Murphy. Marcus loves you—I know he does. He didn't forget you, either. I think, and this is just my own opinion, but I think something went wrong with his operation and he's recovering somewhere. I think he was just saying words when he said he was used to the chair and it didn't bother him. It does. What if they ended up cutting off his legs? Oh, God," she wailed. Murphy growled, the hair on the back of his head standing on end. "Ignore that, too, Murphy. No such thing happened. I'd feel something like that."

She slept because she was weary and because when she cried she found it difficult to keep her eyes open.

"What are you going to do, honey?" Helen Ames asked as Mo closed the door to the office.

"I'm going upstairs to the kitchen and make a chocolate cake. Mom, it's December twentieth. Five days till Christmas. Listen, I think you and Dad made the right decision to leave for Florida tomorrow. You both deserve sunshine for the holidays. Murphy and I will be fine. I might even take him to

Cherry Hill so he can be home for Christmas. I feel like I
should do that for him. Who knows, you guys might love
Florida and want to retire there. There are worse things,
Mom. Whatever you do, don't make Dad wear those plaid
pants. Promise me?"

"I promise. Tell me again, Mo, that you don't mind spending Christmas alone with the dog."

"Mom, I really and truly don't mind. We've all been like
accidents waiting to happen. This is a good chance for me to
laze around and do nothing. You know I was never big on
New Year's. Go, Mom. Call me when you get there and if
I'm not home, leave a message. Drive carefully, stop often."

"Good night, Mo."

"Have a good trip, Mom."

On the morning of the twenty-third of December, Mo woke
early, let Murphy out, made herself some bacon and eggs,
and wolfed it all down. During the night she'd had a dream
that she'd gone to Cherry Hill, bought a Christmas tree, decorated it, cooked a big dinner for her and Murphy, and . . .
then she'd awakened. Well, she was going to live the dream.

"Wanna go home, big guy? Get your stuff together. We're
gonna get a tree, and do the whole nine yards. Tomorrow it
will be a full year since I met you. We need to celebrate."

A little after the noon hour, Mo found herself dragging a
Douglas fir onto Marcus's back patio. As before, she crawled
through the doggie door after the dog and walked through
the kitchen to the patio door. It took her another hour to lo-
cate the box of Christmas decorations. With the fireplaces
going, the cottage warmed almost immediately.

The wreath with the giant red bow went on the front door.
Back inside, she added the lights to the tree and put all the
colorful decorations on the branches. On her hands and
knees, she pushed the tree stand gently until she had it perfectly arranged in the corner. It was heavenly, she thought

sadly as she placed the colorful poinsettias around the hearth. The only thing missing was Marcus.

Mo spent the rest of the day cleaning and polishing. When she finished her chores, she baked a cake and prepared a quick poor man's stew with hamburger meat.

Mo slept on the couch because she couldn't bring herself to sleep in Marcus's bed.

Christmas Eve dawned, gray and overcast. It felt like snow, but the weatherman said there would be no white Christmas this year.

Dressed in blue jeans, sneakers, and a warm flannel shirt, Mo started the preparations for Christmas Eve dinner. The house was redolent with the smell of frying onions, the scent of the tree, and the gingerbread cookies baking in the oven. She felt almost light-headed when she looked at the tree with the pile of presents underneath, presents her mother had warned her not to open, presents for Murphy, and a present for Marcus. She would leave it behind when they left after New Year's.

At one o'clock, Mo slid the turkey into the oven. Her plum pudding, made from scratch, was cooling on the counter. The sweet potatoes and marshmallows sat alongside the pudding. A shaker of sesame seeds and the broccoli were ready to be cooked when the turkey came out of the oven. She took one last look around the kitchen, and at the table she'd set for one, before she retired to the living room to watch television.

Murphy leaped from the couch, the hair on his back stiff. He growled and started to pace the room, racing back and forth. Alarmed, Mo got off the couch to look out the window. There was nothing to see but the barren trees around the house. She switched on more lights, even those on the tree. As a precaution against what, she didn't know. She locked all the doors and windows. Murphy continued to growl and pace. Then the low, deep growls were replaced with high-pitched whines, but he made no move to go out his doggie door. Mo closed the drapes and turned the floodlights on outside. She could feel herself start to tense up. Should she call the police? What would she say? My dog's acting strange? Damn.

Murphy's cries and whines were so eerie she started to come unglued. Perhaps he wasn't one of those dogs that were trained to protect owner, hearth, and home. Since she'd had him he'd never been put to the test. To her, he was just a big animal who loved unconditionally.

In a moment of blind panic she rushed around the small cottage checking the inside dead bolts. The doors were stout, solid. She didn't feel one bit better.

The racket outside was worse and it all seemed to be coming from the kitchen area. She armed herself with a carving knife in one hand and a cast iron skillet in the other. Murphy continued to pace and whine. She eyed the doggie door warily, knowing the retriever was itching to use it, but he'd understood her iron command of *No*.

She waited.

When she saw the doorknob turn, she wondered if she would have time to run out the front door and into her Cherokee. She was afraid to chance it, afraid Murphy would bolt once he was outside.

She froze when she saw the thick vinyl strips move on the doggie door. Murphy saw it, too, and let out an ear-piercing howl. Mo sidestepped to the left of the opening, skillet held at shoulder height, the carving knife in much the same position.

She saw his head and part of one shoulder. "Marcus! What are you doing coming in Murphy's door?" Her shoulders sagged with relief.

"All the goddamn doors are locked and bolted. I'm stuck. What the hell are you doing here in my house? With my dog yet."

"I brought him home for Christmas. He missed you. I thought . . . you could have called, Marcus, or sent a card. I swear to God, I thought you died on the operating table and no one at your company wanted to tell me. One lousy card, Marcus. I had to move out of my apartment because they don't allow animals. I gave up my office. For your dog. Well, here he is. I'm leaving and guess what—I don't give one little shit if you're stuck in that door or not. You damn well took almost a year out of my life. That's not fair and it's not right. You have no excuse and even if you do, I don't want to hear it."

"Open the goddamn door! Now!"

"Up yours, Marcus Bishop!"

"Listen, we're two reasonably intelligent adults. Let's discuss this rationally. There's an answer for everything."

"Have a Merry Christmas. Dinner is in the oven. Your tree is in the living room, all decorated, and there's a wreath on the front door. Your dog is right here. I guess that about covers it."

"You can't leave me stuck like this."

"You wanna bet? Toy with *my* affections, will you? Not likely. Stick *me* with your dog! You're a bigger jerk than Keith ever was. And I fell for your line of bullshit! I guess I'm the stupid one."

"Morgannnn!"

Mo slammed her way through the house to the front door. Murphy howled. She stooped down. "I'm sorry. You belong with him. I do love you—you're a wonderful companion and friend. I won't ever forget how you saved my life. From time to time I'll send you some steaks. You take care of that . . . that big boob, you hear?" She hugged the dog so hard he barked.

She was struggling with the garage door when she felt herself being pulled backward. To her left she heard Murphy bark ominously.

"You're going to listen to me whether you like it or not. Look at me when I talk to you," Marcus Bishop said as he whirled her around.

Her anger and hostility dropped away. "Marcus, you're on

your feet! You can walk! That's wonderful!" The anger came back as swiftly as it had disappeared. "It still doesn't excuse your silence for nine whole months."

"Look, I sent cards and flowers. I wrote you letters. How in the damn hell was I supposed to know you moved?"

"You didn't even tell me what hospital you were going to. I tried calling till I was blue in the face. Your office wouldn't tell me anything. Furthermore, the post office, for a dollar, will tell you what my new address is. Did you ever think of that?"

"No. I thought you . . . well, what I thought was . . . you'd absconded with my dog. I lost the card you gave me. I got discouraged when I heard you'd moved. I'm sorry. I'm willing to take all the blame. I had this grand dream that I was going to walk into your parents' house on Christmas Eve and stand by your tree with you. My operation wasn't the walk in the park the surgeon more or less promised. I had to have a second one. The therapy was so intensive it blew my mind. I'm not whining here, I'm trying to explain. That's all I have to say. If you want to keep Murphy, it's okay. I had no idea . . . he loves you. Hell, *I* love you."

"You do?"

"Damn straight I do. You're all I thought about during my recovery. It was what kept me going. I even went by that Korean grocery store today and guess what? Take a look at this!" He held out a stack of cards and envelopes. "It seems they can't read English. They were waiting for you to come and pick up the mail. They said they liked the flowers I sent from time to time."

"Really, Marcus!" She reached out to accept the stack of mail. "How'd you get out of that doggie door?" she asked suspiciously.

Marcus snorted. "Murphy pushed me out. Can we go into the house now and talk like two civilized people who love each other?"

"I didn't say I loved you."

"Say it!" he roared.

"Okay, okay, I love you."

"What else?"

"I believe you and I love your dog, too."

"Are we going to live happily ever after even if I'm rich and handsome?"

"Oh, yes, but that doesn't matter. I loved you when you were in the wheelchair. How are all your . . . parts?"

"Let's find out."

Murphy nudged both of them as he herded them toward the front door.

"I'm going to carry you over the threshold."

"Oh, Marcus, really!"

"Sometimes you simply talk too much." He kissed her as he'd never kissed her before.

"I like that. Do it again, and again, and again."

He did.

More by Best-selling Author
Fern Michaels

__About Face	0-8217-7020-9	$7.99US/$10.99CAN
__Kentucky Sunrise	0-8217-7462-X	$7.99US/$10.99CAN
__Kentucky Rich	0-8217-7234-1	$7.99US/$10.99CAN
__Kentucky Heat	0-8217-7368-2	$7.99US/$10.99CAN
__Plain Jane	0-8217-6927-8	$7.99US/$10.99CAN
__Wish List	0-8217-7363-1	$7.50US/$10.50CAN
__Yesterday	0-8217-6785-2	$7.50US/$10.50CAN
__The Guest List	0-8217-6657-0	$7.50US/$10.50CAN
__Finders Keepers	0-8217-7364-X	$7.50US/$10.50CAN
__Annie's Rainbow	0-8217-7366-6	$7.50US/$10.50CAN
__Dear Emily	0-8217-7316-X	$7.50US/$10.50CAN
__Sara's Song	0-8217-7480-8	$7.50US/$10.50CAN
__Celebration	0-8217-7434-4	$7.50US/$10.50CAN
__Vegas Heat	0-8217-7207-4	$7.50US/$10.50CAN
__Vegas Rich	0-8217-7206-6	$7.50US/$10.50CAN
__Vegas Sunrise	0-8217-7208-2	$7.50US/$10.50CAN
__What You Wish For	0-8217-6828-X	$7.99US/$10.99CAN
__Charming Lily	0-8217-7019-5	$7.99US/$10.99CAN

Available Wherever Books Are Sold!

Visit our website at **www.kensingtonbooks.com**.

BOOK YOUR PLACE ON OUR WEBSITE AND MAKE THE READING CONNECTION!

We've created a customized website just for our very special readers, where you can get the inside scoop on everything that's going on with Zebra, Pinnacle and Kensington books.

When you come online, you'll have the exciting opportunity to:

- View covers of upcoming books
- Read sample chapters
- Learn about our future publishing schedule (listed by publication month *and author*)
- Find out when your favorite authors will be visiting a city near you
- Search for and order backlist books from our online catalog
- Check out author bios and background information
- Send e-mail to your favorite authors
- Meet the Kensington staff online
- Join us in weekly chats with authors, readers and other guests
- Get writing guidelines
- AND MUCH MORE!

**Visit our website at
http://www.kensingtonbooks.com**